KOPP SISTERS
ON THE MARCH

KOPP SISTERS
ON THE MARCH

Amy Stewart

Houghton Mifflin Harcourt
Boston   New York   2019

For information about permission to reproduce selections from this book,
write to trade.permissions@hmhco.com or to Permissions,
Houghton Mifflin Harcourt Publishing Company,
3 Park Avenue, 19th Floor, New York, New York 10016.

hmhco.com

Library of Congress Cataloging-in-Publication Data
Names: Stewart, Amy, author.
Title: Kopp sisters on the march / Amy Stewart.
Description: Boston : Houghton Mifflin Harcourt, 2019. |
Series: A Kopp sisters novel ; 5.
Identifiers: LCCN 2019002553 (print) | LCCN 2019012330 (ebook) |
ISBN 9781328736543 (ebook) | ISBN 9781328736529 (hardcover)
Subjects: LCSH: United States—Social life and customs—1865–1918—
Fiction. | BISAC: FICTION / Mystery & Detective / Women Sleuths. |
FICTION / Mystery & Detective / Historical. | FICTION / Historical. |
FICTION / Biographical.
Classification: LCC PS3619.T49343 (ebook) | LCC PS3619.T49343 K67 2019
(print) | DDC 813/.6—dc23
LC record available at https://lccn.loc.gov/2019002553

Book design by Greta D. Sibley

Printed in the United States of America
DOC 10 9 8 7 6 5 4 3 2 1

To Michelle Tessler

The national service school was organized by the women's section of the Navy League to train American women for the duties which come to them in wartime and in the great national disasters, which include nursing the sick, feeding the hungry, making bandages and other surgical supplies, and comforting the sorrows and relieving the necessities of those dependent upon the defenders of the nation at the front. . . . There was no intention of producing a modern Amazonian corps.

—*Richmond Times Dispatch*, April 1, 1917

KOPP SISTERS
ON THE MARCH

❧ 1 ❧

BEULAH KNEW IT was over when she returned from lunch to find her desk cleared and a little box placed on the seat of her chair, like a gift.

PINKMAN HOSIERY, read the foil stamping. THREE DOZEN ASSORTED. It was the very style of box that Beulah had been hired to paste together when she started at the factory six months earlier, before she was promoted to office girl. She didn't have to look inside to know that it held the contents of her desk drawer: her comb, her lip-stick, her extra handkerchiefs, and a subway token, along with the silk sheers that Mr. Pinkman bestowed upon every girl he fired as a final, guilty, lily-livered parting gift.

Beulah lifted the box slowly, as if in a dream, and looked around at the rows of desks surrounding hers. Mr. Pinkman employed a dozen office girls in a high-ceilinged but nevertheless cramped room, so that they were obliged to push their desks together and work elbow to elbow. There were no secrets among the typists and billing clerks.

Every eye in the room darted briefly up to Beulah and away again. Typewriters clattered, order forms shuffled, and chairs squeaked and groaned as the girls went about their business. Beulah knew that the dignified course of action was to clutch her little box to her chest and to skitter away quietly, blinking back a few repentant tears as she went out the door for the last time.

That's how she used to do it, back when she first arrived in New York. She thought it was a requirement of the job to behave politely as she was being put out on the street. But then it occurred to her that once she'd been dismissed, she was free to do as she pleased.

What pleased her at that moment was to have a word with Mr. Theodore Pinkman, who was peeking out at her from behind the blinds in his office, like the petty and spineless man that he was. He loved to hide away in that wallpapered den of his, and pretend not to watch the girls in the next room.

He drew away when she caught him staring at her. Of course he did. He could never own up to anything. He was already fumbling to lock the door as she marched over, but he couldn't manage it. For a man who manufactured ladies' undergarments, he was utterly inept with handles, knobs, buttons, clasps, and other small fittings. Beulah had found it endearing at first, but lately she'd come to believe that there was something deficient in a man who couldn't properly undress a woman—or fire one.

She gave the still-rattling doorknob a hard turn and shouldered her way in. Mr. Pinkman fell back against his desk, all two hundred and fifty pounds of him, blushing, sweating, his curly hair resisting his daily efforts to slick it down, those blue eyes, round as a child's, registering a look of perpetual surprise.

He stumbled to his feet and tugged at his vest. "Ah—hello. I—"

"A little box on my chair, Teddy? Like I'm any other girl? I fixed your dinner last night. I made those damn little French potatoes that take an hour to peel because you won't eat the skins. I ironed your collar—the one you're wearing right now! And you send me away with a box of stockings?"

She tossed it down and it fell open. The contents were exactly as she'd expected, except for a folded bill on top. To her parting gift he'd added ten dollars.

Did Mr. Pinkman honestly think that would satisfy her?

He did. "There, you see? It's not only stockings. You . . . you've been so much more to me . . . you know that . . . only, it seems that Mrs. Pinkman . . ."

He trailed off, finding himself unable to make the simplest of explanations for a circumstance that was as old as marriage itself.

"Mrs. Pinkman need never have found out, if you knew one thing about keeping a secret, which you don't," Beulah said. "What'd you do, leave a coat-check tag in your pocket? Come home with perfume on your handkerchief?"

He didn't answer. He didn't have to. It was always one or the other, the ticket or the handkerchief.

Beulah crossed her arms and paced around his office in a circle, as if she owned it, which she did, in that moment. "Well. What are we going to do now? You've dismissed me, because she insisted on it, and she'll know if I'm still working here. She'll come around and check. But she doesn't know about our flat, does she? And you signed a lease through December. So I have ten months left on that lease, and I intend to enjoy every minute of it. It's nice, living by the park, even if it does take half an hour to get down here every day. Although I don't suppose I'll have to do that anymore."

"But Mrs. Pinkman already—" he injected.

Beulah ignored him. "And you can keep your ten dollars, Teddy. You're going to find me a new position at a good firm uptown, so that I can walk to work on nice days. And if I'm not satisfied with the arrangements you've made for me, I will take my services elsewhere. You will write me a letter of commendation so that I may do so."

It was a fine speech, and Beulah delivered it with her pointy little chin held high. But she'd underestimated the depth of Mr. Pinkman's desperation, and the extent to which Mrs. Pinkman had already unraveled the very threads to which Beulah was clinging.

He went around behind his desk and dropped heavily into his chair. "It's no good, missy."

"Don't call me missy no more." The southerner in her always came out when she was angry.

He pressed a handkerchief to his face. Sweat tended to accumulate just above his eyebrows and across his nose when he found himself under pressure. "All right, I won't. What I'm trying to tell you is that the flat is gone. Mrs. Pinkman saw to that. She boxed up your things—"

"My things? Your wife has been through my *things*?" She was shouting now. Outside his office window, every typewriter stopped clattering at once. She didn't care. "When did she do that? Today?"

Mr. Pinkman stared, wide-eyed, at the half-opened blinds, through which every girl in the typing pool was watching him. He lacked the gumption to lean over and tug them closed, so Beulah did it for him. She did everything for him.

He looked at her with something like gratitude and went on. "She was there this morning. She didn't touch your things herself. She had her maid do it."

"Oh, well, that makes it better," Beulah snapped. "And where may I collect my possessions, Mr. Pinkman?"

He looked over at the little box she'd tossed on the floor. "The train station. There's a key in there."

She snatched it up and tucked it under her arm. "And where am I to go tonight?"

He was more in command of himself, now that the situation had been made plain and the worst was past. He stood up and went around to open the door for her. He smelled of the sarsaparilla candies he chewed habitually.

"That's what the ten dollars is for. Go on, now."

WHAT ELSE WAS she to do, but to march out with her head held high? Every girl in the place watched her go with delighted fascination. They knew exactly what had just transpired, and what details they didn't know could have been found out easily enough, if any of them dared jump up and run outside to offer Beulah a sympathetic ear. She would've happily poured out the whole sordid tale, from the day Mr. Pinkman noticed her on the box line and promoted her to the office, only to find that she could neither type nor write nor add a column of figures and was therefore entirely unsuited to the sending and receiving of invoices, to the way he took pity on her and arranged for her to put in her time at the office in the completion of correspondence courses aimed at teaching her something in the way of stenography and clerksmanship.

"I want to see you make something of yourself, missy," Mr. Pinkman had told her.

They were in his office when he said that, but he'd left the door open. Anyone could hear what she said in reply. Beulah knew that would make it all the more exciting for him.

"I'd like to make something of you, too, Mr. Pinkman," she had said, in that breathy way Richmond girls did when they had something to offer a man. She made sure to sashay out before he was forced to fish around for a clever retort that she knew he never would find.

But now he'd dismissed her, and no one did rush out after Beulah to hear about it. She didn't blame them: it wasn't worth losing a place in a good office for one salacious story about the boss. There were enough of those in circulation already. She was only the latest.

It was a chilly afternoon in late February, but Beulah—thanks to Mr. Pinkman's largess—wore the first good wool coat of her life, trimmed in white rabbit fur and lined in heavy silk that rustled pleasurably as she walked. Mr. Pinkman had been a generous benefactor: every time she bestowed a pleasure on him that he had never before known, he bestowed one on her. Owing to his timid nature and unwillingness to make untoward demands on his inexperienced wife, there were any number of new pleasures to grant him in exchange for a coat or a gold bracelet or a furnished room of her own.

Although he never knew it—or never dared to ask—Beulah did, in effect, take him on a private tour of Richmond's cathouses, saving him the threat of a police raid or the moral stain of the world's oldest transgression. There weren't even words for some of the things she did to him, or so Mr. Pinkman claimed, breathlessly, into the pillow they shared.

Oh, but there was a word for everything. Beulah never told him that. Why ruin it for him?

It was terrible to be fired right after lunch, when Mabel was still at work. Mabel, her only true friend in New York, plunked down cups and saucers at a horrible little tea-room up on Broadway. Beulah had never seen a room so overfull of chintz and toile, wicker and silk flowers, ceramic figurines and embroidered tablecloths. The owners—two men, to Beulah's everlasting confusion—behaved as if they'd heard of women but had never actually met one. They seemed to have determined that the way to make a success of a tea-room was to gather every trapping of Gilded Age femininity and to cram it together in a riot of lace, ribbons, and ersatz gold.

The place was absurdly old-fashioned, and the tea tasted of dishwater. The cakes were stale, too, although Beulah wasn't above eating them directly from the box when Mabel was given extras for her dinner.

As much as she detested the tea-room, Beulah found it unbearable to be alone after what had just happened to her, so she wandered up Broadway anyway. It was her good fortune that Mabel had stepped outside for a cigarette just as Beulah came into view.

Mabel saw the box in her hand and laughed as she blew out the smoke. "Has Mr. Pinkman had enough of you?"

"Well, Mrs. Pinkman certainly has. I'm dismissed from my position and I've been put out of my place. How's that for a morning's work?"

Mabel ticked off the day's events with her fingers. "You've lost a man, a job, and the roof over your head. That's a record, even for you." She had round cheeks and the kind of sweet dimples that grandmothers loved, but her sympathetic smile only made Beulah more despondent.

"Oh, what am I going to do?" Beulah took the cigarette from Mabel and leaned against the wall. "I'm so tired of this city. When did I come here—four years ago?"

"Well, you moved in with me just before Christmas of 1911. That's five years, dearie, and a couple of months."

Beulah looked at her in shock. "Five years? Look at me. I'm exactly where I started. Tonight I'll have to go around door-to-door, begging to be let into some boarding-house or another, with no references and no suitable explanation as to where I've just come from. I'll have to be Betty off the train again, just like I was the night I met you."

"You were Lucy back then," Mabel reminded her.

"Oh, that's right," she said. "I liked Lucy. What was my last name?"

"Lane. Lucy Lane. I could tell you'd made it up on the spot."

"Then why'd you offer to share a room with me?"

"I thought you'd have an interesting story to tell."

Beulah choked on the cigarette and passed it back to Mabel. "Well, didn't I just."

Mabel leaned over and looked in the window. The tea-room was empty. "I'm going to tell the boys to save themselves a few pennies and turn me loose this afternoon. We can walk uptown and eat shortbread."

"You know I hate that shortbread."

"Well, you'd best get used to taking free food, unless you're going to sell that fur collar to buy us dinner."

Beulah tucked her chin into the white fur and waited while Mabel made her excuses and collected her things. She returned, as promised, with a box of shortbread and three cucumber sandwiches wrapped in a napkin.

"Eat these," she said, pressing them on Beulah. "You'll need your strength."

"I'm not going to get my strength from a cucumber," Beulah said, but she took them anyway.

They crossed over to Park Avenue because it made them feel elegant to walk among the finer shops and the women who frequented them. They stopped to admire hats in the windows, including one so festooned with striped feathers that it appeared that an entire flock of guinea fowl had been sacrificed.

"That's a church hat where I come from," Beulah said.

"I think it's a hat for the opera here," Mabel said.

"I wouldn't like to sit behind the lady who wore that hat."

They went on that way, criticizing the impractical finery that they couldn't afford, until another wave of misery came over Beulah and she said, "What am I to do, Mabel? I thought I'd be married by now, or in a more established position, anyway. I've done all the jobs in this town, at least the ones I'm qualified to do. I've been every sort of packer and spooler and carder and labeler."

"There was that nasty oyster house."

"Picker. They called me an oyster picker. Never again. I was done with fish and meats after that."

"You enjoyed stencil-painting," Mabel offered.

"Well, I enjoyed the fellow who managed the concern, but I can't say that I enjoyed stencil-paintings so's I'd make a life from it! I'm talking about . . ." She blew a little steam from between her lips. "I'm talking about becoming someone else. I came here to bury that business back in Richmond and to start again." She said it quietly. It was not her habit to talk about her past.

Mabel put an arm around her waist. "You did start again. This is what it looks like to start again. This is exactly how it feels to earn an honest living, darling."

"But I wanted—I just want something to change."

"Then you have to change! You need some kind of education if you want to advance. I thought Mr. Pinkman put you into a correspondence course."

"Oh, he pretended to care about my learning, and so did I," Beulah said irritably. "I sat at my desk and contrived to look busy, but I never could make heads nor tails of those courses."

Mabel drew back in surprise. "For three months you've been sitting and pretending?"

"Six months, more like."

"I could've helped you. You could've brought the courses over to me at night."

"I had business with Mr. Pinkman at night."

"Of course you did," Mabel muttered.

They had, by this time, reached the Armory, where a crowd of young women, all arrayed in the fine winter coats of New York's social set, waited at the wide red brick entrance.

"Is this where they hold the fashion shows now?" Beulah asked.

"It looks like a luncheon for the League of Ladies in Furtherance of Something-or-Other," Mabel offered.

A banner hung above the entrance. They had to push their way through the crowd to read it.

"'National Service School,'" Mabel read. "'Enrollment for Spring 1917.'"

Beulah looked around at the well-heeled young women in line. "These girls aren't going into service," she said.

"I don't think it's domestic service," Mabel mused. "It's . . . something to do with the war. Look, they're all wearing flag ribbons."

"Everybody wears a flag ribbon these days. I even have one somewhere."

Somewhere. It came back to Beulah in a sickening rush that her things had been packed up by Mrs. Pinkman's maid and shoved in a train station locker. Which of her possessions had been left behind? What drawers went unopened, what cupboards ignored?

Beulah didn't like to speak to girls of refinement and breeding —they would see right through her, she believed or, worse, they would recognize her. Her face had been in every paper in 1911. It was only the patchy quality of the image that kept her from being stopped on every street corner.

But a lonely kind of desperation had come over her, and she worked up her nerve to say to the nearest girl, "What's this about? What sort of school is it?"

"Haven't you heard? It's an Army camp for girls."

Mabel whipped around. "They're taking girls into the Army? And all of you are going?"

A chorus of giggles rose up around them. "Oh, she's teasing you," another girl said. "It's not a real Army camp. It's something the generals' wives put together. They say that we're to have our own part in preparing for the war. The troops are going to need us in France."

"What for?" Beulah asked. "Are you all going over to dance with the soldiers?"

That brought a delighted gasp from the group. "Oh, I suppose so, if they ask us," one of them said. "But the idea is to train us in nursing, or mending, or how to cook for a battalion."

Mabel rolled her eyes at this and started to walk away, but Beulah stared at them. "And then you'll go to France?" She looked around at the masses of young women waiting to register. "All of you?"

One after another, the girls thrust their chests out and gave a little salute. "I'll go."

"I'll go."

"Me too."

They collapsed again into laughter, but as far as Beulah could tell, they meant it.

Mabel took her by the elbow and pulled her away. "What a lot of nonsense," she said. "Let's find you a place to stay for the night."

But Beulah shook her loose. "This is what I should do. I should go to this camp."

Mabel snorted. "With these girls? Look at them! It must cost a fortune. You don't see anyone who lives below Fourteenth Street in this line." She marched over and spoke to one of the women, and returned triumphant.

"There, you see? The fee for six weeks away is forty dollars, and you have to bring your own uniform. This is nothing but a summer camp for swells."

Beulah fingered the bracelet around her wrist. Mr. Pinkman hadn't thought to ask her to return it. "I could raise the funds."

"Oh, pish! Save your pennies." Mabel tried to lead her down the street again. "You're just tired and cross after the day you've had."

Beulah turned and looked back at the women milling about the Armory, in their good serge dresses and smart kid boots. She could see them on the deck of a ship, waving good-bye to New York, French phrase-books in their pockets. What a thrill it would be to watch the city grow smaller as the ship sailed east. Her troubles would vanish right over the horizon.

Mabel could see her wavering. "You'd have to give your real name. This all looks very—governmental. They will know."

"These ladies? They're not asking any questions," Beulah said. "You simply go up and tell your name and they write it down. If there's anything more to it than that, I'll find a way."

Over the years, Beulah had forged any number of letters of introduction when she adopted a new name. She wondered if the maid had packed her papers. That was just the sort of thing Mrs. Pinkman would throw into the stove if she found it.

"But what if someone did figure you out?" Mabel said. "You'd have reporters following you all over again."

"No one's recognized me in years," Beulah said. "I've outgrown that picture in the paper. I can manage. Don't you see? I could go to Paris, and get on with the Red Cross or some outfit, and wear a uniform, and when the war's over, I'll sail home on the arm of a soldier, and it'll be like the war erased everything. Not just for me, but for the whole country! I'll go in with everyone else, and wash out the other side a new—"

Mabel shook her head. "This camp—it's for nice girls who've

lived under a chaperone their whole lives. You're not like them, and they'll know it."

But Beulah was staring dreamily at the sea of elaborately trimmed hats around her. "Look at them. They're all fired up about going off to the war. Who, at a place like that, would ever bother looking twice at me?"

⊰ 2 ⊱

CONSTANCE KOPP WAS not in the habit of agreeing with her sister: it was never a good idea to concede territory to Norma. But as they rounded the bend and the camp came into view, Constance couldn't help but be stirred—just as Norma said she would be— by the sight of a hundred or more young women, congregated in an open meadow on a chilly March morning, to register for wartime service.

She sat atop a horse-drawn cart that jostled pleasantly toward the entrance, alongside all the other vehicles delivering campers and their trunks. Even from a distance, she could sense from the girls' posture and their bearing a fine sense of purpose and forward movement. Some type of forward movement was exactly what Constance, at that moment, required.

Norma had insisted that this camp in Maryland would put her back in her tracks, as if she were a derailed train that merely needed to be hauled upright and have its wheels greased. There was something to that, Constance had to admit. The events of the previous year had indeed thrown her off. She'd spent the winter housebound, stranded and stuck. It had taken Norma (forcefully, and without the consent of the other parties) enrolling the three of them in this camp to dislodge her from their small farm. If Norma meant for her to feel like a train put back on its tracks, the experience to Constance was more like that of a bear evicted suddenly from its winter cave.

Hibernation was abruptly over, and the isolation of the past few months gone along with it. Norma clucked at their harness mare and tried—unsuccessfully—to maneuver their wagon down a road already clogged with autos, buggies, and traps delivering young women to the camp. Most vehicles had pulled off to the side, but some were simply stopped in the road, as if for a picnic.

In her old job back in Hackensack, Constance would've hopped off the wagon, blown a whistle, and directed the drivers off the road. She even patted down her pockets, searching for her whistle, before she remembered that she wasn't the deputy in charge.

That little gesture didn't escape Norma's notice. Nothing escaped Norma's notice.

"Go ahead and order them out of the way. You like to be in charge."

I used to like it, Constance nearly said, but didn't. It would only invite a lecture about burying the past before it buried her, a lecture Norma had delivered so many times that Constance had it memorized. Instead she craned her neck and said, "I don't believe they're letting any vehicles through the gate." She sat considerably higher in the wagon than her sister did and had a clearer view of the scene ahead.

Norma urged their harness mare on. "They have to let us in. Ours is the only vehicle here for a military purpose."

Norma's horse-drawn cart served a military purpose only in her own mind, just as Constance was still a deputy only in her own mind. What a pair they made!

Fleurette, meanwhile, labored under her own illusions. While

Norma and Constance sat next to each other on the coachman's seat, the youngest Kopp walked alongside, having refused to be seen approaching camp in such a contraption.

"There is an art to making an entrance," she'd declared half a mile back. "You've put a barn on wheels and attached it to a worn-out mare. I wish you could see what a sight you make."

It was true that they were arriving in the most unlikely of vehicles. Every other camper had been delivered by wagon, truck, automobile, or small cart pulled by some manner of mule or pony. The Kopp sisters, however, traveled by mobile pigeon cart. It was half again as tall as anything else on the road and resembled a miniature cottage on wheels.

"If I can't approach by automobile," Fleurette continued, "I'd rather come strolling in as if I've only just been let out of one." With that, she hopped off and proceeded by foot.

She had outfitted herself in a dusty pink coat with a fox fur collar, which she swore was the warmest coat she owned, but it also happened to be the most outlandish. Even in this crowd of debutantes and bankers' daughters, she made an impression. Heads were turning. Constance saw a chauffeur purse his lips as if to whistle, and she reached once again for her pocket. How satisfying that handgun used to feel, at moments like this.

All around them, young women were disembarking from their vehicles and hopping up and down in an effort to ward off the chill. Many of them stood on top of their trunks and suitcases to get a better look. Wicker hampers were being emptied of sandwiches, children were organizing games for themselves, and mothers and fathers stood by, wearing expressions of fatigued indulgence. A woman in uniform walked between the families, greeting campers and issuing instructions as to the disposition of trunks and bags.

Constance recognized her at once. "Is that Maude Miner?" she called.

The woman looked around in surprise. "Constance Kopp! I should've known you'd turn up here!" She pointed a camper in the direction of the entrance and walked over.

Constance had met Miss Miner the previous fall at Plattsburg, a military camp for men intending to join the Army. Miss Miner had been in charge of making sure nothing untoward went on between the men and the local girls, as the success of the Plattsburg camps depended on them remaining free of scandal. She'd tried to convince Constance to work for her as a camp matron, but at the time Constance still held her post as deputy sheriff. She could remember, as clearly as if it were yesterday, telling Maude that she couldn't imagine a better place for herself than the Bergen County Sheriff's Department.

Maude remembered it, too. "I'm just sick over what happened to you," she said. "What did those leaflets say? Troublesome lady policeman? I can't imagine how that man expects to hold public office after plastering that nonsense all over town. The fact that the voters elected him anyway is something I'll never understand. What was his name again?"

Maude meant well. Constance saw in her face that mixture of sympathy and outrage she'd come to expect from anyone who knew what had happened to her. It was only just now occurring to her that she'd have to confront it here at camp, not just once, but over and over.

She took another look around at the crowd. Was that a lady reporter, going from one family to the next, and a photographer alongside her?

As Constance seemed to have lost her tongue, Fleurette stepped up quickly and said, "His name is Mr. Courter. We don't dignify him with the title of sheriff. Constance doesn't like to speak of him at all."

"Oh, I didn't mean—"

"We've had a rather difficult winter," Norma put in, "but she's in fine form now."

Constance wished mightily that Norma wouldn't talk about her as if she were an invalid.

"I'm terribly sorry," Maude said quietly, in the tone she probably employed with disgraced girls. Constance recognized that tone —she'd used it herself, many times.

"You needn't apologize," Constance said, "only I'd rather start fresh and avoid any talk of the past."

Maude patted her arm, still dispensing more sympathy than Constance would've liked. "I won't say a word. But someone's bound to recognize you, after all that business with the election. You were in the papers down here, too."

Of course she was. She'd been in the papers as far away as California. *Girl Deputy Fired. Politics Takes Job from Girl Cop.* And this one, so succinct in its humiliation: *Miss Kopp Loses.*

Norma grunted. "I'd put no stock in this crowd reading the papers. Most of these girls turn right to the ladies' pages and never go further."

"Perhaps you're right," Maude said, although she didn't look convinced. "Now, what are we to do with this . . . this . . ." She looked up at Norma's cart and searched for the proper term.

"Mobile pigeon transport cart," Norma said. "I've come to teach a class."

"Ah, yes," Maude said vaguely. "I do recall hearing something about a last-minute addition to the curriculum, but I didn't know it had to do with . . . birds, is it?"

"They're trained to deliver messages from the front," Constance put in.

It sounded absurd, but Maude managed to answer graciously. "Of course! The telephones do fail from time to time. How practical. Did you ride in it all the way from New Jersey?"

"We took the train. Horse and cart followed by box-car," Constance said. "We've only just ridden in from the station." The truth was that neither she nor Fleurette had been willing to undertake a journey of some two hundred and fifty miles in a horse-drawn wagon filled with unhappy pigeons. Norma had relented only after she realized that she was physically unable to wrestle Constance aboard—and she did try, but Constance outweighed her by a good thirty pounds and stood her ground.

"Well, we have a stable at the very back of the camp," Maude said. "I'll clear the way and you can ride on in."

With that, Maude marched ahead, waving campers and their vehicles out of the way. Someone nearby was whistling a tune. A few girls took it up and started singing.

Fleurette was about to join in, but Norma silenced her with a glare. "One has to be awfully far away from the fighting to treat war like a carnival."

"We aren't at war yet," Fleurette said, "unless you picked up the news at the train station and decided not to tell us. And I'm glad to hear that some of the girls can sing. I've written to Freeman Bernstein and asked if May Ward can come and give a show. I promised I could round up a chorus here at camp and teach them the songs."

"You never said anything about writing a letter," Norma snapped.

"I'm telling you now," Fleurette said lightly, as if the subject of Freeman Bernstein had only just occurred to her.

Norma harbored a smoldering dislike of Freeman Bernstein, a vaudeville manager whose wife, May Ward, took Fleurette on tour with her the previous spring. Fleurette's abrupt disappearance sent Norma marching into Mr. Bernstein's office, demanding to know her whereabouts. Mr. Bernstein dismissed her worries and lectured her on the proper way to bring up a young girl in modern times. As Norma disliked both lectures and modern times, the meeting ended badly.

Time had not softened Norma's animosity toward the man—but time rarely did. Norma didn't just hold grudges, she feathered a nest for them and kept them warm, like a broody hen.

"That man is not going to set foot inside my camp," Norma sputtered, when she could, at last, find the words.

"It isn't your camp," Fleurette said. "May Ward's been performing at all the men's camps this year. If they're given a show of patriotic music, why shouldn't the women have the same?"

Norma ignored her and urged their horse along.

The reporter was still making her way through the crowd. When the cart started moving, she dashed over. "What a cunning little wagon," she cried, walking all around it and taking in its windows with fitted shutters, its rear door with retractable steps, and its ladder to the top. It was a perfectly crafted vehicle, built entirely by Norma and her friend Carolyn.

Norma would've told the reporter all about it—it was, after all, her mission to convince the public of the benefits of pigeons to wartime communication operations—and Constance wouldn't have minded, except that the man with the camera followed closely on the reporter's heels and set up his stand to take a picture.

"Let's have all three of you girls pose in front of it," he proposed.

"Yes, and I'll need your names," the reporter said.

The headline wrote itself: *Defeated Lady Deputy Dons Khakis.*

"No pictures!" Constance called, rather frantically. "No pictures, and no names."

The reporter looked up at her through delicate gold-rimmed spectacles. "It's all in furtherance of the camp and its ideals," she said sweetly.

If Constance had learned one thing about reporters, it was that a story was only ever in furtherance of its readers—and readers wouldn't pay a penny for another story about preparedness camps and high-flown ideals. It was trouble they liked, but Constance was no longer in that business.

"We'd like to get settled," she said. "We've come a long way. I'm sure there are plenty of other ladies to interview."

"Oh, you must be simply exhausted," the reporter said, still pleasant, still sympathetic. "How far have you traveled?"

"My sister's too polite to refuse directly, but I'm not," Norma said. "Go on, now." It wasn't entirely clear whether she was talking to the reporter or the horse, but both moved along.

They made their way at last to a high cattle fence and a gate with a banner strung across it. CAMP CHEVY CHASE, it read in bold hand-painted letters. NATIONAL SERVICE SCHOOL.

At the gate stood a camp official wearing a blue sash over her brown Norfolk jacket. She looked to be about fifty and had the vigorous air of a club woman about her. Constance could imagine her organizing church suppers and auctioning off cakes for charity. She'd surely run any number of instructional campaigns in her time, on subjects as varied as hygiene for invalids and the advantages of uncolored butter. She was exactly the sort of woman Constance expected to find running a camp like this.

"Geneva Nash, camp matron," she said by way of introduction. From a card file on a table next to her, she extracted their registration forms. "I'll take down your particulars and you can go find your tent. Why don't we begin with the eldest Miss Kopp?"

Constance hadn't expected to be questioned so soon. She was seized with a rising sense of dread over the entire camp knowing that the disgraced former lady deputy from New Jersey was among them. But if she didn't want anyone to know, then what was she to say about her past?

There was no time to decide. Mrs. Nash and her sharpened pencil awaited.

"Name in full," Mrs. Nash said.

"Constance Amélie Kopp."

"Address in full."

She gave it.

"Are you a member of the American Red Cross?"

Constance was not.

"Are you native-born? Place of birth and year, please."

"Brooklyn, 1877."

"Are you married, single, or widowed? Single, I suppose."

"Yes."

"Have you any children, parents, or others who are dependent upon you?"

Constance looked over at Norma and Fleurette. "I suppose not."

Mrs. Nash gave the three of them a quick smile. "You all look quite self-reliant. Can you furnish a health certificate?"

"I suppose so."

"Languages spoken other than English?"

"French." No one admitted to speaking German.

"Have you any training along the following lines? Dairying, farming, fruit-raising, market gardening, or poultry-raising?"

"We live on a small farm and I do the vegetables."

Norma raised an eyebrow at that half-truth. Constance had only ever been nominally in charge of the vegetable patch but hated doing it. As soon as she could afford to hire a boy from the dairy to take care of it, she relinquished her responsibility. She realized with a prickle of dread that if she didn't leave camp with some idea about her next endeavor, she'd be back at home, putting in the cabbage starts.

"That's fine," Mrs. Nash said. "What about household work? Care of children, cleaning, cooking, knitting, mending, sewing?"

"Some of it," Constance admitted. That got a little laugh from Mrs. Nash.

"It's a superfluous question at a women's camp. I wonder who thought to put it down. What about clerical work, such as book-keeping, stenography, or typewriting?"

"I keep the household accounts."

"And mechanical work, such as motor cars, telegraphs, telephones, or wireless?"

"No, none of that." Her throat tightened a bit as the questions veered in the direction of professional experience. Fleurette shuffled her feet and Norma crossed her arms over her chest.

"Any other training, such as nursing, pharmacy, dentist, or lawyer?"

She said nothing about police work, did she?

"No."

"That's fine, dear. And your present occupation?"

Well, that was straightforward enough. Constance told the truth, and betrayed no emotion as she did so.

"None. I haven't any occupation."

3

"YOU OUGHTN'T TO lie like that," Norma said as they dragged their trunks and bags into the campground.

"I didn't lie," Constance said.

"You hid the truth. There's no reason for it. You've no cause for shame."

"I just don't want to have to answer to it," Constance said crabbily. "You've brought us here to live among two hundred strangers. Do I have to tell everyone my business?"

"You already did, when you decided to serve in a public office."

"Well, I'm not serving anymore, and if there's to be one advantage in that, it should be that I don't have to discuss it with you any longer."

"Humph" was all Norma said to that.

It was impossible to argue with Norma, and it was no good telling her that she couldn't possibly understand. Norma had never held any sort of job, much less been fired from one. She'd never been accused of wrongdoing and been unable to clear her name. She'd never had to walk down the street and meet pity on one face and scorn on the next, day after day.

Furthermore, it was inconceivable to Norma that she might not understand her sister's troubles. Norma believed herself to be an authority on all matters Kopp-related and wouldn't entertain ideas to the contrary.

She did, however, know how to let a subject drop when she'd exhausted it. She cast a critical eye over a row of newly constructed privies, which still smelled of fresh-cut wood and sawdust.

"I shouldn't like to be close to the latrines," she announced, in a voice far too loud for the subject under discussion. "These girls will be up at all hours." Norma prided herself on her sound constitution, which allowed her to sleep solidly through the night. She considered it a character weakness to hop up and down to the toilet in the dark.

"We're supposed to be in number seventeen, but I don't see it," Fleurette said. She wasn't looking, either: she was far too busy watching the khaki-clad soldiers carrying tent poles and rolls of canvas to each campsite. Constance hadn't considered the possibility of any kind of male presence at the camp.

"It's just over here," Constance said, and marched them over to their spot.

Norma deposited her bags with relief. "I heard a girl came all the way from Texas. She didn't reserve a place, but Miss Miner took pity on her and let her in."

"How fortunate for the girl from Texas," said Fleurette.

"It doesn't speak well for the military order of the place. They've only room for two hundred, and everyone who applied has turned up or sent a replacement. I don't see how we make room for the odd girl from Texas."

There it was. Already Norma sounded as if she ran the camp.

"She's no odder than anyone else who signed up for this affair," said Fleurette.

"I mean to say that it's five to a tent. The figures don't come out right."

"Five to a tent? But there's only three of us," Fleurette said.

"That's right," Norma said. "We're to share with two others. I can only imagine . . ."

But Norma couldn't imagine, could she? The three of them had lived together in relative isolation on their farm outside Hackensack for so long that it was impossible to contemplate two more women—complete strangers, no less—under their roof. Norma in particular was such a creature of routine. Constance wondered how she'd manage.

All around them, women in pairs or small groups were settling in. Some simply sat down on their trunks and waited for the young men to bring their tents over, but an insurrection of some sort was under way, led by a woman in her thirties—Constance was relieved to see anyone over the age of nineteen enrolled in the camp—who insisted that the women should pitch their own tents.

"I didn't come clear from Fort Worth to have a man set up my tent," the woman shouted, as she wrestled a bolt of canvas away from an unsuspecting soldier. "If we can't put a few pegs in the ground, you might as well send us home now."

"There's your girl from Texas," Constance said.

"Well, she's right about one thing. They're not pitching my tent." Norma dashed over and took hold of their tent, nodding at Constance to carry the tent pole.

"Look at that," the Texan said. "Already we've organized a brigade." She was tanned and sturdy, with a gap between her front teeth and a hat that looked like it had been trampled by a horse. "I'm Margaret Day. Pleased to make your acquaintance."

"Constance Kopp. This is my sister Norma."

"Constance Kopp? Have I heard that name before?"

"It's awfully common," Constance said, in a tone meant to brush the idea away. "Let's show these boys how to raise a tent."

• • •

THEY SPENT THE rest of the afternoon pounding tent stakes into the ground and raising the central pole to support what turned out to be a round tent meant to house eight men, or, as one of the newly unemployed soldiers said, "Five of you girls and all your things." He introduced himself to Fleurette as Hack, but his friend corrected him.

"He's Private Fred Hackbush, but we call him Hack. I'm Clarence Piper." The two of them were, to Constance's eye, about as handsome as all boys of nineteen, which was enough to render Fleurette temporarily incapacitated and in need of help in arranging her trunk and cot in accordance with military protocol. Constance sent them away before Fleurette started setting up housekeeping with one or the other of them.

After much muttering, tugging at ropes, and stomping on pegs, Norma surveyed their living quarters and pronounced them satisfactory. "We're missing two cots and the girls who sleep in them," she told Constance. "Make yourself useful and go find them."

Make yourself useful. That was all Constance had been hearing from Norma lately. Every time Norma caught her gazing into the distance, dozing behind a newspaper, or standing in front of a sink full of dishes with no idea what to do about them, she came up alongside her and gave her a little push with her hip. *Make yourself useful,* she would say. *Try washing those dishes instead of staring at them.*

She didn't want Norma to think that she was at all prepared to take orders, so she tried to make it appear as if it were her idea to step out of their tent and have a look around. She pushed the flap closed behind her and stood blinking in the fading late-afternoon light, taking in the tumult all around. A miniature city had sprung up at Camp Chevy Chase. From every direction the pounding of stakes into the ground created a chorus of percussion, a disjointed but strangely musical drum line.

The campers hauled their trunks and cases to their new living quarters, shrieking and laughing as they struggled (and sometimes failed) to raise their tents, and calling out to newly arrived friends. The place had the air of a summer party, in spite of the early March chill, and seemed far removed from the fighting in France or, for that matter, the very idea of war.

Having no idea how to secure the missing cots and their occupants, Constance made her way down the avenue, dodging trunks and carpet bags, and stopping to inspect a spotted dog that had already appointed itself camp mascot. Just before she reached the central commons, from whence cots and other supplies were issuing forth, she heard a voice behind her.

"Are you looking for tent seventeen?"

Constance spun around and found herself facing a woman of about twenty-five. She was long-limbed and angular, with generous brown eyes and hair to match.

"Sarah Middlebrook," she said. "I'm from Baltimore."

"Constance Kopp, from Wyckoff."

"Where's that?"

"New Jersey. Near Hackensack."

"New Jersey! You've come far. I've never been anywhere until now." She couldn't stop grinning. "If I could only find my tent."

"You have," Constance said. "I'm in tent seventeen. I'd just gone out to look for our missing tent-mates." They walked back together.

"Am I the last to arrive?" Sarah asked, as she followed Constance into the tent.

"We're still missing one," Constance said. "These are my sisters, Norma and Fleurette."

The other two Kopps looked up in unison.

Sarah said, "Sisters! Aren't you lucky to have each other."

"Are we?" Fleurette asked.

"I wonder," Norma said.

Fleurette had brought far too much in the way of luggage and was engaged at that moment in a tug-of-war with Norma over the arrangement of cots and trunks. They were still bickering, mostly under their breath, about the invitation Fleurette had extended to Freeman Bernstein and May Ward.

"You won't be allowed to turn this camp into a vaudeville spectacle," Norma muttered.

"It isn't up to you to decide what's allowed," Fleurette returned.

"They're delightful company when they remember their manners," Constance assured Sarah.

"Well. Put me wherever you like," Sarah said. "I copied out a diagram from an Army handbook on the arrangement of cots and trunks in a field tent. It looks like the trunk belongs at the foot of the cot, just so."

As she put her things in order, Norma hurried over to have a look at her diagram. "We should've each had one of these, if they expected military order," she said.

"The soldiers were here to provide military order," Fleurette said, "but you sent them away."

"I'll take my instructions from the manual," Norma said.

"If you won't take orders from a man standing right in front of you, then why listen to the man who wrote the manual?" asked Fleurette.

"I don't believe anyone in the military takes orders from a private," said Sarah, to warm approval from Norma. As unlikely as it seemed, Norma might've found an ally.

They were nearly finished unpacking their trunks, and making ready to light the first lantern of the evening, when the flap parted and their fifth tent-mate walked in.

Every eye turned to her at once. She was a pretty girl, with a pointed chin and a little bow-shaped mouth. She wore a handsome wool coat with white rabbit fur at the collar.

Constance noticed at once that her shoes were scuffed and nearly worn through at the toes, and ill-suited for walking through the grass. They were the shoes of an office girl.

There was also, in her eyes, a most unexpected flash of terror. Constance saw that, too, before the girl blinked and hid it away.

"Am I the last to arrive?" she said, with a light little laugh. "My driver gets terribly lost on these country roads. He's useless outside of Manhattan. Now, who are all of you? Make yourselves known."

Constance couldn't place her accent, but it certainly didn't come from Manhattan. "I'm Constance Kopp, and these are my sisters, Norma and Fleurette. That's Sarah Middlebrook."

The new girl pulled off one white glove and tucked it into her coat pocket. "Roxanna Collins," she said, extending a limp hand. "My friends call me Roxie."

⚔ 4 ⚔

ROXIE? WHAT WAS she thinking? She invented a nickname for
herself on the spot, out of sheer panic, and now she was stuck
with it.

Beulah had practiced her new name all the way from Manhattan: Roxanna Collins. Miss Collins. Roxanna. It needed to sound
so familiar that she'd turn around instinctively every time she
heard it. In the past she'd chosen tricky false names on a whim,
and never could keep them straight. This one had to roll off the
tongue.

Why, then, did she walk into that tent and spit out a brand-
new nickname that she hadn't once rehearsed?

Because rich girls have nicknames, that's why. This occurred to
her as soon as she found herself in the spotlight, standing with the
tent flap draped around her shoulders and four pairs of questioning eyes upon her. Rich girls never use their full names. They're
never Margaret or Elizabeth or Beatrice. They're Peggy and Lizzie
and Sissy. Nonsensical names, names that Beulah wouldn't inflict
upon a cat, but that's what they liked.

It's nothing to panic over, she told herself. Just a last-minute
adjustment. She'd get used to Roxie, and she wouldn't mind if any-

one called her Roxanna. "My mother always does," she would say, with a lightness in her voice when she exhaled the word *mother*. Just gloss right over it, she told herself. Don't bite down on that word. Let it all come out in one easy stream: *My mother always does*. Just like that.

She had to convince herself that she had an ordinary mother, and a father, too. Two polite, well-mannered people who sat together in a parlor in the evenings and smiled sweetly when their daughter walked into the room. If such people existed, Beulah had never known them, but now she had to conjure them, and place them firmly in her past, like nailing a picture to the wall.

Beulah had retreated so far into these thoughts that she'd failed to notice that her tent-mates were all watching her curiously. Instead of a trunk, she was dragging three enormous carpet bags stuffed with everything that Mrs. Pinkman's maid had deposited in the train station locker. She would've left her belongings there and come back for them six weeks later, but the locker fee had only been paid through the end of the week. She couldn't afford the storage, as she needed every penny for the train. Not just one train, but three, and a streetcar, and then a hack to carry her from Washington over to Chevy Chase. She never would've managed a trunk, but somehow she was able to lug three bags by slinging one over her right shoulder, carrying one in her right hand, and dragging the third one behind her.

"You must've brought a clean uniform for every day of the week," said the youngest and prettiest of the three sisters, eyeing those overstuffed bags. Beulah hadn't expected to share a tent with older women. Two of them were nearly forty, and one was in her mid-twenties. Only the little one, Fleurette, looked to be about twenty, the age Beulah was pretending to be.

"Oh, they can't be serious about those uniforms," Beulah said. "Five dollars for a khaki skirt and a jacket? It's nonsense." She saw her mistake immediately. What wealthy girl complains about the price of a plain-sewn skirt?

"I had my mother's seamstress whip one up for me," she added —lightly, carelessly, breathing right past that word *mother*—"but then wouldn't you know, our girl forgot to pick it up from the seamstress. So I rummaged around in the back of my closet and found the oldest and most dreadful things I own. If any of these rags get dirty, it'll only improve them."

That didn't get the sympathetic laugh Beulah had been trying for.

"I hope those rags are the regulation shade of khaki, because we start tomorrow morning with a uniform inspection," said the sour-faced sister, Norma. She had the unflattering habit of tucking her chin down when she spoke, turning what was already a thick neck into a double or even triple roll of fat. She was one of those women who would have a trough of flesh around her neck when she was older.

"Tomorrow? Oh . . . well, I'm sure I can put something together." Still Beulah didn't open any of her bags. She hadn't considered the fact that she'd have to unpack in front of all her tent-mates, who apparently had nothing better to do than to sit on their cots and watch her.

The eldest of the three sisters, Constance, was also the most fearsome of the trio. She was as tall as any man Beulah had ever met, and every bit as stout. She wore her hair up, in a style favored among women of Beulah's grandmother's generation: a flat bun, set just high enough on her head to fit under a hat, with the locks in front pinned loosely so they wouldn't fall out of place. She spoke in a manner both forthright and commanding, her voice deep enough to convey some authority. She reminded Beulah of the ladies who used to patrol Monroe Square downtown, looking for wayward girls in need of correction.

But she showed surprising tenderness when she spoke to Beulah. "We couldn't talk Fleurette out of bringing her sewing machine, and now I see why. I'm sure the two of you can put something together in the way of a uniform before morning."

Tears came suddenly to Beulah's eyes. At first, she couldn't understand why. But as she submitted to Fleurette's care, and allowed herself to be stripped down to her bloomers and turned this way and that, and to have her bags rummaged through and fabric draped over her, and pins put around her collar and a measuring tape run up her spine, Beulah felt unexpectedly welcomed, and cared for.

She was pulled suddenly back to the first time she'd ever turned up, unannounced, with all her possessions in a bag dragging the ground, hoping to be let in. Hoping to be welcomed.

It was only a dim memory, one she hadn't allowed herself to revisit in years.

SHE COULDN'T HAVE been older than six. Claudia was ten: they'd only just celebrated her birthday a few days earlier. That was when they knew their mother was gone for good. If she had any intention of coming home, wouldn't she have been there for Claudia's birthday?

On the day that realization came to them, Claudia led her through Richmond's muddy streets, past a fruit market and a butcher, past the horse stalls where the older boys played cards in the afternoon, up one unfamiliar, tree-lined lane and down another, until they came at last to their grandmother's house.

It occurred to Beulah, as she thought back on it, that Claudia must've had no idea how to get there. She had simply marched them up and down every street, in an ever-expanding radius from the flat their mother rented, until at last they came to the front porch she recognized: the one with the dark red railings along the

34

stairs, and the black iron boot scraper with the cutout of a race-horse above it.

There was a bell next to the front door, but Claudia had never rung it. Their mother always used to walk right in, calling out, "It's your baby!" as the screen door rattled behind her. But that didn't seem, to Claudia, like the right thing to do in this instance, so she stood uncomfortably on the front porch until Beulah grew impatient and rang the bell.

"Meemaw!" little Beulah called through the screen door. It was summer and the flies were fierce. Her grandmother was right to keep the screen door closed. They'd be all over her pies and her honey cakes, treats Beulah had come to expect and was eager to get her hands on.

Their grandmother was slow to come to the door. She was old, even for a grandmother, and whatever spirit she had in her had been broken in the last few years, when two of her older sons died, one right after the other. One of them was a stone cutter and he had an accident at work that Beulah wasn't allowed to know about. The other died of coughing up blood. He was a grown man, older than Beulah's mother, almost old enough to be a grandfather himself.

Meemaw took to her bed more often after she buried those sons. They were her fifth and sixth children to go into the grave, out of nine that had been born to her. She had also lost a husband, way back when she was young, and before she married Beulah's grandfather. As hard as she tried to breathe life into the world, death kept beating it back.

She found the afternoons unbearable and preferred to sleep through them, except when Beulah and Claudia were expected. On those days the baking kept her busy for hours. Meemaw used to chide them over how quickly the honey cakes would be gone, how she spent all morning baking them and then they were devoured within minutes. But every time they came to visit, she made more, so she mustn't have minded too much.

On that day, however, she hadn't been baking. Beulah knew it because she couldn't smell the burnt sugar through the screen door. Meemaw wasn't dressed for company, either: she had her hair up in a pink kerchief of the kind that women of her generation wore to bed.

Beulah rushed to open the door and to bury her face into her grandmother's apron, but Claudia held her back, having some idea that a negotiation should take place first.

"Mama went off on Tuesday," Claudia said, believing it best to present the facts plainly and to let her grandmother make up her own mind about them.

Meemaw opened the screen door, the better to see them, but still neither of them crossed the threshold to the other. "Do you mean to say you've been without your mama for three days and three nights?"

"Yes, ma'am," Claudia said.

Meemaw looked out over the tops of their heads at the neighbor lady across the street, who was pretending to fuss with her crape myrtles but was in fact watching them surreptitiously.

In a quieter voice meant only for them, she said, "And what about that daddy of yours?"

Claudia only shrugged. Beulah, watching her sister, shrugged as well. They'd hardly ever seen the man answering to that name. Beulah wouldn't recognize him walking down the street.

Her grandmother pushed the screen door open a little wider and stepped aside. "You can come in, but you live here now. You understand? If your mama comes back, you won't go with her. You'll stay here with me and Poppa."

Claudia looked down at Beulah, who was small for her age,

and put a hand on top of her head the way their mother did some-times.

"Yes, ma'am," Claudia said, and that was all. Their grand-mother swept them inside and pressed both of them up against her pillowy chest.

"You're mine," she whispered into their hair. "You're my little girls."

And they were. Their mother didn't even come looking for them until eight or nine days had passed, and when she did come inside and saw the girls at their grandmother's kitchen table, wearing new dresses that had been sewn just for them, in the same style that Meemaw had been making for little girls since the first one was born way back in 1851, she knew that her daughters wouldn't be going back to live with her anymore. She didn't even remark upon it, except to ask if they had all of their things, to which their grandmother replied that nothing the girls might've left back in that cheap old rented room was worth keeping anyhow.

She said the word *rented* as if it meant something worse, which it did.

FLEURETTE TUGGED TIGHT at the fabric around Beulah's waist. Beulah hadn't felt a seamstress's strong, light fingers on her since those early days back in Richmond, when her grandmother made every stitch of clothing she wore.

"Did I stick you?" Fleurette asked when Beulah gasped.

"Not at all," Beulah said, her eyes flying open. The lamp-lit in-terior of the tent swam back into view. "Just tickled, that's all. Go ahead."

❧ 5 ❧

"WELL, WE WON'T starve," Constance said as she mopped up the last of the pork sausage and Spanish rice that comprised their first supper of military-style rations. Constance liked food generally and rarely complained about it. Norma declared the stuffed tomatoes superfluous ("No one will have the time to stuff a tomato at the front," she grumbled), and Fleurette found the mashed potatoes wanting, due to a scarcity of butter. Still, every plate was emptied, thanks in part to a rumor making its way around the mess hall that an hour of drilling and setting-up exercises could be expected before breakfast in the morning.

It was nearly nine o'clock by the time the tables were cleared. Constance stood up, stretched, and said, "I'll sleep like a stone tonight, even on that little cot."

"Sit down," Norma said. "They haven't even begun orientation. We're running at least an hour behind."

So ordered, Constance sat. Her time was not her own, she realized, and wouldn't be, for the next six weeks. She had to admit that she'd grown soft over the past few months, while she did little more than sulk over the sudden and humiliating loss of her position as deputy sheriff. She slept late, retired early to bed, read novels on the divan in the afternoon, and rarely managed more than a walk around their property. To have to follow a military-style schedule, after such a lazy winter at home, would come as something of a shock to the system.

Norma, of course, was eager to see a regimen imposed upon her sisters. Fleurette would complain about it ceaselessly. Constance would tolerate it if she possibly could. But what of their tent-mates?

Sarah seemed to have something of Norma's veneration of the military about her, and looked forward to the rigors of camp life. Over supper she and Norma had conferred on the practicality of deploying a cavalry overseas, and Sarah found herself quite at ease discussing methods of signaling during night operations. She'd obviously read her share of Army manuals—more, perhaps, than Norma had, which gave Constance some small satisfaction. To see Norma outmatched, for once, might turn out to be the great reward this camp had to offer.

And what about Roxie? This was not the first time Constance had seen a young woman veer so wildly from light-hearted gaiety to nervous tics and small flights of panic. She reminded Constance of the girls who used to pass through her jail on charges of waywardness and incorrigibility. They never knew, at first, whether they could trust Constance, and as a result would fly from a pretense at nonchalance to an absolute terror of having their wrongdoings uncovered, exposed in the papers, and used against them in court. Roxie seemed, at first glance, just like one of her jailhouse girls.

Then again, she claimed to come from a family of some wealth and substance. It wasn't unusual for girls of her background to be high-strung. Perhaps Roxie had never been on her own before.

But what of her failure to bring a uniform along? Most of the girls were, to Constance's eye, almost too well-equipped, with plain but perfectly made uniforms, boots so new that there was still a shine on the toes, and cunning little canteen kits slung over their shoulders. To have shown up with nothing at all in the way of a uniform seemed awfully careless for a girl who didn't want for anything.

At least she was friendly to Fleurette. The two of them sat together companionably, their heads bent over a little song-book Fleurette carried in her pocket. With two hundred campers assembled under the mess tent, all of them chatting at once, Constance couldn't hear the two of them, but she could only assume that Fleurette was teaching Roxie a song.

At last Mrs. Nash took the podium and rang a bell to call them to order. "You have an early morning tomorrow, so we must start at once," she said, in the kind of broad and bosomy voice that came from years of addressing crowds at clubs and churches. She picked up a card and read from it. "'The National Service School is the first modern attempt to mobilize women for wartime service, organized with the aim of training women for the duties which fall naturally to them in these times, including nursing the sick, feeding the hungry, sewing bandages and other surgical supplies, as well as comforting the sorrows and relieving the necessities of the families of our men serving bravely at the front.'"

She put down the card and added, "And I remind you that it is war that lies ahead, and that even in victory we pay a terrible price. Just like the men who train for battle, every one of you has a part to play. There is no such thing as an inconsequential job or a meaningless task. Every soldier learns that, and you will, too."

This burst of speech was followed by vigorous staccato applause, whistles, and cheers from the more enthusiastic among them. They were a funny-looking group that evening, as many had not yet put on their khaki camp uniforms and all were still wearing their civilian hats, which is to say that there was quite a lot of ribbon and plumage bobbing around.

"Our school is organized according to military principles, with military drilling and discipline a part of everyday life," she continued. "We take this approach to obtain immediate response, prompt obedience, to have a sure way of gaining time in going from place to place, and to give an understanding of how superfluous are many of the things we have for a long time considered the ordinary necessities of life."

The applause began more hesitantly and died out distractedly as the audience was called upon to wonder what, exactly, might be the ordinary necessities of life that would become superfluous over the next six weeks.

"However, there is no intention of producing a modern Amazonian corps. Yes, you will rise at dawn to reveille and begin your day with the same setting-up exercises performed by the men at Plattsburg. You'll do the same drills and marches, and eat the same meals in mess halls that your brothers and husbands wrote home about. But then you'll spend your days learning the skills most suited for women who wish to be intelligently useful in times of national stress."

At the mention of an Amazonian corps, Fleurette nudged Constance and smiled. Constance answered with a look of despair. She didn't know what, exactly, Mrs. Nash believed to be the skills most suited for women, but she would never forgive Norma if she'd brought them all the way to Maryland to learn to cook and sew.

"Before we issue your field campaign hats and send you back to your tents for the night, I am pleased to introduce your instructors, who will come to the front and take their sashes," Mrs. Nash said.

Norma was poised at the very edge of her chair with her hands on her knees. It looked like a posture that she might've seen in a book. Constance had never seen her stand before a crowd before

41

and wondered how she'd handle it. The instructors rose, one by one, from around the room to join Mrs. Nash on the platform.

"Mrs. Hastings, knitting, plain sewing, and bandages."

Fleurette took particular interest in Mrs. Hastings, who had yet to meet her star pupil.

"Nurse Cartwright, elementary hygiene, home care of the sick, and scientific bed-making. She will also run our infirmary."

Nurse Cartwright had trouble working the sash around her Red Cross badges but managed after a brief struggle. She was red-faced in the manner of all older women who tended to overheat easily, but there was something jolly about her, too: a glimmer of mischief in her eyes, perhaps. In Constance's experience, nurses were champion rule-breakers if it meant getting their patients what they needed.

"Mrs. Billings, home dietetics and cooking for the convalescent."

Norma whispered that Mrs. Billings was far too slender to be any kind of cook. Constance wearily anticipated the afternoons she'd be forced to spend learning Mrs. Billings's recipes for celery soup and soda cracker gruel.

"Mr. Turner, map-drawing and wireless."

That was better, thought Constance. She could learn how to draw a map or run a radio, and Mr. Turner seemed like exactly the sort of angular, bespectacled man who could teach it to her.

"Miss Kopp, raising and dressing pigeons and small game."

Norma was halfway out of her chair before she understood what had happened. "Dressing?" Fleurette whispered. "We're not going to eat them, are we?"

Norma didn't dare to look at them, but Constance could see from the wobble in her chin that she couldn't decide what to do. A rumble went around the room as heads turned in search of her.

"Miss Kopp?" called Geneva Nash, turning their surname into one long musical note.

"Don't keep her waiting," Constance whispered. "You're making it worse."

Norma was rendered temporarily speechless over the idea of roasting her birds and feeding them to soldiers. The sight of her sister in such agitation lifted Constance's spirits considerably. She was secretly delighted over the misunderstanding and resolved to befriend anyone who spoke of serving Norma's pigeons for dinner.

"Go on," Constance whispered, and nudged her shoulder.

Without a glance backwards, Norma marched stoically to the front, where she took her sash and stood alongside the others. She kept her shoulders back and stared across the room, just over the top of everyone's heads.

There stands my sister, Constance thought, in what should have been her moment of triumph. Constance had been nothing but dismissive toward Norma's ideas about a military pigeon messaging service. She'd watched Norma write one letter after another to any Army or Navy commander whose name she spotted in the newspaper. Norma even typed a letter to President Wilson himself. There came no response but one: this invitation to teach a class at Camp Chevy Chase, where she could only hope that her contraption would be spotted by a military man and passed up the ranks. It was such a foolish idea, but what would Norma do without it? Even a staid and unimaginative woman like her sister needed a bit of hope to cling to.

Maude Miner stepped up on the platform next, along with a man wearing a uniform made bright with medals and bars.

"I met most of you earlier today," Miss Miner said. "You won't see me around the camp, because I'm assigned to Washington now, to work with the War Department on furthering the cause of a role for women in the fight which has become almost inevitable. I want you all to know that this camp did not come about by accident. It was not handed to us by the gentlemen in Washington. No one woke up one morning and decided that women should train just as men do—well, no one of the male persuasion woke up and thought that."

To enthusiastic laughter from the audience, she said, "In fact, when a few wives of officers got up a little committee and went to Washington to present their ideas, do you think they were welcomed in and invited to sit at the table alongside the generals? They most certainly were not."

This was received with boos and hisses from the campers. "So they went ahead on their own! Without anyone's permission, without anyone's approval, and with no money or land on which to camp, and no idea whether women would actually turn up and train, they built the National Service School program. Now we have generals attending our graduation exercises, and even the President himself, from time to time. Do you know why?"

"Why?" shouted Margaret Day, to the laughter of those sitting around her.

"Because if we set about doing what we know, in our hearts and minds, must be done, then we will be impossible to ignore. We will take our seat at the table because it belongs to us."

Now everyone was on their feet, cheering and whistling. Constance had never seen such stirrings among a crowd of women before. Fleurette stood on her chair and raised her arms in the air. Sarah, Constance noticed, was laughing and clapping, but crying, too. Miss Miner knew how to rouse an audience.

She waved them back into their seats. "Now you know how hard-fought our gains have been. I must remind you, however, that the fate of this camp, and of every camp like it, rests with you. It's up to you to comport yourselves in a manner that puts us all in the best possible light. I don't have to tell you that reporters have been here all afternoon. We want them here, to tell our story and to encourage other women to join in.

"But they will tell whatever story you give them to tell. That's why you must all hold yourselves to the very highest standards of virtuous womanhood. There is to be no mischief or misbehavior. Breaking of curfew will not be tolerated. Smoking and drinking are absolutely prohibited. Any behavior that could tarnish your reputation will likewise tarnish the reputation of not only this camp, but of the others taking place all over the country. Do you know that when we printed up postcards inviting women to register their willingness to serve in wartime, we received over half a million responses?"

Half a million! That drew a great deal of murmuring. Constance could only imagine the astonishment in Washington when all those cards arrived in the mail.

"That's right. But these camps are looked upon as an experiment, and if that experiment fails—if there is even a whiff of impropriety or moral degeneracy—it puts an end to the possibility of wartime service for women—not just for you, but for all women. Is that entirely clear to each and every one of you?"

There came another round of applause, but also quite a lot of smirking at that idea. Sarah leaned over to Constance and said, "I'm quite certain that one or two men get into trouble at the Army camps. Has anyone declared that men can't go off to war because a few of them behaved badly at camp?"

"She's saying it for the benefit of that fellow with all the medals on his uniform," Constance said. The military man looked decidedly ill at ease in front of a room of women, and something about his demeanor suggested that he thought he had better things to do. It gave Constance the unsettling feeling that she—and the two hundred others—were imposing upon his time.

Miss Miner finished by introducing the man. General Murray took the podium long enough to introduce Privates Hackbush and Piper, who would remain for the duration of the camp to guard the entrance.

"At the conclusion of this camp," he said, "I shall return for your graduation exercises and bestow upon each of you a medal just like this one." He held up a small silver badge, engraved in some manner that couldn't be made out from a distance. "On behalf of the United States Army, we thank you for your service."

As they stood to applaud, Fleurette caught Constance's sleeve. "What happened to Roxie? Did she duck out?"

Constance looked around. Her place on the bench was empty. "I didn't see her go."

"I didn't either. I stood up to cheer, and when I turned around, she was gone. Do you suppose it was the speech that made her ill, or the dinner?"

⊰ 6 ⊱

IT WAS THE speech.

Beulah darted back to the rear of the mess hall. One of the soldiers—the handsome one, Hack—stepped into the exit to block
her way. "Orientation is mandatory, miss."

"I only want some air," Beulah whispered, but when every girl
sitting nearby turned to look at her, she settled for taking her air
indoors, on a vacant bench in the back of the tent. She dropped
down in what she hoped was a posture of exhaustion, loosened
her collar, and fanned herself with her hat.

It wasn't the stifling air that sent her into a swoon: it was the
moralizing. Every girl in camp had just been told to watch for
wickedness among them. And who more perfectly personified im-
morality than the notorious Beulah Binford? Her name was so
synonymous with moral degeneracy that it was still invoked without explanation in the papers. Just the year before, a salacious
crime in Boston had been described as "a Beulah Binford–style
case involving an alluring young lady and a prominent banker."

Beulah had no intention of misbehaving at camp. She'd spent
every penny just to get there, and she'd borrowed from Mabel,
besides. She couldn't leave if she wanted to. She hadn't fare for
a hack or shoes that would carry her far on a muddy farm road.

To make a success of herself at this camp and to win passage to France was her only hope. She wasn't about to throw it away over a stolen cigarette or a wine bottle.

But it didn't matter what she did, it mattered who she was. Anyone might recognize her from the papers and point a finger at her. What was she to do about that?

Beulah saw all too clearly why Mabel had tried to warn her away from this place. She was trapped here, for all practical purposes, with two hundred pairs of eyes upon her. In New York, she could slip away. She could dart down a side street, pull her hat over her eyes, evade a curious landlady, or walk out on a job. What was she to do here, but to pretend to be someone she wasn't, and hope no one noticed?

Now it did feel stuffy and close in the tent, with every girl cheering and clapping. Beulah kicked her feet a little to push some air up her skirts. Miss Miner finished speaking, the general made his remarks, and then they were released, at last, to rush out into the cool night air and back to their tents.

"What happened to you?" came a voice at her elbow. It was Fleurette, tender and solicitous. She was a sweet girl, and eager to please, but Beulah could already see that she'd have trouble shaking her if she ever wanted a minute alone.

"I needed a little air, that's all," Beulah said. Remembering the character she was to play, she added, "Although I suppose it's to be nothing but fresh country air, morning and night. I'll take a nice town house on Park Avenue any day, and a good leaded window that stays closed."

"Do you live on Park Avenue?" asked Fleurette, as they made their way outside with the others.

"Only in the winter," Beulah said carelessly, as if to live anywhere both winter and summer would be uncouth. It was true that the better blocks uptown were virtually empty in the most sti-fling weeks of summer.

"You'll have to show me your house sometime," Fleurette said.

Beulah considered the power she could hold over a girl like Fleurette. As long as the possibility of an invitation to a Park Avenue town house was dangling before her, what would she do? Would she keep a secret, if she had to? Would she tell a lie?

It was a mean-spirited thought. Beulah tried to banish it as they reached their tent and made ready to settle in for the night. But once they were in their cots, with the lamp extinguished, her mind kept circling the question of who misbehaves and who keeps the secrets. Who kisses and who tells. Among sisters, you were always one or the other. And now, with Beulah surrounded by sisters, she couldn't help but think of Claudia—Claudia, whose name had vanished from her lips, whose presence had been driven from her mind.

As much as she fought it, as she drifted off to sleep, it was Claudia who came back to her.

THE FIRST TIME Beulah awoke and found her sister gone, she was too terrified to say a word. Beulah was a fearful child, prone to nightmares and convinced that disaster lurked around every corner, usually in the form of a family member gone miss-ing. But this wasn't a nightmare. She was awake, and Claudia was, in matter of fact, missing. Beulah pushed a toe over to Claudia's side of the bed and found it cold. She'd been gone for hours.

It was Beulah's belief that if she woke her grandparents, Clau-dia's disappearance would be made all the more real, but if she stayed in bed, and closed her eyes, and allowed any sort of dream to overtake her, even a terrible one, that when she awoke, there was at least a possibility that her sister would be restored to her and that the terrors of the night would be vanquished.

Much to Beulah's surprise, that was precisely what happened. Claudia was back in bed before dawn. Her hair smelled of smoke and when she opened her mouth, there came from it a spoiled raisiny odor that reminded Beulah of their mother. She tried to ask Claudia where she had been, but Claudia only put a finger to Beulah's lips and said, "Hush, baby."

That went on for almost a year. Beulah was only nine and would do anything her older sister asked of her: lie, keep her secrets, and even live with the dread that burrowed inside of her every time she turned over in bed and discovered Claudia to be away on what had become her routine midnight absences.

One night, she awoke and knew something was different. Their grandfather was up and waiting in the sitting room. She could hear him cough and scratch his beard. His chair squeaked faintly when he shifted around in it.

Beulah slipped out of bed and crawled just far enough down the hall to see that he was sitting in the dark, with his constable's coat on and a rifle across his lap. Poppa—that's what they called him, having never grown accustomed to calling their own father anything—had fought in the War between the States, and after that was over he found that he enjoyed marching back and forth with a rifle and wearing a uniform, so he took up constabulary work. He liked the house run with a certain amount of order and precision, which suited Beulah just fine, as she regarded predictable meals, a clean bed, and washed and folded clothes to be luxuries never previously afforded to her.

But Claudia chafed at it. When she came home that night and found Poppa waiting for her, she was ready for a fight and she got one.

"If you want to go out there on the streets like your mother, you ought to stay gone," Poppa said.

"You don't know where I go," Claudia said.

"I know exactly where a pretty girl like you goes at night," he said. "You're not the first one to live under my roof and try a trick like that, but you will be the last. Your grandmother took you in after I told her not to. I said you girls couldn't stay here unless you behaved like the Lord's own angels. If you're done behaving, you can leave. Both of you."

"Beulah's got nothing to do with this."

Beulah sat up in the dark when she heard her name.

"Beulah will do just like you in a few years. I see it every day. If there's one in the family, all the rest of them go rotten."

"Nobody's going rotten. I go to school. I do my chores."

"If you've got time for school and chores and running around all night, then you've got time to work. I'll put you on at a cotton mill and you can see how you like that. You'll be too tired to sneak out at night. Maybe that's just what you need."

"What I need is to be left alone once in a while," Claudia snarled. Her footsteps moved toward the bedroom where Beulah cowered in silence, but then there was a smack and a stumble, and Claudia cried out, and then their grandmother was awake. She shuffled out of the bedroom and told Poppa not to lay a hand on the girl, but then she said to Claudia that she ought to be more grateful for what had been given to her.

"I took you in," Meemaw said. "I didn't have to, but I did."

"You did have to," Claudia said. "We were children."

"You still are." Meemaw was crying now. "You're my baby girls."

Claudia couldn't bear to see her grandmother cry. No one could. Beulah, still curled up in a knot in the dark, pressed against the blackened oiled wood in the gloomy hallway. She could hear the sounds of Claudia comforting her grandmother and making promises that she had no intention of keeping.

The trouble with Claudia was not that she was a bad girl, but that she was restless. She had nothing but contempt for the kind of future she'd been told to expect for herself: a few years of seam-stressing or factory work, to be followed by a marriage to a man who could afford nothing but a little shotgun house, just two rooms and a hot, cramped kitchen in the back.

That just wouldn't do for Claudia. In that respect, she was like her mother, Jessie.

Jessie Binford always wanted something better: a better dress, a better pair of shoes, a better complexion, a better man. She wanted money and nice things, and she didn't want to work for them. Anyone would desire a life like that, but the difference was that their mother—and Claudia, turning out to be like her —believed herself to be entitled to just about anything she could dream up. If she could imagine it, she deserved it, and the world was a cruel place for denying it to her.

Beulah unwound a little as the sounds in the parlor subsided. She told herself, as she always did, that if only she could go to sleep, she would awake in the morning with her sister next to her and it would be as if none of this had happened.

She was still young enough, back then, that she could just crawl into bed, close her eyes, give herself over to sleep, and it would rise up and carry her mercifully away.

NOW, AT THE age of twenty-four, sleep was no longer so merciful to Beulah. She was once again wide awake on her cot inside the tent, listening to Norma's snoring and the breathing and sighing and stirring of the others.

There was something else her grandfather said to Claudia that night—something Beulah used to turn over and over in her mind, trying to make sense of it. What was it?

With a shudder she recalled it, like a nursery rhyme she'd forgotten.

"The hemlock in the soup does not know it's the poison," Poppa had said. "It just thinks it's a bunch of green leaves, because it don't see what it does to others. You're the poison in the soup, Claudia Binford. You just don't know it. Your momma didn't know it, neither."

❧ 7 ❧

THE HIGH AND distant note of the bugle insinuated itself into Constance's dreams. Before she could yawn and stretch herself awake, Norma jumped out of the cot next to her and shook her by the shoulder.

"That's reveille," Norma said. "Jump out of bed like a soldier or I'll turn you out."

When Constance and Norma were girls, they shared a bed, and even then Norma liked to thump her in the ribs when the sun came up. Norma couldn't envision such a thing as a leisurely start to the day: she greeted the dawn with the sort of smack one gives to a newborn baby to start it breathing. Constance sat up obediently, as there was no percentage in resisting.

Sarah was up already, brushing out her hair and wrapping it into a braid at the back of her neck. Only Fleurette and Roxie were still abed. Fleurette had one eye open, and kept it fixed on Roxie, who feigned sleep through the commotion with the practiced air of a girl who knew how to get her way by pretending. Constance could already see that Fleurette intended to follow Roxie's every move, which meant that she would sneak an extra five minutes in bed if Roxie did.

Norma was having none of it. In one quick gesture, she pulled

54

their blankets off and gave each girl a swat on the soles of their feet.

"Ow!" Fleurette scrambled out of her cot to get away from her.

Roxie stretched and rose at her leisure. "I hope that horrible trumpet means that breakfast is to be served."

"Not until your calisthenics," Norma said. "Get up. The whole tent earns a demerit if any of us are late."

Constance lifted the tent flap just enough to see a pale strip of pink light along the eastern horizon. It was cold out, in that cruel and damp way that was particular to March. She didn't dare complain for fear that Norma would deliver a lecture on how much more unpleasant conditions were in the trenches in France.

They'd draped their uniforms over the ropes that extended from the central tent pole, there being no other place to air a skirt and jacket. Constance suspected that most of the girls at the camp would be lost without wardrobes and chiffoniers for their clothing, but in her days as deputy sheriff, she had slept in a jail cell often enough that she knew how to organize her attire anywhere it could be hung.

The five of them dressed silently, their backs turned to each other, exchanging night clothes for uniforms as hastily as they could. As everyone's uniforms were homemade, they resembled each other only superficially. Fleurette had sewn hers, Norma's, and Constance's from the leftover runs of light wool and heavy muslin she'd once used to make Constance's deputy uniforms, and cobbled together what she could of sturdy buttons and warm linings from the scraps in her sewing room. Fleurette was fond of pleats and darts and put them everywhere, even on a camp uniform. She even managed to impose a waist on Constance, who disliked the constriction and preferred her garments to hang straight.

The skirts fell just above the ankles, with buttons down the front and deep pockets on the sides. The campers were permitted to wear men's regulation riding pants under the skirts, both for warmth and for practicality, as some exercises were best performed with the skirts unbuttoned near the bottom. Constance wasn't in the habit of wearing riding pants but was glad to have them: already a wind was whistling around the tent flap, and she didn't like the idea of it rushing up her skirt before she'd even had a look at a pot of coffee.

"I wish the contingent arguing against skirts had won the day," Sarah said. "I'd rather wear nothing but pants. Even a skirt like this is a hindrance in the field."

"They weren't going to put us in trousers, were they?" Roxie asked. Fleurette had stitched together a fairly respectable uniform for Roxie, by taking apart a brown dress and fashioning it into a skirt, and adding a collar to one of Roxie's dingy shirtwaists.

For a Park Avenue girl, Constance thought, her clothes were in tatters, and her story about digging them out of the mending basket didn't hold up. They weren't worth mending: they were too cheap to begin with. She considered the possibility that Roxie had run away from home and purchased second-hand clothes along the way, but it sounded far-fetched. It was none of Constance's business, anyway. What concern of it was hers if the girl had a secret to keep?

Norma, having dressed first, stood at the tent flap. "One of us will have to go out every morning to pump water," she announced, taking up the bucket that had been issued to them for that purpose. "Since none of you have given a thought to that, I'll do it today. Roxanna will go tomorrow, and we'll follow the alphabet from there."

Having established a protocol and offering no opportunity for rebuttal, Norma went out with the bucket. When she returned, the five of them gathered outside, behind the tent, dipping into water to splash their faces and then drawing up cups of it so that they might brush their teeth. All around them, the girls from the other tents were doing the same. There was quite a bit of thin, nervous laughter as the light came up in the sky and revealed them, in the middle of their ablutions, in the company of strangers, out in the open air.

For just a moment Constance thought she might know something of what a soldier felt on his first day away from home, awakening with a fine feeling of adventure in the unfamiliar surroundings of a military camp. Theirs was such a smaller kind of adventure—only six weeks away, and then what? A return home, for most of them, to their familiar friends and obligations. And for Constance—what waited for her? A Red Cross course, and then back to the farm to cut field dressings?

The bugle sounded again, but this time it was first call, which was to be their summons to calisthenics. All two hundred women (two hundred and one, including Margaret from Texas) trundled off at once, stumbling over tent lines and bumping into each other in the half-dark. Taken as a group, Constance couldn't imagine that they'd ever look like any sort of military regimen. She wondered if they'd be marching in straight lines by the end of their training, or if they'd always bumble along like children on their way to a sledding party.

In a field just beyond their little city of tents waited Mrs. Nash, a walking-stick in hand and a whistle around her neck. The sun was now up over the horizon, and it shone just enough to warm them slightly. Constance hoped Mrs. Nash would have them running relays, or hopping up and down, or anything that might bring a little warmth. Instead, the first business of the morning was to organize themselves into four companies.

Mrs. Nash blew a whistle and started shouting commands that the group was not entirely prepared to receive. The idea was to count off by fours, and then for each group to arrange itself by height, with the tallest in the back. This gave Constance no trouble as she had only to stand in the very rear of her company. Fleurette readily took her place in the front. The rest of the girls had a great deal of difficulty in sorting themselves out, with many of them perching on their toes to stand next to a friend, or taking off their hats and mashing their hair down to get closer to the front. Mrs. Nash used her walking-stick to nudge the girls into line.

"We have only half an hour for our setting-up exercises, and we've lost most of it already," Mrs. Nash called, but that only encouraged the girls to delay further.

At last they were standing at attention in their rows. Mrs. Nash shouted her commands from a drill-book she carried with her.

"Right, dress!" she called. Norma stood several rows ahead. Constance could see from her vantage point in the back that Norma was one of the few who knew what to do. Had she been marching and drilling behind the barn all winter?

They spent half an hour turning this way and that, heeding commands intended to get them in line and facing the direction in which they were to march. Constance saw little point to it, as the one thing they wouldn't be asked to do for France would be to march in formation. Women might play a role, certainly, but it would be nothing as militaristic as this. She surrendered to the deflating feeling that the camp was more of an entertainment than a practical training ground.

At last came the mess call. The companies fell apart and rushed to breakfast. They were supposed to enter by separate doors according to company and stand at attention until ordered to sit, but there was such a scramble that Mrs. Nash's instructions, barked out over the din, went unheeded.

Constance couldn't help but feel a little pity for her. She was trying to impose order on girls who, for the most part, were accustomed to viewing life as a series of amusements—girls who would only follow a command if it was part of a game, and then only if they felt inclined to play it.

She was glad not to be in Mrs. Nash's position. The last time she had charge of a group of women, they were locked in their cells and had little choice but to do what was expected of them. These girls were running amok.

They descended upon the breakfast that had been set out on long tables: boiled eggs and cold potatoes, bread and butter, and shredded wheat. A girl going around with pitchers of milk and coffee announced that they should've had bananas, but the truck had been waylaid. No one seemed bothered by it.

Constance sat next to Sarah. Fleurette and Roxie came dashing over, and Norma made her way to them eventually. Every company, it seemed, had dissolved and re-formed according to tent-mates and other prior associations.

"Norma's without her cabbage," Fleurette shouted over the racket in the mess hall. "If the ground starts to shake and opens up and swallows us all, it's because my sister has broken with her most sacred of traditions and angered the gods."

"We're in a military camp," Norma said. "Eat your rations."

Years ago, Norma developed a peculiar habit of eating pickled red cabbage on toast for breakfast, and she had never since strayed from it. If the three of them had cause to stay in a hotel for a night or two, she would bring a jar of it from home and set it prominently in the center of the breakfast table like a fetid purple flower arrangement. But military order was all she cared about now. She couldn't be bothered with her old routines.

In between bites of bread, butter, and smashed egg, Sarah said, "Are any of you taking the first-aid course this afternoon? I'd rather practice on someone I know."

"Oh yes, I'll be there," called a girl at the other end of the table who introduced herself as Tizzy. "I'm to learn first aid and hospital cooking. There's a group of us girls in my building back home who want to volunteer in the hospitals as soon as the men start coming back. A pretty face is the best medicine."

"I'm entirely certain that medicine is the best medicine," Norma said, "and we haven't sent a single man overseas yet, so I don't know why you're already expecting them to return home injured. Isn't there something you can do now, while the French and the British are in the trenches on their own?"

"Well, we get together once a week and do our comfort bags," Tizzy said.

"I've seen those bags go out by the barrel at the train station," Fleurette said. "I always wondered what went in them."

"Oh, you know. Handkerchiefs and soap, toothbrushes, cards and little games. But it's the notes from America that mean the most. We tell them that we're proud of them for fighting, and that we admire their bravery and think of them every day. They love hearing from American girls. Some of them write back. It's a fine entertainment to open their little notes and try to read past the censor's marks."

Fleurette looked puzzled for a minute, as if she might be trying to work out in her own mind whether anything a soldier might say about the war should be considered an entertainment.

"Well," said Sarah briskly, "what about the Kopp sisters?"

Constance looked to Norma, who had taken the responsibility of enrolling them in classes.

"Fleurette goes to plain sewing class, of course," Norma began, but was quickly interrupted.

"That's a perfect waste of my time, unless I'm to teach the class." Fleurette sounded appalled, and Constance was appalled on her behalf. What could anyone tell Fleurette about making a uniform or knitting socks?

But Norma was unmoved. She cut her toast into little trian-gles, buttered them along the edge, and said, "The Red Cross is very particular about its bandages. If anyone can learn them quickly and teach others how to do it, it will be you. I've no doubt you'll be bored, but only after you see what's required and settle on the best way to get them done."

Fleurette sighed and surrendered to it. "Bandages."

"I will take the signaling course," Norma continued, "as it is not entirely unconnected to my work, although I hardly see the point of standing on a hill and waving flags around when we can send a bird with a message."

"A bird?" asked Sarah, who, having only been a tent-mate of Norma's for a night, was not yet acquainted with her ideas on messenger pigeons and was still under the impression that Norma was to teach a class on raising and dressing small birds and game.

Constance, eager to cut off this line of discussion, hastily put in, "What about you, Sarah? What do you hope to do for the war?"

Sarah looked up brightly and said, "Ambulance work. I want any kind of first-aid training, and a course on driving and mechan-ics."

"Why would we drive them around in ambulances?" Fleurette asked. "By the time they're sent home, aren't they ensconced in a hospital and out of trouble?"

"Oh, I won't drive it here in the States," said Sarah. "I'm going to France. The American Field Service isn't going to wait for Mr. Wilson to go into the war. They're already running ambulances, and—"

"You're going to France?" Fleurette said, nearly spitting her coffee across the table. "Right now? Before we've even sent the Army, or—or—anyone?"

Sarah took a little breath and touched a napkin to her lips. She looked at some spot in the air between them and said, "It isn't true that we haven't sent anyone. My brother volunteered in January. He couldn't wait. He's driving an ambulance at the front now."

They were a little island of silence in the middle of a noisy mess hall. The last corner of toast stuck in Constance's throat.

"He's my twin," she said, smiling bravely into a platter covered in broken egg shells. "We've never been apart. I'm going to follow him."

Fleurette turned bright red and Roxie's mouth formed a little oval. For once in her life, Norma didn't utter a word.

At last Sarah turned and put a hand on Constance's wrist. "What about you?"

"Me?" She was still imagining Sarah's twin, slight and brown-headed and quick to smile like his sister, driving an ambulance in Verdun or the Argonne because he could not wait to go and serve. She felt very still and strange all at once.

"Yes, you. You look like a woman who has something to offer her country. What is it?"

⊰ 8 ⊱

BEULAH WAS REMINDED, that afternoon, of how capricious spring could be in the South: wintry one minute and unexpectedly sensual the next. The day had started with the kind of bone-chilling damp that seemed to rise right out of the ground, but after lunch, a warm breeze pushed the chill away and suddenly the air was almost tropical. Her mother used to say that those breezes came from Cuba, although what Jessie Binford knew about Cuba was anyone's guess. Nonetheless, the temperatures rose until Beulah found herself sweating under her collar in the steamy tent where she was to learn bandage-rolling and first aid from the Red Cross.

She'd never been good at sitting in a classroom, although she hadn't had much of a chance to practice. Her grandmother couldn't see the use of schooling except as a means of keeping her out from underfoot. Once Beulah was old enough to roll out biscuit dough on her own or to operate the mangle on washing day, she was welcome to stay at home and help her grandmother to do exactly what Beulah herself would be doing, as far as either of them could guess, for the rest of her life. There would always be a washing day, and a day for bread, and one for scrubbing floors.

Nothing they could teach in the classroom was going to change any of that.

Beulah fidgeted in the Red Cross tent as Nurse Cartwright delivered her first lecture, but the words wouldn't come together in Beulah's mind to form any definitive picture that might tell her how to take a man's temperature or dress a wound. When each girl was given an instruction manual to read and memorize, she paged through it and looked at the diagrams, and wondered how she might trick Fleurette into telling her what it said without coming right out and admitting that she couldn't quite follow it.

This was not a promising start. No mention had been made yet of shipping off to France, apart from Sarah's admission at breakfast, and it had not yet been explained what each girl would have to prove she could do before she was allowed to go. In fact, her classmates seemed to find the classes amusing, and at times a bit dull—but didn't treat it as preparation for work they might soon have to carry out on their own.

They were younger, Beulah had to remind herself. Most of them were only eighteen or nineteen and had never worked a day in their lives, apart from helping in their mothers' kitchens. Plenty of them hadn't done that much. They had servants. The purpose of a paid staff was to render the children of the house useless, or at least to make their contributions more of a sentimental nature than a practical one.

Beulah couldn't imagine a life like that. She was pretending to be twenty but she was twenty-four, and had already done every sort of work. As she watched the other girls in class, whispering when the instructor had her back turned and drawing silly pictures in the margins of their books, it occurred to her that perhaps she shouldn't expect the others to take their lessons so seriously. She'd been out in the world, surviving on her wits, and they had not.

That night, after dinner, the entire camp was at its liberty until curfew at nine o'clock. The balmy weather held and made for a pleasant evening to be out among the tents, mingling and laughing with the other girls. Beulah allowed Fleurette to make a few small changes to her improvised uniform—it was satisfying to be fussed over, and Fleurette had a way of understanding just how a body wants to move inside its raiment and to make it do so with grace. Once they were satisfied with their appearances, they went out together into the purple night.

Lanterns glowed orange from the tent flaps, and a few small fires were lit in improvised pits of river rock, giving the place the appearance of a gypsy caravan come to rest for the night. It was lovely to walk among the tents and hear the idle chatter of so many girls at their leisure. Freed from the strictures of the lives they'd left behind—parents, teachers, tutors, bosses if they had them—and without a man in sight apart from Hack and Clarence, who patrolled the perimeter but otherwise stayed away, there was an easy camaraderie among them. With no one watching, they could let their hair down, as a manner of speech but also as a practical matter. It was a great relief to pull out pins, untie ribbons, and shake combs loose.

Fleurette hopped around in the kid slippers that she'd changed into—against camp regulation, Beulah had to admire that—and spun around in the grass to see if her skirt would fly up, which it did.

"The pattern called for a flat skirt that hangs straight," she said, "which is good enough for Constance and Norma, but we need a little life in our wardrobes, don't we?"

"Did you say you live out in the country with your sisters?" Beulah asked. "On a farm?"

"Yes, and it's just as awful as it sounds," Fleurette said. "I'd live there forever if they had their way. But I intend to take a room in town as soon as I can put a little money together. What about you? You must live with your mother and father, if you're up on Park Avenue."

"It isn't so bad," Beulah said noncommittally. "I'm left to my own devices. Which one of you had the idea to come here?"

She was learning to turn the conversation away from herself. The fewer questions she answered, the fewer lies she'd have to keep track of.

"It was Norma's doing," Fleurette said. "She has an attachment to those pigeons that no one else can fathom, nor do we want to. She thinks they're going to be of use in the war, but Constance and I both know that the Army won't have anything to do with Norma and those ridiculous birds. We only put up with them because they keep her amused. She'd be ordering us around if she didn't have the birds to keep her busy."

"I don't suppose there's any chance of marrying her off?"

Fleurette groaned. "Who would marry Norma?"

"Are you the only marriageable sister of the three?"

Fleurette looked at her curiously. "Why would you say that?"

"Well, Constance seems awfully . . . imposing. To a man, I mean. She must've towered over them at dances."

"I don't think she went to many dances. She didn't want to marry and keep house. She'd rather work."

Beulah pounced on that. There was something unusual about Constance, something that suggested that she had a life that she was keeping hidden. "Why doesn't she have a career, if she wants one? She's old enough to have had two or three."

"She's forty, but don't tell her I said so," Fleurette said. "Ask her yourself if you'd like to know."

It was quite apparent to Beulah that there was more to be said on the subject of Constance, but Fleurette wasn't going to tell.

At the edge of the campground, Fleurette spotted Tizzy, the girl who'd spoken to them at breakfast about putting together comfort bags for the soldiers. From her tent came the faint scratchy sound of a phonograph.

"Did you naughty girls smuggle in a Victrola?" Fleurette squealed, rushing over to have a look.

Tizzy was out of her uniform: she wore a peacock-blue kimono with silk knickers underneath, and had stepped out to smoke a cigarette attached to a long ebony holder. "Oh, it's just one of those little portable affairs," she said languidly, blowing out the smoke. "Come and have a look. You're Florine, is that right?"

"She's Fleurette," Beulah said. "I'm Roxie Collins."

That was better. Her new nickname slipped right out, in one long easy breath: *I'm Roxie Collins. Roxie Collins, how do you do?* She'd been practicing it silently all day. The practice paid off.

"Well, come on in, Roxie." Tizzy lifted the tent flap. "Girls, meet the girls."

Inside was a tent equipped like no other. Atop the dusty wooden platform was an Oriental carpet, the kind that wealthy people kept around long after it had been worn through in the middle, for garden parties and barn dances. Every cot was out-fitted with a matching brocade coverlet, obviously sent from a household overrun with such things, and topped with feather pillows. None of the girls wore their uniforms: they were attired as if to be arrayed around a swimming pool at a house-party, all in loose silks and scarves and beaded slippers.

Tizzy said, "You might've met one another in class today. I'm Tizzy Spotwood, over there's Dorina Bingham, that's Ginny Field, this is Liddy Powell, and of course Ellie Duval." She said their names as if they meant something, as if they had weight and import that Beulah ought to understand. She tried to act as if she did.

"Pleased to meet you," Ellie said, rising and giving them a little bow. She seemed to be the royalty among them. She was the prettiest, in that fragile, carved-from-ivory way that wealthy girls could be pretty. Her nose turned up at the very end, and when she smiled, the corners of her mouth lifted beguilingly.

Fleurette hardly saw her. In the very center of their tent, against the tent pole, was a phonograph player the size of a hat-box.

"Isn't that the most cunning little rig!" Fleurette gasped, rushing over to admire it. "Does anyone sing?"

The girls all looked up from their cots at once with expressions of bemused fatigue.

"After all those years of music academy, who can help it?" said Ginny. "But I'm finished with all that. I told Father that I can't be bothered anymore."

The others made murmurs of agreement. Fleurette had started to dance—she made one half-turn, quite stylishly—when she glanced around and saw the others staring at her.

"Then I suppose you all dance as well, but you can't be bothered with that, either. I didn't think I'd hear a single note other than that bugle for six weeks. We'll have to bring it out to the mess hall and have a dance. We could hold one every Saturday."

Ellie rearranged her features into a tender expression of regret. "I promised the owner of this particular machine that I wouldn't let it out of the tent. The very thing he warned against was a loud party and lots of girls stomping around."

Fleurette looked a little suspicious of that excuse, but said, "I suppose it's awfully delicate."

"It is," Ellie said. "Do you remember the night they set one up at Sherry's and a girl fell right into it and smashed the whole thing to bits?"

Tizzy, Dorina, Ginny, and Liddy all groaned in unison. Beulah hated them for it. Of course Fleurette hadn't heard about a night at Sherry's! She lived on a farm in New Jersey. These girls were practiced in the art of making outsiders feel unwelcome.

"Nobody bothers with Sherry's anymore," Beulah said dismissively, but it was a miscalculation. Ellie pounced.

"Oh, no? You don't come from New York, do you? You sound like . . ."

"Of course she's a New Yorker," Fleurette put in. "She lives up on Park Avenue, and she's going to have us all over when we're back in town."

Ellie kept her eyes fixed on Beulah. "We know everyone on Park Avenue," she said. "What's your father's name again?"

"Collins," Beulah muttered. It had seemed so aristocratic at first, but she realized now that the name sounded common. "He's a bore, and so is New York. I can hardly wait to get out."

At last she'd appealed to their sense of stylish ennui.

"New York is a bore," said Tizzy. "The war's ruined everything. There's no one going over to Europe in the summer. You just can't! Even the dress shops in Paris are closed. We're expected to go around modeling hats to benefit an orphanage, when we should be in Venice for the spring balls. It's dull and awful."

"Then I suppose you can't wait to get over to France," Beulah offered.

Tizzy shrugged and blew a perfect smoke ring from her cigarette. "When the war's over, I suppose. If they haven't bombed the place to bits."

"But aren't you going when we finish our course? To help with the war effort?"

Tizzy laughed. "We're not going to the front, if that's what you mean. I think we'd put every one of our mothers in an early grave if we went. There wouldn't be a Junior League left! They all would've died of shock."

Dorina reached into a trunk at the foot of her cot and pulled out a box of crackers and a few tins of anchovies. "I couldn't look at that mess they called dinner tonight. Who's having some?"

Fleurette was distracted by all the contraband Dorina had hidden away, but Beulah was still staring at Tizzy.

"Do you mean that you've come all this way to camp, you're taking all the courses, and then at the end you're just going to tell them you're not going?"

Tizzy looked at her, puzzled. "Tell who? Going where?"

"Tell . . . why, tell Mrs. Nash, or Miss Miner, or whoever's going to be here to ship us off to France."

A general shriek went up around the tent. "Mrs. Nash is not shipping us off!" Dorina cried between bites of cracker. "I'm sure a few of these girls are hoping to join up with the Red Cross or some dreadful thing, but they'll have to get up a subscription and raise the funds to go. Their fathers won't pay for it."

There were nods all around. Liddy said, "The Red Cross is only taking trained nurses, and that's a three-year course. There's a church group on Long Island that sent a girl last spring, but she only lasted two months. My mother knew one of the ladies at that church. It cost them a fortune and the girl never got out of Paris. They decided they'd rather donate to the refugees."

"Would your mother let you go?" Ellie asked, turning to Beulah.

The rest of them fell silent. Every eye was fixed on her. Just the word made something catch in her throat. *Mother.*

"Well?" Ellie asked again. "Would she?"

❦ 9 ❧

CLAUDIA AND BEULAH were under orders never to let Jessie Binford step inside their grandmother's house, but what were two daughters to do when their mother called to them from the other side of the screen door?

She swayed back and forth a little as she crooned to them: *Claudie! Binnie! Mama's home!*

Binnie was the name Beulah gave herself when she was too young to say her own name. No one ever called her that but her mother. The sound of it brought back the sensation of her mother putting her cool fingers over Beulah's eyelids as she fell asleep. It brought back the taste of cornmeal boiled in sweetened milk, with a little pool of bacon grease in the middle, the only dinner her mother ever made for her. Those were the singular comforts Beulah knew from the years before she and Claudia turned up on their grandparents' doorstep. How could she refuse them now?

But Jessie Binford had nothing like that on offer anymore. She stumbled through Meemaw's front door with an avalanche of excuses: She'd lost a job, a good job, and it wasn't her fault, or maybe she'd been put out of her furnished room and just needed a night or two while she looked for another, or she'd been abandoned by the man she'd taken up with most recently, although it was also possible that she abandoned him, and was prepared to swear that she'd never let a man like that bring her to ruin again.

And she was a ruin—a graceful, beautiful, sharp-as-knives ruin. She carried a brown glass bottle in her bosom and sipped out of it from a dropper. "My medicine," she told the girls as soon as Meemaw was out of earshot.

"Did you get sick, Mama?" Beulah asked, turning her face up to her mother, as if to the sun.

"No, baby," her mother said. "The medicine's to keep Mama well."

Jessie's medicine made her buoyant but droopy-eyed, and talkative in the most meaningless way. What started as an elaborate account of her ambitions—a move out West, a marriage to a promising older gentleman, a position in a department store—dissolved into mumbles, until her chin came to rest on her chest and she fell asleep right there, in the chair where she was sitting, in the middle of the afternoon.

It was a sin to sleep in the afternoon. It was a sin to wear perfume. It was a sin to accept a gift from a man: an ivory comb, a stickpin with a glass ruby, a pretty silver snuff-box. Jessie Binford should've crumbled under the weight of her sins, but instead she was elevated by them, and left them on display for anyone to see.

She had been smart to come around during the day, when their grandfather was out on patrol. He'd never let her inside if he was there to put a stop to it. Meemaw should've known better than to grant Jessie admittance when his back was turned, but she was a sentimental old woman who would not pass up a chance to lay her eyes on any of her three remaining children, for as long as she lived. So their mother was let back in. Poppa shouted about it in the evening—they hollered at one another until the cups rattled in their saucers and the neighbors came and pounded on the door for them to keep quiet—but it made no difference. Their mother was allowed to stay.

But she didn't stay long, as she tired of the yelling and chafed against the rules of the house just as Claudia did. In fact, what pained Beulah the most about seeing her mother again was the way that Jessie and Claudia quickly came to be more like disobedient sisters, trading stockings and trying on each other's ribbons and combs. Claudia took on airs in a way that never would have been tolerated when her mother wasn't around. She refused to help with the washing for fear that it would ruin her delicate hands, and she wouldn't get down on her knees to scrub the old pot-black stove because her hair, piled in a delicate top-knot, would come tumbling down if she bent over that far.

Little trinkets turned up for Claudia during Jessie's visit—a cameo portrait of an unknown lady in profile, tied to a blue ribbon, a powder puff and a pretty round box to put it in, a silk scarf. Claudia handled these gifts carelessly, as if they'd simply blown in on the wind and another batch might drift in behind it. She learned that attitude from her mother.

None of those trinkets were meant for Beulah. From the bedroom (Claudia and Beulah's bedroom, taken over by Jessie, so that Beulah slept by herself in the parlor, across two chairs shoved together) would come a trill of laughter, and then a hushed whisper that sounded like the shuffling of feet on a bare floor, and then another flurry of high-pitched giggles.

After a week or so of this, Beulah woke up one morning and found her mother gone, vanished in the middle of the night, having slipped out with Claudia, except that Claudia had the sense to steal back to bed before dawn and Jessie did not.

• • •

73

AFTER THAT, ANY mention of Jessie Binford was forbidden at Meemaw's house. Beulah, aiming to please her grandmother, did her best never to mention or even think of her mother. She did, however, expect to see her when Poppa died.

He went in his sleep one night, which Meemaw said was the best way to go, and she would know about that, having lost so many. She laid him out for viewing in their parlor for three days leading up to the funeral, so that the neighbors and the town constables might pay their respects. Beulah was glad when that came to an end and he was put into a box and taken away. She'd never lived in a house with a dead man before and hoped she would never have to do it again.

Beulah guiltily looked forward to the funeral because she longed to see her mother in a good stiff black dress, her hair done up nicely under a veiled hat, bringing soothing words for Meemaw and a fresh handkerchief to cry into.

But her mother was quite jarringly absent from the church, and so was Claudia. Beulah was, therefore, the only relation to sit alongside her grandmother during Poppa's funeral. All she remembered of it was the dark church, the black wax on the pews that she could dig into with her fingernails, and a tiny window with a pane of red glass that didn't let in the light.

Where was Claudia? She had vanished on the night he died, just slipped out as the doctor slipped in with his black bag. She didn't return to see her grandfather laid out. Her absence at the funeral was enormous and inexplicable. Beulah tried to make excuses for it.

"Claudia just run off 'cause she's scared," she whispered to Meemaw right before the service began, by way of explanation, but Meemaw wouldn't even look at her, and seemed not to have an opinion one way or another about Claudia.

A few of the neighbor ladies came back to the house after the funeral and carried out their obligations as they related to pans of chicken and dumplings, and a Polish dish of sausage and noodles that was unfamiliar to Beulah but worth investigating. None of the food was to be eaten that day, though. Meemaw insisted that it all be put away in the cold room. She wanted to be left in peace, and to put her head on the pillow for a few hours in the gray late afternoon.

The neighbor ladies did as Meemaw asked. Beulah saw them out and thanked them for their kindness. She was twelve by then, and knew how to behave like the lady of the house when circumstances required it. After they were gone, she sat on the front porch with the darkness crowding in around her and a little pecan pie in her hand. She was not terribly surprised to see Claudia coming up from the end of the street after a while, slowly, carefully, putting one foot directly in front of the other as if she were walking on a railroad track.

At sixteen, Claudia looked like a woman. She wore her dresses a little shorter so that her ankles showed, and she didn't mind it when a glimpse of petticoat could be seen from underneath her hem. Her hair was long and full and rich enough to be pleasing in its abundant arrangement of curls and knots, while Beulah's was still as thin as string and good for nothing but braiding. Claudia didn't look anything like their mother—she was prettier, with a pink little mouth pursed into a bow, and eyes too big for her heart-shaped face—but she carried herself like Jessie Binford did, with a certain sway to her walk like she was blowing around in the wind. She had the tiniest waist Beulah had ever seen, a feat that could only be accomplished by a girl of that particular age, when the bone stays were more tolerable and the ribs were soft enough to give way to ever-tighter corset ties.

She was, in every way, a pleasing picture of young womanhood. Beulah hardly knew what to make of her anymore.

Beulah watched as this body containing the spirit of her sister picked its way over the cobblestones and up onto the wooden sidewalk in front of Meemaw's house. She put the last corner of the pecan pie in her mouth and brushed away the crumbs.

"He gone now?" was the first thing Claudia said to her.

"You'd know that if you'da been here," Beulah said sullenly.

"I knew it," Claudia said. "It wouldn't a done me any good to be here, and it wouldn't a made a difference to him, 'cause he's dead."

"Meemaw went to lie down," Beulah said. "You ought not to bother her right now."

Claudia stood looking down at Beulah and then up at the front door where she'd peered through the screen, all those years earlier, asking for admittance that first time. Beulah was still a little peach of a girl, with cheeks that had only just lost their baby fat and eyes that naturally curved upward in a way that made her look just a little more flirtatious than a girl of twelve should be. She was too young for mourning and instead wore a somber dress of dark blue with a little red carnation tucked into the pocket.

That flower made all the difference. It was like a flame burning in a window, late at night.

"Why don't you come with me," Claudia said.

Beulah started to tell her that it wouldn't be right. She intended to say that if she went with Claudia, even to the end of the block, she wouldn't be allowed to come back home. She thought that she ought to remind Claudia about all the terrible things Claudia had shouted to her grandmother over the last few years, when Meemaw wanted nothing but a peaceful home and two good girls sleeping under her roof. She wanted to remind Claudia that there was only so much heartbreak an old woman could take, and to tell her that she ought to think more kindly toward the people who had tried to do right by her.

But when it came time to say any of that, the words just slipped away. All Beulah could see was her sister standing over her, with a hand outstretched. What could she do—what could she ever do, her whole life long—but to take that hand and to go wherever Claudia would lead her?

MONROE SQUARE WAS, in those days, a genteel pleasure ground for city-dwellers, equipped with flower beds in the English style, privet hedges pruned to a knife edge, and wide swaths of gravel where young ladies strolled with their parasols, their chaperones trailing behind.

It was the very civility of Monroe Square that allowed for such uncivilized goings-on. A girl could walk unaccompanied, and anyone might assume that she was under the watchful eye of some older woman sitting nearby on a park bench. There were always enough of them about.

A man could walk unaccompanied, too, and no one would think anything of that. He might be on his way to his place of business, or waiting to meet a friend. It was the most ordinary thing in the world for a man to make arrangements to meet a colleague at Monroe Square, so the men didn't attract any attention, either.

In this way, a young girl could make a friend. She might never be permitted inside a saloon or a hall for dancing, but in a park she could catch a man's eye, deliver a clever retort, and take a surreptitious sip of whatever was offered to her from a vest pocket. Claudia showed Beulah how to take a drink, and how to stop herself from shuddering when the fiery spirit took hold of her.

When they did meet a man, it wasn't much of a walk, after that, over to Mayo Street, where the police would leave them alone. That one narrow street was Richmond's own little pocket of lawlessness, a sanctioned red-light district, a place where a man didn't have to give his name and a girl wasn't asked her age. There were rooms for rent, and bowls of punch and jugs of ale right out on the sidewalk, and little player pianos that would grind out tunes for a penny.

Mayo Street was near the train station, close enough to draw men arriving from all over the country. It was an attractive place for girls, too, especially girls who were expecting a baby and wished to hide themselves away until it was born. There were houses where a girl in a certain kind of predicament could rent a room, and birth her baby in peace, and even keep it with her, if she wanted to, as long as she was willing to stay on and earn her keep afterward by entertaining the men invited in by her landlady. In this way, formerly respectable girls learned how to earn their living through the attentions of men, and Mayo Street flourished.

But for Claudia, it started over in Monroe Square, in the bright sunshine, right under the watchful eyes of the town constables who once patrolled with her grandfather. And it was there that Claudia took Beulah on the night of the funeral, and for many nights after.

Beulah didn't much care for the other girls in Claudia's circle. There was Henrietta Pittman, a fat-cheeked, curly-haired, gossipy girl who laughed too loud and told jokes Beulah never understood. There was another one named Geraldine, too tall and too skinny, all elbows and knees and a tendency to stutter. When Claudia introduced her to a third girl called Josephine, Beulah couldn't help but wonder why all the girls hanging around Monroe Square bore a feminine version of a man's name. Had they all been disappointments to their fathers?

The girls—and the men, for that matter—made for unpleasant company, as far as Beulah was concerned, but she had to admit that Claudia had spirited her away at just the right moment. There was nothing for her at home. Her grandmother stayed in bed most days, and told Beulah not to bother her. "I've buried two husbands and six children, and I don't know how many other relations," Meemaw said. "Just let me be for a while. You go on and take care of yourself now."

In fact, Beulah could've taken care of herself and Meemaw, too. She could've put a meal on the table three times a day, and done the washing and mending, and swept out the house, and aired the bedding on Saturdays. But Claudia wanted Beulah to come with her, and Beulah was irresistibly drawn to anyone who wanted her.

She and Claudia still came and went from Meemaw's house as they pleased, taking their baths there and eating their supper when nobody else would buy it for them, but that wasn't often. Someone always had a dollar in his pocket. Mayo Street was their home now.

Beulah was thirteen before she looked up one morning and recognized the flat her mother had rented, all those years ago.

It was only then that she understood that she and Claudia had been born on Mayo Street.

⚔ 10 ⚔

OF ALL THE courses on offer at the National Service School, Constance thought she might find Mr. Turner's class on telephone, wireless operation, and map-making the most useful. None of the other occupations suggested by the camp's curriculum held much interest for her. She hadn't the patience for sewing, she was a terrible cook, she hated vegetable gardening, and while nursing was a noble calling, she wasn't sure she had the temperament. Wasn't there anything for which she might be particularly suited—any job that called specifically for a woman of her talents?

She was convinced that her days in law enforcement were over. Just before the Kopps left for camp, two notices appeared in the newspaper advertising new positions for policewomen, one in Newark and one in Morristown. It would be impossible to travel back and forth from their farm in Wyckoff for a job in either of those cities. If she wasn't allowed to sleep at the jail, as she had in Hackensack, she'd be forced to rent a room nearby and become an infrequent visitor to her own home. The extra rent would consume enough of her salary to make the enterprise unprofitable. Norma and Fleurette both urged her to put in an application anyway, although their reasons were quite different.

"You could rent a room in Newark," Fleurette said, "and I'll stay there when you come home for the week-ends."

"But I'd be coming home to see you," Constance said, a notion dismissed by Fleurette as implausible and overly sentimental.

"It's impractical for you to go all the way to Morristown, when there are criminals just up the road in Ridgewood you could catch all day long," Norma said, "but you ought to go and have them offer you the job anyway, so you can retire this ridiculous notion that you're unemployable."

"I'd like to retire this argument with you," Constance said, "and it would be worth writing a letter for that reason alone. But there's no time for that, if we're about to leave for camp."

They were due to depart on Wednesday, and the notices had appeared in the Sunday paper.

"A letter isn't the way to go about it," said Norma, who had never once applied for employment or responded to any sort of notice in the newspaper. "Go tomorrow, and present yourself in person. They're going to want to have a look at you anyway. You can reach both by train in a single day if you start out early enough. Stay the night in Newark if you have to."

Constance felt that her sisters were a little too eager to put her out of the house, but she went regardless, setting off before dawn dressed in her old deputy uniform, which she'd avoided wearing or even looking at since her dismissal from the sheriff's department. Fleurette had patched it, pressed it, and let out the waist just slightly to account for a lazy winter spent indoors. She did feel smart in the long tweed skirt and Norfolk jacket, even though the badge was missing from her chest. Her pockets were uncommonly light without the revolver and handcuffs.

She appeared in person, newspaper notice in hand, just as Norma advised her to do, starting first in Newark and then proceeding on to Morristown. In both cases, the results were as dispiriting as they were humiliating. Word of her firing had reached both offices—of course they had. She had only to give her name, and to answer a question about her previous experience, for the police chief in each city to know exactly with whom he was dealing.

"Terrible mess back in Hackensack," said Newark's chief, looking embarrassed about it. He was a jowly man who reddened easily. "How's Johnny Courter getting along in the sheriff's office over there? I never thought he'd want to run a jail, but who would?"

"I wouldn't mind it myself," Constance said, ignoring the police chief's inquiry regarding the man who'd fired her. "It was my pleasure to look after the female section, and I had reason to help with the other inmates, too, from time to time. I could serve as a translator, or go and interview female relations who had some knowledge about the case, or—"

"Yes, well, what I'm expected to do is to hire a lady to go around to the dance halls and keep the girls in line," the chief put in. "Put a watchful eye on the train stations, that sort of thing. I don't much see the need for it, but the ladies in this town got up a committee, and before I could say a word about it, I'd been given three hundred dollars a year to hire a policewoman."

Three hundred? Sheriff Heath had paid her a thousand dollars a year, the same as the male deputies.

The chief must've seen her hesitation, because he said, "It isn't a salaried job so much as a . . . a sort of charitable endeavor. Something for a widow, maybe."

"Three hundred doesn't put a roof over anyone's head, but I can see that's not your aim," Constance said. "I can do the very same policing your other officers can do, for the same salary. Would you consider a thing like that?"

The chief looked genuinely puzzled by the idea. "What's the point in hiring a lady, if you're just going to do all the same things the fellows do? We have plenty of them already."

She saw no reason to argue the point and made her excuses to leave. The position for which she'd worn a badge before—one in which she had all the duties and responsibilities of any other officer (although admittedly with more attention paid to the female criminals and inmates)—was not necessarily on offer elsewhere. It was all too plain that her position in Hackensack had been a rarity, and that to take up police work in any other city would require her to step back in time by a decade or two, and to serve as a kind of public chaperone, watching out for hemlines and lip-stick, not thieves and murderers.

Morristown was, if it were possible, only worse. The chief of police in that town looked Constance over once, heard her all-too-brief description of her previous employment, and then made the astonishing pronouncement that he was looking for someone less experienced.

"We'd like a new girl to come in and . . . well, to make the position her own," he said. "It wouldn't do to have a lady barge through the door with a head full of ideas put there by some fellow in another county."

He clearly meant to say that Constance was that lady. She had by then braced herself for all sorts of objections, but hadn't conceived of the possibility that having professional experience would be considered a hindrance. Still, she managed to corral her thoughts in time to answer, "But surely Morristown hires officers from other cities. In fact, one of Paterson's policemen moved over here just last fall. He must've brought some ideas with him from his previous job."

"Oh, the policemen, sure. They move around all the time. But we've heard about some of the experiments that have gone on with lady officers, and we'd just like to try our own ideas, owing to some of the difficulties that have . . . ah . . ."

He allowed his voice to trail off, hoping, Constance thought, to be interrupted before he had to say another word about the difficulties. She didn't give him the pleasure. After allowing his unfinished thought to hang in the air just a moment too long, she said, "You run a police department. It's your business to handle difficulties. I wish you luck with it."

A packet of Norma's ham-and-butter sandwiches kept her company on the train ride home. Constance silently thanked Norma for having the good sense to pack three of them. When she arrived home, defeated, in the dark hours long after suppertime had passed, she said only this to her sisters: "Today I met two police chiefs who didn't want to hire me. I expect there are others."

Norma and Fleurette made no argument to that. There was nothing to do but to pack her things for Chevy Chase.

What, then, was left for her? In Mr. Turner's class she thought she might find out.

FORTUNATELY, SHE DIDN'T have to share the class with Norma, who considered herself an expert in all Army communications and liked to lecture anyone who dared venture an opinion on the subject, even if he was the instructor and she the student. The course was offered four times a week, and it just so happened that Constance landed in the Monday morning class and Norma attended on Tuesday afternoons.

Mr. Turner was a man who believed in getting on with business. When the class began, at the stroke of ten, he launched right into a discussion of conventional telephone signals with no preliminaries whatsoever.

"It being easy to confuse letters with others that sound similar, the Army has devised a list of words to be used in their place for the sake of clarity. This is of particular importance when transmitting cipher."

He paused and looked out at his students with the air of a man who had just made an especially good point and wished to be recognized for it. A few girls were taking notes. Their pencils could be heard scratching.

"We begin with these because they are the very simplest sort of code, and necessary for the operation of any switchboard. It will give you each a taste of the work involved. We'll see at once who among you has the aptitude for it. I've written out the alphabet here," and he turned a blackboard around, revealing each letter with its corresponding word alongside. "I'd like a volunteer to help me demonstrate."

Margaret Day, the woman who'd insisted on setting up her own tent, accepted the offer.

"Thank you, Mrs. Day," Mr. Turner said. "Now, have you any experience in the use of a telephone?"

"Would you believe it," Mrs. Day said, "those wires run all the way out west. We just had one put in."

"Then you know the difficulties with making oneself understood over the wires."

"'Deed I do," she said.

"That's fine. I'll write the word so the others can't see it, and you'll spell it using the Army codes. We'll see who can guess the word."

It wasn't a particularly exhilarating start to the class, but he seemed pleased with himself for having made a game of it, so the students shifted in their seats while Mr. Turner scribbled the word and showed it to her.

Margaret studied the board for a minute, then said, "Boy item easy love able sail king item." She looked down at the note Mr.

Turner had handed her again, mouthed the words one more time to be certain, and nodded satisfactorily.

"There!" Mr. Turner beamed. "Who has it?"

There was some muttering and confusion and more scratching of pencils, but one at a time, the girls sounded it out. "Bielaski?" they asked, hesitantly, each trying a different pronunciation.

"Precisely!" Mr. Turner said. "Now, imagine if Mrs. Day had simply spelled the name. You might've thought it started with a V rather than a B. Or you might've thought that the letter S was an F. It's impossible to hear over the wires. And she couldn't just give you the name, could she? No one spells Mr. Bielaski's name right the first time. Just look in the papers."

Apparently no one had looked in the papers. "But—who is he?" asked a girl in the front row.

Mr. Turner, who was already paging through his code manual to launch into the next lesson, looked up, the creases in his forehead rising in confusion. "Who is Mr. Bielaski? Is that what you asked?"

Constance didn't like his arrogant tone. "It's a fair question," she said. Her voice carried easily from the back. Constance had the sort of intonation that allowed her to make herself heard without seeming to put any wind into it.

Mr. Turner squinted to the back of the room to find her, then said, "Why, he's the man who's going to get us out of this mess."

"Which mess specifically?" Margaret inquired, having returned to her seat.

Did everyone who taught codes enjoy speaking in them as well? Constance wondered. He seemed to relish the idea that he knew more than the rest of them.

"Why—the war. This mess with the Germans. Haven't any of you read about him? Surely your brothers and your fathers have. It's actually quite thrilling, what he's done. I'm not giving away any military secrets by telling you about it, because the papers have already written it up. Mr. Bielaski has charge of a division at the Department of Justice called the Bureau of Investigation."

He paused for a moment, anticipating some reaction. His students watched him curiously. Some held their pencils in mid-air, waiting for more, but no one said a word.

"Well. Yes. He goes all over the country, searching for German spies and saboteurs. There are those who believe the war could never arrive at our shores, and those who think it already has. Mr. Bielaski is of the latter group. Every time a munitions depot goes up in flames, and every time one of our ships sinks before it can leave the harbor, it is evidence that the Kaiser's agents are already afoot. They're not just destroying our factories and our naval yards. They're listening, and planning."

He leaned forward and put a hand to his ear, to dramatic effect. At last, Constance thought, he was warming to his subject.

She was warming to it, too. New Jersey had already seen more than its share of explosions at munitions plants. One of John Courter's first duties as the new sheriff was to investigate an explosion in Kingsland. It had pained Constance greatly that she hadn't been able to join in. One of her inmates had formerly been employed at that plant, and Constance was certain that she could've gathered some useful information from the inmate, if only she'd still been a deputy.

"Mr. Bielaski has gone about," Mr. Turner continued, "with very little in the way of taxpayer money, and assembled a network of volunteer agents all over the country who keep a watch out for suspicious activities."

"What sort of suspicious activities?" Margaret asked.

"Anything that might undermine the United States government. If the Germans are allowed to gain a foothold here, and to persuade sympathetic minds to join in their cause, then the Kaiser has only to give the command and turn his army against us, right here at home. Mr. Bielaski's men look for any sign that such a movement might be forming."

Constance stiffened at this. Such ideas were at the root of the distrust of German immigrants, as well as Austrians, Poles, and anyone else toward whom law enforcement took a dislike. It was the reason none of the Kopps dared admit to speaking German anymore. Mr. Courter had even flung such an accusation at her during the election, wondering aloud in his speeches whether a deputy with a name like Kopp could be trusted.

"That's why we must have our own network," Mr. Turner said. "The Department of Justice started with the idea of hiring Pinkertons who spoke French and German. It took them a few years to realize that there is no such man. But Mr. Bielaski . . ."

No such man? Was the government really unable to find a single detective who spoke French or German (or, as Constance did, both)? She was drumming her fingers on the table now, but it attracted attention, so she stopped.

"Mr. Bielaski wasn't about to give up so easily. He got wind of the trouble—he was in a more junior position back then, you see—and he went directly to his division chief to propose a new scheme. The division chief was of the mind that no one who had lived less than half a century was capable of having a good idea, but Mr. Bielaski wouldn't be turned away. After showing up at the fellow's office for three mornings in a row, his idea was finally heard, and it was a good one. Mr. Bielaski now commands his own bureau, and relies not upon Pinkertons for hire, but upon an ingenious volunteer network of postmen, hotel clerks, and even elevator boys, to follow any suspicious doings and report to him. He maintains a card file with the names and addresses of every man with seditious tendencies discovered to be operating within our borders. In a moment of crisis, he can wire the police in any city and have a man brought to him for questioning."

He slumped back a little and mopped his forehead with a handkerchief, having exhausted himself with the vigor of his speech. As he wiped his spectacles, he added, "You might think that only the Europeans use spies and secret agents. But we do, too, and we will beat them at their game. That, girls, is why you should know how to give the proper spelling of his name."

Without glancing back at the blackboard, he said, "Boy item easy love able sail king item. Bielaski."

⊰ 11 ⊱

"WHAT DO YOU know about a Mr. Bielaski at the Department of Justice?" Constance asked Norma the following morning, as they trudged to the field for their setting-up exercises. It was a fair day, brisk but clear, and Constance found it invigorating to be out in the sunshine. Fleurette and Roxie, having stayed up far too late whispering to one another, trailed behind.

"Only the same rumors everyone else repeats," Norma said. "He's thought to have intercepted the Zimmermann note at the Mexican border a few months ago. Why are you asking about him? Has he turned up at our camp?"

"Mr. Turner said something about him in our wireless class. I thought his job was to go after German propagandists. What was he doing in Mexico?"

"Oh, the Germans have been sneaking back and forth over the border for months now," said Norma, with a fatigued air, as if she herself had been watching through binoculars all the while. "We don't know precisely how Washington got hold of Zimmermann's note, but it appears Mr. Bielaski was waiting in El Paso and took it off a diplomat."

"I suppose that's why Mr. Turner considers him a hero," Constance said. "If Mexico had taken Germany up on its offer, we'd have German submarines in the Gulf of Mexico right now."

"I doubt it," Norma said. "The Germans offered to let them take back Texas if they co-operated. Those Texans would've put up a fight."

Constance had no opinion on what the Texans might do, but she thought more highly of Mr. Bielaski after that. It was one thing to keep an eye on German insurrectionists from behind a newspaper in a train station, and another entirely to intercept a coded message between two governments in wartime. For once, Constance missed Norma's stack of daily newspapers. There were none at camp, and she found herself curious about what other news of Mr. Bielaski's doings might have come out since they left.

The campers arrived at the training field, where they were to put themselves into formation and go through their exercises. Mrs. Nash demonstrated from a raised platform, elevated on stilts and accessible by a ladder, so that she could be seen by everyone. The exercises consisted mostly of rising on the toes, squatting and standing up again, and bending to the left and right. All around Constance, girls were groaning and huffing and giggling a little as they dropped to the ground, kicked their legs out behind them, and jumped back to their feet. Some of them looked to be accustomed to hard work, but none were in the habit of hopping up and down in a synchronized fashion in the company of two hundred others. Constance felt silly doing it herself, and wondered whether the Army men were given the same routine and whether they got through it without laughing or spinning around and catching someone else across the ear with a loose shirt-sleeve.

They'd been working on their marching and had learned how to step, halt, quick time, and double time. That left most of them panting and whistling for air, and wanting to drop down on the grass to get their breath back. Two girls had already fainted and had to be sprung loose from their corsets and lectured on the benefits of an unrestricted diaphragm. Several more staggered about, dizzy from the exertion, but recovered and went back to their places. They marched in double time for five full minutes, until even Constance found herself winded and overheated from the effort.

"The men do the drills every day for two months," Mrs. Nash called out to them, with a naval megaphone to her lips. "By the end of their training, they can march at a double-time rate for as much as twenty minutes without fatigue."

Some of the girls tried to laugh at the very idea of marching for twenty minutes, but it came out in the form of more panting and coughing. Constance was relieved when it was over, and eager to begin the next drill, because Mrs. Nash announced that they were at last to be trained with rifles.

Here is something interesting and useful, she told herself. Constance had her own history with firearms, having been trained in their use by Sheriff Heath himself, long before he ever hired her as a deputy sheriff. It was her skill with a pistol, and her willingness to use it, that had first impressed him and given him the idea that she might succeed as a deputy sheriff. In fact, she rarely had a need for her revolver when she held the job, but she liked wearing it at her side and appreciated the fact that she'd been equipped in precisely the same manner as the male deputies.

It came, therefore, as something of a shock when Hack and Clarence pulled a canvas cover off the back of a wagon and Constance had a good look at the rifles they were passing around.

"They're just toys!" Fleurette said.

Norma turned one over in her hands, puzzled. "It's a wooden model. You couldn't kill someone with it unless you bashed them over the head."

The girls took great delight in pointing them at one another and at kneeling down to take aim at the far horizon, one eye squeezed shut and a hand placed somewhere near where a trigger might be.

But Constance could barely touch hers. What was to be gained by training with toys? The militaristic aspects of the camp—the marching, the drills, the wooden rifles—were more like play-acting than serious preparation for war. If the real intent was simply to train women in sewing, cooking, and first aid, why not hold those classes in church basements? There was no need to live in a tent and wear a uniform if they were only to be taught how to make soup.

Sarah mistook her silence for fear. "You can touch it! It's only wood. They'll have us practice with these until we're ready to shoot. Jack learned on a rifle just like this one, although he already knew how to fire one, of course."

Jack was her brother, the one driving the ambulance in France. Constance had never known a twin before and could see that there might be something to the idea that they speak to one another telepathically. Jack seemed to be constantly present in Sarah's thoughts. She spoke about him as if he'd only just walked out of the room. "Jack misses a hot bath more than anything else," she might say, as they waited in line for one of the two showers, which were fueled by an old and unreliable copper boiler and offered up to each demerit-free girl according to a weekly lottery system. "Jack hasn't seen a banana in months either" came her answer when they had no fruit at breakfast again. The idea seemed to be that if Jack was living without it, so could she. Perhaps she felt obligated to share in his deprivation, Constance thought, so that their experiences might be as similar as possible.

She had never known a woman so torn apart over the absence of a brother. She found it a bit of a relief to be a few hundred miles away from her own meddlesome older brother, but he was safe at home, not overseas in the line of fire. Although every one of her siblings grated at her from time to time, they were as indispensable as her own arms and legs. She couldn't imagine sacrificing any of them to a war in a distant country.

Sarah handled the rifle thoughtfully, holding it first in one hand and then the other, and aiming it carefully at the ground as if it might actually go off. "I wouldn't think that an ambulance driver would have any use for a rifle, would you? Even in war, the ambulances should go about unmolested."

"What does Jack say?" Constance asked. She had already grown accustomed to the idea that Jack was quite nearby and could be consulted on any matter.

"Oh," she said, her eyes wandering to the tops of the trees around the edge of the field, "he doesn't like to say anything that might worry me. Besides, if he goes into very much detail, it wouldn't get past the censors anyway."

"Well, I'm not so convinced that we're going to be given actual rifles next," Constance said.

"Of course we will!" said Sarah. "Otherwise, why bother with these?"

Why bother, indeed? Constance leaned against her rifle as one would a walking-stick and tried to think of a single useful thing she'd learned at camp thus far. All that came to mind was Mr. Bielaski chasing down diplomats at the Mexican border. It was the most intriguing sort of war work she'd heard of in some time. It sounded far more worthwhile than marching into battle with a rifle, real or wooden.

At last all the girls had their rifles and they were ready to begin. Mrs. Nash picked out one for herself and climbed back up the platform to demonstrate.

"Stand at order arms with the butt of your rifle square on the ground," Mrs. Nash called, "sights to the rear, toe of the butt in line with your own toes."

After some fidgeting, they all managed it.

"Port, arms," she called, and they raised the rifles up in their right hands and clasped them in the center with the left, then moved their right hands down to the small of the stock. A few girls tossed their rifles very smartly from one hand to the other, but Mrs. Nash was quick to discourage the throwing of rifles, even wooden ones.

Order arms was the next maneuver, which involved reversing the movements and sliding the gun back down into place with its butt on the ground. This proved trickier than it should have been, owing to the coordination required to let go with the right hand, slide the rifle down with the left, and take it back up again with the right. They went through the sequence five times before Mrs. Nash, looking somewhat dubious, decided to move them along.

"Present, arms," she called next, and hoisted the rifle straight up, with the very end of the barrel even with her eyes and the left hand holding it at the balance. There was no special trick to it, but somehow Constance kept ending up with the wrong hand on the balance or the rifle at an angle. She wasn't the only one—from the back of the company, she watched a forest of wooden rifles at jaunty and un-militaristic angles, all rising and falling with little regard to the commands Mrs. Nash shouted through her megaphone.

"Well," Sarah said brightly, "I'm ready to take on the Germans now, aren't you?"

Constance turned around to answer her. It was at precisely that moment that a gasp rose up among the company of women and a crash was heard from the direction of Mrs. Nash's platform. When Constance whirled back around, their leader was gone.

Here was a moment for a policewoman's instincts. Without

hesitating Constance rushed to the front of the crowd, shoving a few girls out of the way as she ran. When she drew closer, she saw that the rail around the platform had broken loose, and Mrs. Nash had stepped backwards and fallen into the ravine behind her.

It was there that Constance found her, face-down in the bramble. A breathless crowd of anxious girls looked down at her from the ravine's edge.

"Go and call Clarence and Hack," Constance ordered. Several girls ran off at once to find the soldiers, who'd returned to guarding the front gate. "And bring Nurse Cartwright."

Constance stepped out of her skirt—never had she been gladder for those riding pants—and passed it to Sarah, who'd run up right behind her. "We might need this to pull her up," she said.

Mrs. Nash was moaning now, and trying to turn herself over. "Stay where you are," Constance called. She was only a few feet away, but the terrain was steep and muddy. Constance lowered herself into the ravine and was relieved to find the flattened end of a stump against which she could anchor her feet. She bent down and put a hand on Mrs. Nash's shoulder.

"Can you move your arms?" she asked in a low voice.

"I think so," Mrs. Nash said. "It's my leg that—oh, I don't know!"

"Stay where you are. The boys are coming."

"I don't want them handling me," Mrs. Nash cried. "I can get up on my own."

"You most certainly cannot," Constance said.

"Don't let them climb down here and make such a fuss. I'm sure I'll be fine once I'm on level ground. I don't want everyone to see me being carried around like an invalid."

Constance had seen women in crisis like this before: fearful of being exposed, afraid to take help, wanting to draw a curtain of privacy around their pain. She would carry Mrs. Nash out herself if she could, but if she'd broken a bone, the risk was too great. Fortunately, there came from behind her a skidding sound, and then Nurse Cartwright's figure loomed over them from above.

"The nurse has come," Constance said to Mrs. Nash, her voice still low and reassuring. "The two of us can manage you ourselves." Turning to look up at Nurse Cartwright, she said, "Sarah has my skirt. Will it serve as a stretcher?"

It would serve. Nurse Cartwright scrambled down with it tucked under her arm.

"We'll haul you right up ourselves, Geneva," Nurse Cartwright said. She had an intimate quality to her voice that was naturally reassuring. "Just don't try to help us. I want you limp as a rag doll. Let us do all the work."

Mrs. Nash was of a smaller frame than either Constance or Nurse Cartwright, but she made for an awkward bundle. Constance's skirt, unbuttoned and unrolled, proved both voluminous and sturdy. It wasn't much of a stretcher, but they were able to roll Mrs. Nash on top of it and drag her out of the ravine, headfirst, with Constance doing the heavy lifting from Mrs. Nash's shoulders, and Nurse Cartwright guarding her legs to make sure they didn't move.

Constance fought the mud and bramble, ever the more grateful to have stripped down to trousers and boots. The damp earth threatened to give way every time she planted her heel. Mrs. Nash looked up at her wildly and gripped the sides of her improvised stretcher as if she feared tumbling back into the abyss.

With a mighty effort, Constance planted one foot on higher ground and pulled Mrs. Nash up with her. The force was such that Constance dropped to the ground and Mrs. Nash ended up in her lap. They remained there for a moment, practically in each other's arms, panting, while Nurse Cartwright prodded the injured leg.

From the edge of the field came Hack and Clarence, running with their hats in their hands.

"Why didn't you let us carry her out?" Hack said, when he skidded to a stop and saw what had happened.

"She hadn't fallen very far," Constance said.

"There's a stretcher in the infirmary," Nurse Cartwright said. "Bring it here."

The privates ran off. Every girl in camp was gathered around, making the air still and close.

Constance stood up and called, "Back to your tents. We'll suspend our morning exercises while we look after Mrs. Nash. I don't want any of you out of your tents until the dinner bugle. Go and study, or write your letters home, but don't take a step outside. I'll be watching."

Constance knew how quickly a situation like this could get unruly. Order had been maintained in the camp through nothing but Mrs. Nash's authority and the patrolling of two privates. Without anyone in charge, it would be too easy for the girls to run wild.

Her harsh tone had its intended effect and the crowd dispersed. Constance knelt down and took Mrs. Nash's hand. The older woman was panting a little, and beads of sweat stood out on her upper lip. Constance suspected that shock was setting in.

"Take a long, slow breath," Nurse Cartwright said. "I'm going to open your collar." She loosened Mrs. Nash's shirt and blotted a handkerchief against her neck.

"I've gone and ruined everything," Mrs. Nash groaned.

"Not at all," Constance said. "Nurse Cartwright will take good care of you, and we can send for a doctor if it looks like—"

"Oh dear, not a doctor!" Mrs. Nash was of that generation who harbored a mortal fear of doctors and saw them only as harbingers of death.

"Try to stay quiet," Constance said. She stood back, with some relief, when Hack and Clarence returned with the stretcher. She and the nurse slid Mrs. Nash over—eliciting a fresh yelp of pain —and they walked alongside as Mrs. Nash was carried to the infirmary.

Constance returned to her tent for a clean skirt (the riding trousers drew abashed stares from Hack and Clarence, who tried not to look but could not help themselves) and found Norma waiting.

"Is the leg broken?" Norma asked, as Constance rummaged through her trunk.

"I suspect so," Constance said. "She was in a cold sweat by the time they carried her off."

"You look like a madwoman. Half the ravine is stuck in your hair."

Constance reached up and realized she'd lost her hat, and her hair had tumbled down in the commotion. No wonder Hack and Clarence had looked at her so strangely.

"We'll have to take up a patrol," Norma said. "I'll do the east side and you can take the west."

Constance stepped outside and looked around at the neat rows of tents. Apart from a few girls coming and going from the latrine, no one was out and about. "Why? They can't get up to too much trouble before lunch."

"That's only because you barked at them like a woman who wears a badge." Norma thrust a hairbrush at her. "You'd best follow through on your threats. Pull yourself together and go."

With that, Constance took charge.

⤙ 12 ⤚

"MRS. NASH WAS taken to the hospital," Constance announced at breakfast the next morning. "Miss Miner is expected this afternoon with news of her condition. Classes are to proceed as usual."

The girls took her orders unquestioningly. Constance had that effect on people, whether she intended it or not. She'd already deputized Sarah Middlebrook and Margaret Day to patrol the camp and make sure that stragglers were rousted from their tents and classes were conducted as usual.

If it was a momentous morning for Constance, having found herself unexpectedly employed in a role for which she possessed abundant qualifications but little interest (hadn't she already turned down Miss Miner's offer to serve as matron at a Plattsburg camp?), the day had even more import for Norma, who was to teach her first pigeon class. With some assurance that her deputies could keep the camp in order, Constance stepped out behind the barn to observe. There she found her sister, standing alongside her pigeon cart, her hands on her hips and a kind of glowering furrow to her brow. She addressed the forty or so girls seated before her on camp stools as a general addresses his troops.

"We face serious shortcomings in France when it comes to the dispatch of messages from the front," Norma began. "What the Army lacks is a program to train pigeons to fly at great distances through gunfire to deliver messages from the trenches. A flock of pigeons can be raised inexpensively with nothing more than the ordinary equipment used to keep chickens or geese. You might not know it, but pigeon fanciers all over the country have been breeding pigeons that can fly at greater altitudes, at higher speeds, and over longer distances, than have ever been seen before."

With that, she lifted a little door on the side of her pigeon cart and extracted a bird. It occurred to Constance that she didn't know if Norma had any favorites among her birds, or if some were better suited for carrying out demonstrations of this sort than others. In fact, Constance knew as little about Norma's birds as it would be possible to know and still live in the same house with her. As she stood at some distance and watched, she was struck by the authority with which Norma handled the opalescent gray creature. She heaved it just slightly into the air with its feet pinched between her fingers, so that it spread its wings and made an alarmed burble that elicited a murmur of sympathy from the onlookers.

A freckle-faced Virginian girl, her red hair in pigtails, raised her hand. "Don't they go back to the place they were born? What good does it do us to send pigeons to the front if they're only going to fly home to Maryland?"

The pigeon stretched out its neck and preened a long feather on its breast as if it knew itself to be the subject of discussion. That raised another ripple of interest as the girls sat up a bit taller to have a look at it.

Norma said, "They'll be raised at Army headquarters, or at any encampment where communications are to be established. A flock will go from there to the front in a cart like this one"—and she turned to wave her arm in the direction of her cart—"so that our soldiers can send messages back to their commanders without any fear of interference from German spies or untrustworthy French telephone operators."

Sarah, having finished her patrol, had come to stand next to Constance in the back. "Are the French operators terribly untrustworthy?" she whispered.

"Well, Norma doesn't trust them," Constance said.

"Then I won't, either."

"Couldn't the Germans just shoot down the pigeons and read the messages?" another girl asked.

"We expect them to try," Norma said grimly.

Constance wasn't sure whom Norma was thinking of when she said "we," but she spoke as if she had the concurrence of the entire United States Army behind her.

"A certain number of pigeons will give their lives in service to their country, just as a certain number of soldiers will," she said. "That's why it's so important that we have a robust breeding program and send an ample supply to the front. As for the messages being read, they'll naturally be in code."

The red-headed girl asked, "Where is the Army raising its pigeons now?"

The bird in Norma's hand was getting restless, so she put it back in the cart and said, "That's just the problem. The Army hasn't done a thing to prepare and behaves as if the telephone and telegraph are in any way sufficient to deliver messages in wartime. By the time they realize how many pigeons are needed, and the work involved in putting the entire program in place, it will be too late. That's why we're moving forward now, without waiting to be asked."

That raised even more of a murmur from the crowd. A few girls rose to their feet. "Do you mean to say that the Army hasn't any interest in messenger pigeons and hasn't asked citizens to do anything concerning them? What about the Red Cross? Have they any need of them?"

None of this flustered Norma. "The Red Cross will need more pigeons than the Army does," she said, as if it were a well-known fact. "They could use them to send back counts of the wounded and ask for supplies. Why, even doctors—"

Before she could finish, a girl from Philadelphia named Alice rose and said, rather self-righteously, Constance thought, "We've already been asked to knit mufflers and plant vegetables, and now we've come to learn first aid and convalescent cooking. Shouldn't we do that before we take up bird-keeping, if no official request has been made?"

Something along the lines of a mutiny was under way, but Norma acted as if she hadn't heard. "We'll begin today with the basics of pigeon husbandry," she announced. "Inside this cart is a perfectly outfitted pigeon loft, with everything you might need to start a flock at home. You may come and have a look. I can take in three at a time."

That was enough to distract the students from the practical difficulties posed by Norma's scheme. Everyone jumped up at once, and soon a line went around the cart to the little door at the back, where each girl was obliged to remove her hat and bend down to step inside and take a look at the miniature house Norma had built for her pigeons.

Alice and a few of the other girls decided that they would rather roll bandages, and drifted off in pairs toward the sewing tent.

Constance was glad Norma didn't see them go. Sarah noticed her watching and said, "Don't bother about them. Not everyone is suited for working on plans so secret that the Army doesn't even know it has them."

She winked at Constance and they took two empty stools in

the back, where they waited for the rest of the girls to have a look inside the pigeon cart before they took their own turn.

It was there that Maude Miner found them.

"I'm just in from Washington," she said quietly, putting a hand on Constance's shoulder. "Come and walk with me."

Miss Miner was dressed in a fine blue suit with a ruffled shirtwaist entirely unlike anything that had been seen at the camp in the last week.

"You look like you've come from some kind of affair," Constance said, as they left the barn and strolled around the edge of the training field.

"Just another meeting at the War Department," she said. "I've never seen such a mess. We couldn't send fifty thousand troops today if we had to. Everyone thinks we can rely on British Navy ships, but why on earth would they send a ship all the way over to collect us? And they expect the French to arm us. The French can't arm themselves!"

"At least Norma's pigeons stand at the ready," Constance offered.

"And now this camp has come undone," Miss Miner continued, as if she hadn't heard. "Mrs. Nash won't be back. She managed to break her leg in that fall, and twisted the ankle on the other. She'll be laid up for weeks."

"I'm sorry to hear it," Constance said. "I take it you've returned to run the camp?"

"No, I've returned to tell you that you're to run the camp," Miss Miner said crisply. "If I leave Washington, there's not a single woman at the table as we ready for war. I'm needed there. You're already here."

"So are two hundred other women," Constance said. "Couldn't you find one of them to take Mrs. Nash's place?"

"I couldn't find one who's worked as a deputy sheriff and knows about keeping girls out of trouble, and could haul a wounded woman out of a ditch if she had to. I don't believe we have any others of those, Miss Kopp."

"I'm no longer suited for matron work," Constance said. "I've put it behind me."

"Then you picked a terrible time to quit. You've prepared yourself for a life of service, and now you're being called upon to serve. Just keep doing what you've already done. See to it that the girls follow a schedule. Maintain order. I'm told you've already appointed two deputies. You see, it comes naturally to you."

"Couldn't you bring someone in? Who's been running all the other camps? There must be another Mrs. Nash somewhere."

Miss Miner looked at her, puzzled. "I wouldn't have thought of you as a shirker."

"I'm not a shirker." She said it quite forcefully. Constance could be fearsome when she wanted to. "Only the camp ought to be led by someone who is more in tune with its . . . well, its general intentions."

Maude Miner said, "Why wouldn't you be, unless you're a pacifist and never bothered to tell me?"

"The war's a terrible thing," Constance said, "but that isn't it. The marching exercises are treated as little more than a game. Yesterday we were given wooden rifles as if we were children. There's talk about progressing to real firearms next, but we won't, will we? There's to be no serious military training."

"Not with guns," Miss Miner admitted. "I suppose it is a bit theatrical, with the marching and the uniforms and the wooden rifles."

"That's just the word for it," Constance said. "It's nothing but theater. I might as well audition for one of Fleurette's plays."

"But don't you see? The reporters take photographs, and the generals come to watch our graduation exercises. Before women can be admitted to the military—before we can be trusted with a rifle, or put into a trench—the commanders must have a picture in their minds. They couldn't even imagine it, before we started these camps. Now they see girls in khaki, marching in a straight line. Isn't that a start?"

"A start toward what? Are you saying," Constance asked, hardly believing it herself, "that your aim is to convince the Army to make soldiers of these women?"

"My aim is to plant the idea in the minds of the generals and the congressmen and the President that women are capable of military service. Right now there aren't very many women who would join the Army, regardless. But perhaps we're putting the idea into women's minds, too."

Constance looked out at the rows of drab tents, so like a military encampment. Could Miss Miner possibly be right? Was it first necessary to put on a performance, to sneak into the minds of generals through the back door of their imaginations, before they might someday take the notion seriously?

She couldn't say with any certainty that she took it seriously, either. Only a few years earlier, she couldn't have imagined herself as a police officer, much less as a soldier in the trenches. But perhaps that was because she'd never had an opportunity to imagine it. She'd never read about such a thing in a novel, or seen it performed on a stage, or even heard it sung about in a song.

Still she wasn't convinced. "It's too much like play-acting for my taste."

"Then take charge over the week-end. Let me see who might be persuaded on short notice. It's either that or we close down the camp this afternoon. I suppose you're the one to decide about that. What's it going to be?"

Constance didn't like to hear it put that way. Norma would

never forgive her: she'd only just started in with her pigeons. "There's no need to close it down. I can run things until you find someone else."

"If I can find someone else," Miss Miner said.

"You will."

≈ 13 ≈

"SARAH WENT OUT after curfew. Why haven't you arrested her?" Fleurette was lolling on her cot, buffing her fingernails. She had the long, nimble fingers required of a seamstress.

"The one I'm going to arrest is you, if you make trouble while I'm gone." It raised Constance's spirits to even make the threat of an arrest. There might be something to this matron business after all.

Fleurette rolled her eyes over to Roxie, who was brushing her hair with the air of a girl preparing for a night out. "I'm not staying in. Even Norma's out wandering around."

"Norma has never wandered around in her life. I've allowed her to go look after her birds. I'll be back in half an hour."

With that, Constance went out into the gathering darkness and walked among the tents with Mrs. Nash's walking-stick in her hand. The stick was useful for pushing open tent flaps, and for rapping on the ground to call an unruly crowd to attention. There was no doubt in Constance's mind as to how a camp matron behaved. Having agreed to play the role (for only a few days, she reminded herself, until Miss Miner secured a replacement), she threw herself into the part.

The girls were fairly subdued following the announcement

that Mrs. Nash wouldn't be returning, and seemed willing to observe the rules and keep up appearances until some permanent arrangements could be made.

As she went between the tents, the campers asked her about those arrangements. "Couldn't you stay on as matron, Miss Kopp? There's nothing to it," a freckle-faced Irish girl said.

"If there's nothing to it, why don't you volunteer?" Constance asked.

"Oh, I couldn't get anyone to listen to me," she protested. "But they're all afraid of you."

"I'm going to look for the compliment buried in that remark," Constance said, but she knew what the girl meant. A woman either carried herself with authority or she didn't. The girls responded to that: it was why Maude Miner put her in charge.

At the edge of camp resided a particularly noisy group, all with names that Constance couldn't keep straight: Tizzy, Kitty, Mimi —frivolous names born from summer cottages along the beach in Cape Cod or Long Island, names that they'd carry with them long after they'd outgrown them. Constance had seen it among the friends of Sheriff Heath's wife, Cordelia. A woman with stiff white hair and a sturdy tweed suit would nonetheless answer to Sissy or Bunny, as she had from childhood.

The difficulty tonight with these girls arose not from their names, but from their extravagant flaunting of the camp's rules. Among their transgressions: they'd smuggled in a phonograph that they played at all hours, they were often seen in the evenings out of uniform, and they deposited enough confection wrappers and empty tins of smoked fish in the rubbish bins to let the entire camp know that they had treats no one else had.

There was a reason for rules against contraband, and it was one that Constance respected: No one should flaunt their wealth in wartime. They'd have to live together as equals.

Here was one advantage to taking command of the camp for a few days. She could right this particular wrong.

She poked her walking-stick inside the tent. Tizzy rushed to put out a cigarette and turn off the Victrola.

"Is it nine o'clock already? We wouldn't want to miss lights-out. It's so enchanting when the lanterns all go dim at once."

Constance looked around at the lavish rugs and pillows, the half-hidden contraband, and the flimsy dresses tossed about like rags. She said, "You're out here by yourselves, holding your own little party every night. You stay to yourselves in class. You eat every meal together at your own table."

"Well . . . we don't want to be in anyone's way," Ginny put in.

"Besides, we've known each other so long, we're practically sisters," Liddy added.

"And the others are so badly behaved," Tizzy said. "The girls in tent eight are running a card game, and I assure you they're not playing for buttons. That's to say nothing of what goes on with the Tuesday-night kitchen crew. They're a bad influence."

"You have quite the eye for misbehavior," Constance said. "To-morrow morning I'm moving you to the tent next to mine. You'll be right in the center of camp, so you can tell me all about the doings of the girls in tent eight. The Victrola goes into storage un-less it's to be played for everyone. And I'll take whatever treats you have left and set them aside for our graduation party. I'm sure most everything you brought will keep for another month or so. If I see any of you out of uniform again, the entire tent goes on la-trine duty for a week."

The protests were loud and heartfelt, but it gave Constance a great deal of satisfaction. The entire camp would know what had happened. They'd know that she had been the one to lay down the law. Even if she was only to run the camp for a few more days, she wanted to see it run well and with authority. This ought to do it.

She left Tizzy and her friends to wail and moan over their diminished fortunes and went to take a walk along the perimeter fence. The front gate was locked at night. Hack and Clarence kept up a light patrol, stepping out from their tents a few times each night to watch for signs of trouble. There never were any. The camp sat on a peaceful and remote stretch of land, and the road was only ever traversed by farmers.

Nevertheless, she enjoyed an evening beat. Like an officer poking down alley-ways and beating his stick into the bushes at the perimeter of the city park, she walked along a little path next to the fence, taking note of the quiet of the woods beyond and the congenial hum from the campsite. The mess tent had only just been buttoned up for the night. The latrine saw a few visitors, girls picking their way through the grass along a path lit here and there with lanterns. An outburst of laughter rang out from one tent or another, but it was only just nine o'clock and Constance wasn't going to hand out any warnings about noise so early.

Just as she rounded the edge of the camp nearest the barn and started to come up the other side, she heard a noise in the woods. There was a little footpath leading into the sparse trees right there, and a break in the fence that she hadn't noticed before. Constance stood still and listened for just a minute more. There were footsteps, certainly, and the sound of some object being shifted from hand to hand. She saw no light, but thought she might've caught a glimmer of metal between the trees: a button, perhaps, or a belt buckle.

For the longest time there were no voices, just the shuffling of feet. They didn't seem to be leaving or drawing near. Were they merely walking back and forth?

Then, at last, she heard a whisper, and another.

"Port, arms," the voice said. "Order, arms."

It was a woman's voice. Someone was conducting rifle drills in the woods.

Constance looked around and realized that the barn blocked the view from camp. No one could see her duck into the forest. She hopped over the fence and walked as quietly as she could down the path. After only a few minutes she came to a little clearing, and there saw Sarah, Margaret Day, and three other women in a circle, their wooden rifles hoisted at attention.

"Are you planning an invasion?" Constance called. Her voice was unnaturally loud in the woods and the women jumped.

"I didn't mean to scare you." Constance stepped away from the trees and lifted her lantern to give them a look at her.

"Oh, I'm glad it's you," Sarah said, one hand still over her heart from fright. "We were just out here . . . ah . . . taking a little extra practice."

"At this hour of the night?" Constance couldn't help but feel somewhat betrayed: why hadn't Sarah simply told her what she intended to do?

There was some mumbling and shuffling of feet. They were obviously reluctant to confess. At last Margaret stepped forward.

"Before she was injured, Mrs. Nash told me that there was to be no real firearms training at the camp. She seemed to think we could get by on one day of drilling with wooden rifles, to give us an idea of what the men got up to in training. But some of us do intend to go to France. We ought to be able to look after ourselves."

Constance looked around at them, each one in a perfectly turned-out uniform, standing, as it were, at attention. They seemed entirely prepared to go into battle.

"Are every one of you bound for France?" she asked.

Margaret eyed Constance evenly. She was the eldest woman in the group and, in Constance's opinion, the one least willing to bend to camp rules. "Well, you know that Sarah intends to join her brother in the ambulance corps. My husband's a pilot. He's gone over to help the British, and I intend to follow him. I've nothing and no one to keep me at home. Now, these girls—well, Bernice and Hilda come from military families. Fern just feels called to serve. They'll need more than a turn around a field with a wooden rifle."

Fern looked a little hesitant. She fidgeted with a button on her collar. Bernice and Hilda stood rigidly upright, with their hands at their sides, like the daughters of soldiers might do. Sarah stood apart, watching the scene with a little half-smile, which told Constance that she'd been the ringleader. These were her troops.

"But wooden rifles are all you have," Constance said. "Why be so secretive about it?"

"We'll train with these for now." Sarah held up a pocket-sized book. "We're just following the manual. But I have an idea of how we might get hold of a few real rifles."

Constance's heart leapt at the idea, but then she steadied herself. "Under no circumstances are you to fire off a rifle in these dark woods. Do you all understand that? Anyone could be out here."

Margaret turned and nodded over her shoulder. "There's a larger clearing just over the next hill. It's a bit of a march to get there, but we can set up a target on a clear night and hold a practice without disturbing anyone."

She meant that they could hold a practice without being found out. Constance looked around at them, five women eager for adventure. "Have any of you ever fired a gun before?"

Margaret shook her head. "My grand-daddy lived on a ranch," she said, "but he only ever took the boys out shooting."

"My brother likes to hunt," Sarah said. "I have some idea . . ."

"You don't have any idea," Constance said. "I want you to promise me that you won't bring a gun into these woods. There's plenty to learn at camp. First aid, wireless, codes, and map-making—it'll all serve you, if you go overseas. It wouldn't hurt to study your French, and even learn a few words of German so that you can speak the language of the enemy. You don't need to gather in the woods at night to study a phrase-book. You ought to know how to drive an automobile, too, if you don't already. And you might practice some holds, and some combat moves, in case you find yourself overpowered. What does that Army book have to say about fighting hand-to-hand?"

All five women were staring at her. It was not lost on Constance that she'd just rattled off the broad outlines of a real military training program for women.

Sarah cocked her head, crossed her arms over her chest, and said, "You seem to know an awful lot about it. Why don't you show us?"

⚜ 14 ⚜

BEULAH AND FLEURETTE hadn't, of course, stayed inside while Constance made her rounds. They were both a little restless and struck out for the edge of the campground. Back in New York, Beulah could stroll the city's wide and crowded avenues when her room felt too cramped. But here, there was nothing to do but to circumnavigate their miniature city of tents. On all sides they were hemmed in: by the fence, the gate, the woods beyond. Outdoor living, in an open field beneath an expansive sky, should've felt spacious, but to Beulah, a bustling city was far less cramped. She could disappear in a city.

It occurred to her that wartime duty in France might mean living in the countryside, in such makeshift conditions as they now endured. She'd entertained vague thoughts of an assignment in Paris, perhaps in a little office, but it was far more likely that she'd be in a tent, with girls like these—if any of them went at all.

"Did you know, before you arrived," Beulah asked, "that you wouldn't necessarily be sent to France at the end of the course?"

"Necessarily? I wouldn't have left the house if I thought they were sending me to France. You do know they're at war over there, don't you?" Fleurette took Beulah's cigarette and touched it to her lips: it was all she dared to do. It was obvious that she didn't know how to smoke but didn't want to let on.

"Well, I intend to go." Beulah took the cigarette back and gave it a good hard draw. She loved the dry bitter hit of smoke in the back of her throat: it was an old friend, a steady companion that had seen her through some terrible times. "That's the reason I'm here. Otherwise, what's the point?"

It had taken her all day to work up to this question, although she asked it casually. All her hopes had been pinned on France: she imagined herself on board that ship, she pictured a bustling port and someone—a French version of Constance, perhaps—awaiting her disembarkation with a bundle of papers that contained her orders, and after that . . . well, she wasn't sure what might happen after that. She was quite certain about getting away. She was absolutely in love with the idea of disappearing into a country where nobody had ever heard the name Beulah Binford. But how she might serve, where she might work, how she would even put a roof over her head—she hadn't considered any of that. She'd assumed the camp organizers would take care of practical matters.

"I haven't met anyone who actually intends to go," said Fleurette, "except Sarah, and I suppose Margaret. Norma would go if they'd let her."

"I don't know how they'd stop Norma," Beulah said. Should she ingratiate herself to Norma, in the hopes that they might travel as a pair, and make their way through France together? She couldn't imagine how anyone fell into Norma's good graces—it appeared that one had to be born there, and even then, there were no assurances.

They were perched along the fence, just up a slight hill, so that they could look down on the tents and the lanterns flickering in and out of view.

"There goes your sister," Beulah said, pointing at the unmistakable figure of Constance marching toward Tizzy Spotwood's tent. "Do you suppose they're about to lose their Victrola?"

"And their tins of crackers, and the chocolates," Fleurette said. "If she takes their kimonos, I'm sneaking one into my trunk."

"I don't suppose you got away with much, if you had those two watching over you. Or did they spoil you?"

Fleurette made another attempt with the cigarette. She managed to take in a little smoke and hide the cough demurely behind the back of her hand. "I do as I please."

From the other side of camp, the figures of Hack and Clarence approached. They always took their first patrol together, right after curfew. Every night they made the same clockwise loop. It was not a coincidence that Beulah and Fleurette were perched at that particular spot. The soldiers had no choice but to pass them on their route.

"What do you make of these two?" Beulah asked.

Fleurette shrugged. "They're nice boys. It's a shame to send them off to war."

"They'll come back heroes," Beulah said. "They'll be men."

"Won't they be men if they stay here?"

One of them was whistling as he approached: it was a marching tune, one Beulah couldn't name. They all sounded alike: the same bouncy beat, the endless repetition of the chorus. It served to keep men moving, she supposed. The two of them stepped in perfect time as they drew near.

"You girls are out after curfew," Hack called when they were still a good thirty or forty paces away.

"My sister's the new matron," Fleurette said. "She knows where we are."

"I'll bet you a dollar she doesn't." Clarence grinned at them in the dark. He didn't look like he had any intention of telling Constance about them. Clarence was one of those round-faced boys who hadn't quite grown into manhood. His eyes were quick to betray uncertainty or confusion, but he would learn to mask that if he went to France. Hack already had: he was taller and leaner, the type who won at any sort of sport and had a wall of trophies at home to prove it. He would be good at soldiering because he'd always been good at things.

"How'd you get stuck out here in Chevy Chase?" Beulah asked. "Where's the rest of your unit—not out guarding another camp for girls, are they?"

"You saw General Murray at orientation," Hack said. "He's in Washington right now, and we're assigned to him. After this little tour of duty, we'll be back at Fort Monmouth."

"In New Jersey?" Fleurette asked. "Don't tell me you're with the Signal Corps."

"How do you know about it?" Clarence said.

Fleurette put a hand over her forehead as if she could hardly bear to think about it. "My sister can't stop talking about the Signal Corps. She wants the Army to take up pigeons."

"I heard about that," Clarence said. "We went around and looked at her cart. Who built that for her?"

"Nobody does a thing for Norma. She built it herself."

He whistled. "That's a fine piece of work. But we can't take birds into battle. They'll drop dead of fright if they hear the artillery. You wouldn't believe the noise those French 75s can make."

"Oh, but she's already fired a rifle at hers and they did just fine. She's tried every test imaginable. You can't rattle those birds any more than you can rattle Norma."

It was touching, Beulah thought, the way Fleurette defended her sister, even though they bickered ceaselessly with one another. She and Claudia were like that once.

Hack and Clarence had already lost interest in the pigeons.

They leaned against the fence, watching from a distance as Constance made her rounds and the camp settled down for the night.

"What do you girls get up to when you're not learning how to march in a straight line?" Hack asked.

"I'm on the stage," Fleurette said—a little too eagerly, in Beulah's opinion.

"Oh yeah? Clarence here plays the piano. You two should work up a duet."

"I would, if we had a piano," Fleurette said. "I've written off to my old vaudeville troupe and invited them to put on a show for us."

"It's not an Army camp without a show," Clarence said. "Why don't you sing a little something? I'll hum along."

Fleurette would have, but just then Beulah saw Constance making her way up the hill to the barn. They'd be spotted in a few minutes.

"We'd best get on back," Beulah said. She hopped off the fence and offered her hand to Fleurette, who was shorter and had a harder time managing the rails.

"All right, girlie," Hack said. "Mind your curfew."

Girlie. Beulah froze, then spun around on one heel and peered at him through the dark.

"Girlie?"

"Pardon me," he said. "Miss—"

"Collins," she said. "Roxanna Collins. You may call me Miss Collins." Only one man ever called her *girlie.*

"Yes, ma'am. Good night, Miss Collins. Good night, Miss Kopp."

⊰ 15 ⊱

DURING ALL THOSE years in New York, Beulah had managed to keep the past at bay. She learned how to squeeze her eyes shut at night and replace one memory with another, one face with another, one voice with another.

She visited a spiritualist once who told her that she could make a ghost from her past vanish if she only summoned a convincing replacement every time he showed up. She tried it, and it worked, mostly: she simply buried her memories of Richmond, and planted New York memories on top of them.

But now, even the most careless remark sent her hurtling back to those days. Was it because she'd returned to the South? She was not far from Richmond, just across the Potomac, really, breathing in the sweet southern air she'd been raised on, with the same rich black soil under her feet. Many of the girls at camp came from Virginia, and talked like she used to. Their voices took her right back to her days in Richmond.

And then Hack had to call her *girlie*. Henry Clay was the only one who ever called her that.

Who came first, Henry Clay or Claudia's baby? It was all mixed up in her head, the events of that year. She had to count backwards to figure their ages. Claudia had been seventeen, a fine age for a mother. Beulah was only thirteen—no age at all for meeting a man like Henry Clay, but who was going to tell her to stay away from him? All eyes were on Claudia that year. Nobody paid a minute of attention to Beulah.

Claudia hid her pregnancy well. You could do that, in those days, with the dresses they wore. To any stranger passing on the street, it looked like Claudia was dressing more modestly, or like she'd finally sat down to a decent meal for the first time in her life. And some girls just carried that way, where nothing showed for seven months. Claudia was like that.

But Meemaw knew. Meemaw could smell it. She leaned over and put her nose right into Claudia's neck and came away convinced.

"You're going to have a little bastard baby right here in this house," Meemaw pronounced, right in front of Beulah, who hadn't understood about Claudia's condition until that moment, even though she'd noticed the way the bed sagged on her sister's side.

"I don't have to have it in this house," Claudia said.

"Oh, but you will, and then we'll take it right over and give it to the Catholic home," Meemaw said.

"But we're not Catholic," Claudia argued.

"It don't matter. They do the best by their babies."

"What if I want it for myself?" Claudia said.

"Then you have to marry the boy that done it to you."

Claudia looked down at her ever-expanding belly. "I don't want him to see me like this."

"Not now. You wait until you have that baby, and you go show it to him. Show it to his mama, too. She won't turn a grandbaby away if it's put into her arms."

"I don't know his mama. They live out in the country."

"Then you'd better hope it's a boy, because a farming family needs boys."

It went just like Meemaw said. One night in August, Beulah awoke and the bed was wet and Claudia was moaning. Meemaw was already up, building a fire in the stove. It was hotter than Hades in that kitchen, but Meemaw told Beulah to stay there and to keep boiling rags until Meemaw said to stop.

Upstairs was nothing but Claudia yelling and Meemaw yelling right back at her. Beulah had no way of knowing if a baby's birth was always so raucous, but this one was. The rags coming out of the boiling water were so hot that Beulah lifted them out with the fire poker and carried them upstairs in one of Meemaw's iron skillets. She carried a bucket of water up, too, when Meemaw asked for it.

Claudia wouldn't look at Beulah and shouted at her to stay out of the room. Sometimes when Beulah stood in the doorway, Claudia was on her back, red-faced and crying, but mostly she was down on all fours like an animal, and Meemaw was down there with her, rubbing her back and putting her gnarled old hands against Claudia's purple-veined belly as if it might burst if she didn't hold it together. When the baby came, Beulah was just outside, in the dark hallway with her eyes closed tight as she heard it gushing out from between Claudia's legs in a river of blood. Never in her life had Beulah seen so much blood as she did when Meemaw called her in to help clean up.

"It looks bad, but it ain't" was all Meemaw said. She was too busy with the baby, a puckered, oily thing that screamed just like Claudia did when she birthed it. Beulah took away the sheets, and all the rags, and even the braided rug that Meemaw had pulled out from under the bed to push under Claudia's bottom before the baby came. Beulah carried it all out back to be burned in the yard when it dried, according to her grandmother's instructions.

It was a boy, just like Meemaw said it ought to be. Claudia wanted to name him Luther after his daddy, but Meemaw wouldn't allow it. "He can't have his daddy's name until his daddy marries his mama," she pronounced. "You'll call him Temple after your grand-daddy."

Claudia didn't like that one bit, and countered, through her sweat and panting, that she would at least like to call him Crenshaw after her own daddy, but that, too, was unacceptable to Meemaw.

"That Crenshaw has been no father to you. He never had a dime for your keep and you've hardly ever even seen him. He don't deserve it. This baby was born in Temple's bed and he will take his name."

That was all there was to it. The baby had a name, and Claudia was a mother now. Meemaw tried just once to take the baby over to the Catholic home, but Claudia wouldn't let go of him and, if truth be told, Meemaw never tried very hard. She still loved the feel of a baby against her chest and carried little Temple with her every time Claudia would relinquish him. He was a sickly baby, yellow and prone to colic, and for that reason Meemaw insisted on waiting before he was presented to his father's family. "Just let him pink up a little first," she would say whenever Claudia asked about it.

That suited Claudia fine. She was in no hurry to marry the man, or to join his family. Luther Powers was nothing but a farm boy, raised in the cotton fields and unschooled to the point of being unable to write his own name. He was a brute, Claudia said. An animal. Beulah tried to ask her sister why she'd gone around with him if she didn't like him, and Claudia only sighed and said that she hoped Beulah would never understand the appeal of a man like that.

As long as they were keeping the baby a little longer, Claudia said she wanted to show him to their mother. Jessie Binford hadn't been seen nor heard from since before their grandfather died, but surely she could be found and brought back to set her eyes upon the infant.

Meemaw was reluctant to summon Jessie Binford back to her house, but she understood Claudia's reasoning. A woman should know her grandchild. If Luther agreed to marry Claudia, Jessie would never be a suitable visitor to Luther's family's home. If he didn't marry her, the baby was to be deposited with the Catholics and none of them would see the child again. This might be the only opportunity for four generations of Binfords to be together.

Meemaw was too old to go out looking for Jessie, and Claudia wouldn't leave the baby, so Beulah was sent out to search for her mother, beginning with a series of old addresses that Meemaw had saved from envelopes and postcards over the years. Jessie had long ago abandoned each of those places, but from various landladies, roommates, and neighbors, Beulah picked up a theme: Jessie was described by her old acquaintances as a woman increasingly ill, desperate, and dependent upon her medicine. She heard that Jessie had gone to a hospital, to an asylum, and that she disappeared down to Mexico for some kind of exotic treatment. Jessie Binford had been everywhere, apparently, but where Beulah went looking.

Finally it occurred to Beulah that if Jessie's medicine was all that mattered to her, she ought to ask at the druggists. In Richmond, there were druggists, and then there were the druggists a woman like Jessie Binford might frequent. Beulah, even at her tender age, knew the difference.

Several of the white-coated men behind the counters seemed

like they knew her mother, but wouldn't say. Finally, on her way out of a tiny druggist run out of the back of a barber's shop, a delivery boy stopped her. He claimed that he had been running packages over to a woman named Jessie Binford, and for a dollar, he'd take her there.

Beulah didn't have a dollar and told him so. The boy, who was sixteen to Beulah's thirteen, looked her up and down and said that she could keep him company, and that would be payment enough.

Beulah had, by then, spent enough time on Mayo Street to know exactly what he meant. She told him that there was a family emergency and she had to hurry. If she found her mother, she'd return to him that night.

What did he have to lose? He led her to an old abandoned brick building, once a tobacco warehouse, with the roof half caved in and the front door missing. Beulah couldn't believe he delivered to a place like that.

"What kind of druggist would make a delivery over here?" she asked.

"He don't," the boy said. "I take whatever he won't miss and bring it over myself. If any of them have a dime, they pay me."

"Well, you delivered me, so go on, now," Beulah said. The boy reminded her, half-heartedly, that she'd promised to return to him that night, but Beulah just spat and waved him off.

She stepped inside alone. She'd been in enough disreputable houses by then that she wasn't too surprised by what she saw. The warehouse had been made into a series of small rooms without walls, only rugs and sheets hanging from rope, and from within those makeshift chambers came the moans and sighs of Richmond's opium addicts. Beulah crossed her arms and stepped carefully among the broken brown glass and the empty tobacco tins, crossing from one side of the cavernous space to another until she found her.

She hardly recognized her mother. Jessie Binford was nothing but a skeleton. Her hair hung down in oily strands, and she wore a dress that was plastered to her skin, she'd been wearing it so long. Her mother didn't recognize her either, and couldn't understand what she was saying about Claudia. The place smelled of the sewer, and up close, her mother smelled, horribly, of sex. It was the very end of summer, still steamy in Richmond, and there were flies everywhere, and enormous beetles and roaches scampering across the floor.

Beulah did try to pull her up, not knowing what she would do with her after that. Meemaw wouldn't take Jessie back in this condition, but how could she leave her own mother in a place like this?

In spite of Jessie's emaciated state, she was as limp and heavy as a sack of coal. Beulah couldn't heave her to her feet. Jessie screamed and spit and fought when Beulah touched her—she said her skin hurt and to leave her alone—and soon others came running, women who looked just as bad as her mother, and men with long crusty beards and filthy trousers. "Leave her be," they said. "She don't want you. She knows where to find you if she does."

She don't want you. Those words sliced through Beulah like a razor. She didn't stay to hear any more. She rushed out with a hand to her face so she wouldn't take another breath of that poisonous air, fled through town, and ran back home to Meemaw and Claudia.

She refused to say anything about what she'd seen. She claimed that she couldn't find Jessie, and only repeated a few of the more promising rumors. She'd probably gone out West, Beulah said to a skeptical Meemaw. She might've married and moved on.

After that, Claudia, Meemaw, and Beulah settled back down, just the three of them, tending to a baby who cooed and smiled and occupied their hearts and minds. As for her mother, Beulah tried not to think about what she'd seen. *Your mother's sick,* she told herself, when the image of that broken-down woman rose before her, like a specter, late at night. *She can't live here and you can't go there.* It was as if Jessie Binford had entered some netherworld, and resided not quite on this Earth but not in heaven or hell, either. She was in between, living in a room of locked doors. Beulah could not guess what door might someday open and offer her an exit.

It was just before Christmas when Meemaw decided that the baby was ready to be seen by his father. She and Claudia rode out to Luther's family farm with the baby in a basket between them. Beulah wasn't allowed to go.

"They won't take her if they think she's got family obligations," Meemaw said.

But didn't Claudia have an obligation to her sister? Beulah didn't dare ask for fear of what the answer might be. She stayed behind, but she learned the story later from Meemaw, and from Claudia's infrequent letters.

Under Meemaw's instructions, Claudia wore a plain dress suited for farmhouse work, and kept her hair—all the more luxurious since baby Temple came into the world—in a tight knot at the base of her neck. She complained that she looked like a scullery maid. Meemaw told her that was all she'd ever be, and if she didn't like it, she could stay behind and Meemaw would deliver the baby to Luther's family by herself. But Claudia wasn't about to wait at home. She was unable to resist the high drama of showing Luther Powers the baby he'd made.

Meemaw knew her business and made sure they turned up in the middle of the afternoon, when the men would be out in the fields and Luther's mother would be in the kitchen making supper. She went around to knock at the kitchen door and held up little Temple by way of greeting. Claudia hung behind her, looking guilty. Mrs. Powers didn't have to ask who the baby belonged to.

"God damn that Luther," she said, and pushed the door open so they could step inside.

Meemaw made the introductions and handed the baby to Mrs. Powers. She unwrapped him and looked him over, checking his fingers and toes and running a finger inside his mouth.

"He's a Powers, all right" was all she said. She left him on the kitchen table, writhing around bare, and turned back to Meemaw with the air of a woman brokering a business transaction.

"Do you intend to leave him here?" she said.

"And her, if you'll have her," Meemaw said.

They both looked over at Claudia dubiously. "She don't look like she's done a day of work," Mrs. Powers said.

"No, but she will now," Meemaw said. "And she'll give you another boy if you want one."

"She better hurry," Mrs. Powers said. "Harrison don't have more than ten years left in him, and we got forty acres out there. Never had but one boy myself. You can see what good he done me."

"Then you'd best take her," Meemaw said. "Get your trunk, Claudia."

Just like that, it was done. Claudia's trunk was put into Luther's bedroom, and when Luther came in from the fields to wash up for supper, he learned that he was a father and a husband-to-be.

Claudia had forgotten what a flat face he had, and how one eye never quite looked at her.

"Where will she sleep until the wedding?" was all he had to say, when the situation was made plain to him.

"It don't matter about that," Mrs. Temple said. "You all get started on another boy, and we'll call the preacher over here after Christmas."

That suited Luther just fine. He was too shy to take Claudia's hand in front of his mother, or to smile at her or give her an idea of whether he had any affection for her at all.

Luther's father had even less to say. He was already old—not as old as Meemaw, but old enough so that he didn't have to bother with polite conversation anymore. He put another peg on the wall for Claudia to hang up her coat alongside theirs, and that was all there was to it.

Claudia had a new family now, and a new life.

❧ 16 ❧

IT WAS RIGHT around that time that Henry Clay Beattie turned up on Mayo Street. He was just like any man looking for a good time with a girl, but it was obvious to Beulah that he came from a different world. He wore smart suits and crisp collars, and his hat was always blocked and brushed. Under that hat was a fine head covered in thick dark hair that never would stay slicked in place. He smelled of a barber's tonic and that sweet, smoky fragrance of wet tobacco and burnt orange peel.

Most of all, though, Henry Clay was devastatingly handsome, with mischievous eyes and wide, full lips that looked like they might devour you and enjoy doing it. From the minute she laid eyes on him, Beulah wanted to know what it might be like to have those enormous hands—smooth, clean hands that hadn't done any work—holding on to hers.

Beulah wasn't the only one drawn to Henry Clay. Every girl up and down the street had her eyes on him. But Beulah was the youngest and the prettiest—or maybe she was just the youngest, and that made her the prettiest in the eyes of most men. There was something a man couldn't resist about a girl who was still growing. Beulah knew that already.

She was living on Mayo Street most of the time now that Claudia was gone. She stopped in to see her grandmother and stay a night or two when it suited her, but mostly it didn't suit her. After Claudia left, the girls on Mayo Street became sisters to her, trading clothes and secrets, telling her what she needed to know about what men might expect of her, and sharing a bed with her when she didn't have a way to pay for one of her own. Beulah had been wrong to think that Mayo Street was a lawless place. It ran according to its own set of laws, and Beulah had learned them and found a way to be comfortable there.

Henry Clay was too good for Mayo Street. He was twenty-two and had discovered plenty of ways to get into trouble, but his version of trouble centered around boating parties and summer trips to vacation cottages. He didn't have to go down to Mayo Street to find a girl, in other words. He didn't have to spend his money to have a good time. In the wealthier circles where he traveled, the son of one of Richmond's most powerful merchants found that his desires were easily met, without him having to expend any effort at all to satisfy himself.

But one night, in the company of a cousin who'd come in from out of town, he wandered over to Mayo Street on a dare. The cousin didn't know anything about Richmond except its notorious red-light district and couldn't believe Henry Clay had never ventured down the lane of disreputable houses and saloons. With a five-dollar bet on the table from the cousin, Henry Clay did his best to make himself unrecognizable and went along.

He didn't meet Beulah on his first night there. He found, to his surprise, that Mayo Street was a comfortable place for a man like him, a man who chafed at the strictures of good family upbringing and resented the pressure to marry well and go into business with his father. On Mayo Street, nobody cared about a thing like that. His whims could be catered to without any guilt or obligation, and without fear of reprisal or second-guessing. If he wanted to play cards and drink whiskey all night, nobody thought anything of it. If he wanted to go upstairs with two or three girls, Mayo Street could accommodate that particular wish, too.

He met Beulah in May Stuart's parlor, having been delivered there late one night after he and his friends had been thrown out of another place for being too rowdy.

"May won't mind," one of them pronounced, and off they went, to the shambling three-story boarding-house where Beulah sometimes resided. She happened to be in that night, nursing a sore throat, wondering if she ought to go home to Meemaw but not wanting to have a fuss made over her. So she stayed, and took a cup of May Stuart's curative tea, which was bitter and required Beulah to pick the twigs out from between her teeth. But the girls said it worked for everything, from fever to monthly pains to stopping a baby before it took hold in the womb, so she drank it.

She was just about to go upstairs with another cup when Henry Clay Beattie stepped in her way.

"Hey, girlie," he said, smiling down at her.

"Hey" was all she could think to say back.

"You live here?"

"Sometimes."

He looked around, as if he were marveling at the place, although it wasn't much to marvel at. May Stuart favored floral wallpaper in any pattern she could get her hands on. She put it up herself, and did it badly, so that each layer peeled away and revealed another. Atop this pastiche she nailed gold frames—any kind of frame, with any kind of picture in it, as long as the frame itself was gold—and hung mirrors anyplace she could find the room. It looked glorious to Beulah the first time she saw it, but now she thought it was a mess and wondered why May didn't bother to fix her place up and try to bring in a higher class of customer—customers like this fine specimen standing before her.

"How old are you, girlie?" Henry Clay asked.

"Sixteen," Beulah said. She was thirteen.

"Where does your mama think you're at right now?" For some reason, the men on Mayo Street liked to believe that the girls came from good homes, and had mothers who would be scandalized if they knew what their daughters were up to.

"My mama knows right where I'm at," Beulah said, just to defy him, but she flinched a little as she said the word *mama*.

Henry Clay took a step back. Even in his compromised moral state, this seemed too much. "Does she live here too?"

That made Beulah remember the part she was to play. She laughed and smacked his arm. "No, silly. I'm teasing you. Does your mama know where you're at?"

Henry Clay looked shocked, like he didn't care to hear mention of his mother, that pillar of Richmond society, in a place as low as this. But all he said was "My friends are getting up a little party. Why don't you come along?"

Beulah mustered all her boldness, looked him right in the eye, and said, "I haven't got a thing to wear."

"Well, then, you'll do just fine, girlie," Henry Clay said, and took her hand.

⊰ 17 ⊱

CONSTANCE DID NOT, upon discovering Sarah and the others in the woods, take up the challenge and begin immediately to train them for war work, as much as she might secretly have wished to. She ordered them to bed, as any self-respecting matron would do. But she was not immune to their pleas, particularly Sarah's, for whom this was no escapade, but preparation for a future both imminent and treacherous. She entreated Constance to return the following night, and to teach them whatever she knew, if only for one night.

"An hour in the woods won't harm anyone," Sarah said. "We only want to improve. Come and show us what you can do, and give us a chance to show what we can do."

"Yes," answered Fern, the youngest of them, and so like Fleurette, but without Fleurette's utter disinterest in military or martial arts. "Give us a chance. Don't let us go off to France without —well, anything that might be of use."

Who could resist a tiny creature like that, begging to be taught? Wanting more than the camp curriculum had to offer? Whether she might ever make it to France or not was another question, but her desire to serve was sincere. Constance agreed, warily, to meet them once more in the woods.

What bothered her the most was not the curfew violation, of course, but the prospect of their getting hold of real weapons. The very least that anyone expected of a camp matron was to return the girls to their families alive, entirely unbesmirched by gunshot wounds. The prospect of untrained hands on a rifle, a misfire in the dark woods — it was unthinkable.

And it was always the most unthinkable dread that visited in the middle of the night and demanded to be thought about. Such was the case for Constance that night, who was visited repeatedly by images of rifles slipping to the ground, of pistols carelessly handled, of a bullet tearing through one of her own charges, before they even laid eyes on the fighting in France. She made it her first order of business the following morning to find out why, exactly, Sarah believed it would be so easy to put her hands on a gun.

This did not prove at all difficult, and required almost none of Constance's ability (however rusty it had become over the winter) as an inquisitor and investigator. Sarah believed Constance to be sympathetic to her cause — and she was, even if she disapproved of the methods proposed — and told her with very little prompting exactly where the rifles could be found.

"I can't believe you don't know about them already," Sarah said, "now that you're the camp matron. They're kept in the supply shed behind the mess hall. I spotted the case myself, the last time I was on kitchen duty."

Constance wasted no time. During supper that night, when everyone was gathered together in the mess hall, she slipped outside to the supply shed and rummaged around to see the guns for herself. The shed was by this time nearly filled to capacity with unused and discarded equipment: oilcloth tarps and tent stakes, a broken chair, a row of lanterns missing wicks, and shovels and axes in varying sizes. Ellie Duval's portable Victrola was stored there, at Constance's insistence, perched atop an empty wooden barrel. There were crates of potatoes, too, and tinned milk, which she was obliged to move in order to step inside.

Finally, feeling her way in the near-dark, her fingers struck a wooden case. It was under a heavy and unwieldy canvas tent, but she was able to shove enough of that aside to take a closer look. What she had before her was certainly a gun case, and it was Army-issued. It looked only large enough to hold two or three weapons, but as the case was locked, Constance couldn't see what was inside.

If anyone had a key, it would be Hack or Clarence. She could ask them about it directly, but to do so would only raise their suspicions. One gun case in a supply shed was easy enough to keep an eye on, she told herself. Let them train in the woods. What harm could come from it?

"I DIDN'T THINK we'd see you again," Margaret said, when Constance burst in on them later that night. It had taken her longer than expected to settle the camp down after curfew, owing to the coincidence of three different girls celebrating their birthdays, and festivities popping up between the tents like small fires. Constance went around extinguishing them as gently as she could — birthdays, after all, were worthy of commemoration and merited a little rule-breaking, especially when the girls were so far from home. She paced around the camp twice after everyone had gone to bed, just to make sure they stayed put. It was almost ten o'clock before she stole into the woods.

"You shouldn't be seeing me again out here, and I shouldn't see you," Constance said, brushing pine needles from the hem of her skirt. "I was on the verge of handing out demerits to girls who were only celebrating their birthdays, and here are all of you, carrying on in secret."

"It isn't a secret now that you know about it," Sarah said.

"What I mean to say," said Constance, "is that it's my obligation as matron to put a stop to this. If there's to be any trouble at the camp, it mustn't happen under my watch." She thought it best to begin sternly, to put a little fear into them.

Sarah had been bunking with Constance long enough to have some idea when she wasn't being entirely sincere. "But you enjoy it, don't you? You've been waiting all day to come out in the woods with us."

This was, of course, correct. The truth was that it gave Constance a fine feeling of adventure to sneak out at night. She'd been thinking all day about teaching her band of outlaws (already they were her outlaws) a little jiu-jitsu, just the simple moves that every deputy who worked inside a jail had to know. If she could only show them how to step up decisively and strike a blow, she'd give them a weapon almost as powerful as a gun. No one could protect them from bullets, but Constance could, at least, teach them to fend off attacks of the kind any woman might face in wartime.

Nonetheless, the rules were the rules.

"Couldn't we train in the daytime?" Constance proposed. "We have a half-hour before supper, and if you don't mind being last into the mess hall, you'd have a little more time than that."

"Do you really want us to practice our rifle work in the middle of the training field?" Sarah said. "Or hand-to-hand fighting?"

"There won't be any rifles," Constance put in quickly.

"But what about the rest of it? Learning French and German phrases? I don't think Miss Miner would approve of German being taught at an American military camp. You'd be booted out of the country for espionage."

"But how are you to fight the enemy if you don't speak a word of his language?" Constance argued, furious now, but nonetheless falling very neatly into Sarah's line of reasoning. "Never mind about the training field. Someone would write home and complain that we're not following the approved curriculum. These girls love to write to their mothers and air their grievances."

With that, she surrendered to the inevitability of this secret night school. How could she refuse? Nothing about camp interested her but this. In fact, nothing at all had interested her for months, but at that moment, out in a field on a clear and chilly night with five women eager for a bit of trouble, she felt like her old self again—or, even better, like her new self. She wasn't going backwards in time, retreating to better days long past. She was moving ahead, and that felt exhilarating.

The five of them were watching her, and waiting. They were as eager for adventure as any boy in a khaki uniform. Why not give it to them?

"I'll start by showing you how to throw a man down to the ground," she said. "Hilda, we'll begin with you."

Hilda was a dark-haired girl with a pleasingly prominent nose and front teeth that sat out over her lower lip when she smiled. She stepped forward and spread out her arms. "Is someone going to catch me when I fall?"

"I'm the one who's going to fall," Constance said.

"But I could never put you on the ground! You're so much bigger—no offense, ma'am."

"There's nothing wrong with sizing up your opponent," Constance said. "Knowing his size tells you what to do. If he's so much larger than you, you'll take his strength and use it against him."

She grabbed Hilda's wrist, roughly, and pulled. Hilda resisted and tried to back away, but she couldn't, and allowed herself to be dragged along, her heels in the dirt.

"You see? I'm no match for you," Hilda said.

"But look at what happens if I pull on you forcefully, and you use all that force to come toward me," Constance said. "Now I'm going to yank on your arm, and you're going to fling yourself at me. I'll even be helping you do it, although I don't yet realize that I'm pulling a lethal weapon toward me."

They all giggled at that and grouped themselves in a half-circle behind Hilda to watch the action. Constance took her wrist again and pulled. This time, Hilda flung herself right at Constance's chest, knocking her back a step.

"There, you see?" Constance said.

"But I didn't push you over," Hilda said. "I couldn't."

"I haven't shown you how yet. This time, when you come in close, put your right leg between mine, like so. When you fling yourself at me, I'll be unsteady on my feet, and you'll kick my leg out from under me. Be prepared to fall with me. I might still be holding on to you."

There was quite a bit more nervous laughter and uncertainty from the spectators, but Hilda was engrossed in the problem. She practiced it once or twice, taking a run at Constance and putting one leg between hers and just behind, so that Constance would stumble over it when she went backwards. Hilda wore a fine look of concentration as she worked it out in her mind. It pleased Constance enormously to see her study the problem.

When she was ready, she said, "But I don't want to hurt you."

"Only a minute ago you didn't think you could do it at all," Constance said. "The trick is that we're going to go down slowly. I know what to expect, and you're going to do it gently. It's only practice, remember."

Hilda did remember, but just barely. When Constance took her arm and gave a good hard pull, Hilda flew at her, planted a leg behind her, and only at the last minute remembered to kick softly when Constance stumbled backwards. The two of them went down into the damp grass, panting, to the carefully muffled applause of their spectators.

Hilda stood up first, and offered a hand to Constance. "I never would've thought of a maneuver like that."

"Of course not," Constance said. "It has to be taught."

"And if it hasn't been taught to you," Fern said, "something else happens when you get grabbed."

Everyone turned at once to look at her. Fern was the smallest of them. Constance was reminded again of Fleurette—they were the same size and had to be about the same age. A man would have no trouble in overpowering her. Constance shuddered to think of it.

In the silence that followed, Fern looked around defiantly. "Surely I'm not the only one."

"You're not," Constance hastened to say. "And you're entirely correct. If you don't know what to do, something else could happen—but it won't tonight. You're next, Fern."

❧ 18 ❧

IT WAS FIVE days before Miss Miner returned with news of Constance's replacement. In that time, Constance had made a few changes at camp, with an eye toward simplifying her responsibilities.

Some of the girls tended to wander and get up their own entertainments. Some of them would, if permitted, spend the entire day in bed, reading magazines and napping on and off, as if all of life was simply too exhausting to contend with. In spite of a full schedule of classes and training exercises, a few of those girls did manage to wander off, so that Constance had to go around and poke Mrs. Nash's walking-stick into tents all day long to look for shirkers.

When she took over the supervision of chores, she realized that the girls would expand any job to fill the time available. In response, she split two shifts into four, which meant that chores occupied double the time on the schedule that they had previously. If the girls were willing to spend thirty minutes scrubbing pots when fifteen would've sufficed, she reasoned, why not allot the entire thirty minutes and keep them occupied?

With this modification, kitchen duty took place four times daily now, and latrine duty twice. Tents and uniforms were inspected more often, drills and setting-up exercises ran longer than before, and she instituted a strict prohibition on releasing students from class early, which the instructors tended to do in fair weather.

None of these changes, Constance supposed, were a great deal of fun for the campers, but it was easier on her if everyone was kept busy. She found that there were fewer goings-on at night if they were exhausted by the end of the day.

And if they didn't like it, she told herself, they could complain to Maude Miner, who had it within her power to find another matron.

On the night Miss Miner reappeared, Constance had kept the girls in the mess hall after dinner to write letters home, and was walking among the tables, making sure her charges were applying themselves to the task.

"You're quite the mother hen," Margaret Day said. Constance flinched at that. She used to know a policewoman in Paterson who described her role that way: a mother hen watching over errant chicks. It didn't sound like any kind of law enforcement that Constance wanted to do back then, and it didn't sound any better now.

"It keeps them occupied," Constance said. "I don't suppose you're writing to your mother?"

"I'm writing to my husband," she said. "His last letter hardly made it past the censor at all. He's a mechanically minded man, so he likes to tell me all about his location and his training and the kind of aeroplane he's flying, none of which is allowed. I have to teach him how to write about all the little things — the dinner rations, the friends he's making, the weather."

"But he doesn't enjoy the art of small talk?" Constance asked.

"He never did. He's just like his daddy. That man hardly said a word to me the first three years we were married."

Sarah was writing to her brother, as she did almost every day. "I'm telling him about our training," she whispered as Constance walked by. "He doesn't want me learning to shoot, but I told him I wouldn't go overseas unless I could look after myself, and look after him."

"You're too fond of those guns," Constance whispered back.

"I'm not at all fond of guns," said Sarah, "but I am coming to like some of those holds. I hope I didn't leave a bruise."

Sarah had been a little rough with her the night before, forgetting that she was supposed to merely pantomime an elbow jab to the gut. Her aim was off, and Constance took a blow to the ribs.

"I've had worse," Constance said, smiling down at her, and walked on.

She was standing at the back of the mess hall, surveying the faces bowed over their letters, when Maude Miner walked in. She watched the heads lift and turn toward her, then go back to their work. Miss Miner was heading straight for her.

"Have you come to introduce my replacement?" Constance asked.

"Step outside and I'll tell you," Maude said. They went out the back way and rousted a couple of girls sneaking cigarettes.

"Two out of two hundred isn't bad," Maude said.

"If I had to confiscate every cigarette, I'd never get anything else done," Constance said.

Maude waved that subject away. "I'm not worried about it. But you know I can't find a replacement on short notice."

"I wonder if you even tried."

"Not particularly. I just gave you a few days to get used to the job. It looks to me like you have everything in hand."

Constance was prepared to offer up her usual protests: She hadn't come to camp looking for a matron job. It wasn't her aim to chaperone society girls. The camp was (by Miss Miner's own admission) a bit of theater anyway, not seriously engaged in teaching its enlisted much beyond a slightly more militaristic version of domestic work.

But now there was subterfuge afoot. Five women training after dark in the woods didn't make for much of an insurrection, but it was enough. She had something to offer these women, and she found that even a few stolen moments after dark satisfied her greatly.

Besides, there was Norma to consider. She was still marching her students through her pigeon curriculum, convinced that a general would drop by at any moment and conclude that the Army simply couldn't function without her and her birds. If the camp closed for want of a matron, she would hear about it from Norma for the rest of her days.

For all those reasons, she found herself saying to Miss Miner: "It wasn't what I came here to do, but you're right. We all have our duties."

Maude clapped her hands together. "I knew you'd come around! Just keep them in line for a month. Turn the camp back over to me without a scandal attached to it, can you do that?"

She said it lightly, as a kind of a joke, but it gave Constance pause. Maude would never trust her with the job if she knew that Constance was sneaking out at night and teaching her campers to fight. The mere possibility of women wearing trousers at this camp had raised an outcry in the papers. Hand-to-hand fighting —much less those rifles Sarah had her eye on—would ruin them.

Maude seemed not to notice Constance's hesitation and went on in the same airy tone. "Do that, and you will have acquitted yourself as well as anyone could. I'll look for another posting for you after this, and I promise it'll be more interesting than camp matron. I'm in the thick of it in Washington right now. Something will turn up."

"That's good of you," Constance said. Having already been rejected by two prospective employers, she felt herself to be in no position to turn down any post Miss Miner might have on offer.

"Then it's settled. You'll be paid the balance of Mrs. Nash's wages, of course." Maude marched back inside the tent before Constance could say another word. She stood on a chair—even in a skirt and high boots, she didn't waver but jumped right up as if she did it every day—and clapped her hands together.

"Ladies, I'm pleased to announce that Miss Constance Kopp has agreed to stay on and serve as camp matron for the duration. Mrs. Nash is expected to recover, and we hope to see her at graduation. Miss Kopp has my wholehearted support and I know she'll have yours as well."

There were a few good-natured groans—Constance already had a reputation for being harder to fool than Mrs. Nash—but Norma and Fleurette stood up and led the applause, and everyone soon followed.

Constance had nothing prepared in the way of a speech and decided to set the tone with a straightforward order. "Finish your letters, and be back in your tents by nine."

Miss Miner had an auto waiting. Before she left, she said to Constance, "There's something else, now that you have charge of the camp. I have a letter from the manager of a vaudeville act, a Mr. Freeman Bernstein. It seems he's been sending his performers around to the Plattsburg camps, and someone with the last name of Kopp wrote to him and suggested he bring them here."

It was too late to keep the news from Fleurette: she'd been making her way through the crowd to Constance since the applause died down, and she heard what Maude said.

"I wrote the letter," Fleurette called out, "because we simply must have May Ward at our camp. She puts on a light comedic act with patriotic songs, just like what you saw at the Plattsburg camp last year."

"I remember it well," Maude said. "But this"—here she glanced down at the letter she pulled from her pocket—"this May Ward wasn't with you, was she?"

"No, she was making a moving picture just then, but now she finds herself able to return to the live stage. I know all the songs and I intend to train some of the girls to sing in the chorus. It'll be every bit as good a program as the men had." Her arguments, all so carefully crafted and rehearsed, gave Maude little room to argue.

"It's up to the camp matron. What does Miss Kopp have to say about it?"

Constance wasn't about to be responsible for refusing Fleurette her turn on the stage, even if it was only at a camp for girls. She'd be insufferable if she was denied this small pleasure.

"Mrs. Ward is known as a respectable actress," Constance said. "I can't imagine that any of the parents would object."

"I'm not concerned about the parents," Miss Miner said. "You're the one who has to manage the entire production."

"The girls deserve a little entertainment, after how hard I'm going to make them work," Constance said. "I'll reply to Mr. Bernstein myself."

Fleurette frowned at the mention of hard work but raced back to her table to deliver the news.

❧ 19 ☙

"YOU DON'T EXPECT me to get up there and sing, do you?" Beulah said, when Fleurette came bouncing back to the table with news of May Ward's concert.

"It's only a few little lines of the chorus," Fleurette said. "Anyone can do it."

"I never had a talent for singing," Beulah said.

"But you must've been taught music and dance," Fleurette said. "Didn't you go to a girl's academy? Even I was sent to one in Paterson."

"Oh, of course I went," Beulah said, with the air of fatigue she'd been cultivating. Wealthy girls were always fatigued. "I was forever being carted off to Mrs. Dimwit's or Miss Featherbrain's, but I couldn't be bothered to learn the steps. What good would it do me?"

"It might've won you a place in my chorus line," Fleurette said, "but if you're as terrible as you say, I'll put you in charge of the footlights."

"Couldn't I sit in the audience and throw rose petals?" Beulah asked. It put her in a sweat just to think about standing up on a stage and having all eyes on her at once. Fleurette couldn't possibly know it, but Beulah had a rather ruinous history with the stage. She couldn't bear to return to the spotlight, here at camp.

Where have I seen that girl before? Every single camper would have time to think about it. One of them might just snap her fingers, stand up, and call out her name.

That's Beulah Binford!

Beulah could just imagine a voice floating out from the dark. She'd heard it before. When she first moved to New York, people used to spot her on the street. One woman even ran up to her with a picture cut out of the newspaper. She'd obviously been carrying it around in her pocket for weeks.

"I heard you were in New York," the woman hissed, shaking the picture at her. "I've been watching for you. They banned you from the stage, didn't they? There's nothing for you here. Go on back to Richmond."

Fortunately, Mabel was walking with her that day, and came to her rescue. "She only looks like Beulah! Don't hold her looks against her. Throw that picture in the trash where it belongs, and leave us alone." Mabel had to rush Beulah down the street to get away from the growing crowd of spectators. They ducked into a hotel that was known to be generous with the sherry in the afternoons and sat in the lobby, taking curative sips until Beulah stopped trembling.

She would not be setting foot on a stage. Not now, not ever.

"What's this lady's name again?" Beulah asked when she realized Fleurette was still watching her.

"May Ward. She has a traveling act. It's May Ward and Her Eight Dresden Dolls. Haven't you've heard of her?"

"I used to see the posters in New York," Beulah said. "Were you one of the Eight Dresden Dolls?"

"For a while," Fleurette said. She looked around and saw that the mess hall was emptying. Beulah's letter-paper was still blank in front of her.

"I thought you were going to write to your sister," Fleurette said.

Beulah pushed the paper away. "I couldn't think what to say."

WHERE WAS CLAUDIA now? She didn't last long with Luther Powers's family, Beulah knew that. She was too restless for farm life, and unwilling to take orders from Mrs. Powers or to follow her ideas on child-rearing. She didn't take to the rigors of farmhouse chores and found Luther to be dull company, seeing as how he was always coming in after dark, exhausted and filthy, good for nothing but a silent dinner and an early bed-time.

But she couldn't get away by herself. She didn't have a dime to her name, and she wasn't about to go crawling back to Meemaw's. There was no convincing Luther to leave his family's farm. The boy didn't know much, but he knew his duty.

Then luck arrived for Claudia in the unlikely form of her father-in-law's demise. After Mr. Powers dropped to his knees in the field and proved immune to any effort to revive him, it became immediately clear that Luther could not carry the burden of running the farm on his own, nor could he afford to hire on laborers.

Beulah wasn't there and didn't know how many nights were spent arguing over it, but it must've been quite a few, because after a reasonable mourning period, the farm was sold. Mrs. Powers kept a parcel of land on the edge of the property closest to town for herself, and Luther built her a small cottage on it. Then he and Claudia moved to Washington, D.C., where Luther hired on at a steel factory.

Four years after that, Beulah had a baby of her own. Claudia had by then moved on from Washington and hadn't left a forwarding address. Meemaw had a letter from her but refused to show it to Beulah. "Don't go writing to her," Meemaw said, as fiery and blunt as ever. "She's gone off to a teacher's college to make something of herself. That don't concern you."

Beulah was by then seventeen, the same age Claudia had been when she had her baby. She'd always imagined that Claudia would come back for her pregnancy, and would tell her what to do and help her through it. Where was Claudia, when Beulah most could've used a sister?

The baby belonged to Henry Clay Beattie. Of course it did. Beulah never went more than a month or two without sharing a bed with Henry Clay. A baby was bound to be the result, and she was glad of it. She wanted to give him one, after everything he'd given her.

She'd amassed a little collection of trinkets he'd bestowed upon her over the years. He had the endearing habit of turning up with some small girlish treasure: a tiny rose-colored perfume bottle with a glass stopper, a delicate gold lorgnette on a chain, a double-ended lip-stick in a silver case. They were obviously lifted from his sisters' bureaus—imagine a life so filled with baubles that one could disappear and not be missed!—or, in the case of a pristine packet of silk stockings, taken right out of his father's department store.

He would undress her first, and then, at the very moment of wildest anticipation, he would dangle the tiny gift before her eyes and take his own fulfillment from her, all at once. It delighted her to catch only a glimpse of some sparkle, and to feel it drop to her bare chest, cold and mysterious, at the very moment that their bodies came together. She felt so utterly swept away on those nights, lifted breathlessly above her circumstances and set to sail into some new life, where it was only her and Henry Clay, and all his riches and good looks to carry them along. She was someone else on those nights. She was his.

Of course she would marry him after the baby came, and live with him in a big white house with columns in the front and a porch that wrapped all the way around. She remembered how it went with Claudia. Once they see the baby—and in particular, once the man's mama sees the baby—it will be understood that there is nothing to do but to make a marriage, and quickly.

But Henry Clay had different ideas about it. If there was one thing the promiscuous son of a well-to-do family knew, it was how to send a girl away when she got into trouble. His cousin told him of a place down in North Carolina where a girl could have her baby in private and leave it with the nurses to be placed with a good family.

Beulah had no intention of handing her baby over and didn't think she needed to go any farther than Mayo Street to give birth, and told him so.

"May Stuart won't care if I have a baby up in her room," Beulah said, but Henry Clay was adamant about it.

"They have good nurses down there," he said. "They'll look after you, and you won't have to worry about anybody around here gossiping about it."

Beulah didn't mind about the gossip. She had every intention of returning with their baby—it would be a boy, she felt sure of it —and presenting him to Henry Clay and his mama right there on the Beattie's grand front porch. Anyone walking by would be able to see exactly what she was doing, and she wouldn't mind at all.

But she allowed Henry Clay to put her on the train for North Carolina, if that's what he wanted to do. Once they were married, she'd have to do whatever he wanted, all the time, and she wouldn't mind that, either.

They didn't say good-bye in Richmond. Henry Clay borrowed his father's trap and drove her to another station, two towns away, where he hoped he wouldn't be recognized. (Make sure you put the girl on the train yourself, that was the advice given to him by his cousin. Don't hand her money for a ticket and expect her to go where you tell her.)

Following his cousin's advice, Henry Clay bought the ticket, and kept it in his hand until it was time for her to get on board. Beulah carried her baby low and close, like Claudia had, so it wasn't difficult to hide her condition under a high-waisted dress. For a little extra concealment, she wore a cape even though it was late in the spring. If any of the other passengers waiting on the platform suspected, they didn't let on.

"I'll see you back here in a few months," she said as the train screeched into the little station, nothing but a barn roof over a rickety platform.

"You might find you like it down in Raleigh," Henry Clay said, but not unkindly. He didn't have it in him to be unkind. There was always an air of gentility about him, even to a girl like Beulah, and that's what Beulah appreciated. He'd make a good husband to her. Of course he wanted to marry her, and only needed the baby as an excuse to do so. Why else would a man of his wealth be twenty-five and unmarried?

"I think I like it better here," Beulah said. She gave what she hoped was a flirtatious smile, but with a baby crowding against her rib cage, she couldn't tell anymore how she came across to men. It was distracting, trying to carry on a conversation with Henry Clay while his baby was kicking inside her.

Henry Clay looked over the top of her head, watching the platform. "Well, there's your train," he said, and picked up her trunk. The porter took it, along with a few coins from Henry Clay, and heeded his words about where the trunk and the girl were to be deposited.

Beulah never touched the train ticket. Henry Clay passed it directly into the conductor's hand, and Beulah found herself whisked aboard, the ticket punched and tucked into the back of her seat, another crumpled bill pressed into her hand from an ever more guilty-looking Henry Clay, and then he was back on the platform, and the train was moving, and Beulah had nothing to do but to wait. To wait for the baby to come, to wait for her return to Richmond, to wait for Henry Clay's mama to see what her boy had made, and to make the arrangements for the wedding. It didn't seem at all daunting, only tedious. Such a great deal of waiting when they could've walked into any church and been married in an afternoon.

Sleep came easily to Beulah now that a baby was growing inside her. As soon as the train set to rocking back and forth out of the station, she put her head back and slept, and dreamt of Henry Clay's son and the white house with the columns in front.

BUT SHE NEVER did have a chance to present her baby to Henry Clay's mother. The subject was hardly even discussed. When Beulah returned to Richmond with her boy, in August, about a month after he was born, her grandmother didn't register any surprise at all over the fact that she didn't leave him in Raleigh as she'd been told to.

"I hope you didn't name him after his daddy" was all she said when Beulah appeared on her front porch.

"I did," Beulah said. "I gave him the same whole name. Henry Clay Beattie Jr."

"That better not be them Beatties that own Beattie's department store," Meemaw said.

"Of course it is. After we're married, you can come around and see him anytime you want. Him, and all the other ones I'll have."

Meemaw chuckled a little at that. "If this is a Beattie like you say it is, you won't be marrying him or having no more of his babies. I don't mind going to have a word with that boy, but that's all it'll be."

"But—why can't you do like you did for Claudia? Don't you think when his mama sees this boy she'll want him? He's the spitting image of Henry Clay. Couldn't she use a grandson, to take over the running of their store someday?" Beulah had it all worked out in her head: how the boy would learn the family business from his daddy and his grand-daddy, and grow up in the merchant class, and wear a suit to work every day.

"Oh, honey, them Beatties don't want nothing to do with a girl their son messed with down on Mayo Street. That's not their way. Like I said, I'll speak to the boy that did this to you, and we'll find a place to put that baby."

Little Henry Clay Jr. was sweet and warm, like a loaf of bread, and he had a fine head of dark hair like his daddy. But it hadn't occurred to Beulah that she'd have to nurse him and hold him and look after him all day long, every day, after he was born. She always thought she'd have some help. She'd marry Henry Clay, and there would be a nurse to take the baby. Or Claudia would come home and invite Beulah to move in with her and Luther and whatever children they had. Or Meemaw—even Meemaw would help to raise a baby. She loved babies. Beulah had seen it when Claudia brought hers home, four years earlier.

But this was different. Maybe Meemaw knew better than to get mixed up with another baby that was only going away. She never helped with him, or held him for long, or called him by his name. She left Beulah to look after him all by herself. That was too much to manage.

There seemed to be three times as much washing to do. The kitchen smelled of boiled diapers morning and night, such that Beulah couldn't bear to touch her food. She was tired and cross and couldn't have a minute to herself, even on the toilet.

If the baby loved her, he showed no sign of it. He was hot and tearful and prone to rashes. He wanted nothing but her sore and bloodied breast, and would not accept a milk-soaked rag as a substitute, not even once. She cried when she fed him, and sometimes bit into her fist just to feel another kind of pain.

This could not go on. She begged Meemaw to go looking for Henry Clay like she promised to.

"Either you bring him here," Beulah said, "or I will march this baby right over to his doorstep." If the Clay family would not receive her, she was prepared to set that baby down on the porch and walk away. She'd already been dreaming of it, in those rare moments when the baby let her dream. She would hand him to a stranger, if it bought her a moment's peace.

Meemaw looked at her doubtfully. "Don't you want to wait until he's weaned?"

"We can wean him tomorrow," Beulah said. She hardly knew what that meant, only that if he was weaned, she could wrap her breasts in bandages and never let another human touch them. "Go get Henry Clay."

"I'll do it," Meemaw said, "but you clean yourself up, and get the stink out of here, and chase out those flies."

"Are you really going to bring him here?" Beulah asked, so relieved that her chin wobbled and her eyes watered.

"'Course not. A Beattie man won't be seen coming into this house. You make it tolerable for me, and I'll take care of your troubles, like I've done for every one of you girls."

Beulah couldn't argue with that. She put the baby down on the floor and let him scream, and she did what she could to make Meemaw's house decent again.

Meemaw, for her part, went out to look for Henry Clay, not wanting to approach him at the Beattie mansion if she could avoid it. She asked around down on Mayo Street and in some other disreputable establishments nearby. He wasn't there, but everybody knew Henry Clay, and everybody had an idea of where he might be found: a hotel, a cigar shop, a barber with a card game in the back room. She visited them all, without success.

She eventually tracked him down, not in May Stuart's parlor like he'd been so often over the last few years, but at his club, with his more respectable friends. Meemaw wasn't allowed inside and had to go in through the kitchen and persuade a friendly dishwasher to pass a note to Henry Clay, along with a handful of coins to be deposited in every palm through which the note passed: from a waiter to a bartender, from a bartender to a shoe-shine man, from the shoe-shine man to the attendant in the billiards room. She had no idea how often Henry Clay turned up at his club. The note named a time and place one week later in case it took that long to reach him.

On the appointed day, Henry Clay arrived as instructed and in fact turned up early.

"Where's Beulah?" he asked when he saw only Meemaw waiting for him near the rose bower at Monroe Square.

"You're a free man. Go see Beulah anytime you want," Meemaw said. "I'm here to find out how you plan to keep your mama from ever seeing Beulah, because that girl's ready to go knock on your door with a baby in a basket."

Henry Clay spat on the ground and said, "She wouldn't dare."

"Dare? I understand you took up with my granddaughter when she was thirteen years old. I guess you know about daring."

"She told me she was sixteen! She must be twenty by now."

"Well, she ain't. She's seventeen, so count up the years yourself. If she stays in Richmond, you'll mess with her again, won't you? Best to send her away, maybe up to a school in Alexandria, where nobody'll know her."

"Maybe that is best," Henry Clay said, with evident relief.

"I'm fixing to get married anyway. They've got a girl all picked out for me."

Meemaw ignored the part about the marriage—men like Henry Clay were always about to be married—and said, "It costs a fair bit to send a girl off to boarding school, not to mention finding a home for that baby of yours somewhere far away where nobody asks no questions. That boy looks just like you. We don't want him running home from school right past your house, do we?"

"No, ma'am, we do not," Henry Clay admitted. "But don't you think the baby ought to be shown to me before I'm made to take responsibility for it?"

"Like I said, ain't nobody stopping you from visiting with Beulah or that baby. Go right on over there. But she's going to make a scene. She was all ready to have letter-writing paper printed up with the name of Mrs. Henry Clay Beattie at the top."

Henry Clay spat again. "I never promised her a thing like that."

"Oh, but you did, when you gave her a baby. Now, would you like to make her your responsibility for the rest of your life, or just for this one year, and be finished with her?"

That's how it came about that Henry Clay Beattie agreed to pay for a year at St. Mary's School for Girls in Alexandria, and offered up a lump sum intended to cover the baby's upkeep for the first year of his life, to be settled in cash so that the Beattie name was not attached to a single penny of it. They met a week later to conduct that bit of business.

"That's the last you'll ever see of Beulah Binford," Meemaw said.

A flicker of shock registered across Henry Clay's face. Then he said, "You tell her I said to be a good girl."

⤚ 20 ⤙

"OH, JUST STAND up and sing a line," Fleurette said, when it came time to hold auditions for May Ward's chorus.

"I told you, going on stage gives me a nervous stomach," Beulah said. She was beginning to tire of the girl's insistence. Clearly no one had ever told Fleurette no. Beulah wished she'd made more of an effort to take up with some of the girls in the other tents, but it was too late now. Social circles formed quickly in a place like this, and they'd already tightened and closed.

It was her misfortune to have ended up in a tent with a girl five years her junior, who wanted nothing more than to be admired and praised. Fleurette made much of very little: she dressed herself in beautiful fabrics and fine tailoring, which was no small feat, considering that her sisters seemed to be of limited means. She sat up every night making small repairs and improvements to their uniforms and working on bits of costuming for May Ward's concert. Beulah had never done more than sew on a button or repair a ripped seam, but she could see now that it took considerable effort to keep a fine wardrobe in good repair. Beulah did admire her for that.

But that was also the trouble. Fleurette put in the effort because she wanted to be noticed. She wanted to be seen. More than that, she was perfectly convinced that she was worthy of being seen. Beulah had watched her dance—just a few little steps when they were in formation, waiting for their setting-up exercises to begin—and judged her to be competent but not extraordinary. She sang in a fine, clear soprano, and knew a good many songs, but no one would ever line up to hear her at a concert.

She was, in other words, as capable as any other girl who had ever gone through a music and dance academy, but no more. Why, then, was she so eager to put herself forward, and so at ease in front of others? How could she accept praise and adoration as if it were her due?

Her sisters didn't seem overly sentimental about her. Norma in particular hardly had a kind word for anyone, and Constance was careful and reserved in her praise for the girl.

But it was obvious that no one had ever told Fleurette that she wasn't worth a damn, and nothing had happened yet to allow her to come to that conclusion on her own. She sought out love and got it, just for being her ordinary self.

Beulah found Fleurette a little hard to take sometimes.

But she came to the auditions nonetheless, because Fleurette was an irresistible force, and because her sister was the camp matron (what horrible luck for Beulah!) who would've been suspicious had Beulah disappeared just before the auditions began.

Gathered in the mess hall that night were about fifty girls who professed some interest in singing and dancing. The others were made to attend a field bandaging demonstration put on by Nurse Cartwright. It gave Beulah some relief to know that a good three-quarters of the campers would rather watch a nurse bandage a volunteer than stand up on stage and sing a song. At least she wasn't alone in that.

Constance had confiscated the portable Victrola. It had been locked away in the supply shed until it could be put to some communal use, and this was just such an opportunity. Fleurette would've preferred an upright piano, with Clarence banging out tunes at her request, but such an instrument could not be had on short notice.

"I'll write off to my sergeant and see about getting one here in time for your concert, miss," Clarence promised. "I wouldn't mind putting my hands on a piano again."

Without the piano, there was nothing to do but to sing along to the Victrola. Constance carried it into the mess hall and allowed Ellie Duval, the owner of the player, to set it up. Beulah had the impression that Tizzy, Ginny, Ellie, and the others wouldn't have come to the auditions either, but Ellie seemed to want to keep an eye on her Victrola and the others followed along.

Fleurette stood up on the speaking platform at the front of the mess hall. "I've sent away for the sheet music, so that whoever is going to sing in the chorus will have time to learn it. May Ward usually travels with eight girls, but she'll be by herself this time. She said that we could cast more than eight if we wanted to. We once had twenty up on stage in Pittsburgh."

Beulah could tell that Fleurette was showing off. Had any of the other girls traveled with a vaudeville act? Here again, Beulah marveled at how easily she put such a small accomplishment before an audience. From what the other girls said, May Ward was a minor actress, past her prime and unable to get a foothold in the moving pictures business. It wasn't much to have traveled with her, but Fleurette thought it a fine achievement and believed everyone else would, too.

"If you don't mind singing unaccompanied, you can come up and perform whatever you've prepared," Fleurette said. "Otherwise, you can sing along to the Victrola, but you'll have to choose from among the music that comes with it. Who wants to go first?"

A few girls queued up and took the stage with their own music: sweet, pretty songs that they'd been singing for years in their mothers' parlors. A few others sang "The Star-Spangled Banner" or "My Old Kentucky Home," and performed them quickly and nervously, as if their only interest was in getting it over with so they could sit in the back and avoid that Red Cross bandaging lesson.

It was all innocuous enough, until Tizzy took the stage.

"I believe there's a song on the Victrola I could sing," she announced with a note of daring in her voice.

Ginny put the music on. It wasn't a song Beulah recognized —she didn't keep up with the new music—and she was surprised when a man started singing. What was Tizzy doing with a man's song?

She sang loudly and clearly, drowning out the man's voice on the recording with her own. It was a bit of a dirge, the way he sang it, but she made it into a comical song, and embellished it with winks and elaborate vocal flourishes.

I love you, I love you,
You're just the kind of girl for me,
But there is something 'bout you, makes me doubt you,
Why, oh! why must it be?

You dare me, you scare me,
And still I like you more each day,
But you're the kind that will charm, and then do harm,
you've got a dangerous way.

"You're a Dangerous Girl." That was the song. It had been popular just last year. Beulah remembered walking past a sheet music shop on Fifth Avenue and hearing the salesman sing it for a customer.

"I wonder who they wrote that one about," the man said, and the salesman only winked and kept singing.

Beulah rushed on before she heard her name invoked. There had been a rash of songs like that after the trial. Songs about wanton vixens who lead men to their ruin took hold among vaudevillians and theater producers. Everyone wanted to put her story out in front of the public again, reformulated only slightly, so as to make it seem like dangerous girls and tawdry affairs had only been invented for people's amusement.

The theaters wouldn't allow Beulah on the stage, but they would put up another girl with another name and a story only slightly different from hers. That was enough to sell tickets. That was enough for someone to get rich, as long as it wasn't her. It could never be her.

The songs only got worse from there. Tizzy and her friends, it seemed, were obsessed by Binford-style scandals. Dorina and Liddy, two girls so alike that they might've been twins, with their pink cheeks and dimpled smiles, linked arms and delivered a clownish rendition of another lurid tune.

If I hadn't-a shot young Mary
I'd have loved her all my life
If I hadn't-a shot young Mary
I'd still have her for my wife
But she's dead and buried, Lord, she's gone
And soon I'm going, too.

If I hadn't-a met young Annie
I never would've thought to run
If I hadn't-a met young Annie
I never would've bought that gun

But Annie led me down that path, Lord, it's Annie's fault
And now I've lost her, too.

Beulah went cold all over. The room seemed to swim around as the girls finished their vile song, to great laughter and applause from the others.

She dropped to a bench and looked around at the faces surrounding her, all of them grinning monstrously, their teeth bared, their lips red and wet.

Did they know? How could they? And why would they take this moment to put it in front of her?

From behind her, a hand clamped down on her shoulder and she nearly screamed.

"Roxanna?" It was Constance, taking a seat alongside her, pressing her body solidly against Beulah's. It was evident to Beulah that Constance had done something along the lines of a matron's duties before. She knew how to use her size to her advantage, and to put herself right up against a girl in trouble, offering her comfort, perhaps, but also giving her no way out. Beulah gave into it and sank against her.

"It's that song," she whispered. "I don't know why they sing such wicked, awful songs."

Constance looked down at her in surprise and put a hand on her forehead. "I didn't think you shocked so easily. But you're right, it's a—well, it's what my mother would've called an ode to iniquity. Go on out and get yourself some air. I'll put a stop to it."

An ode to iniquity. As long as she lived, Beulah would keep learning new words for what she was. Her stomach turned over, sharp and sour, and she ran out of the tent with her hand over her mouth.

⚹ 21 ⚹

HAVING BEEN LIBERATED from the auditions, Beulah found it a relief to be out in the chill of early evening. No one else was about. From inside the mess hall came laughter and a pair of voices raised in song. They were singing decent songs now, about a sweet home far away and a mother praying for her son. Constance must've seen to that.

Across the field, a Red Cross demonstration was under way in one of the classroom tents. The campers inside were mostly quiet. Beulah could hear only Nurse Cartwright, who was lecturing in a loud, clear voice. "If you can't find anything that will answer for a splint," she was saying, "take his belt and lash his legs together, like so."

Beulah shuddered at the thought of it. What gave nurses the courage to tend to wounded and dying men? Beulah was probably more at ease with the bodies of men than any girl at camp, but not when they were suffering. Not when they were in agony.

She'd known every kind of man during her years down on Mayo Street. At first, when she was only thirteen and looked it, men would try to have their way with her, but they would only go so far. They liked to hold her on their laps, and bounce her up and down, and rock her back and forth. They liked to put their hands on her, and to go all the way up her skirt, and to put a finger somewhere they shouldn't. Sometimes they'd take her hand and put it down their trousers. Beulah always kept her eyes closed at those moments. That made it seem more like a game, or something she was only imagining.

She couldn't remember exactly when it progressed beyond that, but Henry Clay wasn't her first. He didn't get that privilege. She couldn't remember who did. They were all like him, though: fresh-faced, milk-fed, strong-jawed southern boys raised on fried chicken, biscuits, and sorghum syrup. They came to Mayo Street with sharp haircuts, clean shirts, and pockets full of their daddy's money. Beulah sought them out particularly: she couldn't stand an older man, or one who wasn't clean.

Even though Henry Clay wasn't the first man to take her to bed, he was her first in another way. He was her first love and, to this day, her only love. He was the only one she ever thought of when she was apart from him. He was the only one who talked to her—really talked to her, about his innermost thoughts—and the only one who seemed interested in hearing hers.

"Strange as it seems," he said to her one night, when they were up in her room at May Stuart's, "you and me have something in common. We don't want to live the lives we've been given. I don't want to run my daddy's store, and you don't want to keep house with your Meemaw."

"That's exactly right," Beulah said. She had her head on his chest and she was smoking his cigarette. "What are we going to do about it?"

"Run off, I guess," he said.

Beulah's heart turned over when he said that. That was how she knew she loved him.

· · ·

HOW, THEN, COULD Henry Clay ever marry another woman? She was so astonished to hear about his nuptials, only a year after Henry Clay Jr. was born, that she had to see it for herself.

Beulah had been off in Alexandria, at the school Meemaw chose for her, although she only lasted a month at St. Mary's before the teachers there realized exactly what sort of girl they had in their possession and told her she wasn't welcome. The rest of the tuition money stayed in Meemaw's pocket, as did most of the money for the upkeep of the baby, until a home was found for him.

Meemaw never could bring herself to deposit the baby at the Catholic home as she'd sworn she would, nor did she have the wherewithal to place him in another town, far away from Henry Clay's family. She kept him for so long that Beulah thought Meemaw wanted him for her own, and never imagined that she'd give him away.

But just before Christmas, a neighbor girl came over to say that her family was looking to adopt a baby, and pointed out that Meemaw seemed to be in possession of one that could not possibly be her own. It took very little convincing for the child to change hands. Beulah wasn't told about any of it until months later, in the middle of summer, when cholera took the baby away. The funeral was over by the time she knew a thing about it.

Beulah returned to Richmond to lay a wreath at her baby's grave. With that wreath she also laid down all of her regrets: her regret for surrendering the child at all, and making it so that the baby would never know its mother, and her regret for not taking seriously Meemaw's intention to give the baby away. What made her think that an old woman could raise an infant by herself, or would want to?

She could hardly imagine what those last months must've been like for little Henry Clay Beattie Jr. (she called him Clay, during the short while that she had him), being passed from one family to another, with such a bewildering array of new faces to look up at through those deep blue eyes, blinking at each face like a star winking in and out. For his life to be over before it started—it was terrible to think of. What had she done by abandoning him, and to what end? School had nothing to offer her. She knew it wouldn't. She'd lost her little boy, and gained nothing by it.

She laid that wreath down for her mother, too, although she hadn't any idea whether her mother was alive or dead. Meemaw didn't want to hear Jessie's name spoken in her presence. That was another regret: Why hadn't Beulah ever gone looking for her mother again? Couldn't she, at the age of fourteen or fifteen, have found some kind of steady work and rented a room for the two of them? If her mother was so terribly ill, shouldn't Beulah have provided her with a bed, at least?

It was a mournful day in the graveyard. All of Richmond seemed gray and drab. She couldn't stand to stay in that town for another minute. She would've left right away, but then she heard about the wedding.

Henry Clay was to marry Louise Welford Owen, a girl from a good family, a girl who wore the approval of Henry Clay's daddy like a garment label. Beulah remembered hearing Henry Clay talk about a girl named Louise, a girl so bland he couldn't ever find a word to say to her. Louise and Henry's mother could talk endlessly of old family connections, of grandmothers' china patterns, of cousins who married well and nieces who didn't. It bored Henry to tears, all this talk of lineage and inheritance and propriety. Henry couldn't imagine how his own father had seen fit to marry a society girl.

"He must never have known a girl like you, Beulah," Henry said to her one afternoon, as they lay in bed together passing a bottle of wine back and forth between them. "If he had, he would've known what he was missing, and that would've been intolerable. I have never once seen my father laugh at a single thing my mother said, and you make me laugh all the time, girlie." He chucked her under the chin when he said it.

No wonder Beulah felt special. No wonder she harbored particular expectations as to their future.

No wonder his wedding was such a strange and stilted affair.

Half of Richmond turned out for it—the rich half, that much was plain. Beulah had never seen such finery and flowers inside a church before. The pews were overfull, and Beulah was compelled to stand in the back, which she didn't mind at all, as she had no right to be there anyway. Instead of giving her name at the door, she said only that she was "a Beattie neighbor girl," a phrase that somehow insinuated that she might be the daughter of a servant, and for that reason she was admitted inside as long as she didn't take up a family pew.

Beulah wore black for a month after her baby died, which was the reason why she wore a black veil to Henry Clay's wedding. She would've gone in an ordinary afternoon dress, but Meemaw had declared that to give up her mourning only a few weeks after little Henry Clay Jr. went into the ground would bring a curse upon the entire family. Beulah didn't know about curses, but she wore her black crepe nonetheless. It was an effective disguise. Besides, she was not the only woman in black at the wedding. It had been a terrible summer for cholera and others had lost family, too, most of them small children.

From the rear of the church she could only see the hats and the backs of the necks of Henry Clay's mother and sisters. His father must've been one of the men alongside them, although they all looked the same from this distance and she couldn't guess which one he might've been. She recognized some of his ne'er-do-well cousins. One or two of them might've recognized Beulah, even behind her veil.

As for Louise, Beulah saw nothing but frills and lace, and a bevy of similarly attired attendants. What did she matter, anyway? She meant nothing to Henry Clay and was only lucky enough to marry him because Henry Clay's parents had prevailed at last. It wasn't a love match. She would never have Henry Clay, not the way Beulah had. And Beulah carried the secret pride of having borne his first (and so far, only) son. What did Louise have to put up against that?

The ceremony was overly long and the church was hot. Beulah dozed off, leaning against the back wall. When she came to, there was organ music and a great rustling of petticoats, and the couple was walking back down the aisle to a waiting coach. Henry Clay had the side of the aisle nearest Beulah. She edged over a little to get a better look at him. There was a smile across his face, but his eyes were blank. He shook hands with the men along the aisle, and accepted kisses from the women.

When he reached Beulah, his gaze passed across her but did not stop. The corners of his mouth twitched downward for only a second—not so you'd notice, unless you were watching for it— and Beulah was.

He saw her. She was certain of it.

AFTER THE WEDDING, it was almost a year before Beulah saw Henry Clay again. In the time that had passed, she had decided that if he could get married, she could, too—and she almost did. Mayo Street held no appeal for her anymore, but the ball park proved a wonderful place to meet men and find entertainment. She came so close to love and marriage behind the dugout that she went around calling herself Mrs. R. T. Fisher, wife of the in- fielder, even though they never did marry, even though he'd been traded to Danville and she was back in Richmond. There were certain advantages to going through life as a married woman, chief among them that she could take a furnished room under his name on a more respectable street than Mayo. She even held a job in a shop for a few months and earned an honorable if meager living. Marriage gave her all of that, even if it was a sham marriage.

The fact that Bob Fisher never did manage to put his signature to a piece of paper concerning Beulah, and that he sent her home after she trailed behind him to Danville for an ill-fated month-long stay—none of that mattered, as long as she could lay some claim to him. Bob Fisher was tall and good-looking, with a substantial nose, a toothy grin, good deep lines around his mouth when he smiled, and a sunburn from all those afternoons at the ball park. He was twenty-five, which seemed a solid and reliable age. He carried himself with swagger and confidence, and he was genuinely kind to Beulah. She, in turn, behaved like a perfect little wife, and understood only later that a perfect wife was not what Bob wanted Beulah to be.

After he'd been away for six months without a word to her, Beulah had to own up to the fact that she was not, in fact, Mrs. R. T. Fisher, and might not even see him again, unless his team came through town for a game.

She wished she could call herself a widow, but she'd already made too much of the fact that she was married to the great Bob Fisher, who was doing so well out in Danville that he was rumored to be under consideration to join the Brooklyn ball club. Anyone who read the sports pages would know that she couldn't possibly be a widow, because the man she claimed as her husband was at that moment kicking up dust in the infield.

She found that she liked ball players, though—their easygoing camaraderie, their muscled shoulders, that way they had of breezing through life. They played a game for a living, the only game they ever wanted to play, and because of that they were entirely at their ease and comfortable in their own skin. They took pretty girls as their due, welcomed them easily, said good-bye without even feigning regret, and made no promises they couldn't possibly keep.

Beulah loved them for all of that. She loved their beer, their tobacco, the sand in their shoes, the way they'd come off the field hot and dusty, and emerge from their clubhouse an hour later, scrubbed and fresh-faced, with open collars and rolled-up sleeves. Everything about them was easy and good. Beulah couldn't stay away.

When Henry Clay turned up at the ball park, this time with Louise's brothers (a far more respectable group of men than his old friends), Beulah was shocked at how he'd changed. After almost a year of marriage, he hadn't grown fat, exactly, but he was swollen, somehow, and red-faced, and dull-eyed. There was an angry set to his jaw that Beulah didn't remember seeing before. When she compared him now to the ball players she'd come to know in the last year, he wasn't nearly the specimen of man they were. What had she ever seen in him?

Beulah sat behind the dugout with the other girls, as she always did, and kept her head turned so Henry Clay wouldn't spot her from his place in the bleachers not far away. After the game, though, she forgot herself, and milled around behind the clubhouse with her friends, and there Henry Clay spotted her. Louise's brothers were out on the street, ogling a friend's new automobile, so Henry Clay took a chance and ran to her.

"I thought you'd left Richmond for good," he said, panting, when he reached her.

"You don't own Richmond," she said. Her friends giggled at that and she walked a little ways away from them. Henry Clay followed.

"I thought I'd never see you again," he said.

"I don't know why it matters whether you do or not," Beulah said.

"I can't stand to be in that house any longer," Henry Clay said. "You don't know what it's like."

"If you're asking if I know what it's like to be Mrs. Henry Clay Beattie, you are correct," Beulah said. "I don't. But it don't matter to me now. I married a ball player last fall, and I've been all over the country with him, watching his games."

Henry Clay hung his head. Beulah couldn't believe she could hurt him so easily. "Which one is your husband?" he mumbled.

"He's back in Illinois right now. But I still like to watch the games."

Henry Clay snatched up Beulah's hand. She looked around to see who might be watching. His wedding ring dug into her palm. "Meet me tonight, Beulah," he begged. "Just give me one more good night with you. That's all I'll ever ask."

Beulah jerked her hand away. "Why are you still after me? Go on down to Mayo Street and find yourself whatever you like."

Henry Clay whispered, "I can't go down there, don't you see? I have a hawk for a mother-in-law. She's got it in for me. She knows all about—what I used to do. Don't ask me how she found out. But she pulled me aside on my wedding day and told me that if I ever so much as looked at another girl, that would be the end of it between me and Louise."

"You talk like you don't much care for Louise," Beulah said. "Why don't you just walk away?"

He put his palms against his temples and then ran his fingers through his hair, frantic. "Don't you remember? If I make one wrong step—I'm out. I'm out of the family, and that damned store, and there's not one penny for me. My daddy's got me on an allowance, if you can imagine that. A grown man, and I have to go over and beg for what's due to me, every Sunday!"

"You could try earning your money," Beulah said. "You could be your own man and not wait for your daddy to hand you everything."

Beulah couldn't believe she had the nerve to say such a thing to Henry Clay. Then again, she'd been running around with these ball players, and to a person they were all their own men. Free spirits, making their way in the world on the strength of their sweat and their talent. What would they make of Henry Clay, crying about his daddy and his pocket full of money, all of it unearned and unappreciated?

"Go on home to your wife, Henry Clay," Beulah said.

Henry Clay was by then even more red-faced, breathing heavy and almost crying. There was something wrong with him. Something had changed, but Beulah didn't want to ask what it was.

He grabbed her again, this time by the elbow. "They're watching me all the time, Beulah," he panted. "I can't ever get away from them, not for a minute. I can't hardly take a breath in my own house without someone looking at me funny. You've got to come with me. Just give me one afternoon. Let me be my own man again, for just a few hours."

Beulah picked his fingers off her elbow, one at a time. "Is that Louise of yours expecting a baby yet?"

Again he hung his head. "She's just a couple months away."

"And do you intend to raise this one, or are you going to throw it away like you did your first-born?"

He was crying now, really crying. Beulah had never seen a man weep and found that the sight of it made her queasy. "Of course I intend to raise it," he said, sniffing and shaking like a little boy coming out of a nightmare. "And I never did throw that other one away. I wanted to see him, but your Meemaw wouldn't let me."

Beulah knew better. She knew her Meemaw told him he could come around and see that baby. He never did. "It don't matter what you wanted to do. It only matters what you did. You stayed away."

"I wish I'd seen him once. Your grandmother sent me a note after the funeral and told me I wouldn't have to worry about a baby anymore. I keep thinking it's my fault, what happened to him."

"Your boy took the cholera like so many babies did. I shouldn't have said you wanted to throw him away. I know you didn't."

That seemed to placate Henry Clay, who wiped his eyes and looked around for his brothers-in-law.

"Go on back to your people," Beulah said, "and stop making yourself so damn miserable. You have a wife and a baby and a house and plenty of money. You ought not to cry and complain and make such a mess of everything. Go on home."

The ball players were coming out just then, and the other girls were starting to gather around. Beulah was eager to get away from Henry Clay.

"But how can I find you?" Henry Clay said. "Just—if I need to. Not to bother you again like this. I just want to know where you are."

Beulah was distracted watching those ball players and didn't think much about how to answer Henry Clay. "I'm Mrs. Fisher now," she called, an easy lie to toss off as she walked away. "But don't come around looking for me. You had your chance."

❦ 22 ❧

NURSE CARTWRIGHT WENT to town for supplies, having discovered that two hundred girls could make short work of a carton
of aspirin, several packets of mustard plasters, and rolls of gauze
and cotton. She was distributing more than the expected number
of hot water bottles, and found herself entirely depleted of cough
syrups and sleeping powders. She returned with all of this and
one other item that interested Norma a great deal: a newspaper.

Constance never would've believed that her sister could survive without her daily infusion of newspapers from every nearby
city and as far away as New York. Norma didn't just read her papers, she quarreled with them, shook them at her sisters for em-
phasis, and even gave them a smack when she couldn't otherwise
resolve her disputes with them.

For that reason, the arrival at camp of a single newspaper
made for a momentous occasion in their tent. Norma sat up with
a lantern, digesting the news from Washington and passing on
whatever might be of interest to the others.

"They fought back the Germans in Verdun," she announced to
Sarah, who had reason to believe her brother might've been sent
there. "Someone even brought down their aeroplanes with those
enormous machine guns. It doesn't say whether it was the Brit-

ish or the French." She rattled her paper to make her displeasure known over the reporter's lack of specificity.

"Shooting down aeroplanes doesn't leave much for the ambulances to pick up," Sarah said curtly. "It's becoming another kind of war over there, and we're not doing a thing about it."

Constance looked up from her ledger-book, where she kept a record of the day's activities. It was a habit from her years on the women's floor of the jail. She recorded demerits issued, classes skipped, sick days taken, and work shifts completed.

Her pencil was poised in mid-air, but she was watching Sarah, who was readying herself for a night in the woods. "What's the matter with you?" Constance asked.

Sarah shoved her feet into her boots and wrapped her braided hair around her hand, then began to pin it up. "I haven't had a letter from Jack in nearly a week."

"They get delayed," Norma said authoritatively. "The rail system's a mess, and the ports are overfull. Even our ships have to drop anchor and wait. Over half the letters aren't getting through at all."

Sarah was usually so tolerant of Norma's overbearing ways, but her patience had worn thin. "That could be the explanation, or it could be something far worse. None of us know, not even you."

With that she stormed out. Constance would've run after her, but she was only half-dressed herself and had her nightly rounds to make. Besides, what could she say? None of them knew what might become of Jack. It wouldn't be fair to Sarah to pretend otherwise.

Norma went on as if nothing had happened. "Here's something for you. Your Mr. Bielaski's in the papers again. They're calling him the most remarkable investigator in the country. He says that the United States needs an independent and secret organization that will work in closer co-operation than the men we are hunting."

"And who is he hunting this week?"

"Oh, the usual. Russian revolutionaries, German propagandists, pacifists, insurrectionists, and saboteurs."

"I wonder how he manages it all in secret," Constance said.

"Well, they don't explain that, for the most obvious of reasons," Norma said, and put the paper down to go out and check on her pigeons before curfew.

When she was gone, Constance picked up the paper. There was a photograph of Mr. Bielaski at his desk, looking pointedly at the camera. Arrayed around that picture were five or six fanciful drawings of his secret agents: a postman flipping through the mail, a businessman hiding behind a newspaper on a train, a waiter carrying a tray of drinks, and a society lady covering her face with a fan.

How many society ladies had Mr. Bielaski enlisted, and how had he accomplished it?

Constance took the entire page and stashed it in her pocket for further consideration.

Curfew was by then only half an hour away. The tent was empty: Sarah and Norma had both stepped out, and Fleurette and Beulah were out socializing. There were by now long-running card games in some of the tents, and in one tent a girl dressed as a fortune-teller and read palms for a dime. She did a brisk trade that way, predicting war hero husbands, obedient children, and exotic journeys. Constance should've shut the little enterprise down, except that it kept the girls lined up around the tent where she could keep an eye on them. Better they stay at the campsite and fill their heads with nonsense than run off into the woods, she reasoned.

Constance made her rounds in great haste, still thinking

of Sarah and wanting to catch up with her. The front gate was locked, which meant that Hack and Clarence had already been by. There was a larger than usual gaggle of girls around the latrines, owing to one of them being occupied for the last hour by a girl with cramps. It fell to Constance to help her to her feet and deposit her at the infirmary with Nurse Cartwright, who was glad for the company and for a chance to put her new hot water bottles to use.

Constance took one last walk between the tents, calling a halt to the card games and the fortune-telling. Within half an hour, the camp was quiet.

Low clouds hid the moon that night. There were no lights around the perimeter of the campsite apart from the lantern Constance carried. She doused the light and slipped behind the barn into the gap between fence posts, which led to her usual rendezvous spot with Sarah and the others. She could hear them faintly through the trees and rushed down the path, worried all at once that she never should've let Sarah out of her sight. She'd never seen Sarah so disconsolate.

But she arrived and found everything in order. Everyone was present: Sarah, Margaret, Bernice, Hilda, and Fern. They were practicing the halter hold Constance had taught them, which required the girl to approach from behind, hook his right elbow (assuming the opponent was right-handed) with her own, pin it behind his back, then throw the other arm across the man's neck, pinning down his left arm in the process. Then it was a simple matter to kick a knee into the back of his leg. Even a large man would go down face-first, if the move was done quickly and with confidence.

It was a difficult maneuver to practice, because the recipient of the hold would, in a practice session, know what to expect, but they ran through the first half of the move over and over, ending with a gentle nudge to the back of the leg but not going so far as to push their partner down. "If you ever have to use this move, you won't have any trouble with the last part," Constance had assured them. "Once you've gone this far, you'll know exactly how to overcome him."

She stood at the edge of the clearing and watched them with some pride. Here was the Amazonian corps Geneva Nash had warned against. They weren't large, most of them, but they were fierce, and utterly determined to learn every move Constance taught them.

She'd once imagined, back when she was deputy sheriff, that she might have a role to play someday in training women for law enforcement work. There was no such academy in existence anywhere that Constance knew of, and no formal instruction of any kind for women going into the profession. Most of the sheriffs and police chiefs hiring women had no idea what they might do, and therefore no plan for how to train them. Only a woman who had done the job could prepare another woman to do it.

Constance lost her chance to carry out a scheme like that, but this—wasn't this the next best thing? Even if these women never went to France, she thought, look at what they've learned to do. Who could say how they might put their training to use?

Hilda spotted Constance and ran over to her, still out of breath from her drill.

"How do we look?" she asked Constance.

"You look like warriors." There was no other word for it. Even in their skirts and shirtwaists, and their hair pinned up, they'd become soldiers.

Hilda's cheeks were flushed, and her countenance was triumphant. "Tonight we are. Look what Sarah brought." She pointed to the edge of the clearing.

Constance knew before she turned around to look. The guns.

There they were, four of them: two rifles and two revolvers, placed carefully in the grass atop a pile of jackets.

"What did I say about weapons?" Constance said furiously.

Sarah stood her ground: there was no other way to describe it. Her feet were planted as staunchly as tree trunks, her arms crossed stubbornly over her chest. "I've had a week to imagine what might've happened to Jack. You know as well as I that a German could've put a bullet in him by now. I intend to return that bullet the first chance I get."

"Oh, Sarah," Constance said. "Don't let yourself think that way. Surely the mail's been lost. You'll hear from him—"

"You don't know that. If it were your brother, you'd feel just as I do."

"I might," Constance said. "But these guns—they were locked away. I checked them myself."

"Locks have keys," Sarah said. "Nobody's going to miss them. The case was covered in dust and shoved under a pile of tent stakes and ropes. No one's so much as looked at that case since we set up camp. Hack and Clarence have probably forgotten it's there."

"They most certainly have not!" Constance said. "They're soldiers. I can assure you they're well aware of the gun case. It was issued to them, for their use."

The other women were all standing around her in a semi-circle now. Margaret said, "I wouldn't blame you if you were opposed to what we're trying to do. Plenty of people were against rifle training in these camps. That's why we don't have it."

"I never said I was against—"

But Margaret pressed on. "I remember what they said. Why not learn to knit, instead of shoot? As if any of us are untrained in knitting."

"That's preposterous," Constance said, "but you've stolen these weapons. I can't allow it."

"We've only borrowed them," Sarah said. "We can have them back in an hour, if we start our training now."

"Or you can put them back immediately," Constance said. "Camps have closed over less than this. You heard about what happened in Newark. They shut down a camp over six girls misbehaving."

"Those girls were drinking cocktails with their wireless instructor," Sarah said. "I'm talking about training for war, which is precisely what this camp is intended to do."

"And we are," Constance said. "We can train without weapons. There's plenty to learn."

"Maybe she's right," Hilda said. "Do you remember the anti-suffragist cartoons last fall? One of them showed women soldiers stopping in the heat of battle to powder their noses. What a distraction we'd be!"

"No one's going to war to powder her nose," Constance said stormily. She was being worked over by all of them and she knew it.

"But your point is taken," Margaret said. "We don't need to train with guns. Let the men meet the enemy."

"They're our enemy too," Constance said. She knew, at that minute, that she was sunk.

Margaret held her breath. All of them did. They were so young, some of them—just barely Fleurette's age, but with such seriousness of purpose.

Constance couldn't help but wish she had the last twenty years to live over, starting right at that moment, with these young women for comrades. What a life she could've led alongside them! It was foolish of her to think of forty as old, of course, but she couldn't help it, when she considered the two decades that stood between her and the youngest of these women. For most of those years she'd been at home, keeping house, helping to raise Fleurette, and doing her mother's bidding. These girls had such bold and brilliant prospects ahead of them.

She had to admit that women made awfully good shots. They were more methodical than men, and more practiced in the kind of fine and precise work that was the secret to good marksmanship. They weren't brutal or careless with a weapon, as a man might be. Every one of these women would be cool, calculated, and competent—if they were shown the way.

And what a thrill it would be for them, to put a target in their sights, to squeeze the trigger, and to see how perfectly they could hit it!

"One hour," Constance said. "And you won't fire tonight. I'll show you how to handle them, but that's as far as we go for now."

No one wanted to give her time to change her mind, so all five women rushed over to the guns at once. Constance had them sit in a semi-circle around her. She settled down on her knees, her skirt in a pool on the ground, and looked over the weapons.

They were wonderfully heavy and cool. Although she hardly ever fired a gun as a deputy, she missed the security of wearing it against her hip.

She started by unloading each of them.

"Who taught you to do this?" Bernice asked.

Constance pretended not to hear. "I want you all to see that the chamber is empty." She lifted her lantern so that they could each have a look. "Never trust what anyone tells you. If the gun's in your hands, it's loaded until you prove otherwise. Look inside the chamber yourself."

She passed the revolver around and they each took their turn. Constance was pleased to see that each one of them handled it carefully, and pointed it down at the ground without her having to tell them to do so. They were thinking about the consequences, as she knew they would.

"That's fine," she said. "Now let's do the rifle. Did any of you hunt with your fathers?"

None of them had.

"My brother took me out once or twice," Constance said. "Now, this might not be the rifle you'll see in France. They're using artillery guns over there. But you know they're fighting out in the countryside, among villages and farmhouses. I have no doubt that rifles like these are in circulation."

Once again, she showed them how to break it down and make sure it was unloaded. The rifle was well-oiled and in good form. It made a satisfying sound as it came apart and locked together in her students' hands.

"Your stance is a little different with a pistol than it would be with a rifle," she said. "I want you all to stand up and put your feet just so."

She was in the middle of demonstrating, and had the pistol out in front of her, aimed into the trees, when she heard a rustling in the shadows and a feminine shriek.

"Don't shoot!" came a familiar voice, followed by laughter.

Into the circle of yellow light cast by the lantern stumbled Roxie and Fleurette, followed by Hack and Clarence.

The girls were grinning, delighted at having caught Constance in an illegal act, but Hack and Clarence were wide-eyed and terrified.

"Are those— Do you have— Are those our guns?" asked Clarence.

⤜ 23 ⤛

THESE BOYS ARE going to make terrible soldiers, Beulah thought. They abandon their posts to walk in the woods with us. They can't keep track of their own weapons. Now a woman twice their age in long skirts has a pistol in her hand, and they're absolutely terrified. What are they going to do when they're facing down the Germans?

Constance tucked the pistol in her belt as if she did it every day. Fleurette had been awfully coy about her older sister, but Beulah was ever more suspicious that she'd done something in the line of police work before. She carried herself that way, and it wasn't just because she'd been appointed camp matron.

But if that was true, why was it such a secret? Who would want to hide a thing like that?

Constance said, "The guns aren't loaded. These girls are all planning to go to France directly, as soon as camp is over. They wanted some training in firearms for their own protection. I told them I would give a demonstration, but nothing more. This is entirely my responsibility."

Hack took a few steps forward and peered down at the other guns, still arrayed on the pile of jackets. "Are these ours? We never took them out of the supply shed. They've been locked, and we carry the keys."

He felt around on his belt for a ring of keys and held them up to the light of Constance's lantern.

"Your keys are there," Sarah said, "and Constance shouldn't be the one to take the blame. I stole the guns. I borrowed a key from Clarence and returned it right away."

Clarence fumbled for his own keys. "They're on me all the time, Hack! I swear I never take them off. Unless . . . You didn't come and get them while . . ."

"I did," Sarah said. "I lifted them while you were in the shower. But I didn't look."

Beulah couldn't help but laugh. That sounded like something she would do. One of the first things she learned on Mayo Street was how to slip her fingers into a man's pockets, whether he was wearing the pants or not.

Every girl turned around and looked at Beulah when she laughed. They were taking this far more seriously than she was. Even Fleurette looked horrified. It took a minute for Beulah to understand why: she and Fleurette, too, had been caught doing something wrong.

"It doesn't matter who took the keys," Constance said briskly. "I'm the matron of this camp and I should've put a stop to it. You can take the guns back now. I don't suppose I have to ask what the four of you were doing in the woods after curfew."

"We only went out for air," Fleurette said. "The boys were escorting us back to our tent. Isn't that their job?"

"I've heard enough from you," Constance said, just sharply enough to make Beulah shrink back, too. "But Privates Hackbush and Piper should've known better. You're here to guard the camp, not to carry on with girls in the woods."

"Then I suppose we're all in a bit of a pickle," Hack said.

Beulah had to give Hack some credit: the boy could think on his feet. He was about to bargain his way out of this mess.

"I'll tell you what, ladies," he said. "If you're serious about going to France, we'll show you how to fire a weapon. But you won't put a hand on these guns unless we're right here with you."

"And you won't put a hand on these girls," Constance said.

"We never did!" Clarence protested.

"They really didn't," Fleurette said, with just enough disappointment in her voice to make everyone laugh this time.

But Constance didn't look convinced. She stood with her arms folded across her chest, frowning down at the two men. What must it be like, Beulah wondered, to tower over everyone else like that? A woman of her size might actually stand a chance against the Germans.

"Did you say," Beulah asked, as long as everyone remained silent, "that all of you are going to France?"

"I've already booked my passage," Sarah said.

"I'm trying to get on the same ship," said Margaret, "and I've written to some friends back home to take up a fund so that we can bring Fern and Hilda with us."

"I'll be leaving from Florida," Bernice said.

It was starting to occur to Beulah that she'd been sneaking out with the wrong crowd after curfew. If she still intended to go to France—and what else was she to do when camp ended?—she needed a woman like Margaret on her side.

"A battalion of ladies invading France," Hack said. "I don't think they intended that when they organized this camp."

"Well, we intended it all along," Margaret said.

"I think it's awfully brave of you," Clarence said. "I have three sisters at home and I can't imagine any of them out here doing what you're doing."

"They might surprise you someday," Constance said. "I'll allow another night of training, and this time you can bring the guns. But one of you has to stay behind and guard the camp. We've left it unattended, and that can't happen again."

"Hack's the better shot," Clarence said. "I suppose he ought to be your rifle instructor. I'll take guard duty."

"You can take turns at guard duty and I'll give the lessons myself," Constance said. "These girls are my responsibility."

Hack cleared his throat and said, "I hope you don't mind me asking, ma'am, but where did you learn how to handle a pistol?"

"Our brother taught her," Fleurette said, before Constance could answer. "He taught all three of us, when he got married and moved away from the farm. He thought we ought to be able to protect ourselves. But I didn't take to it. Of the three of us, Constance is the best shot."

⇥ 24 ⇤

IT WAS ABUNDANTLY clear to Constance that there was no privacy at camp, not even in the woods. If Hack and Clarence could find them, anyone could. And it was all too easy for the girls to be spotted returning to their tents after curfew. To avoid the appearance that any of them were sneaking around on their own, Constance insisted that they walk out of the woods with her. She could always claim, if asked, that they had merely extended their night patrol.

But Hilda and Fern trailed behind, and peeled off, unnoticed, from the group to make their own way back to their tents. It was their great misfortune to be recognized by Tizzy Spotwood, who was at that moment walking back from the latrines.

Tizzy was still stewing over the confiscation of the Victrola and the other privileges Constance had taken away from her and her friends. Constance had made good on her threat and relocated the girls to the very center of camp, which Tizzy believed to be an unfashionable neighborhood. As she was now situated right next to Constance's tent, she didn't hesitate to complain, loudly and often, about the injustice that had rained down upon her and her friends.

Constance regarded Tizzy as the kind of girl who was accustomed to being given the very best of everything. If she was put in inferior accommodations or given anything less than the very finest on offer, she assumed it was the result of neglect or incompetence on someone else's part, and saw it as her duty to step forward and demand that to which she was entitled. In fact, she seemed to believe it to be a special skill of hers to go around finding fault, and took pride in doing it well, which is to say, loudly, frequently, and always within earshot of her friends. She liked an audience.

So when Tizzy spotted two girls across the campground, moving between the tents, she went directly to Constance, who was only just then returning to her own tent.

"I suppose you noticed those two on your rounds," Tizzy said.

Constance straightened and looked around. She would not be intimidated by this girl. "I saw them."

"Well? What are you going to do about it?" She jutted her chin out in the manner of a mistress berating a servant.

"You ought to be in bed," Constance said.

But Tizzy wasn't put off so easily. "They'll have to have a demerit. They weren't going to the latrine. No one else is permitted to be out after nine."

"I'm aware of the rules, Miss Spotwood. Good night."

Tizzy gave an aggrieved little *tsk* but went into her tent anyway.

The next morning, after breakfast, Norma caught up with Constance on their way to pigeon class. "Moving those girls next to us was your first mistake."

"And what was my second mistake, and my third?" Constance asked.

Norma was so surprised to be asked that it took her a minute to compose a list. Before she could recite it, Constance said, "The least you could do would be to keep Fleurette and Roxie in the tent at night."

"If they don't sneak out while I'm putting the pigeons up for the night, they wait until I'm asleep," Norma said. "I'm not in the habit of sleeping with one eye open."

"I noticed," Constance said. Norma's snores were legendary. No one slept as soundly as she did.

"You're going to have to punish Fleurette, and that Roxanna. I never did like that girl." *That Roxanna* was the only way Norma ever said her name.

"Oh, but she speaks so highly of you."

"There's something out of kilter about her," Norma persisted. "She can't seem to make up her mind about where she comes from. Half the time she sounds like a southerner, but she claims to have grown up on Park Avenue."

"She says her mother's from Georgia," Constance said. "I suppose that might explain the accent. But have you noticed how she handles a knife and fork?"

"No finishing school," Norma said.

"Exactly. And she doesn't have that walk."

"Toe-heel, toe-heel."

"It's a ridiculous way to walk," Constance said. "I don't know why girls are taught it. But they all do it."

"It's so they can balance a book on their heads."

"Well, I've already spoken to Fleurette and Roxie. We have an understanding."

"You always have an understanding with Fleurette. What's called for here is a punishment. You ought to cancel May Ward's concert."

"Doesn't that punish the entire camp? You just don't want Freeman Bernstein coming around."

"Surely he won't show his face," Norma said.

"It's quite likely he will. He's May Ward's husband and her manager." Constance enjoyed taunting Norma with this possibility. Norma's grievance against Freeman Bernstein was so massive and unyielding that she could've built a granite monument from it.

"He won't set foot on my campground," Norma said.

"If it's anyone's camp, it's mine," Constance said, "and I'm not going to call off the show. It would only bring unnecessary attention to . . . a minor infraction."

Norma noticed her hesitation: Norma noticed everything. "You were out for quite a while yourself last night," she said.

They'd arrived at the barn by then, as had most of Norma's students. "They're waiting for you," Constance said, with great relief. She wasn't ready to make a full confession to Norma.

Hilda and Fern were among Norma's students. Constance took Hilda by the arm and motioned for Fern to follow. They came along eagerly, obviously expecting to hear daring new plans for their after-hours target practice.

"You were seen last night returning to your tents unaccompanied," Constance said. "I warned you to stay with me, but you didn't. I'm putting you on kitchen duty tonight by yourselves."

"But it takes eight girls to do the kitchen after dinner!" Hilda said.

"Won't we miss our—"

Constance put up a hand to silence Fern before she gave everything away. "This is going to be a good lesson to you. When you go to France, you're simply going to have to follow the rules, and do what your commander tells you, whether you like it or not. And you're going to have to learn how to keep your mouths closed and your secrets to yourselves. Word's already going around this morning that you broke curfew. If anyone asks, you're to confess that you were out, and say that you're on kitchen duty by yourselves as punishment. Don't offer any other explanation."

"But—"

Constance wouldn't hear their arguments. "If you can't obey a straightforward command, then you aren't in any way prepared to go to war."

That was enough to put an end to the complaining. They were good girls who understood at once what was expected of them. They each gave a silent nod and returned to the class, with Constance on their heels.

Norma's lesson that morning concerned the method for affixing messages to the legs of pigeons, and removing those messages when they returned to their loft.

"A bird has to be handled firmly, and with authority," Norma was saying as Constance came back around to the other side of the barn. She sat next to Sarah, who was scratching away in her notebook with a stubby pencil. She was taking the subject of Norma's pigeons far more seriously than Constance ever had.

"If you've handled a chicken, you know how to take hold of a pigeon," Norma said, to scattered laughter from city girls who had only ever handled a chicken after the butcher had plucked and dressed it.

On a hastily knocked-together wooden table next to her was a wire cage holding four birds. Norma reached in and grabbed one from its backside, pinning the wings down under the palm of her hand, and held it out for the class to see. Its feet hung down uselessly and its head bobbed up and down, trying to stay level as Norma waved it around. Several in the class cooed at it affectionately: the creature did look small and helpless in a manner that inspired sympathy.

"You'll each take a turn at handling one before we put the bands on," Norma said, "but we'll have to go inside the barn and close the doors to do that. I can't risk any of them getting away. They might take it upon themselves to fly home. I need them here."

"They wouldn't fly all the way back to New Jersey, would they?"

came a voice from under the eaves of the barn. It was Hack, who had wandered over to watch the class.

Constance bristled at this: the aim of the camp was to put women into classrooms by themselves, where they could learn without interference from the opposite sex. But she was in no position to go against Hack. She'd only just negotiated a truce with him and didn't know how long their fragile peace would hold.

Norma didn't mind, of course. Her purpose in bringing the pigeons was to attract the attention of the Army. There weren't any generals around, as she'd hoped there would be. A private was better than nothing.

"It's two hundred and fifty miles back to Wyckoff, more or less," Norma said. "That's an easy flight for them. You'd know the answer if you attended class more regularly."

Sarah fought a smile. "She can't help herself, can she?" she whispered.

"She thinks she's being helpful by letting him know what he missed," Constance whispered back.

"Can they really fly that far?" Hack asked.

"They can comfortably manage five hundred miles in a day. Our national pigeon racing club has been setting records in excess of two thousand miles," Norma said.

Hack whistled. "Well, that ought to get them across France."

"Correct. France hardly exceeds six hundred miles across in any direction, so they won't have any trouble with it," Norma said briskly.

Soldiers were accustomed to gruff treatment, so Hack wasn't put off by it. "Supposing we turned them loose at the front," he said. "Wouldn't the Germans just shoot them down?"

"We took care of the Germans in our second class, which you also failed to attend," Norma said. It didn't appear, for the moment, that she had anything else to say on the subject.

Sarah took it upon herself to rise from her seat in the back and whisper to Hack, "They can fly as high as any aeroplane. In fact, they've been dropped out of aeroplanes before and they do just fine. From the ground, they'd only be a little speck in the sky. Of course the Germans would get a few, but with a cart this size, you could take a hundred pigeons to the front. You'd have plenty to spare."

"A hundred in that cart?" Hack said, walking over to take a closer look. "Can you pull it with an automobile, or does it have to go by horse? Because I don't think we're fighting this war on horseback."

Norma was losing control of her class. Constance thought about interceding on her behalf, but wasn't this what Norma wanted—to demonstrate her cart for the Army?

"It can go by horse or auto," Norma said, "but a noisy engine has no place in the French countryside. A horse is nearly silent. You wouldn't be noticed."

"Sure, but a horse can spook," Hack said. "Say, we have an auto for bringing supplies back and forth. How about I drive it over here and we take this cart of yours for a ride down the road?"

There was such a flurry of excitement over the prospect of leaving the campground that every girl in the class jumped up and started talking at once.

"I don't suppose we're going to get around to banding any pigeons today," Sarah said.

"I'd better make a round through camp," Constance said. "Keep an eye on this business for me. I don't want a single one of them late for their next class."

THAT NIGHT, THE entire camp knew that Hilda and Fern had been punished for being caught out of their tents after curfew. Great whoops of joy came from the crew of eight who'd been relieved of kitchen duty so that the miscreants could take their punishment. When Constance walked back to the mess hall after dinner to check on them, she found Sarah, Margaret, and Bernice in the kitchen as well, helping Hilda and Fern scrub pots and wash two hundred sets of dishes.

"We're a unit," Margaret said, when she turned around and saw Constance watching them. "We stay together."

Constance let them go on with what they were doing. Outside, under a vast and inky sky, she thought: We might've just formed an army.

⤙ 25 ⤚

IT WOULD BE cold in the woods that night. Beulah warned Fleurette not to wear the filmy green dress she'd chosen for the evening, but Fleurette was always beautifully turned out, even when it meant sacrificing comfort. She had her sights set on Hack, the tall one, the good-looking one, if you liked a man who looked like he'd been cut out of a page in a magazine.

Beulah didn't care for him herself. He would want something from her: men like Hack always wanted something from girls like Beulah, eventually. Soldiers in particular were a little too expectant for Beulah's tastes. They made much of the fact that they might go off to war and never come back, which is to say that they wanted a little something extra from a girl purely out of sympathy. There was nothing in it for the girl, unless she could justify an act of intimate generosity on patriotic grounds, which Beulah could not. The soldiers made it sound as if they might never see a girl again once they left for France, but as far as Beulah knew, Paris was full of pretty girls. They hadn't all been evacuated in advance of the Germans.

She liked Clarence. He was barely eighteen, and still a little soft. He wasn't embarrassed to say that he missed his mother and his sisters, which Beulah appreciated. Any man who spoke well of the women in his family could be expected to behave honorably toward other women. It occurred to her, when Clarence talked wistfully of his younger sister, to whom he'd only just begun to give piano lessons the summer previous, that Henry Clay never said a kind word about his mother or any other woman in his family, even his wife. Especially his wife.

That should've been a sign.

But how different was Henry Clay, really, from any other man down on Mayo Street? Most of them were just like him, except that they never went on to do what Henry Clay had done. They lived out rather ordinary lives. They never made the papers.

Beulah shuddered. She'd managed to go years in New York without ever letting Henry Clay's name flit across her mind, without ever summoning his face or trying to recall the sound of his voice. She wanted nothing more than to put him behind her, but something about being at this camp, within spitting distance of Richmond, brought him back.

It wasn't good for her to relive the past like this. That's what Mabel told her soon after they met. Beulah wasn't as adept, back then, at hiding her identity, and Mabel quickly came to understand that Beulah had been lying to her. It took the better part of a bottle of cheap wine—nasty stuff, far worse than anything she drank back in Richmond—for Mabel to extract a full confession from Beulah. Once she did, she made it her job to help Beulah craft a new identity for herself.

"You have to tell yourself a different story," Mabel insisted. "Every time you think about the past, put something else in your head."

When Beulah asked what, exactly, she ought to put in her head, Mabel said, "Imagine yourself as another girl, with a different name, who had good parents and a nice apartment uptown."

Beulah did just what Mabel told her to do, and it worked,

mostly. After a while, she felt a little less dirty. A little less tainted. She wasn't the poison in the soup anymore. She could look people in the eye, give them one of her new names, and let slip a little about an imagined past, one that held no shameful secrets. She discovered that as long as she believed the story she was telling, everyone else did, too.

But now it was as if the curtain had slipped, and Beulah could see directly through a window into those old days. She couldn't convince herself that she was Roxie Collins of Park Avenue, and she probably hadn't convinced anyone else, either. In class, her mind tended to drift. At night she dreamt about Meemaw, and woke up wondering whether her grandmother was dead or alive. If she had died, who would tell her? No one from Richmond even knew where to find Beulah.

Sidling up to her old terrors was turning Beulah back into the fretful and anxious girl she'd once been. She'd forgotten how hard it used to be for her to eat, and how her wrists were like sticks when she came out of jail. Now she was back to her old habits, nibbling on a roll while everyone else in the mess hall devoured their rations. She could live on tea and crackers. It was the only thing that ever settled her stomach.

And she had to force herself to smile at the other girls, much less to talk to them. When she first arrived at camp, she thought she would make a sensation, with her glamorous stories and her light-hearted laugh. She expected to be at the center of the camp's social life. It would be a game to fit in with these girls, a deceptive little entertainment that would lift her spirits after she gave up on New York.

But in fact, she could hardly stand to be around them. It was painfully obvious that she wasn't one of them, and never would be. To make matters worse, as the weeks went by, it was ever more apparent that a voyage to France was not on offer—at least, not for her. She tried not think about what she'd do next, but the future pressed against her just as urgently as the past did. That made the present a miserable place to be.

She didn't even particularly want to go out with Fleurette to watch Constance and the others take their target practice, but she also didn't want to be left alone in the tent with Norma, who had a tendency to raise her right eyebrow at everything Beulah said. She'd never met such a mistrustful woman in her life as Norma Kopp. The less time Beulah spent under her wary gaze, the better.

So she waited while Fleurette put on her green dress and did up her hair. She wore most of her uniform over it — the jacket, the long skirt, the canvas hat, but she intended to slip out of it once they were in the woods.

Beulah resisted Fleurette's efforts to dress her up for the evening. She'd taken a liking to her uniform, finding it a relief not to have to think about her style of dress anymore.

"Wear a pin, at least," Fleurette said, and pressed a red cotton geranium into her collar.

The two of them left the tent about fifteen minutes before curfew, so they could slip away without attracting attention. It was a bright night, with a clear sky and a half moon. There were still plenty of girls going back and forth between the tents. Constance would be busy for quite a while, rounding them up and herding them all to bed.

"Oh, there's Hack, down by the mess hall," Fleurette said. She floated down the hill toward him, like a leaf dropped into a fast-moving river. Beulah went along. They caught up with him just as he was going into the supply shed. It was just a little wooden lean-to, knocked together when camp opened and meant to be taken down when it was over.

"You girls shouldn't see where these are hidden," Hack said, but he did nothing to conceal what he was doing. The guns were kept in a wooden case behind some paint cans and covered up by tarps and tent stakes. Hack hauled the case out with him.

"Why bother with the case? Don't you soldiers know how to wear a firearm?" Fleurette asked. She managed to sound flirtatious when she said it, but Hack was taking his responsibility seriously.

"When it's a training exercise, we keep them in the case," he said. "I don't recall Miss Kopp inviting you two along."

"She told me just now that she expected us out there with the others," Fleurette said. "She thinks we ought to have the training, too. I told her that I wouldn't be doing anything but seamstressing during the war, and wouldn't need to know how to shoot a German, but she insisted." Fleurette looked almost sorrowful about it, as if she hated to sacrifice a good night's sleep for a shooting lesson in the woods.

Beulah admired how effortlessly Fleurette told lies. They had that in common, at least.

She followed Fleurette and Hack—walking side-by-side, as if they were already a pair—around behind the camp and into the woods. There was no guarantee that they hadn't been seen, but Fleurette seemed to feel that she was immune from punishment because she was Constance's sister. Beulah decided that she, too, would be afforded some protection because of her association with the two of them.

Behind the barn, past the broken fence post, down the little trail, and into the clearing they went. Margaret was waiting for them there, as were the other women Beulah had seen a few nights earlier when she stumbled into their training session. Only Constance and Sarah were missing, but they came along a few minutes later, having finished nightly rounds together. Clarence was back at camp, standing guard.

"I don't have to tell you how easily you can be spotted coming and going," Constance said, once they were all gathered together. They stood in a circle around her lantern, which cast up a yellow light on their chins. From above came the thin blue light of the moon. It made for an otherworldly effect. Beulah wouldn't have been surprised if one of them had started chanting a spell.

But they all listened quite seriously to Constance. "The camp was designed to keep anyone from sneaking in and out, for good reason. But it means that we must all assume that someone will see us going in and out of the woods. To that end, I'm going to appoint each and every one of you to take up a nightly patrol as my deputy. You'll work in shifts, but occasionally we'll go out together. Tell anyone who asks that you're in training to run a camp like this one someday, and that's why I've put you all on duty. That way, it won't be as obvious if you're spotted out after curfew."

The women seemed satisfied with that.

"Tonight we'll go deeper into the woods and work on our stances and the handling of unloaded guns. I'll let you each fire off a single shot, but no more. I've asked Norma to listen from camp and tell me if we can be heard. If we can, that's the end of it."

"You didn't tell Norma!" Fleurette protested.

Constance shot a look at her of the type that passed between sisters and said, "She's the only one in this entire camp whom I can trust completely with a secret, and that includes you. I don't know why the two of you are here tonight, by the way."

Hack said, "I brought them, miss. I thought they were to train with the others."

Constance wasn't fooled. She frowned at that but said, "Well, they're not, but you might as well come along. I don't want you going back by yourselves."

Margaret was the one who found the route deeper into the woods, and she showed them the way. The others followed silently, in a straight line, putting their feet down in each other's footsteps as Hack demonstrated. He led the group with his lantern. Constance took up the rear with hers.

It seemed to Beulah that they trudged for hours in those dark woods, but when they emerged in a wide, flat, hilltop clearing, Hack checked his watch and announced that only twenty minutes had passed.

"Let's get on with this," Constance said. "First let me see your stances."

Constance went from one girl to the next and showed them how to put one foot in front, and to anchor the other foot behind. Fleurette and Beulah tried to stand alongside and imitate them, but Constance said, "Go sit over there where I can see you, both of you," and they did.

While they worked on their stances and passed a pistol around, Hack walked the edge of the clearing.

"There's not a house or a road or anything out here," he said to Constance. "You won't wake up anybody but the birds."

Constance nodded but went and checked for herself.

"Your sister doesn't trust a soul," Beulah whispered to Fleurette.

"Not when it's her responsibility," Fleurette said. "If she can be blamed for it, she does it herself."

That gave Beulah an idea about Constance and her mysterious past. Perhaps she'd been blamed for some mishap. "Sometimes people blame you for things that aren't your responsibility," she proposed.

Fleurette nodded. "She doesn't like it when that happens."

It was cold on the damp grass, but they'd been ordered to sit there and didn't dare move now that guns were being passed around. Fleurette never did relieve herself of her uniform to show off her green dress: there wasn't a minute to do it when Hack wasn't watching, and it would've been awfully strange, even on this already strange night, for her to start stepping out of her clothes. A little bit of green silk hung below the hem of her uniform, and she fingered it absently as the girls took their places in line.

Beulah was sleepy, in spite of the cold. She leaned against Fleurette for warmth. The sensation of a shoulder and elbow next to her, faintly reminiscent of those early years when she shared a bed with Claudia, was so soothing that her eyes started to droop.

She'd hardly slept the night before: she'd awoken several times in a terror over what she would do when camp ended. Where would she go, on the very last day? When the gates opened and the parents came to retrieve their daughters, what would happen to her? If she could make her way back to New York, she could borrow a few dollars from Mabel and resume her old life, but if that was all she had waiting for her, why stay at the camp? She was doing poorly in her classes. She hated to sew and couldn't manage the telegraph codes. She was too squeamish for nursing and bored by cooking. There was nothing for her, if France was out of reach. But she'd have to walk back to New York if she wanted to leave now. She hadn't a penny in her pocket.

Such were the thoughts running around in her head at night. Sometimes they raced into the past, too, where they hadn't been allowed to go for so many years: back to Meemaw, and Claudia, and Henry Clay, even, when he was sweet and tender to her, before everything went so terribly wrong.

Nestled against Fleurette, she was halfway back to her dreams when the first girl fired her gun.

Beulah jerked away from Fleurette and gasped with such force that she nearly choked.

⊰ 26 ⊱

THE PAPERS ALL claimed that Beulah was the last one to see Henry Clay. That must've been right, because he took her driving on July 17, 1911, and she told him that it was her birthday.

"It hardly seems possible that I'm nineteen already," she said as she wrapped a scarf around her hair. He liked an open-topped auto in the summer, no matter how dusty or windy. "It's just so strange, because in my mind Claudia is always nineteen, but now I've caught up to her and Claudia's a mature and married woman of twenty-three."

Henry Clay didn't hear a word she said, he was driving so fast. Since the day they met back up again at the ball park, she'd allowed him to come around and see her once or twice a week. This felt like a triumph, on one hand, because she'd wrestled him away from Louise, but Henry Clay himself had become so unpleasant that it outweighed the sweetness of that small victory.

He was half-crazed over his predicament and obsessed with the idea that he'd been trapped for life. He believed he was, in every meaningful way, already interred in a grave dug for him by his very own family. They had put him in a box and meant to keep him there. Increasingly, Henry Clay saw this not as the sort of warm and comfortable strait-jacket that a well-to-do southern family might wrap around its errant son, but as an active conspiracy, aimed at strangling him quite literally to death.

On their drive that day, he could talk of nothing else. "They do mean to kill me. They mean to crush my spirit and to stifle my soul and then to smother me in the night until I can't hardly breathe. Why, they're already doing it. I believe Louise put a pillow over my mouth last night. I woke up gasping for air."

Beulah was puzzled and a little alarmed by this kind of talk, but also, she had to admit, ever so slightly fascinated. She kept him talking about it.

"Now, why would your own wife do a thing like that, now that y'all have a little baby to bring up?" she said. It stung to even think of the new Beattie baby, but Beulah conjured him up anyway, if only to bring Henry Clay to his senses.

"Don't you see?" Henry Clay raged. "That's precisely the reason! She has everything she needs now. A son with the Beattie name, a house to call her own, her share of her parents' fortune and mine. What purpose do I serve in any of it?"

"Well, what purpose did you expect to serve when you married her?" Beulah said. She was growing tired of all this talk about Louise. She resolved, once again, to refuse to see him the next time he came around. He wasn't the man she remembered, but she had trouble keeping this newer version of him fixed in her head when he was away. It was only after she'd stepped into his auto that the truth came to her: something had gone seriously wrong with Henry Clay. Or maybe something had been wrong with him all along, only he used to be better at hiding it.

They were on their way to an old stock pond he liked to frequent. It was long abandoned and overgrown with high grass that summer, as there weren't any cattle on the land anymore. The place was private but not hidden. He explained that he did not like to be sequestered behind a stand of trees. Even a canopy of branches made him feel smothered. Here, on this old dirt road, miles away from any living thing and under an open sky, he could relax.

He stepped out of the auto and stretched out on the grass, not having bothered to bring so much as a blanket for the two of them. Romance was not on his mind. It didn't matter: Beulah hadn't had relations with him in some time. He was often ill and feverish, and said he didn't like to take his clothes off in the daytime, which was the only time he could visit with her. At night he was expected to be at home, "in my place," as he put it, spitefully, as if there was anything at all wrong with a man being in his own home with his own family in the evening.

He was still muttering about all of this as he stretched out in the grass, but he did not stay there long, and did not call for Beulah to come and lay with him. Instead he was up again, restless, pacing, pleading with Beulah to try to understand him, to see things his way, to help him find a way out of the mess he'd made for himself.

"Her mother knows everything I do," Henry Clay said, kicking a rock into the mud around the edge of the stock pond. "She knows every step I take when I leave the house. She even knows I've been seeing you again."

"Now, how did she find out about me?" Beulah demanded.

"She's got somebody following me, I know she does."

Beulah didn't like that one bit. She had no interest in tangling with Louise's mother or anyone else of her ilk. She was living on her own now, working as a laundress, and enjoying a nice quiet life. If Henry Clay wanted to make a mess of his marriage, he ought to do it on his own.

"I have no part in this, and if you were any kind of man, you'd leave me out of it," Beulah said. "You come by and pull me out of my house, and haul me out here to listen to you rant about your family, as if any of it matters one bit to me. Well, it doesn't, and you don't."

It had been a terrible idea to be out with him like this, all alone in an empty field. What did she hope to gain by running around with him? He'd brought her nothing but trouble and heartache, and that was still all he had to give.

He dropped down on the grass again and pulled at her skirt, as if she would find that enticing. "We had something together, didn't we? Doesn't that matter?"

She jerked her skirt away from him. "What did we have? A room in a whorehouse? A baby you threw away? You paid me to go with you, Henry Clay. Did you ever think of that? Whatever we had between us, it was because you paid to have it."

"Don't be like that," he moaned. His eyes were dark and liquid and should've moved her to sympathy. They did not.

"Now you're the one being paid," she said. "You're living on your daddy's money and Louise's money, and you have to do what they say and act how they say to act, don't you? How's that any different than what I had to do for you?" She wrapped her scarf around her hair again and looked down the road, making it obvious that she was thinking about walking off.

Henry Clay was furious. He scrambled to his feet. "Don't you dare call me a whore."

Now that word was offensive? Beulah would've laughed if she wasn't so desperate to get away. "Go on back to Louise. Next time you come by, I won't be at home."

Was she really going to walk all the way home? How far could it be? She didn't know, but she'd walk down that old dirt road and take it all the way back into Richmond, if only it carried her away from Henry Clay.

She didn't look back. She could hear him rummaging around in his automobile. He could chase after her if he wanted to. She wasn't about to climb back in that machine with him.

For the first time she thought it might've been for the best that her baby didn't live. What if he'd been crazy like his daddy? She wondered how she could've missed this side of him before.

It was peaceful, walking down that country lane by herself. Crickets sang in the grass and bumblebees tumbled through the air. She'd only been walking for a few minutes when she heard the shotgun.

She jerked forward as if she'd been hit. Never once had Beulah feared for her life as she did in that moment. She found herself down on the ground, running a hand over her legs, across her shoulder and the back of her head, expecting to find blood. When she determined that she was alive and unhurt, she slumped facedown on the ground, wanting to wrap her arms around the entirety of the earth in gratitude.

Was he still behind her? *Don't turn around,* she told herself. But then she did. There he stood, silhouetted against a blazing afternoon sky, with his rifle up over his head, pointed at the heavens.

"Is that what I have to do to get your attention, Beulah Binford?" he shouted, although she could hardly hear him with the wind carrying his voice away.

"Don't you know you have everyone's attention, Henry Clay?" she shouted back. "You're driving everyone around you crazy, including me."

He put the gun down at his side, but he didn't make a move toward her, nor she toward him.

"What do you intend to do with that thing?" she called. She stood up on shaky knees and brushed the grass off.

This time his voice was more subdued. "Nothing," he said. "Just fire it up at the clouds."

"All right, then, why don't you put it away? And don't ever go shooting it off around me again." She was more afraid than she let on, but she stood her ground, and waited until he went around to the rear of his automobile and put the rifle back where it must've been all this time. Beulah hadn't even suspected that he carried a gun with him.

She walked away again, the dust kicking up into her skirts, thinking that she might pass a farmer going into town who would give her a ride. Henry Clay called after her a few more times, with such sorrow in his voice, but Beulah refused to turn around. He was a haunted man now, governed by his own misery, ruled by demons Beulah couldn't even fathom. How a man could have everything a person might reasonably want, and still go around so aggrieved and wounded, was something she would never understand.

Just seeing what a wreck he'd made of his life made Beulah want to do something with hers. She would stop chasing after ball players. They were only ever passing through town anyway. It wouldn't do her any good to try to go to school now, after all this time, but maybe she could find Claudia and ask for help securing some kind of better work for herself.

It had never before occurred to Beulah to imagine what she wanted her life to be, or what kind of person she hoped to become when she was twenty-six like Henry Clay was then. All she knew was that she didn't want to end up like him.

It was too far for her to walk all the way home. She followed the road quite a ways, until the sun started to sink into a low hill on the horizon. She might've kept going in the dark, except that Henry Clay managed to settle himself down eventually and came driving up behind her, slow as he pleased. He asked her very politely to climb back in and let him take her home.

"I won't bother you again," he said. "I know you don't want to see me like this. You won't. I promise. I'm going to go home and take care of my own mess. You'll see."

"I don't want to see, is my point," Beulah said.

"I know. I know. You won't. Just let me take you home. You'll be out here all night if you keep walking."

She bent down and squinted at him, and saw how tired he was. He'd worn himself out with all that ranting and raving. There wasn't any fight left in him.

"All right," she said, wary but willing. "You take me directly home, and then go put your own house in order."

"That's exactly what I intend to do," Henry Clay said.

⊰ 27 ⊱

LATER, BEULAH WOULD look back on that night and recall the scent of murder in the air. They say a hound can sniff a raw kill in the wind. Beulah didn't have a nose like that, but something smelled wretched. It wasn't rot and decay: this was a fresh horror. It had a tang to it.

She'd allowed Henry Clay to take her back to the little room she rented, but she couldn't stay there. The air was oppressive, even long after dark. She sweated, not from the heat but from nausea, the kind that always came over her at the sight of blood. There was an unbearable pounding at her temples. She couldn't be alone in that state. Around midnight, she crept over to Meemaw's, slipped inside, and passed a sleepless night on her divan, waiting for whatever was to come.

It was a neighbor lady who told her. Beulah was sitting on Meemaw's front steps the next morning, sewing a strap on an apron because Meemaw couldn't see to do it herself anymore.

"Lady got murdered out on the Midlothian pike last night," said the neighbor, stepping outside to dump a pail of washing-water. "They sent the dogs out looking for the man that did it."

Beulah knotted the thread, snapped off the needle, and said, "Was she just out walking by herself and somebody got her?"

"Oh, no, she was in a motor car with her husband. A man stepped right out into the road and shot the lady. The husband got out and wrestled the gun away from him, but the fellow ran off. It was too late anyway. The wife was already dead. He drove all the way back into Richmond with her leaning up against him, him driving with one hand and all covered in blood."

"Haven't they caught the man who did it?"

"No," said the neighbor. "I'm staying inside until they do. Looks like a sweet young couple, too. They were only married last August, and the wife had a baby a few weeks ago. Poor little thing don't have no mama now."

Beulah tried to make it sound like she had only a passing interest in the story. "Who was it—the lady who died?"

The neighbor shrugged. "She don't live around here, if that's what you're wondering. Last name Beattie. Must be the same ones that own the department store, because I heard they closed down today so all the men could join the manhunt."

The neighbor went back inside her house and locked the door rather loudly, calling attention to herself by rattling it. Beulah stood up off the step, slowly, and stretched, as if she was in no hurry. When she turned around, Meemaw was standing just inside the screen door, her arms folded across her chest, looking down at her with an expression that Beulah could not read.

"Do not bring the police to my house" was all Meemaw said to her.

"Then I guess I'll have to go," Beulah said. She handed the apron back to her grandmother, and wandered on down the street to her own rented room.

It was a strange day, because she stayed inside and did so little. She thought she ought to clean the place, as long as she was housebound, or see what she could salvage from her mending basket, but she found that she could hardly move. She sat in a chair most of the day, near a window but not too close, looking out on the street and wondering if the police had found what they were looking for.

She didn't dare stir. She had never been so still and quiet for an entire day.

The news came to her in whispers and rumors: a pair of voices floating in from the street through her half-opened window, a glance at the news-stand when she rushed out with a quarter for the egg and butter man. It was impossible not to hear about the Beattie murder. The whole town was swimming in it: the gossip started as a ripple, then swelled to a current that tugged at all of them.

And the story going around town was that Henry Clay's explanation didn't add up.

Louise hadn't been shot by a man standing over her in the road, came the whispers from the coroner's office. She'd been shot by someone standing at eye level, who very nearly pressed the barrel right up in her face. She hadn't been shot inside the automobile, either. Her blood was all over the road. There was hardly any in the auto, according to the sheriff who impounded it, except right up underneath where she lay in Henry Clay's lap while he drove her dead or dying body back to Richmond.

Most damning of all were the dogs. There wasn't a Virginian alive who wouldn't believe a bloodhound over a guilty-looking husband. The dogs picked up the scent of the blood where it soaked into the ground, but there was no trail leading in any direction to point out which way the killer went. The dogs just ran in a circle, yipping in frustration.

It was almost as if the killer had driven away in an auto, the newspapermen speculated, tartly.

The worst came the next day, when Louise had been dead only forty-eight hours. An old Negro woman walking along the railroad tracks found a rifle. She took it straight to the police. Henry Clay had claimed that he'd wrestled the gun away from the attacker and thrown it into his auto, only to have it jolted out on the street as he drove hell-bent for Richmond with Louise's head across his knees. That was a fine tale, except that this gun was found quite a ways down the railroad tracks, suggesting that it had been thrown, not merely dropped, from a speeding vehicle. Now it fell to the police to decide whose rifle it was, and whether it had been used to kill Louise.

Beulah didn't so much hear the story as she breathed it in, like a poisonous gas that seeped under the door. What kind of man puts a gun to his wife's head like that? She closed her eyes and tried to picture it: bland, blameless Louise, standing in the road begging for her life, and half-crazed Henry Clay with that rifle he'd been brandishing all afternoon.

If he could kill his own wife like that, the mother of his child, what might he do to Beulah if she displeased him? She didn't dare think on it overlong. He might yet come after her, if the police weren't already watching his every move.

When a tap came at her door, she feared he'd done exactly that. Did he think he could hide from the authorities, in her single room? Would he expect her to run off with him?

She wouldn't answer. She couldn't. She sank down, silently, into the little wooden chair where she ate her supper every night. With one knee tucked under her chin she held her breath and waited.

Another tap, and a little scratch, like a fingernail against the paint. And then a voice that she knew.

"Beulah, honey? It's Henrietta. Let me in, quick."

Henrietta Pitman, her old chum from her days down on Mayo Street, one of the girls Claudia ran with. Beulah wouldn't call her a friend, exactly, but Henrietta was a girl of her ilk. They were the same—or they had been, at one time.

For that reason Beulah opened the door.

Henrietta rushed in, chased by a cloud of ersatz jasmine perfume. She kept a scarf of yellow chiffon around her head, but that did little to disguise her: Henrietta was a certain type of girl and she looked it. Anyone passing her by on the street could tell exactly who she was.

She closed the door behind her and leaned against it. With one glance she took in Beulah's surroundings, the dust hanging in the air, the pan on the gas plate where she fried herself an egg every day, her only decent dress hung from a peg on the wall.

Beulah saw in an instant that Henrietta would take in these details and relay them to the girls back on Mayo Street. She would peddle them like the unofficial currency they were.

The first words from her mouth were "You didn't shoot that woman, did you?"

Beulah hesitated, thinking she might pretend not to know what woman Henrietta was referring to. She waited too long, because Henrietta said, "The police are over at May Stuart's right now. They think you had something to do with it."

"Well, I didn't," Beulah put in hastily, before Henrietta could infer otherwise. "I was at my Meemaw's all night. Go ask her."

"They know you had something to do with Henry Clay."

"Lots of girls had something to do with Henry Clay." It was true: Beulah had never been the only one. She hadn't been loyal to him, either. How could she, in her line of work?

"Well, it's in the papers that there was another woman. Everybody's saying that Henry Clay Beattie shot his wife because he was in love with a woman who had his baby and gave it up."

"That could've been any girl in Richmond," Beulah said flatly.

"They say it was a woman who wore a black veil to his wedding, and then hunted him down no matter how many times he tried to get away, and refused to let him go." Henrietta looked triumphant about it. How she loved to be in the middle of a mess like this. Beulah hated to give her the satisfaction, but Henrietta was the only one who'd come to her. She hadn't been given a choice of messenger.

"How'd they find all that out?" Beulah asked reluctantly.

"Louise's mother. She knew all about that woman, because Louise went crying to her over it. She told the police everything she knew. And now they're coming for you."

"Well, let them come," Beulah said, although she wasn't at all certain that was the right position to take. "I had nothing to do with it."

"Then you don't know anything about Henry Clay and a gun?"

There was some small sound outside—a door closing, a package dropping on the sidewalk—and Beulah, believing it to be a knock at her door, nearly jumped out of her skin.

Henrietta heard it too and looked around uneasily. "I came to warn you. I didn't have to, but I did it on account of the times we used to have together. You do what you have to do, but I don't want to be caught here."

She put her hand on the doorknob. Beulah said, "I could run off to Claudia's, if I knew where to find her."

If Henrietta knew, she wasn't telling. "Don't bring your sister into this. She got out."

With that, Henrietta was gone. Beulah could hardly breathe. How far ahead of the police had Henrietta been? How many minutes before they came through the door? Those constables were all friends of her grandfather's. They'd find her.

If she could sneak over to the station, she could hop on board any train going out of town. It didn't matter where. Give it a week, she thought. Let Henry Clay confess, if he was man enough to do it, and clear her of any wrongdoing. If he did that, the police might decide they didn't need to talk to her after all. She packed up the smallest bundle of possessions she could manage and set out for her grandmother's.

Beulah didn't have a dollar to her name, but Meemaw was all too happy to make a contribution to the cause of sending Beulah out of town.

"Go on, and don't tell me where you're going," Meemaw said. She didn't try to hug her, but she did put her thumb under Beulah's chin and squint at her, as if she was trying to memorize Beulah's face.

"I'll be back," Beulah said.

"You might not," Meemaw said.

Beulah ran out the door. She was on her way to the train station, with nothing but a little carpet bag under her arm, when a policeman who knew her from her days down on Mayo Street put his hand on her shoulder.

⇥ 28 ⇤

"DID EVERYONE LEARN 'My Little Red Carnation'?" Fleurette called.

"She's not still out singing that sappy old thing, is she?" Tizzy groaned in that languid way she had. Her tent-mates followed suit, rolling their eyes and grumbling about the stilted, old-fashioned songs.

"Of course she is, and they beg her to sing it if she leaves it out," Fleurette said. "It's one of her most popular songs."

May Ward's concert was by then only a week away. An upright piano had been delivered for the occasion, and Clarence had been pressed into service. Fleurette had selected her chorus and begun a series of rehearsals in the mess hall after supper. Beulah refused to take part in the singing and dancing, but she attended rehearsals anyway, and helped with the costumes and whatever other small favors Fleurette asked of her. She wanted the concert to go off well, for Fleurette's sake, but she had to admit that Tizzy was right: the songs were tired and held little appeal for the young women at camp.

The song was written for a man and a woman, but when May Ward performed it, one of the girls stepped up and sang the man's part. Fleurette took that role. The others were supposed to harmonize behind her.

My little red carnation,
Sweetest in all creation,
Why all this meditation?
I love you fond and true;

I'm filled with desperation,
Caused by your hesitation,
My little red carnation,
I love no one but you.

Tizzy couldn't bear the song and led a full revolt. She sang in a squeaky, grotesque voice, aping Fleurette's dance steps behind her, and the others followed suit. Soon their voices dissolved into laughter.

"Oh, that's enough of little red carnations," Tizzy called, jumping down from the stage. "Let's have a look at these costumes."

May Ward liked her chorus in frilly white dresses reminiscent of the Dresden dolls after which her act was named. Fleurette had done her best to put something together with whatever material she had on hand. Even a tablecloth was pressed into service. The result was a set of aprons that could go over the shirtwaists and skirts the girls wore every day.

They were neatly hung from a rope that ran alongside the stage. Tizzy flung herself at them and tossed them to the other girls in the chorus.

It enraged Beulah to see Tizzy behave so spitefully. Fleurette was too stunned, at first, to react, but Beulah had been saving up plenty of sharp words for Tizzy and didn't hesitate to deploy them.

"Get your hands off of her costumes," Beulah said, grabbing the aprons away from Tizzy. "If you're too high-and-mighty to sing the song, you won't be wearing one anyway."

Although Tizzy was surrounded by girls shrieking and laughing, she remained perfectly still herself in the face of Beulah's criticism. Like ice, this one.

"Let's see what you look like in a costume, *Roxanna*," Tizzy said. Beulah didn't like the way she leaned on that made-up name. "How about you try on the bonnet, see if you like it?"

Fleurette had made little white bonnets out of handkerchiefs to go with every frilly apron. They were tucked inside the pockets. Tizzy pulled one out and slammed it down on Beulah's head. This brought more giggles and whistles from those cowardly girls who followed Tizzy everywhere.

"Oh, that's pretty!" shouted Liddy.

"All you need now is a red carnation!" called Ellie.

But Tizzy, once again, was an island of calm among them. "You remind me of somebody in that bonnet," she said. "Who is it?"

There was a mirror propped up across from the stage so the girls could watch themselves dance. Beulah glanced over at it and saw the resemblance at once.

It was the same kind of bonnet she wore in that picture that all the newspapers ran.

There she was again, six years older but not so terribly changed from before: Beulah Binford, the Other Woman in the Richmond Murder Case.

⇥ 29 ⇤

BEULAH RIPPED OFF that bonnet and ran blindly out of the tent, which put her right in the path of Constance, come to tell the girls that curfew was imminent. Because Beulah's eyes were squeezed shut to stop the tears, she hurled herself bodily into Constance. This had no effect on Constance's gait: she probably could've kept walking with Beulah hanging around her neck.

But she didn't. She just swept Beulah up into her arms unhesitatingly. It wasn't an embrace, exactly, but it was not quite as forceful as those holds she'd been teaching her late-night army.

"What's come over you?" Constance asked, pressing her lips right into the top of Beulah's head. "Something's not right."

When Beulah didn't answer, Constance took a step back and held her at arm's length. "I've seen a girl in trouble, you know."

Constance had eyes of a color that Meemaw would've called hazel. She looked at Beulah with a mixture of compassion and scrutiny. Beulah knew that look. It meant that Constance was sympathetic to a point, but reserving judgment.

In that moment, she could've broken down and told Constance everything. She had a feeling that Constance wouldn't kick her out of camp just for being Beulah Binford. But what good would it do for her to confess? All she wanted was to suffer through the rest of that infernal camp and to trudge back to New York, hat in hand, and hope she could put some semblance of her old life back together. She'd have left already if she had so much as a dollar in her pocket. Having already paid her room and board, she had no choice but to see it through.

She couldn't bear to have anyone look at her too closely. She jerked away from Constance. "I'm not in trouble, and I'm not your little sister. I'm just getting myself to bed by curfew is all."

She walked away at what she hoped looked like a normal pace. If she ran, Constance would snatch her right back up again.

THAT PICTURE IN the papers had made it so much worse for her. She didn't understand it at the time—how could she have? —but without a picture, she never would've made the headlines. And without the headlines, she would've been nothing more than a footnote in the Beattie murder trial. Instead, she became the scandal at the very center of the whole mess.

When the newspapers get hold of a good picture, they take a little story and turn it into a big story. Once it becomes a big story, it runs all over the country.

It wasn't her fault that she didn't understand that. What did she know of newspapers, and of how stories spread?

She should've had a lawyer representing her, not a Broadway show manager. That seemed so obvious in hindsight, when she recounted the whole mess to Mabel and saw it through her eyes.

"What you did," Mabel told her, once she had heard it all, "was no different from what a thousand other girls have done. You went around with a man who wasn't your husband. You had a baby and you gave it away. There's nothing so unusual about that."

"Well, there might've been a few dollars that changed hands," Beulah pointed out.

"And some girls have their rent paid, or their dinner bought for them," Mabel said. "There's no difference, not to my thinking. But the way they splashed you across the front page—that's what was different. That's why the whole country knows your name and not the names of every other girl who did the same thing. And I blame that vaudeville man for that."

Mabel was right, of course. Beulah never should've agreed to see him, but she was lonely in jail, and eager for news. The police kept telling her she was only being held as a witness. Once the trial got under way, they assured her, the judge would decide whether Beulah would be called to testify. She might even be released before the trial was over.

Beulah didn't know whether to believe that or not. She didn't know what to think. She wanted to write a letter to Meemaw, but what could Meemaw do for her now? There was nothing to do but wait.

She'd been in jail a week before he turned up. From her cell, she could hear the guards arguing about whether he should be allowed to see her.

"I thought you said no visitors," one guard said.

"She's allowed to see a lawyer," said the other guard.

"The girl says she don't have a lawyer," the first guard said.

"Well, somebody must've hired him. He's come all the way down from New Jersey. Might as well let her see him."

With that, Beulah was led into a little windowless room furnished with two chairs and a table bolted to the ground. She wore the same dress she'd been arrested in seven days earlier, the jail lacking any sort of inmate uniform for women. She must've looked a shambles. She hadn't seen a comb, and had been given only one shallow basin of water per day with which to make herself presentable.

The man waiting for her, on the other hand, was immaculately dressed in a black suit with lapels that must've been silk, the way they shone a little in the light, and a red vest with a tie to match. He wore an enormous gold ring on one hand. A good heavy gold watch hung from his vest pocket.

Beulah had an eye for precious metals. She didn't look him over so much as she appraised him.

"You're no lawyer," she said when they were alone.

The man found that entertaining and leaned back in his chair, his fingers laced together behind his head. "No? What am I?"

She cocked her head and took in his hair pomade, his striped vest, his spotted tie, and his black patent shoes, shined to perfection. They reminded her of a tap dancer's shoes.

"You're a show-man." She pronounced it like that, coming up first with the word *show* and then the word *man*.

He leaned forward and put his hands down on the table, looking over at her from under heavy eyebrows. "You're not too terribly wrong, Miss Binford. I'm a manager. I manage people, and I help them with their image."

"Image?" Beulah patted her hair, which she knew looked terrible.

"Not how they look, although that does come into it. But how they appear. In public, I mean. In the papers. I help people manage how the rest of the world sees them."

"Well, I'm in jail," Beulah said. "Nobody sees me now."

"They don't?" He reached into his pocket and unfolded a page from the *Richmond Times*. "You're on the front page, girlie."

There she was, a full quarter page of her, in a ridiculous ruffled bonnet and a blouse with a sailor collar. She remembered the picture: she'd had it taken at a makeshift studio at a carnival a few years ago and gave it to Meemaw on her birthday. How did the papers get hold of it?

Even worse was the headline: "The Other Woman in the Richmond Murder Case."

She slapped it down on the table, shocked. "I'm not *in* the Richmond murder case! I'm not in it at all. I knew the man, but that doesn't put me in the case. Half the girls in Richmond knew him. I don't see them here in jail with me."

"Well, that's your side of the story," he said.

Beulah was infuriated. "Yes, it's my side of the story! Why isn't my side of the story printed in this paper? Nobody talked to me. Whatever they said, they must've made it up."

"And that's just why I'm here, miss. To make sure that your side of the story gets in the paper, too. You need someone to speak on your behalf, don't you see that?"

"What I need is to get out of this jail. What are you going to do about that?"

"Don't you have a lawyer?"

Beulah patted herself down, as if to check her pockets. "Do you see a lawyer?"

He lifted his eyebrows. "Well. Then you'll need one, and you'll need some way to pay his bills. Has your daddy offered to help?"

"I don't hardly know my daddy."

"Anyone else? Your mother? A grandfather? A kindly uncle? A sister or a brother?"

She shook her head. "Even if a single one of my relations had any money, I don't think they'd spend it on me. Not after this."

"Well, then. Here's what I propose, Miss Binford. I'll handle the reporters. I know how these people work. I speak to the press every day, all the New York papers, the Washington papers, everybody. I've helped many a vaudeville actress through a scandal. Names you'd remember. Good girls who didn't deserve the bad press they'd been given."

"But why? Why would you do that for me? I can't pay you."

"You won't have to. I'll even find a lawyer down here and pay him out of my own pocket. You won't owe me a thing. After this is all over, it can just come right out of my fees."

"Your fees? Fees for what?"

The guard came back just then. Their fifteen minutes had ended. The man stood to go. "Your career on the stage, Miss Binford. Don't you see? You're famous now. You're going to go for your stage tour as soon as this trial ends, and you'll be a very rich girl."

The guard heard that last part and snorted. "Visitin's over," he said.

The man handed Beulah his calling card. "At your service. If you need anything, you can reach me at my office."

The guard led him away and left Beulah locked in the interviewing room. She turned the card over and ran her finger over the engraved letters.

FREEMAN BERNSTEIN, it read. ENTERTAINMENT AND MANAGEMENT.

⊰ 30 ⊱

"VANQUISHING THE GERMANS with Precision Bed Corners," Fleurette said. "I can't believe we're to have a course in making up a bed."

"You've never made up a bed in your life," Norma said.

"That doesn't mean I don't know how."

Constance stood outside the mess hall, ticking names off a list as the girls went inside. Scientific Bed-Making was a required course at camp, at the insistence of the Red Cross. Each camper was expected to make up a bed three times in rapid succession if she hoped to graduate. The difficulty with this requirement was the short supply of beds with which to practice. Only four metal beds had been delivered, and they would be picked up at the end of the week, as soon as the course was complete. To accommodate all two hundred campers, the course had to be held twice a day, every day.

"Where's Roxanna?" Constance asked as Norma, Fleurette, and Sarah passed by.

"She's been in the infirmary all morning," Norma said. "I went over there just now. Nurse Cartwright says it's dyspepsia."

"It was awfully kind of you to look in on her," Sarah said.

"I wasn't intending to be kind." Norma sounded alarmed at the prospect. "I was trying to get her into class, where she belongs. Nurse Cartwright is our instructor. You'd think she'd want everyone in attendance."

"Roxanna's obviously not well. I'll speak to her this afternoon and put her on tomorrow's list," Constance said.

Nurse Cartwright arrived just then, huffing up the hill and pumping her arms. "One of yours is down in the infirmary," she said to Constance, as soon as she came within earshot.

"Will she survive?"

The nurse grinned and lifted her hat to wipe the sweat away. "They'll all survive. They miss their mothers, more than anything. These girls like to be tended to. They just won't admit it."

"I don't suppose I've done much tending," Constance said. Should she have been going around to the tents at night, soothing homesick hearts and troubled minds? Had she thought of them too much as soldiers-in-training and not enough as girls who missed their mothers?

"I don't mind them coming to me," Nurse Cartwright said. "I put them to bed with a cold cloth or a hot water bottle, depending on their disposition, let them tell me their troubles, and after a few hours they come out right as rain. Do you have your list?"

"I do," Constance said. She was to take half the class and tick off each girl's name as she completed her bed-making tasks. With everyone on the roster marked as present, she closed the tent flap and Nurse Cartwright began her lecture.

"Get yourself into groups," she called. "It's five girls per bed."

The dining tables and benches had been pushed to the sides and replaced with the hospital beds. Nurse Cartwright took a folded sheet from one of the beds and held it aloft.

"The lower sheet is the foundation of a hygienic bed," she called in a sing-song voice. "Queen Victoria insisted on having hers sewn fast every day. We might not have that luxury in a field hospital, but we can do the next best thing and tuck a good half-yard of fabric under the top of the mattress, even if that leaves the bottom short. Invalids will tend to slide down in bed and take the sheet with them. As for the upper sheet, it must be tucked well under the foot of the bed, as patients like to pull the covers up. Now, for the coverlet . . ."

She continued in this manner, lecturing on the benefits of a tightly made, wrinkle-free bed, until girls who had never enjoyed making a bed in their lives were suddenly eager to get to it, if only to put an end to the lecture. Constance watched them struggle with the sheets as if competing in an athletic event, running from one end of the bed to the other and heaving the mattress up by its corners. Under the nurse's explicit instructions, Constance issued her check marks only after the beds had been made quickly and competently, even if it meant starting over a half-dozen times. Norma, with her penchant for military precision, passed on the first go, as did Fleurette, which didn't surprise Constance at all. Anyone who'd spent a lifetime handling fabrics could whip a sheet around a mattress as if it were a length of crêpe de Chine around the hips.

Nurse Cartwright announced the final lesson, which was to make up a clean bed while the patient was still in it. At the start of camp, the plan had been to require each girl to complete this task three times, but there was so much mirth and antics among the girls playing the part of the patient that the requirement had to be reduced to one successful attempt per student.

"In making up a bed for an invalid," the nurse said, "the patient must be moved as little as possible, and must be uncovered not at all. This requires you to pay as much attention to the upper sheet as the lower. Deft, rapid, and noiseless is the way to go about it."

Some of the students were rapid, some were deft, but none were noiseless. The girl playing the part of the patient inevitably gave in to laughter as her fellow students tried to maneuver her. Constance could see why Nurse Cartwright put this lesson at the end: it dissolved into a social hour, no matter how stern the lecture or how watchful the instructor.

This didn't bother Constance, who found that in walking among them, she could learn quite a bit about what was going on under her nose.

"I heard they have chocolates over in tent fourteen," one girl said.

"Unless they're filled with whiskey, I'm not interested," said another.

"The nurse will give you a little brandy in hot water if you can summon up a convincing cough."

Constance made a note to speak to Nurse Cartwright about her reliance on medicinal spirits—this was hardly a war zone, after all—and went on down the line, where she heard this, from a group of girls from Pennsylvania:

"I heard those gunshots again last night. It was just after you went to sleep."

Constance froze, and waited for the reply.

"I was up long after you were, and I didn't hear them."

"You weren't up after me. You were snoring. I'm telling you, this is the third time I've heard them."

"It's probably just an auto firing. What do you think, Miss Kopp?"

Constance forced herself to walk on by, slowly, as if it didn't matter. "It's an engine," she said. "I've heard it myself once or twice."

They'd been out three times at night for rifle and pistol practice. Norma swore she couldn't hear them from the center of camp, but these girls were camped along the fringe, closest to the forest — and one of them had sharp hearing.

It was impossible, under the circumstances, to continue. For firearms training they'd have to go back to play-acting.

❧ 31 ☙

BEULAH WAS ALL too happy to skip the bed-making course. She allowed Nurse Cartwright to diagnose her with a severe case of dyspepsia, attributed to the heavy camp meals of beans and sausages, when Beulah was accustomed to cucumber sandwiches and light soups (or so the nurse was led to believe). She was put on a diet of salt crackers and chicken broth, which was about all she could eat anyway, as the memory of those weeks in jail kept floating back to her and turning her stomach.

There was something about the confinement of camp, and the regimented life it demanded, that recalled the last time she'd lost her freedom. In jail the guards' eyes were always upon her. She used to wake up and see their dim silhouettes outside her cell, just standing there, breathing heavy through the bars as she slept.

That was jail: a pair of eyes always upon her. Her misdeeds— whether real or accused or imagined—were always laid bare for anyone to see. She never knew what the guards thought of her, or what fresh rumor had reached their ears the night before. She was a circus animal to them, on display to be mocked and gaped upon. The camp was starting to feel that way too, in spite of her best efforts at concealment.

It was a relief, then, to turn herself over to the camp nurse, a sturdy, wide-bosomed woman with a helmet of tightly curled silver hair around a face that could be stoic and unsmiling when circumstances called for it, but uncommonly warm when she had a patient to tend to. Beulah surrendered utterly to the nurse's care, and allowed her to sit alongside the bed (a proper hospital bed, with two pillows and a pile of blankets, so much more luxurious than her canvas cot), and to issue, in addition to the pronouncement about dyspepsia, a further diagnosis of homesickness, for which she prescribed a daily letter home to Mother.

"I see you in the assemblies," Nurse Cartwright said. "All the other girls are writing their letters, but you never do. You won't miss home so much if you write to them and tell them a little about what your life is like here. Paint a picture of it for them."

"I did," Beulah muttered, "but that only made it worse. We only have a few weeks to go. I'll see them soon enough."

"That's the spirit," Nurse Cartwright said. "Now, how's that cough of yours?"

Beulah had almost forgotten to cough. "It's so much worse when I lie down," she said. To demonstrate, she settled back down to her pillow and offered up a few convincing hacks and wheezes.

"I'll put a kettle on," the nurse said, and reached for her bottle of medicinal brandy. "I might feel a cough coming on myself."

Beulah passed a peaceable day and a half in the infirmary, sampling Nurse Cartwright's curatives and working her way happily through one tin of salted crackers after another. She accepted cool washcloths when they were handed to her, and took a hot water bottle under the covers whenever the nurse decided she looked peaked. No one had ever nursed Beulah before, and she found it delightful. Would a hospital be even better, she wondered. Some sort of minor operation, with a long period of recuperation, sounded luxurious to her at that moment.

Beulah departed reluctantly, and only when another patient

came in: Ginny, from the tent next to hers, doubled over with monthly pains, which in her case were accompanied by fiery headaches and constipation of such intransigence that Beulah made haste to depart before the full explanation was proffered. With Ginny in greater need, she would have to surrender her comfortable bed and the hot water bottle tucked between the sheets, so that was reason enough to rally to full health and return to her tent.

Before she left, the nurse put her cool hands on Beulah's neck, and then on her forehead. She did this habitually to any girl within reach, perhaps to feel the pulse and check for fever. Beulah found it marvelous.

"You're a good girl," Nurse Cartwright said, "and your people back home love you. That's why I know you'll be fine."

Beulah thought about telling the nurse how wrong she was, but there was Ginny with her innards in knots and she thought better of it.

AT BEULAH'S REQUEST, the nurse had refused to allow visitors. That gave her a little break from Fleurette and her sisters. She only wished the break could've been longer.

When she returned to the tent, she learned that Hack had gotten himself tangled up in some kind of argument with Norma over her pigeons. The woman was irrationally attached to those birds and convinced that they were capable of military heroics. The idea of a pigeon serving in the Army struck Beulah as about as comical as a chicken steering a ship in the Navy, but she kept her opinions to herself. The more she said in Norma's presence, the more that woman's distrustful eye would be trained upon her. In her weakened condition, Beulah might just wither under the scrutiny.

"Private Hackbush owes me five pigeons," Norma was saying as Beulah settled down on her cot.

"They flew home!" Fleurette said. "They'll be waiting for you when you get back. You have the boys from the dairy looking after them. Hack doesn't owe you anything."

"I have five fewer pigeons with which to conduct my training," Norma said, "and it's his fault."

"If he did bring you five pigeons," Constance put in, obviously aiming to further annoy her sister, "would you even accept them? What if they weren't of good stock?"

"Oh, they wouldn't possibly be of good stock," Norma said, dismissing Hack's imaginary pigeons before they'd even been presented to her.

"I'm glad you're back," Sarah said when she saw Beulah. "Has Nurse Cartwright returned you to fighting form?"

"I believe so," Beulah said.

Fleurette gave her a little smile and said, "You missed quite a performance. Hack said that pigeons wouldn't fly through gunfire, and Norma wanted to prove it to him. She set five birds free, and we were all made to go out in the field with pots and pans—"

"I wondered what all that clanging was last night," Beulah said.

"Yes, that was us, making fools of ourselves, banging wooden rifles around and smashing pot lids together and any other kind of racket we could get up."

"How did the birds do?" Beulah asked.

"Heroically," Norma said.

"They flew home, which is what they do if you turn them loose," Fleurette said. "The trouble was, Hack wasn't at all convinced. He said that gunfire is a hundred times louder, and the birds would spook."

"Then why didn't you shoot at them?" Beulah asked.

"Oh, you missed that, too," Fleurette said. "Someone heard the shots from camp. Rifle practice is over."

"What a shame," Beulah said. Although she tried to sound light about it, she regretted deeply that there were to be no more training in firearms. Beulah had been paying a little more attention at rifle practice. She hadn't been allowed to touch the guns, but that didn't stop her from watching, and watching closely.

Each time training was held, she and Fleurette sat in the grass at the edge of the clearing, nearly concealed by darkness, the lanterns illuminating only the girls and their targets. Beulah loved to watch them go through their paces. The rifles practically glowed from years of enthusiastic oiling and polishing. When the girls pulled the bolts back to load more cartridges, the mechanism slid open and closed with the satisfying clang of a heavy lock. Beulah couldn't imagine firing one herself: the rifle was almost four feet long, and the smaller girls, Fern especially, struggled to keep hold of it.

But the revolver—that looked like something Beulah could manage. From a distance it appeared to be black, but if she crept a little closer and caught it in the light, she could see a deep blue sheen to the steel. The cylinder slid out so easily that most of the girls could flip it open one-handed, a move so sharp and elegant that Beulah found herself imitating it, off to the side where Fleurette couldn't see, in the dark.

That gun was dead simple to shoot, too. While Margaret and Sarah took great care aligning their feet just so and adjusting their stances to match Constance's precisely, the younger girls developed a little more flair. They'd jut their hips out, put a fist against their waists, and lift their chins so high in a posture of defiance that they could hardly put the target in their sights. Constance corrected them every time—this was not a joke, this was not a pageant—but Beulah loved how brash and bold they looked.

She came to love the sound, too. It had terrified her at first, recalling as it did that awful night with Henry Clay, but after the first time, she wanted to hear it again, and again.

It was the decisiveness of a gunshot that satisfied Beulah. A bullet had the power to end something when nothing else would. She gave herself over to the fantasy of being in brutal, terrifying command for just a moment. She swam around inside of that dream, and imagined how it would feel to be the one who had the final say.

Fleurette didn't notice the way Beulah drifted off—she never did notice when her audience had stopped listening, or perhaps she didn't care—and went right on chatting. "You also missed Hack telling Norma, right to her face, that pigeons couldn't be counted upon to reliably transmit military communications."

"He didn't," Beulah said in mock outrage, trying to keep up with the conversation.

"He did, and now he owes me five pigeons," Norma said. "If I'd known he wasn't willing to believe his own eyes, I never would've released them."

"Well, it's over now," Constance said briskly. They'd obviously rehashed this incident more than once already.

Norma wasn't finished, though. "He had the nerve to tell me that even though the telephone lines are abysmal in France, the soldiers prefer them, because at least they get to talk to a girl every now and then."

"That's exactly what Jack says," Sarah put in, happy to be back in correspondence with her brother, whose earlier letters might've been sunk by the Germans, but who remained unscathed himself, "except that he says he wishes they'd send some American girls over to work the switchboards. The French operators don't even make an effort to say hello in English."

"No, they wouldn't," Norma said, as if she knew all about French telephone operators.

"We might find out soon enough," Sarah said. "Clarence told me they mustered a thousand men to the Armory in New York last night."

"Why did they want them on such short notice?" Norma asked.

"Nobody knows. They were sent home and told to return at eight this morning. But he also heard that an order's been given to enlist another six thousand men in the Navy."

"They're going to need more than six thousand, for all the ships they're building," Norma said. "We could be at war within a matter of weeks at this rate."

Fleurette rolled off her cot and went to stand over Beulah's. "I made some posters for May Ward's show," she said, and unfurled a sheaf of papers. They were surprisingly well-done: carefully lettered in black ink, with a border of stars around the edge in gold paint. Plenty of bills pasted up on the street in New York were only half as good.

"Come and help me put them up," Fleurette said. She held out her hand with absolute certainty that it would be accepted, and Beulah could think of no good reason not to.

⚔ 32 ⚔

THE NEWS THAT Constance had decided to put a stop to the late-night drills was met with strenuous objection by her band of soldiers-in-training. To a woman they were indignant, and insisted upon a fuller explanation. To that end, the six of them met one more time in the woods: Constance, Sarah, Margaret, Fern, Bernice, and Hilda. Fleurette and Roxie weren't invited along and wouldn't have been interested regardless, with all the preparations for May Ward's performance under way.

It was a dark night, with low heavy clouds and no moon. There was a muggy kind of warmth in the air that foretold an early-morning storm, the kind that could send trickles of rainwater down the tent poles and make them all grateful to be sleeping atop a wooden platform—a luxury not afforded to the men in the trenches, as Norma liked to remind them every time they awoke to find themselves high and dry atop a mud puddle.

In every way their suffering was nothing like that of the men in the trenches. Only that afternoon, Sarah had another letter from Jack, remarking—but never complaining, he didn't complain—on the endless chill in France, and the way they had all learned to stuff their uniforms with newspaper for insulation. "We fight over every issue of *Stars & Stripes*," he'd written. "Wraps right around the legs, lasts a week or more in dry weather."

Sarah was passing the letter around when Constance arrived at their meeting place, just after curfew. "He's sleeping in what remains of an old kitchen," she told Constance, "the roof half gone and a crumbling brick oven for fire. These villages hadn't much to begin with, and now they're entirely wrecked. There isn't one intact house to be had for miles, so they bed down in any promising pile of rubble."

"It's unfathomable," Constance said, looking over Sarah's shoulder and deciphering his faint pencil scratch. Ink was impossible to come by at the front.

"What's unfathomable," Margaret said, "is the idea that we can't so much as shoot at a target, when Jack has the Boche firing on him every night."

"Not every night," Sarah said, quaking a little at the thought.

"We simply can't take a chance," Constance said. "We've been overheard already. We're sure to be found out, and that was our warning."

"It doesn't matter if we're found out. I'm not afraid of a girl complaining to her mother," Margaret said.

"It matters to me. I must do as I've promised and conduct this camp according to the program set forth," Constance said. "I shouldn't have let it go this far." What she didn't say was that she shouldn't have allowed herself to be swept up in the excitement of it. To have her own militia, to teach them something of use . . . it had suited her so perfectly. She'd felt like her old self again, on those nights. But her duty was to the entire camp, not to the five of them.

"Then we'll practice on our own," Margaret said.

"With wooden rifles, you're free to do as you like," Constance said. "I've already told Hack and Clarence to put the guns away, and to keep a closer eye on their keys this time."

"Oh, I could put my hands on those keys," Bernice said, a little wickedly.

"Don't you dare," Sarah said. "If you haven't learned to follow orders, you've learned nothing. Jack takes his orders without complaint, and without the benefit of a full explanation and an opportunity to offer up objections."

It warmed Constance to have Sarah on her side. "I'm as sorry as you all are to see it come to an end, but I've bent the rules as far as they'll go without breaking."

Her troops showed little appreciation for how far the rules had been bent already. "I don't see why we couldn't go deeper into the woods," groused Hilda.

"It would take us half the night," Bernice said. "I'm not getting my sleep as it is."

"You won't get any sleep at the front," Fern interjected, to laughter from the others. She did a fair imitation of Norma, answering any complaint with dire warnings of worse conditions overseas.

Their protestations were of no use: Constance was adamant. It occurred to her, in that moment, to think back on all the times Sheriff Heath had stood by the rule of law, the strictures placed upon him by county charter, and his obligations to the public. She used to plead with him for an exception—for her inmates, for the cause of justice beyond what any courtroom could deliver—but more often than not, he stood firm. To the extent that she ever defied him—and she did, more than once—she now regretted it. She was out of a job, and so was he, for that matter. What cause did that serve?

It made her sink a little in her boots to turn her attention back to the duties of chaperone and overseer of camp activities. There were bandages to be rolled, and carrots to be scraped into soups for the convalescent. It all sounded so dreary compared to their late-night target practice. But no one promised that war work would be exciting, or that anything more than a warmed-over vaudeville show would ever be offered up to relieve the tedium.

⚜ 33 ⚜

OVER THE NEXT few days, Fleurette stayed busy with her rehearsals, but Beulah begged off.

"Why don't you want to come out at night?" Fleurette asked,
pleading her case. "It's so dull here otherwise."

"I'm enjoying staying in for once," Beulah said, and added,
with a bit of her society girl weariness, "There is such a thing as
too many gay affairs."

Fleurette raised her eyebrows to indicate that she hadn't yet
had her fill of gay affairs, but said nothing.

Beulah thought it best to keep her distance from the rehearsals. Tizzy had come too close to guessing the truth. Memories
were like ashes in a coal stove: sometimes they flickered back to
life, just when they seemed to have gone cold. Seeing Beulah in
that bonnet might've been just the spark Tizzy's memory required.

But it hadn't been enough to summon the name Beulah Binford to mind, had it? Wasn't that all that mattered? She kept
reminding herself that six years had passed since her picture appeared in the papers. Tizzy, like so many of the other girls at camp,
had been only fourteen or fifteen during the murder trial. How
many other faces, reproduced in black-and-white at two inches
tall, had flown past her gaze since then?

In fact, Beulah couldn't be entirely sure, looking back on it, that Tizzy had even looked at her so pointedly, or meant anything at all by her remark about the bonnet. For too many years she'd lived with the feeling that every eye cast upon her was suspicious. She couldn't bear anyone's gaze. She took any remark, however innocent, the wrong way. Everywhere she went, with everyone she met, the same two words haunted her: *They know.*

Now, at camp, *They Know* might as well be written across the sky. She cringed when her Virginian accent slipped through. Even worse were those moments when the girls from New York noticed that she couldn't possibly have come from the same world they inhabited: she didn't know any of the dressmakers and florists they did, or the restaurants and theaters, or even the songs and dances.

If they didn't know, they suspected. How could they not? Her saving grace was that no one, not even Tizzy, seemed sufficiently interested in her to probe further. Best to keep it that way by staying away from the rehearsals and avoiding gatherings of any kind outside of the classes she was required to attend. The less anyone noticed her, the better. She was determined to be the dullest girl at camp.

Constance kept a close eye on her, and there was no avoiding her gaze. A distraction was required. Beulah found that if she made a great show of studying in the evenings, Constance would merely nod her approval and leave her alone. She practiced her stitchery until she reached a middling level of competence. She studied the Red Cross diagrams until she could fold bandages according to the instructions. She pored over the wireless and telegraphy manual and found that she could read most of it, if she pointed at the words and sounded them out. It began as a charade, but she found that as she persisted, she made some progress. Perhaps she'd learn something of use after all, and in that way prove herself worthy of passage to France.

She was, in measured steps, trying to pull herself together. She might even manage to put the past back to bed, where it belonged. Meemaw, Claudia, her long-vanished mother, Henry Clay, and the little baby she had lost—all of them were like children who could be tucked under the covers, and the lights turned out. If she could keep very quiet, they would not awaken and demand her attention. She'd allowed them to sleep for years back in New York, and she could do it again.

They could sleep forever, as far as she was concerned—even the ones she'd loved.

Come to think of it, she'd once loved all of them.

CLASSES ENDED EARLY on the afternoon of May Ward's concert because so many girls were either performing in the chorus, helping to decorate the stage, or setting up the mess hall for theater-style seating. May Ward herself was to arrive at four o'clock for a short rehearsal, but her train was delayed and it was nearly six before she turned up.

Fleurette had been pressing Beulah to drop by the rehearsal and meet Mrs. Ward before the audience was seated. It was obvious that Fleurette wanted Beulah to see how friendly she was with the vaudeville star. Beulah was touched by the idea that it mattered to Fleurette at all what she thought of her, or that any sort of proximity to a stage actress would raise Beulah's esteem for her.

Beulah was ready and waiting at the appointed hour, but when it became clear that there had been some sort of delay, she went back to her tent. "I'll hear the commotion when she arrives," she assured Fleurette, "and I'll be right over."

But Beulah did not hear the commotion, because by the time Mrs. Ward turned up, the campers were in the middle of collecting their cold suppers on trays, which they were to eat in their tents while the mess hall was converted to a theater. Beulah wasn't much interested in the supper: it was nothing but sliced ham and rolls left over from lunch, cold potatoes that had probably been boiled the night before, and a mealy apple. She was picking at the roll when Constance stopped in and told her that Fleurette was looking for her.

"There's a little changing-room tent behind the mess hall," Constance said, "and Mrs. Ward is waiting there with Fleurette. She's asking if you'll come and say hello."

Beulah tucked the last corner of a roll in her mouth. "The great May Ward. If only I'd brought my autograph book."

"Fleurette adores her," Constance said, as they walked together to the tent. "She used to buy all of May Ward's sheet music, and insisted that we go to see her perform whenever she came through Paterson."

"Did you and Norma bring Fleurette up by yourselves?" Beulah asked. She'd nearly given up on asking the Kopp sisters about their lives back home, because they were so rarely forthcoming. It was also true that she'd stopped asking anyone about their past, for fear that they might reciprocate.

"Our mother died a few years ago," Constance said. "Fleurette was sixteen at the time. She was mostly grown."

"She still is," Beulah said.

Constance smiled at that. "Mostly grown? She wouldn't like that. She's nearly twenty."

It was April by then, and light later in the evening, so that the camp had more of the air of a summer retreat about it, with games of lawn croquet set up between the tents, and canvas chairs propped up outside like rocking chairs on a porch.

The campers were starting to emerge from their tents, still in their uniforms, but just a little more dolled up for the evening. Gauzy scarves appeared around collars, hairstyles were more elaborate, and there was the pleasing fragrance of smuggled perfume and face powder in the air. Constance didn't seem to notice: Beulah had the impression that she'd decided to relax the rules for the occasion.

They arrived at the mess hall just as the doors were opening. It had been transformed with some success into a theater, with Fleurette's posters wheat-pasted to the wooden posts on either side of the door, and a row of lanterns illuminating the entrance. Through the doorway Beulah saw Clarence at his piano, playing a few warm-up pieces, but the music was nearly drowned out by the audience's light, bubbly laughter.

"She's just around here," Constance called, above the noise. Beulah found herself unaccountably happy to follow along, and to be admitted backstage as if she were a visitor of importance.

The dressing-room tent sat just behind the mess hall. It was the same size as the ones they all slept in: large enough for five campers, or one vaudeville actress. Constance pulled the flap aside and Beulah stepped in.

It was as elegantly furnished as Fleurette could manage. Lanterns glowed from every corner, bright bits of fabric hung from the ceiling, chairs and cots were scattered about like settees in a salon, and a table and mirror had been placed in the center. May Ward was seated in front of the mirror, with Fleurette behind her arranging her hair.

The actress was chatting gaily with Fleurette as Beulah walked in. "Everyone's trying to get into films," she was saying, "but I missed the stage. There's nothing like a full house. Give me an audience over a camera any day. And now, with the war coming, we want to be of service to the men going off to fight, don't we, dear?"

"Mrs. Ward," Constance said, "pardon the interruption, but I'd like to present Miss Roxanna Collins."

Fleurette patted Mrs. Ward's hair into place and stood back.

"This is the girl I told you about! Roxie claims she can't sing a note, or she'd be on stage tonight with us."

May Ward turned around, not so much to greet Beulah as to accept her compliments. She was older than Beulah had expected, and wore an overly bright expression of false merriment. She'd once been a freckle-faced young woman, but she'd faded somewhat, and her fine, thin features now only looked pinched. The vivid stage paint on her lips and cheeks didn't help: she looked garish in close quarters.

Beulah felt an urge to curtsy, but thought that wasn't quite right. She did make some awkward little bow, nodded, and said, "Pleased to meet you, Miss Ward. I hope—"

"Oh, don't call me Miss. I'm married, whether I like it or not. I had a husband around here a minute ago. What's become of Freeman?"

Freeman? Beulah froze. Surely not.

Then she heard his voice behind her.

"Just stepped out for a cigar, dear, and to have a peek at the audience. You'll have a full house. If we could only charge them a dollar each, we'd really have something. Now, who's this?"

She couldn't keep her back to him forever. Everyone else had turned around to face him. What could she do, but spin around and look him in the eye?

There he was: the same old Freeman Bernstein. He'd grown a little more jowly, and he'd lost some hair, but he was in every other way the same showman who'd turned up at the Richmond jail all those years ago.

Who'd had the *nerve* to turn up at the Richmond jail.

He'd been grinning behind his stub of a cigar, but when he and Beulah were face to face, the smile faded. A look of panic crossed his eyes. He was remembering, and calculating.

He took possession of himself so quickly that no one would've noticed, unless they were watching for it.

"I'll be damned," he said. "Who let the likes of you in here?"

Fleurette was already starting her introductions when he spoke. She didn't seem to take in what he said.

"Mr. Bernstein, I'd like to present Miss Roxanna . . ."

Fleurette's voice floated along, from somewhere far away, as Beulah bolted from the tent.

She never was much of a runner, but she was behind the barn, over the fence, and into the woods before Constance had time to make her apologies and chase after her.

⪥ 34 ⪤

IT WAS NOT lost on Beulah that she'd made something of a habit of running out of rooms lately. It was a miscalculation, of course: it drew attention to her at the very moments when she most wanted to disappear without notice. But if there was a way to vanish without actually leaving a room, Beulah didn't know about it.

Besides, she wasn't running away this time. She knew exactly where she was going.

By now, Freeman would've told everyone who she was. She'd be kicked out of the camp—Constance would have no choice about that, once everyone knew—and sent, penniless, back to New York.

Or, worse, if she couldn't get as far as New York, she might drift back to Richmond. What would a man pay, on Mayo Street, to take a turn with Beulah Binford? She couldn't pretend to be anyone else if she went back home. They all knew her there.

Whatever might happen next to her, Freeman would be to blame. It had always been Freeman. If he hadn't turned up at that jail with his promises of a lawyer, and his talk of a stage career, and all his high-flown ideas about making a sensation of her in the paper, she might never have been more than a single line at the end of an article about Henry Clay, easily forgotten.

Beulah understood now that she would never get away from her reputation. No matter how many times she moved, or changed her name, or took a new job, or invented a new past, it would come creeping back to her.

Now her past was back in the very bodily form of Freeman Bernstein, Entertainment and Management.

And she could do something about that.

OF THE TRIAL itself, Beulah knew only rumors and scraps from the papers. She was never brought into the courtroom or called to testify. The jail cell was her home for nearly two months that summer. She wasn't permitted to see a newspaper, but the guards couldn't resist telling what they knew.

Once, she heard, her sister, Claudia, had been seen among the spectators. A reporter must have recognized her or asked her name, because she was quoted as saying that she was curious about the goings-on but wouldn't answer any questions put to her. She never went to see Beulah, nor did anyone else, except for Freeman Bernstein.

At the end of July, Claudia's husband, Luther, was called to the stand. He testified only that he was aware that Henry Clay had paid to send Beulah away to school years ago, and that he knew the two of them had recently taken up with one another again. (How did he know that, when neither he nor Claudia had spoken to Beulah in years? Beulah could only guess that he must've gone to Meemaw for the whole story.)

She asked the guards every day if there had been a word in the papers about her mother. If she was still in Richmond—if she was still alive—surely she would've heard about the trial. Wouldn't she come to see her daughter, even after years apart? Wouldn't she at least try to speak on Beulah's behalf, if she was at all capable of doing so?

But there was never a mention of Jessie Binford. She was dead, or she'd disappeared, or she'd deserted the family forever. *Dead, disappeared, deserted.* Those words went through her head in the hours after midnight, when she awoke and turned over on her side, away from the bars of her cell, so she might forget where she was and drift back into sleep. But the incantation would start again and kept her from any kind of rest. *Dead, disappeared, deserted.*

The police even managed to track down Henrietta Pittman, her chum from the old days at Monroe Square, and a couple of the other girls she knew on Mayo Street. They were expected to say that they overheard Beulah and Henry Clay arguing about how he would get rid of his wife, and how Beulah wouldn't see him again until Louise was gone. It was a lie, of course: Beulah could only assume that they were testifying because they wanted to see their names in the papers. When they took the stand, it was apparent even to the judge that they had nothing to add to the proceedings, and they were sent away.

What hurt Beulah the most was not that her own family and friends were testifying. They had their reasons for saying what they did, and none of them helped nor hurt her situation.

No, what cut her most deeply was the way the judge cleared the courtroom of women before any mention of Beulah could be made.

The most dreadful moment came in the middle of August. Beulah could still remember how unbearably hot and muggy it was in that jail cell right then, how sticky and damp she was, how the toilets stank and the men in the other cells all reeked of stale sweat. Right about then was when Louise's mother took the stand.

The judge announced that the women in the courtroom must be escorted out, because the testimony to be given by the mother of the pretty dead wife wasn't fit for a woman's ears.

But hadn't it happened to a woman, and wasn't a woman about to tell about it?

The guards never could bring themselves to tell her specifically what Louise's mother said in court, but Beulah overheard them talking. It was the most sensational moment of the trial. There was no keeping it from her.

Mrs. Owen testified that Louise ran to her, crying, over Henry Clay's infidelity. He'd been seen around town with another woman (presumed to be Beulah, although Henry Clay always went with other girls, too, and Beulah would've been happy to explain that if she'd been given the chance). When Louise confronted him, Henry Clay denied any wrongdoing.

But Louise knew better. She brought the proof to her mother: the evidence of his sin could be seen in his underclothes.

Beulah had never heard of anything so filthy being said in a courthouse before, or anywhere, really, where the public might hear it. That her name could be attached to something so vile — that she could be the very cause of it — well, Beulah could've died of shame right then. She wanted to.

At the time, Beulah didn't know, precisely, what the stain on Henry Clay's underclothes implied. She'd spent a lifetime scrubbing stains out of britches, and they were all a horror. Nothing was more disgusting than the old, dried evidence of some unmentionable filth that had issued, unchecked, from a body and made its mark. At May Stuart's house of pleasures, it wouldn't have been unusual three times a day for Beulah to soak, lather, scrub, or even cut away and patch a stain, be it from wine, mud, sweat, blood, or any other excretion. But whatever remained in Henry Clay's underclothes was, Mrs. Owen implied, far worse. It pointed to his infidelity, to his wickedness. And to Beulah's.

This set Beulah to paging, in her mind, through a catalog of stains and splotches and wondering what, specifically, Mrs. Owen might have been referring to. It was months before anyone had the gumption to put it to her plainly (bless Mabel for her forthrightness!), but that was after the trial, when it was all over, when Beulah was already trying to forget, and didn't want to know anything more.

As loathsome as the story was, the public had a bottomless appetite for it. The newspapers couldn't print their extras fast enough. They sold out by mid-morning and had to run off another batch just to keep up with the demand. Soon there were pamphlets in circulation, reprinting the whole story so much as it was known. Hundreds of spectators arrived every day, hoping to be let into the courtroom. They came by wagon, on foot, and by trolley, so many that the trolley lines ran extra cars and farmers made folding money ferrying people back and forth from the train station. Although Beulah had no window in her cell, she could glance through a window in the hall whenever she was taken out to the shower room or the interviewing room. All around the courthouse were lemonade stands, lunch carts, and other such small endeavors as one might see at a carnival.

"They've come to see the famous Miss Beulah Binford," the guards would say. "I could charge a hundred dollars to let one of them have a look at you."

They ran a hand up her arm when they said that. Beulah would flinch and jerk away.

As far as she could tell, Freeman Bernstein wasn't doing anything to keep her out of the papers. He wasn't trying to protect her good name. He allowed the reporters to make their own label for her, that of the siren, the scandalous woman who shocked and riveted every American that summer. The mere idea that women had to be escorted out of the courtroom so as not to hear of her degradation only made everyone want to see her more. Mr. Bernstein wasn't trying to put a stop to it. He was adding fuel to the flames. That was his only aim. Beulah simply didn't understand that at the time.

"I have good news for you, Miss Beulah," he said one day in August, bustling into the interviewing room.

"Am I to be released?" said Beulah. "Because if I'm not to be released, it's not good news. I don't know how they can keep me in jail when I've done nothing wrong."

"We're working on that, darlin'," Freeman said, but that only further annoyed Beulah.

"You can stop calling me darling and talking like you're a southerner, because everybody knows you're not. I thought you were going to get me a lawyer."

"Well, I have, dar— Miss Beulah, and he's filed a petition with the court to get you released. He's done all he can."

"Well, doesn't he need to talk to me? Can't I tell him that I'm innocent and I ought to be set free?"

"He knows all of that. Don't worry, we'll spring you loose the very minute we can. But you need to understand that you're having more of a success of it inside this jail cell than you ever did out there on Richmond's wicked streets. The press can't get enough of you! Do you know how many of the actresses I represent— stage actresses, I mean, with names you would recognize—do you know how many of them would absolutely die to get the kind of free press you're enjoying?" He waved a sheaf of clippings at her victoriously.

"Enjoying?" Beulah snatched the papers from him: they were the first she'd been allowed to see in some time. Every paper in the country ran the same picture of her, the one with the awful bonnet. "I hate this picture," she sniffed.

"We'll get new ones," Freeman rushed to assure her. "They

won't let me bring a photographer in here, but I'll find a way. Haven't you had any other pictures made of yourself, a pretty girl like you?"

Beulah shrugged. "I can't think why I would have."

Most of the stories took up an entire page and were too much for her to read with Freeman standing over her. She was a slow reader and didn't want him to see her struggling to puzzle it out. But one small clipping, folded in half, dropped to the floor, and it seemed to be all about her.

"What are they saying about me?" she asked as she picked it up.

Freeman tried to take it away from her. "Oh, don't bother yourself with that one," he said. "That's just a little gossip rag. Nobody pays any attention to it."

Beulah turned away to read it. She had to mouth the words to make sense of them. "They say I'm of a pronounced type of certain women who have caused men to become embezzlers and in many cases murderers."

She looked up at Freeman in shock. "I didn't cause Henry Clay to murder Louise! I didn't cause any of this! Didn't your lawyer tell them that I had nothing to do with it?"

"Now, what do you think?" he said, his voice low, trying to soothe her. "Don't you know that's why they haven't called you to testify? They don't want the jury distracted by you when the killer is sitting right in front of them."

"You mean Henry Clay," Beulah said.

"Yes, exactly," Freeman said.

"Well, don't call him the killer. He has a name."

Freeman didn't share Beulah's sympathy for Henry Clay and went on as if she hadn't said anything. "You weren't the one out on the Midlothian Turnpike that night, that's all I'm saying. The prosecutor wants that jury looking hard at Henry Clay. Either he pulled the trigger, or he wrestled the gun away from the man who did. You don't come into it, except as a plausible explanation for why Henry Clay might've done the things he did."

"But I didn't even want to go with him anymore. I never—"

"Now, Beulah, this is just some nonsense in the papers. It's really nothing for you to worry about."

But she read on. "'The woman who has attained such an unenviable notoriety seems to be devoid of sensitiveness or delicacy. Her deportment shows her to be one of the frivolous feminine gender who regard life as a round of frivolity, and have no idea of the responsibilities of existence or the value of money.'"

She threw the clipping down. "Are they talking about me? Do they mean to say that I'm that woman? That I have no—" She bent down and picked the clipping up again. "That I have no sensitiveness? That I don't know the value of money? After what I've had to do to earn my keep?"

Freeman chuckled. "There's a story for the front page."

"Nobody knows a thing about me! I've done nothing but sit in this cell. They've never even seen my deportment."

She slid her chair away from him and pulled her knees up under her chin.

Freeman said, in as soothing a voice as he could conjure, "Miss Beulah, I wish you'd let me show you how that's not really a story about you."

"Not about me? It has my name at the top!"

"Well . . . not really. You see, at the end they speak of how a story like this absorbs the attention of a certain class of readers. They're criticizing the public for lusting after a seamy story, even when one doesn't exist. Don't you see, they're only talking about—"

"They're talking about me. I'm the seamy story. You're supposed to do something about this, Mr. Bernstein. Isn't that your job? To handle the papers? So far, you haven't done a damn thing you said you would. I don't believe I'd like to have another visit from you. How about you go on back to New Jersey and leave me be?"

He took a step away from her. She thought, with some terror, that he really might leave. He was the only visitor she'd had.

"I will go, Miss Beulah, if that's what you want," he said. "I have no need of a long rail journey to Richmond just to visit with a sullen girl in a jail cell. But neither can I leave you alone if I've no idea what's to become of you. Can you tell me that, at least, before I go? What will happen when they release you—and they will release you, my attorney assures me of that—where will you go? Who will take you in? What kind of life do you imagine for yourself after this is all over? Do you intend to find work, or to marry? Everyone knows the name of Beulah Binford. What will you have to say for yourself when asked about the trial? How will you explain it?"

"I intend to go about just as I did before," Beulah said. "Why wouldn't I?"

But all at once, she knew why she wouldn't.

Beulah hadn't considered what might become of her upon her release from jail, if Freeman wasn't there to look after her. She knew Claudia wouldn't have anything to do with her. Her mother had disappeared. Her grandmother was almost bedridden and wouldn't want Beulah around after the trial anyway.

Where did that leave her, especially now, when her name was on the front page of every newspaper in the country?

"Well, I suppose you could walk out of the jail a free woman and find out what happens," Freeman said. "I don't know about you, but I like to have a plan in times of uncertainty, and someone to help me through adversity. Don't you?"

Beulah hadn't a plan or a friend, and Freeman knew it. She didn't bother to answer.

"Now, I thought I saw something special in you, Miss Binford. I saw a pretty face, a fetching figure, and a high, clear voice. You carry yourself in a particular way that suits the stage, with your shoulders back and your chin up. You've got moxie, if you don't mind me saying so. You're a little thing, but you're bold. You'd make quite a sight with the footlights shining up on you."

Beulah sniffed. "But what would I do? I don't know how to sing any songs. I've never been up on a stage. What would you have me do?"

"Oh, you leave that to me," Freeman said. "If there's one thing Freeman Bernstein can do, it's to fill a theater. But first we have to make sure that your name is known. And this trial—whether you like it or not—is putting your name in the minds of every theater-goer in this country. Don't you see what that can do for you? Don't you see the crowds of people with coins in their pockets, just lined up to get a glimpse of Beulah Binford?"

"Am I to do nothing but stand on stage and let them look at me?"

"Oh, no," Freeman hastened to reassure her. "We'll put a show together for you. I'll bring in my writers, and my lyricists, and my costume girls and scenery-painters, and we'll make a show suited to your particular talents, and put you on the stage and let you reap a reward for all the trouble you've been put through. Why, Miss Binford—"

Here he leaned in, pressing his advantage.

"Miss Binford, don't you see? Every story like the one you crumpled up and threw on the floor represents a hundred dollars to you."

She startled and stared down at the wad of paper. "A hundred dollars!"

"More than that," he said hastily. "A thousand dollars. One thousand dollars, every time they make up another scandalous lie about you. Because people will want to see for themselves! They'll line up around the block for a ticket to see the real Beulah Binford, and to find out whether she's that woman they read about in the papers or someone entirely different! Don't you see? You can show them for yourself how wrong the papers were. Now, wouldn't you like a chance to do that?"

The very idea of it exhausted Beulah, who was already weary and downtrodden from her weeks in jail. "I'd rather they not write about me at all. I thought you promised to put a stop to it."

"I promised to manage the press. Honestly, Miss Binford, I believe I've managed it quite well. You're a sensation! Most of the actresses I represent would double my fee if I could deliver this kind of press for them. Do you know how much I'd have to pay to run one of my actress's pictures on the front page, above the fold like this? Why, I'd have to mortgage my house to do it in one city, not to mention all across the country. This is like gold raining down on you, Miss Binford. You might not see it that way now, but you will, when it turns into real gold. How'd you like a gold bracelet for that slender wrist of yours?"

Beulah thought she might like that very much. "Are you entirely certain that people will pay to see me?"

"Of course they will!"

"And that they'll want to hear my side of it, and they'll understand that I'm not the way they say I am in those papers?"

"How could they not understand that, when you'll put it to them so prettily?" Freeman said.

Beulah leaned back against the wall and squinted up at him.

No one had ever shown as much confidence in Beulah's abilities as Freeman Bernstein did at that moment. She was crushed by shame at the way her name was being bandied about in the press. But no one was standing before her speaking of shame. There was only Freeman, and his promises of redemption and riches.

⇥ 35 ⇤

BEULAH CROUCHED SILENTLY in the woods. She knew bet-
ter than to run directly to the supply shed. It was too close to the
center of camp. She would hide here first, and draw Constance
out, too.

From her vantage point behind the scraggly pines, Beulah
watched her running from tent to tent, searching. Constance was
tall enough that it was easy to track her: a hatted figure moving
between the dark triangles of tents, going from classroom to mess
hall to latrine and back again.

It would occur to Constance soon enough to look for her in
the woods. She had only to go and retrieve a lantern—and there
were plenty of them about—and then she'd be right here, squeez-
ing through the gap in the fence and clambering up the little trail
to the clearing where Beulah and Fleurette had first found Constance and the others doing their nighttime drills.

Would she get up a search party? Probably not, at first. Constance knew how to keep a crisis quiet and handle it herself.
All Beulah had to do was to keep an eye on her, and stay out of
her way.

The show was by then under way. From the middle of the campground, Beulah heard Clarence pounding away at the piano, and

the cheers and applause of the audience. The mess hall glowed faintly from all the lanterns: it was a pretty sight, a warm yellow among the darkened tents.

Beulah should have been there with the others, clapping and dancing and maybe even singing along. But she never was, was she? Her place had always been right here, at the ragged lonely edge of the circle, knowing better than to join in. She saw herself as a wild animal just then, huddled in the undergrowth, the smell of rotten leaves and damp earth beneath her, while in the village, there was fire, warmth, and good cheer.

So she crept like a little animal, away from the trail, just far enough back from the fence that she wouldn't be spotted, until she'd circled halfway around the camp and had her target in sight.

Just as she'd predicted, Constance turned toward the woods. Beulah expected her to spend ten or fifteen minutes, at least, going up and down the trail and calling her name.

That was more than enough time.

With everyone at the concert, it was easy enough to climb over the fence and make a run for camp. The supply shed sat just behind the mess hall, not far from the tent they'd put up for May Ward. She slipped inside the shed, wishing for a lantern or even a match, and felt around in the dark. It wasn't hard to find the case. The tent and stakes that usually concealed it had been put to use that night, leaving it sitting on a shelf all by itself.

She pulled it down, which was a battle on its own as it was half her size and nearly as heavy. Once she'd wrestled it to the ground, she settled down to work on the lock. Back in Richmond, she'd had a brief affair with a pickpocket who liked to spend his earnings on Mayo Street. He was something of an amateur lock-picker and thought that the two of them might do a little business together going in and out of the locked rooms at May Stuart's boarding-house and lifting watches and coins from the men who were sometimes left to sleep off their drink alone. Beulah didn't think it right to steal from the other girls' clientele, believing they ought to have that opportunity for themselves. She told him so, but before he went on to find another accomplice, he did show her how much she could accomplish with a hairpin.

"A girl like you might need to break a lock now and then," he said, with nothing but friendship and goodwill in his voice. She couldn't see a reason to argue with that, and accepted a few lessons from him.

But none of that helped her now. The case had only a small lock, easily broken, but she was in a hurry and her hands were shaking from the urgent impulse now propelling her forward. Here was the man who insulted her, who ruined her life once and was probably doing it again at this very moment. She might never have another chance at him, and, by God, she was going to take it.

There were tools in the shed somewhere. She gave up on the hairpin and felt around until she found a box of hammers and pliers and other such things. Her fingers hit something flat—a metal file, maybe, or a crowbar. She pulled it out, along with the heaviest hammer she could find.

She sat still for a minute and listened. Could anyone in that boisterous audience hear her? What if someone was wandering around outside? She popped her head out and found the grassy paths between the tents empty. Everyone was watching May Ward.

The case was just wide enough to stand on its side. She propped it up, stood over it with a hammer, and smashed the lock as hard as she could. The hammer bounced off uselessly the first time, but Beulah liked to smash things and felt that she was only getting going. She hit it again, and again, and again, thinking each time about what had been done to her, and how long she'd lived with the humiliation, and how she wasn't going to live with it anymore.

At last, the wood split and the lock came loose. With all her weight, she pried it open with a crowbar.

The rifles were there, and both of the pistols. Hack and Clarence hadn't bothered to arm themselves to protect Mrs. Ward. Nobody worried about a thing like that, out in the country.

Beulah took one of the pistols and opened the chamber, just as she had seen the others do, and counted the bullets.

Six. She only needed one.

That cool metal felt awfully good in her hands. Here was certainty. Here was finality. The weight of that gun held a promise. She was just wild-headed enough to believe it.

She didn't bother to hide the gun. It was in her right hand when she stepped out of the shed. No one was watching. She practiced the stance Constance had shown the others: right foot in front, left planted firmly behind, arm out straight. Check the little notch on the top of the gun to make sure the target's in your sights. Then squeeze the trigger. Don't pull it, squeeze it.

There might've been some small ripple of doubt that came across her before she struck out, but she pushed that away easily enough.

He ruined her. Now she was going to ruin him.

⊰ 36 ⊱

PEOPLE LIKE ANYTHING SALACIOUS

NEW YORK, SEPT. 7—Freeman Bernstein, a theatrical booking agent, today stated that Beulah Binford, the girl in the Beattie murder case at Chesterfield, VA, will appear at the Liberty theater, Philadelphia, next Monday.

He said that her act probably will consist of a couple of songs, adding: "It does not matter what she does just so long as the people have a chance to see her."

Bernstein said that later the girl will appear in New York, Chicago, Detroit, St. Paul and Minneapolis with possibly some dates in other cities.

FREEMAN KNOCKED ON the door of Beulah's hotel suite promptly at nine. He carried a roll of newspapers under his arm, but when he walked in, he saw that Beulah had already been out to gather the morning papers herself. They were scattered all over the floor.

"'People like anything salacious'?" she shouted when she saw him. "Is that how you talk about me?" She threw the paper at him, but it only fluttered to the ground in loose sheaves.

Freeman ducked anyway: it was a habit of his. "I can see you've never been introduced to that morally corrupt species known as the headline writer," he said. "He has more poetic license than Shakespeare. I don't write the headlines."

"If it doesn't matter what I do on stage, why have I been learning songs all this time?"

"You'll sing them! But it's far better for audiences to come expecting nothing more than to have a glimpse of the famous Beulah Binford, and then to be surprised and delighted by her many talents. If I told them now about your lovely voice and nimble feet, what would be the mystery? People fill theaters to see the unexpected, don't you know that?"

Beulah arched an eyebrow and shuffled through the other papers. She'd only been out of jail for two days, but the restorative effects of a long bath, a visit to the beauty parlor, and a fresh change of clothing had been considerable. She lounged at that moment in a long pink kimono patterned in dogwood blossoms, furnished to her by Freeman in a box tied in satin ribbon, although she suspected she was not the first wearer of the kimono. It frayed slightly at the sleeves and there was a faint fragrance of curling cream at the neck.

Nonetheless, she mustered as much elegance as she could on that shabby divan. It was a second-rate hotel, but it offered suites, and the desk clerk bent the rules about male visitors to the women's floors, allowing Freeman upstairs because Freeman paid for so many of those rooms.

"But that was yesterday. Look at what they're saying today." She waved another story at him. "Is it true that the mayors of these towns where I'm to perform are saying they'll pass a law against me even stepping foot in their town?"

"Well—they might pass a law against you appearing on stage, anyway," Freeman muttered, preparing to duck again.

"Listen to this," Beulah said, reading in her slow and halting way. "'The Binford girl did not even figure in the murder trial. She was not an actress. She had no advertisement save as a woman who had relations with the defendant in a murder case. A stage that would welcome a woman of her type would be more degraded than the sufficiently degraded stage that attempted to exploit other women of her type. That there is a limit to the degradation of the stage is encouraging, no matter where that limit is found.' What do they mean, other women of my type? What type am I?"

"Oh, you know," Freeman said. "Other women in murder trials. These . . . I'm sure you know what I mean . . . these women who . . . like Nan Patterson, or that Yohe girl."

"No, I don't know about other women in murder cases," Beulah said. "This is my first one. What I do know is that you promised me a thousand dollars a week if I would agree to go on the stage. I've done everything you asked. Why am I being cast out of cities when they've never even seen what I can do?"

"Oh, they'll see what you can do. We might just have to make some . . . adjustments."

Beulah looked at him suspiciously. "What kind of adjustments?"

Freeman jumped to his feet and waved his arms with the air of a showman. "How does a motion picture sound?"

Beulah dropped her paper. "You can't be serious."

Freeman went on, undaunted. "We'll call it 'Beulah Binford's Own Story.' Our tale begins with little Beulah Binford dodging her sixty-year-old grandmother and frequenting roller-skating rinks and similar resorts."

"I never went to a roller-skating rink. We went to a park, and then we went to Mayo Street. There were no resorts of any kind, not in my neighborhood."

"People pay to see pretty pictures. We'll put you at a resort. Then you meet Henry Clay, and it finally winds up with the Beattie tragedy. The last scene shows the bars of your cell dissolving while you step forth, your face wearing the expression of a saint, saying"—here Freeman broke into a falsetto that Beulah found most annoying—"'I wish I could carry my story into every home in America.'"

"I would never say it like that, and I don't think anyone wants my story in their home. Isn't that what these papers are saying?"

"It all depends on how we sell it. We have to let the public know that this moving picture is an expression of your desire to make yourself a horrible example."

"A horrible example? I've done nothing wrong. Surely that was proven when they let me out of jail! Why, the trial isn't even over, and the lawyers already decided they had no use for me. The judge agreed. Henry Clay might yet be found innocent. We don't know. Why can't we tell that story on the stage?"

"That's not much of a story," Freeman muttered, and went to the window, where the sound of a newsboy calling an extra drifted into the room. "Anyway, I'm afraid it's not true."

"What do you mean?" Beulah rushed over to the window. Never had she seen a crowd gather so quickly around a newsboy. An entire corner of Eighty-Second Street was impassible owing to the number of people scrambling for the special edition.

"Henry Clay Beattie found guilty," called the boy. "To be executed by Christmas. Extra paper, just out!"

The room swam around, and Beulah dropped to the floor. She was in a sweat, and there were little pinpricks of ice up the back of her neck.

"They aren't going to hang him, are they?" Beulah swore she wouldn't cry over Henry Clay, but the sobs were coming up from inside of her like water bubbling out of a spring.

Freeman had never looked so eager to get out of a room. "You stay right here, Miss Binford. I'll just go and see about this."

He didn't come back. She sat under that window all day, listening to the cries of the newsboys.

⪥ 37 ⪤

A GIRL IN trouble instinctively runs home. For that reason, Constance checked her own tent first. There was no place to hide inside, but she went around anyway, lifting blankets and kicking over the cots. The latrines seemed the next most likely place for a girl in distress to hide, but they, too, were empty.

Inspecting every single tent would take an hour. Nonetheless, she went up and down the paths between the tents, calling out as she went.

"Roxie? You're not in any trouble. Just let me see you. I only want to know you're all right."

Nothing. The concert was starting by then. The cheers and whistles from the mess hall made it harder for Constance's voice to be heard. She didn't want to shout over it: that would only scare the girl away.

She ran to the classrooms and looked inside, which wasn't easy without a lantern, but she ducked into each one and peeked into dark corners and behind desks. There was no sign of her.

It was only then, after a few frantic minutes of searching, that she slowed down enough to wonder how Roxanna Collins and Freeman Bernstein were acquainted. The girl had refused to be a part of Fleurette's chorus, claiming that she didn't know how to dance or sing. Was it possible that she did? Had she performed in one of Freeman's shows? But why hide a thing like that?

Hack was standing guard at the entrance to the mess hall. Constance hurried over.

"Have you seen Roxie?" she asked.

He shrugged. "She might've gone in with the rest of them. I didn't take a head count."

"No, she would've come in late, within the last few minutes."

"Then I haven't seen her, miss. What's the trouble?"

Constance wasn't ready to alarm anyone. A missing girl, connected in any way to May Ward's visit, would be a disaster for the camp.

"I believe she's ill again, that's all. If you see her, would you keep an eye on her?"

"Did you check the infirmary?"

"I will," Constance said, but she didn't expect to find her there. Sure enough, the infirmary was closed, the medicine cabinets locked, with a note that Nurse Cartwright could be found at the concert.

Roxie had to be in the woods. Constance took one last look around, casting an eye over the entirety of their small campground. Seeing no one about, she picked up a lantern and headed for the trees.

It would be easy enough to believe that the girl had some sort of dispute with Freeman Bernstein. There were probably dozens, if not hundreds, of aspiring vaudeville actresses who had pinned their hopes on Freeman's promises. Fleurette herself had done so: she'd joined May Ward's troupe as an unpaid seamstress, hoping to impress Mrs. Ward with her tailoring abilities and somehow win a part on stage.

But that was entirely Fleurette's idea. As far as Constance knew, Freeman had never promised Fleurette a place in the troupe. She saw an opportunity and took it. Norma always held Freeman accountable regardless, and resented him for misleading Fleurette, but Constance never did. Fleurette went of her own accord and could've come home at any time.

But did every girl get away so easily? When Constance had charge of the female section at the Hackensack Jail, she heard far worse stories from the women inmates. Theater owners offered private booths to men on a night out, and those booths came with the promise that girls from the chorus would pay a visit after the show and let the men do whatever they liked to do. The expense of touring was often deducted from an actress's paycheck, making it impossible to earn a dollar, much less to save up enough to leave if it became necessary. And everyone knew that a vaudeville audition wasn't over until the girl agreed to a private meeting in the producer's office.

Any of that could've happened to Roxie Collins. But she obviously hadn't expected to see Freeman. If she'd worked with him before, wouldn't she have known that he was May Ward's husband?

Fleurette had talked about nothing but this concert for weeks. Was it possible that Freeman Bernstein's name had never come up in Roxie's presence?

Constance couldn't remember. It hardly mattered, at this point.

She slipped behind the fence and ran up the trail, swinging her lantern and calling for Roxie. The clearing was empty and utterly silent, save for the faint sounds of Clarence's piano drifting over from the mess hall.

Would it do any good to go deeper into the woods? If that girl didn't want to be found, she could easily stay hidden.

Constance knew she couldn't draw her out by shouting, so she kept her voice soft.

"Roxie, if you can hear me, just let me take you somewhere safe for the night. You can stay in the infirmary again. Tomorrow this will all be cast in a different light. Mr. Bernstein will be gone, and we can decide what's best for you. If you want to go home, I'll arrange your ticket myself."

Not a sound. Nothing but laughter and music from across the way.

"I'm going back to the show," Constance said. "If you're here, come find me. Don't stay out all night in the cold and the damp. We'll look after you."

She waited another minute to let that sink in. She listened for a crackle of dead leaves, the snap of a twig, a soft footstep in the mud. The noise of the crowd died down a little—May Ward must've come to a quiet verse in one of her songs—and Constance held her breath, hoping for any sound that might betray a girl in hiding.

That's when she heard it, from across the camp: the ring of a hammer, coming down hard. It could've been the front gate, it could've been a fence post—she didn't know, but she ran toward it.

Another hit, just as Constance reached the fence, muffled this time behind an audience singing along to a chorus. It wasn't coming from the gate, but from somewhere in the center of camp.

Crack! came the next hit, as she drew closer. What on earth was that girl pounding on? It could be a trunk in any one of the tents. It could be the medicine cabinet in the infirmary—and that was easy enough to check, so she jogged past it. Still dark and deserted.

There wasn't another sound after that, but it occurred to Constance that if a hammer was involved, it must've come from the supply shed.

She picked up her skirts and ran toward it, flying, really, her boots hardly touching the ground. She knew what was hidden in that shed.

May Ward was leading the audience in a rousing rendition of "America the Beautiful." There was no time to go to the shed: if Roxie had a gun, she could be headed straight for the mess hall, and all two hundred campers.

"Hack!" Constance called as she tore around the corner. But the mess hall was unguarded.

Constance ducked inside and saw nothing out of the ordinary. May Ward was on stage with her chorus. Fleurette stood right next to her. The audience was on its feet, singing and clapping in time with the music. Constance ran along the edge of the crowd to see if Freeman was seated in the front row. He wasn't.

Norma was, however. When she saw Constance duck in and bolt out again, she jumped up and followed her.

Roxie had to be right back where she started: in that makeshift dressing-room tent with Freeman Bernstein.

Constance flew around the back of the mess hall and practically threw herself into the tent. Roxie had only just stepped inside. Constance hit her with such force that they both fell face-down into an unyielding wooden platform. Constance heard the crunch of breaking bone, but it wasn't hers.

The gun went off in Roxie's hand, and Freeman Bernstein screamed.

⊰ 38 ⊱

THE LAST TIME Beulah saw Freeman was in the much shabbier hotel room to which she had been shifted after the verdict was announced. He claimed that reporters had discovered her, leaving him no choice but to stow her away in a less prominent location. It was obvious, though, that he didn't wish to pay to keep her in a comfortable suite charged to his account any longer. At the new hotel, she paid for the room herself, using a few crumpled bills he pressed into her hand, the implication being that the responsibility for the hotel charges now rested more with her than him.

She found herself sequestered in a narrow single room with nothing but a twin bed and a writing desk. The window permitted no sunlight: it looked out across an air shaft to a brick wall. She was obliged to share a toilet down the hall with the other women on her floor, all of whom came and went so infrequently that she rarely saw them. She might as well have been in jail, for all the comfort her lodgings provided.

After a week in this dismal room, Freeman arrived to tell her, with a resigned, hang-dog look, that no theater, whether a live stage or moving picture, would allow any sort of performance connected to Beulah Binford. Ladies had formed committees. Town ordinances had been passed, even in places Freeman never intended to send her. It had become fashionable to banish her, as a way of taking a stand against indecency.

"I think you're up against it, sweetheart," Freeman said, chomping on a wet cigar. "I don't know just why New York has gotten on its hind-most moral legs at this late date when it stood for Nan Patterson and others I have booked."

"Why do you keep talking about Nan Patterson? She was nothing like me. She shot a man!"

"That was never proven," he said hastily. "I mean to say that if Nan was welcomed back to the stage after a scandal, there's no reason to push you out. I speak as a practical theatrical man, not as a moralist, but I do stand for consistency."

"Well, what are we to do about it now?" She'd been in New York for three weeks, and had yet to see a penny of the salary she'd been promised.

"I think we let 'em cool off, girlie," Freeman said. "Give it a year. Maybe we try for that photoplay later. I know the best fellow in the business. He'll write your story, and we'll get a girl who can play you beautifully. It'll be grand." He turned to leave, as if he couldn't wait to go speak to that fellow about a photoplay.

"If she's playing me, then what am I doing?" Beulah called.

Freeman's hand was already on the doorknob. "Listen, sweetheart. I can't carry you for another year. I've already put myself to considerable expense on your behalf. No one wants to see you get rich as much as Freeman Bernstein does. But you're too hot right now. Find yourself a nice office job. You're paid up here through the end of the month. There's plenty of respectable houses where a girl can rent a room. Go find one of those, and live a quiet life."

He opened the door. "And stay away from married men, why don't you?"

He was gone before she could say a word. Beulah never saw him again.

⫷ 39 ⫸

THE GUN WENT off, uselessly, into the damp earth beneath the tent. Beulah's face, however, did not enjoy such a soft landing. She hit the wooden platform at full force and saw stars. Her nose felt the way it did when she inhaled a full head of bath water as a little girl. She tried to breathe out of her mouth, but with Constance's full weight on her, she could only cough and sputter.

She felt the gun being jerked out of her hand. After a little fumbling around, Constance shifted off her and pulled her wrists behind her back.

Beulah would've laughed if she could even take a breath. "Are you about to put me into handcuffs?"

"I was thinking about it," Constance admitted. That's when Beulah knew with certainty that she used to be a cop.

Beulah felt herself yanked up to her knees, which allowed the blood to run right out of her nose, and also put her directly in front of Freeman Bernstein, who was crumpled on the floor and staring at her with an expression of wild-eyed terror.

It might've been worth it, Beulah thought, just to see him looking like that.

She craned her neck around—although Constance did not, in fact, possess any handcuffs, she held Beulah's wrists behind her as if she did—and saw Norma standing just inside the tent flap, huffing a little from having dashed in behind her sister. Now there were four of them, but there was no question as to who was in charge. All eyes were on Constance.

She pulled Beulah to her feet and spun her around. Norma gasped when she took in the ghoulishness that was Beulah's face. Constance was unmoved.

"It's only a broken nose." Constance pushed a handkerchief against Beulah's face and turned to Norma. "I'm going to take this girl to the infirmary. You stay here and keep an eye on him. Don't let anyone else in."

"You can't hold me here!" Freeman said, scrambling to his feet. "I was nearly killed, and now I'm to be arrested? You might be able to subdue a man like me, Miss Kopp, but your sister damn well couldn't."

Constance thought about that for a minute and looked down at the pistol in her hand. She passed it to Norma, who took it without expression, as if she handled a gun every day.

"You will stay here," Constance said to Freeman, "and you will not say a word. Norma has the gun."

That seemed to settle it.

Constance stepped outside with her arm around Beulah. Hack came running toward them. Campers were already streaming out of the mess hall, having been excited by the gunshot.

"I went to look for—" Hack was panting from the exertion. "This one."

Beulah turned her head away. She didn't like a young man to see her like that.

"Never mind," Constance said. "Listen to me. You are to stand outside this tent. Don't let anyone in or out. Not even May Ward. Do you understand?"

Hack straightened a little. "Yes, ma'am."

"If anyone asks about the gunshot, tell them . . ." Constance paused. Beulah could see her debating with herself. She wouldn't order him to lie. "Tell them it was a misfire, and no one was hurt."

Hack didn't flinch. "Yes, ma'am," he repeated. "I can see that much for myself."

"Good. We're going to the infirmary. If you see Nurse Cartwright, send her over. Don't move until I come back."

It was quite a sensation to be tucked up under Constance's arm when she was giving orders, much like leaning up against an engine when it starts. Constance moved under considerable power. Beulah yielded to it and allowed herself to be swept along, limp as a rag doll.

Constance spoke into the top of her head as they marched up to the infirmary. "You're going to tell me everything, and you're going to do it tonight."

Beulah could offer nothing but a cough in response to that.

"We'll get your nose set, and then you'll tell me," Constance said.

Beulah managed to ask, "Is it broken?"

"Oh, certainly," Constance said. "But a nose is nothing. It'll be good as new."

They were only in the infirmary tent for a few minutes before the nurse bustled in.

"I am the guilty party," Constance said. "Let's get her fixed up and bandaged, then I'll need a few minutes alone with her."

"Certainly," said Nurse Cartwright, equally unable to resist Constance's crisp orders.

What followed was too unpleasant for Beulah to form a definitive memory of. There was a slug of the nurse's anesthetizing tonic, followed by a great deal of gauze over her face, and Constance's hand in hers so that she could squeeze as hard as she liked, and another terrible whack to the nose, this one twice as painful as the last, because the nose had begun to swell and throb by then. After that, a few caustic and foul-smelling ointments were applied, a bandage was wrapped all the way around her head, and she was eased down into that familiar well-cushioned hospital bed.

Beulah gave a little cough in hopes of another round of medicinal brandy, but was offered only tea and aspirin. She wanted neither, but Constance insisted.

"I'll take one of each," Constance said, having refused any other attention from the nurse over the injuries she might've inflicted upon herself when she threw Beulah down.

As soon as they were alone—and Constance had taken a look outside after the nurse left, to be sure she wasn't lingering around the infirmary—she settled into Nurse Cartwright's chair and put her questions to Beulah.

"Let's start with your name, dear."

"You know my name! It's Roxanna Collins."

Constance looked cross at that and took Beulah's tea away, which pained Beulah a little. It had been lovely and warm between her hands.

"You're out of time, and you've exhausted my patience. That name never did fit you. Tell me the real one, or we'll bring Mr. Bernstein in here and let him tell us."

Beulah had forgotten, already, that the man who knew her secrets was only just down the hill. Could Norma really stop him from talking? Beulah decided that she could: she'd seemed quite at home with that pistol.

"All right, then," Beulah said. "I'm surprised you haven't guessed it already. I'm Beulah Binford."

Constance snorted and wiped the tea from her chin. "Don't play games."

"How do you suppose I know Freeman Bernstein?"

Constance sat back in her chair and stared. "I wish I could take that bandage off and have another look at you."

"Don't you remember the pictures?"

"Not particularly. It's been so long. But I'm surprised Norma didn't recognize you." Constance was still staring at her with such intensity that Beulah wanted to pull the covers over her head.

"That was six years ago. It was an old picture even then. I've lost my baby face, and I changed my hair."

"I suppose you would have. But what are you doing here?"

"What do you think? I wanted to go to France."

Constance stared up at the top of the tent pole. "Beulah Binford wants to serve her country," she mused.

"Don't you go writing headlines," Beulah snapped. "I only wanted to get away. It hasn't been easy all these years."

"Have you been in New York the whole time?" Constance asked.

"How did you know I was in New York?"

"You claim to live there, or was that a lie, too? But I do remember that story just two or three years ago. 'Beulah Binford Makes Good at the Telephone Company,' something like that. They went through exactly what you were paid, and how much it cost you for room and board and subway fare, and wondered if you'd be able to live an upright life on so little, or if you'd fall prey to the first man with money in his pocket."

"Yes, well, that story was the end of the telephone company job, as they also happened to mention that I was working there under an assumed name. You can only imagine the clever little lady supervisors doing their detective work."

"Oh, I can imagine it," Constance said mildly. "Now, what have you got against Freeman Bernstein? I do know that he managed you. Norma was very eager to remind me of that last year, when Fleurette joined up with May Ward."

"Why, because it shows what a shady character he is?" Beulah asked. "I suppose Norma didn't want Fleurette associating with anyone who associated with Beulah Binford."

"It might've been something like that. But Norma was proven wrong. Mr. Bernstein did Fleurette no harm."

"Well, I can't say the same." There were tears in her eyes, unbidden, that rolled into the bandage across her face. Now her nose was starting to swell again, and to throb unbearably.

Constance put a hand on hers. "I'm not going to make you tell it all tonight. But didn't you expect to see Mr. Bernstein? Surely you knew he was married to May Ward."

"I didn't," Beulah insisted. "He mentioned a wife on the stage, but I thought she'd be named Bernstein."

"But the two of them were in the papers together all the time. You must've kept up with him."

"Oh, I couldn't bear to look at a paper after . . ." She choked and put a handkerchief to her mouth.

"I've heard enough," Constance said. "I can guess at the rest. I'm going to call Nurse Cartwright back in here, and I'll put Clarence on guard duty outside the infirmary all night long. I suggest you go right on being Roxanna Collins for the moment."

"What's the use? The entire camp knows by now," Beulah groaned, "and you're only going to show me the gate in the morning."

"If Norma's held fast, the entire camp doesn't know yet," Constance said. "How do you suppose she's handled Mr. Bernstein?"

Beulah would've smiled, but the bandage wouldn't allow it. "I haven't heard another gunshot, but I wouldn't put it past her."

"Nor would I. Get some sleep. We'll sort you out in the morning."

⚅ 40 ⚅

BEULAH KNEW WHERE Nurse Cartwright kept the extra blankets, and she just happened to remember that a spare bottle of brandy was stored in the same cupboard. She took one of each—a blanket, and a generous and (to her mind) well-deserved slug of brandy—while Constance and Nurse Cartwright murmured outside the infirmary. When the nurse returned Beulah feigned sleep, having already made herself entirely comfortable.

She would explain herself to the nurse in the morning. There would be a great deal of explaining in the morning, and decisions to be made about her future. Under any other circumstance she would've stayed awake all night worrying about it, but firing that shot at Freeman Bernstein had cleared her head remarkably. There was a rousing finality to that gunshot, even if the bullet had only gone into the ground. (Was it lodged there forever, or would someone dig it out? Beulah thought she might like to have it as a souvenir.)

Whatever news the morning would bring, Beulah felt that she had, improbably, brought the darkest chapter of her life to an end. Her misfortunes, it now occurred to her, had begun with a bullet. Perhaps it was true all along that a bullet was the only way to end them. If she'd known that, she would've fired off a near-miss in Freeman Bernstein's general direction years ago.

With the benefit of hindsight (for she now viewed the last several years as an epoch that had ended and could be put upon a shelf and studied from a distance), she knew that her situation could've been much worse. She emerged, as it were, unscathed —which is to say that after everything Henry Clay inflicted upon her, he did not leave her with what Louise's mother called the "evidence of his sin."

She learned about that only after Freeman abandoned her. She'd gone around looking for work in New York—he'd left her no choice—and quickly found that she couldn't give her own name. Women drew away from her, and men whistled and called their colleagues to come running over and have a look at "the real Beulah Binford." She rushed out of more than one office red-faced and fighting back tears.

What was that silly name she chose the first time? Lucy Lane. As Lucy Lane, she could secure work as a clasper in an envelope factory. With a week's pay in hand, she found a boarding-house and a girl willing to share a room with her. Mabel was her first friend in New York, and the only one who ever knew the truth.

It was Mabel who told Beulah what the soiled undergarments meant. They'd been living together for about a month when Mabel arrived home with a gallon jug of wine. "Don't ask how I came by it," she said, "but we're going to have us a party tonight."

With nothing to eat but crackers and potted ham, the wine went straight to Beulah's head. They reclined together on her bed, end to end, with their elbows resting comfortably on each other's knees. No circumstance is more conducive to setting free a secret than two women with a bottle of wine and an entire night to themselves. Beulah was all too ready to surrender her real name, and everything that went along with it.

Fortunately, Mabel couldn't be shocked. She'd lived in New York too long to find anything scandalous in Beulah's version of events, and in fact considered herself privileged to share a room with a woman whose name was probably better known to most Americans than Edith Wilson's. "Every one of my roommates had a story," Mabel said, "but you happen to have the *only* story of 1911. You were right not to go on the stage, but I won't pretend I'm not highly entertained to hear the entire business from your side."

Beulah didn't find it at all callous of Mabel to say that her misfortunes were so entertaining, and in fact it lightened her spirits to bring the sordid mess out into the open and to give it an airing. She relished every detail, lingering over her veiled figure at the back of the church during Henry Clay's wedding, and that afternoon at the stock pond when he brandished his gun.

The part about Louise's mother describing the soiled underclothes came out hours later, well past midnight and well into the wine.

"I always wondered why they bothered about his nasty old pants in the middle of a murder trial," Beulah said.

Mabel sputtered. "Do you mean that you don't know?"

"Well, I . . ." Beulah didn't know, and there was nothing to do but wait to be told.

"Surely you've heard, after all those years you spent . . . I mean, from what you're telling me, you lived in a house full of women who . . ." Mabel couldn't quite bring herself to say it. "These were women with experience. Isn't that right?"

"That's what I said, isn't it?" Beulah couldn't help but be annoyed at the way Mabel was dancing around the subject. Hadn't she just told her everything? It had taken them each a hefty portion of that raisiny old cheap wine to work themselves up to this point in the conversation. Beulah didn't think she could keep much more of it down. Hadn't they reached the honest end of the bottle yet?

"Well, they must've told you how to be with a man. How to keep yourself from having a baby, things like that."

"Oh, those horrible rubber bags." Beulah shuddered. "They put the same soap up in there that they use to clean the toilets. Do you know how that stings?"

Mabel didn't want to talk about the soap. Beulah couldn't blame her. "And didn't they tell you about . . . social diseases?"

Beulah said, "I don't recall that term. Maybe they didn't use such polite language, for fear of not being understood."

"I'm trying to ask you if you were ever told what it meant if a man had sores. Did they tell you to look at him when he pulled his pants down, and to see for yourself if he was . . ."

"Clean," Beulah said crossly. "They told me to look and see if he kept himself clean. But I never could stand to look. Can you?"

Mabel reached over and took Beulah's hands in hers. "Beulah, dear, I want you to think about this. Those sores—those were a sign of his disease. That was the stain in his underpants."

Beulah shuddered. Now she felt truly ill. "I can't believe Louise showed that to her mother."

Mabel sighed and tried again. "You told me he was acting crazy just before his wife died. Isn't that right? He was going off like a lunatic?"

"He sure was," Beulah said. "I'd never seen him like that. I hardly knew him."

"Well, don't you know? The disease does that to a person. That could be why he was out of his mind."

Tears came into Beulah's eyes, and she pressed her palms against them. Henry Clay had only been dead a month at that point. They'd put him in an electric chair and burned him to

287

death. She woke up every night thinking about it. There'd been no picture of that in the papers—someone at the news bureaus had a sense of decency—but she could imagine it, and she did, between the hours of two and three o'clock, every morning.

"Are you saying that all he needed was some medicine, and he wouldn't have shot Louise?"

"I think he might've been too far gone for medicine," Mabel said.

"Well, didn't the judge know about it? Couldn't he have brought in a doctor?" Beulah sniffed and looked around for a handkerchief.

Mabel handed hers to Beulah. She spoke more gently now. "What I'm trying to tell you is that he was diseased, and you might be, too. You need a Wassermann test."

Beulah looked up at her sharply. "Do you think I have what Henry Clay had?"

"Well, that is how you get it. Don't you know that?"

Beulah pulled away from her. She didn't like to have all the things she didn't know pointed out to her. "I know that you can get a disease from a man, if that's what you mean. But I don't have one. And I hardly let Henry Clay touch me last summer. Before that, it had been . . . I don't know, a few years."

"And how many baseball players in between?"

Beulah smiled at the thought of those ball players. "Oh, a few, but they're so clean and good."

Mabel put a hand over her mouth to stop from smiling. "I never thought I'd say this, but I'm going to have to teach Beulah Binford a thing or two about men. We're taking you to a lady doctor next week."

Beulah had never seen a doctor of any kind, but there was no arguing about it. Mabel kept every promise and every threat, including this one. She hauled Beulah off for a Wassermann test, and Beulah was found, through some miracle, to be free of disease. The lady doctor gave her a lecture on the evils of social illness and the importance of keeping herself pure until marriage.

"And when you do marry," the doctor said, "*after* you marry, there's a better way to make sure you don't have a baby than a hose and a bag of toilet soap."

She pulled a little rubber cup out of her desk and pinched it together. Beulah didn't require very many words of explanation. "I've heard about those," she said. "How nice for the married ladies."

The doctor dropped it on her desk. "I believe I hear my receptionist calling. Wait right here."

Beulah didn't hear anyone calling. When the doctor didn't return she stood up, slipped that little rubber cup into her pocketbook, and went out into the hall, where Mabel was already paying the bill.

"Did you get one?" Mabel asked on the way out.

"Well, I stole one, if that's what you mean."

"That's what you were supposed to do." Mabel put an arm around her, and they leaned into the wind on Forty-Sixth Street. "You're a New York girl now."

⊰ 41 ⊱

OUTSIDE THE INFIRMARY, Nurse Cartwright was waiting off by herself, leaning against a solitary birch that served as a kind of informal camp message board. Notices of lost items were posted there, and offers from the more enterprising campers (Fleurette not among them) to mend stockings and hems for a fee. The nurse made a show of appearing to read the notices, but came rushing over as soon as Constance walked out.

"Everyone's talking about a gunshot," she said. "I heard it myself, but I thought it was only an auto misfiring. Do I have another patient?"

Constance glanced down the camp's wide central avenue, with tents arrayed on either side. Discipline was starting to fall apart. With the show over, and no one to order them to bed, the campers were running between the tents, a sort of frenetic buzz in the air about the gunshot that brought the performance to an abrupt end. Constance could hear the rumors floating toward her: Hack shot an intruder. May Ward was followed to camp by a jealous lover.

She motioned for the nurse to follow her. They walked a little ways away, behind the infirmary, far enough to be out of earshot.

"You don't have another patient," Constance said. "There was a gun, but it didn't find its mark."

"And who was its mark, may I ask?"

Constance hesitated. Who else could she tell, besides Norma? "You mustn't say a word."

"If it concerns my patient, I'm duty-bound to keep it quiet."

Of course, Nurse Cartwright didn't know her patient's true identity—and Constance wasn't about to tell her that. "I will say only that a gun was fired in the general direction of Mrs. Ward's husband, but he wasn't hurt."

Nurse Cartwright squinted at her in the dim light. "A girl shooting at another woman's husband? I'll wager she had a good reason to put a bullet in him. I wonder if she'll tell me what it was."

"That's for her to decide," Constance said.

"Oh, she'll tell me," the nurse said. "They all do. If you're through with her for the night, I'll mix her up a sleeping powder. She needs her rest."

"Why should she sleep tonight?" Constance said. "She stole a gun and tried to shoot a man. That ought to keep her awake. Mr. Bernstein was very nearly murdered."

"And then you stopped it," the nurse said, with cheerful aplomb. "That's a job well-done."

"But it isn't over yet," Constance said. "Mr. Bernstein's going to want to press charges. I'll have to call in the police, and testify myself. I'm the only eyewitness. I've no choice but to give evidence."

The weight of what had happened was descending upon her. She could picture all too clearly what was coming next: the police arriving, the interviewing of witnesses, Beulah put in handcuffs, taken away to jail . . . and then the reporters, and a round of scandalous stories about Beulah Binford and the National Service

Schools. Beulah's life would be ruined a second time. Constance's own past would be resurrected: the disgraced lady deputy, bringing dishonor to another institution.

But even worse, the cause of women's war work would be set back a decade. A camp meant for wartime preparation, descended into a tawdry feud between a notorious harlot and a vaudeville showman. No mother would ever send her daughter to such a place again.

Nurse Cartwright was watching her: she saw the despair move across her face.

"It'll be a mess, with the police here," she offered.

"It will," Constance said, "but I can't ignore the law."

Nurse Cartwright gave a startled little cough. "The law! What business is that of yours?"

"It used to be my business," Constance said.

Nurse Cartwright stepped back and looked her over. "Oh, I see it now. You have that air about you. What were you? Jail matron? Police lady?"

"Something like that," Constance admitted. Her former profession hung about her like a uniform.

"But you've given it up?"

"You might say it gave me up. But that doesn't change the fact that a crime has been committed, and I have a duty—"

Nurse Cartwright interrupted. "This Mr. Bernstein—what did he do to that girl? Was it lawful?"

"It might not've been," Constance mused. Was he guilty of fraud? Misrepresentation? "Whatever he did, though, the punishment isn't a bullet through the head."

"No, the punishment is a good fright, and that's all he's had," Nurse Cartwright said.

They'd walked around the infirmary three times now, their heads bowed, hands clasped behind them.

Nurse Cartwright blew out a puff of air and looked up at the stars, considering. "You must know the inside of a jail cell, if you've been in police work."

"I slept in one myself, alongside my inmates," Constance said.

"Then you know what's in store for her. Would it help that girl to go to jail?"

"Not at all," Constance admitted. "In my old position, I could put a troubled girl under probation, and keep an eye on her myself. But I can't do that anymore."

The nurse glanced back over at the infirmary and said, thoughtfully, "She does need looking after." Then, turning back to Constance, "There are times when I find the law to be more of a hindrance."

Constance sighed, thinking of her illicit late-night trainings and how dull life had been without them. "I'm getting rather tired of laws and rules myself, but consider the position I'm in."

"It seems to me," the nurse said, "that a great deal depends upon Mr. Bernstein. He's the only one with a grievance. If he has an ounce of shame, he'll scuttle out of here and never say a word."

"That doesn't sound like Freeman Bernstein," Constance said. "And what am I to tell the campers about that gunshot? And the parents, and Miss Miner, when she finds out?"

Nurse Cartwright patted her shoulder and turned to go back to the infirmary. "I told a few of them that it was only a prop, shooting blanks. It works marvelously. Give it a try. Can I mix you a sleeping powder, too? You could use one."

Constance declined the sleeping powder. She made her way back through the tents, ushering girls to the latrines or the water pumps one last time, issuing stern warnings about curfew.

A girl of only seventeen, her hair in two long braids, popped out of her tent in her nightgown.

"Go on to sleep, Roberta. Reveille's at six," Constance said.

"But, Miss Kopp—is it true? Are you the one who fired the gun? I heard there was a bear in the woods. Did you kill him?"

"I heard it was Hack, shooting at a thief who was going from tent to tent while we were at the show" came a voice from inside Roberta's tent.

A little crowd gathered around, most of them wrapped in blankets against the nighttime chill. Constance looked around at their faces, some anxious, some mirthful. This was little more than a bedtime story for them—a bit of adventure, a story to be passed around for a few days until the next bit of drama gripped them. The newspaper-reading public would treat it that way, too, if word got out: an entertainment, to be tossed about the way a cat tortures a mouse, until a more enticing plaything comes along.

Never mind what happens to the mouse. Constance looked back at the infirmary and marveled again at the fact that the notorious Beulah Binford was secreted away there. What had to be going through her mind at that moment?

"It was a gun, wasn't it? It sounded more like an automobile firing." The question came from a girl named Sally who'd attended her wireless class. She had a bit of garish lip-stick still smudged across her lower lip. Constance pulled out a handkerchief—here was one rule she could enforce, anyway—and wiped it away.

"It was nothing but a theatrical prop meant to sound like a gun," she told them. "Flash powder, for dramatic effect. I'm sorry if it startled you. It went off unexpectedly."

Whether they were satisfied with that explanation or not Constance couldn't guess. At least they went obediently back to their tents.

Now she had Freeman Bernstein to reckon with.

⪥ 42 ⪤

NORMA DID A marvelous job of holding Mr. Bernstein at gun-point. It was, in every way, the role she was born to play: Norma was nothing if not indomitable in the presence of a foe.

Hack held up his end of the bargain, too, and didn't allow any-one to come near the tent. Fleurette stayed with May Ward in the mess hall where they were forbidden, under rather stern orders from Clarence, from leaving until Constance gave the order.

The entire operation was conducted so smoothly, Constance reflected, as she looked around the camp, that it almost seemed as if they'd formed a cohesive military unit. It was with no small amount of pride that she thanked Hack and Clarence for their ef-forts and stepped inside the tent to confront Mr. Bernstein.

Norma was at her ease in a folding chair, with one leg crossed over the other and the pistol pointed casually in Freeman's direc-tion.

"Has he been entirely silent?" Constance asked.

"No. I had to remind him twice," Norma said.

"I'm glad there wasn't a third time. I'd like to speak to you pri-vately, Mr. Bernstein, and the walls of this tent are far too thin. Please come with me."

"I'll go anywhere you like, as long as I'm not looking down the barrel of a revolver any longer. A man my age shouldn't be kept in suspense when bullets are involved."

Constance thought otherwise and decided to take the weapon with her. She held her hand out and said to Norma, "That's all for tonight. I'm sure you need to see to your pigeons."

"Pigeons!" scoffed Mr. Bernstein. "What does an Army camp need with pigeons?"

That remark was enough to make Norma look thoughtfully at the gun. Constance took it away gently, and Norma stumped outside.

Constance took hold of Freeman's arm in that proprietary manner she used to employ with her inmates, digging her fingers into the bones around his elbow to let him know that he'd be down on the ground with a nose like Beulah's if he tried to run. He groaned but went along with her, having been given no choice in the matter.

They walked in silence until they reached the training field. No one from camp could hear them, and as long as they were in the open, she would see anyone coming.

She always thought it best to begin an interrogation without any preliminaries. "You weren't expecting to see Miss Binford tonight, were you?"

"I hoped never to see that girl again."

"And what about your wife?"

"Mrs. Ward will not permit her name to be uttered in her presence."

"Does that mean you didn't say her name after she ran out of the tent?"

Mr. Bernstein rubbed his forehead. "I can hardly remember, I was so shocked."

"Of course you remember. Do Fleurette and Mrs. Ward know

that they were in a tent with Beulah Binford no more than an hour ago?"

He groaned. "No. I shut my trap when you ran out. It isn't in my best interests to introduce the subject or the girl in the presence of Mrs. Ward. That Binford girl nearly put me in the poorhouse."

"Yes, I'm sure that whatever happened between the two of you was entirely her fault," Constance said drily.

"I'd like to know why you allowed her into camp. A scandal like that would close this place down. Or—wait a minute. I know her game. She gave a false name, didn't she? She always did, back in New York."

"This camp is not your concern," Constance said. "What matters now is whether Miss Binford is to be given the privacy she deserves."

Freeman stood with his hands in his pockets and rolled his eyes up toward the sky, calculating. "Well, let's see. I know a reporter or two in Washington who could be out here in the morning. What would that headline be?"

Constance yanked Freeman's elbow for good measure. "You know perfectly well. 'Disgraced Lady Deputy Snares Beulah Binford.' Every paper in the country would run it."

Freeman nodded thoughtfully. "I like that. This might just be the little something extra that we need to put Beulah back on the stage. A lady deputy throwing her behind bars when she tries to shoot another man—"

"Another man! When did she ever shoot a man before?"

"Oh, you're right," Freeman said. "It was the wife who was murdered."

"And the husband who did the murdering! You haven't even bothered to remember what transpired."

"Well, there's no need to go into the particulars now. What I'm proposing, Miss Kopp, is to put you in the very center of our little morality play, as a force for good. Now, I don't have to tell you how much this might help rehabilitate your own image after all that nastiness during the election last fall. What I suggest is—"

If Constance hadn't been certain how to handle Mr. Bernstein before, she was now. He hadn't been damaged a bit by that gunshot. He was already trying to put on a show about it. There was in fact no tragedy, no scandal, that he wouldn't exploit for his own gain. She wasn't shocked by it any more than one is shocked by a leopard for wearing its spots, but she saw now that he would never be persuaded to see Beulah's plight another way. He couldn't be persuaded at all—but he could be threatened. That sort of bravado in a man always had cowardice hiding underneath it. She could manage a coward.

Constance—summoning up more of Deputy Kopp now than she had in months—gripped him by both shoulders and gave him a rough shake. "You're not making the suggestions, Mr. Bernstein. You're going to keep quiet about Beulah Binford. You've already ruined that girl's life once. There's nothing to be gained by doing so again."

"But the public deserves to know!"

"Oh, you don't believe that. You do remember that I saved your life tonight, don't you?"

"For which I offer my thanks, if I haven't already."

"You haven't," Constance said flatly. "I just happened to catch Beulah in time. Who's going to be there to stop her the next time she comes after you?"

He paused to consider that. "She's not the first girl to point a gun at me. And I don't imagine she's a very good shot."

"Mr. Bernstein, here's one thing I know about Beulah Binford. She might be quiet, and a little evasive, but she watches and learns. She won't make a mistake next time."

He went very still at that idea. "Then what do you propose?"

"I propose you do your utmost not to aggravate her. Leave her alone, and don't breathe a word about her to the press."

"But she put a gun on me! Don't you throw girls in jail for a thing like that?"

"Leave her to me. I can't appeal to your sense of decency, because you haven't any, but—"

"Now, that's unkind!"

"But what I can do is to remind you that if you go against Beulah Binford, or say a word that would damage the reputation of this camp, you will have Beulah to worry about—"

"That's nothing new." Freeman tried to summon up his bluster and bluff, but it drained away again when he saw something fierce and—Was it possible? A bit of the rogue outlaw?—in Constance's eye.

"And you will have me to worry about. If Beulah doesn't come after you, I will. Am I understood?"

⇥ 43 ⇤

"BUT WHY WOULD you threaten him on my account?" Beulah asked Constance the next morning. She'd passed a comfortable night in the infirmary, in spite of her swollen and throbbing nose. There was no ice to be had in camp, but Nurse Cartwright put cold cloths on top of the bandage, which helped a little, and gave her a restorative sip of brandy now and then, which helped a great deal more.

"He deserved it," Constance said. "I'm going to think of you the same way I'd think of a girl who's been arrested. You're entitled to your privacy until your case is sorted out."

Beulah had, by then, formed a pretty good idea of why Constance knew so much about arrests and cases, but she didn't say anything about it at that moment.

"Well, I am a girl who's been arrested, as you well know, but I'd rather not be again."

"You won't be."

Constance couldn't promise that, and Beulah knew it. "What did you tell everybody, then?"

"I said that a gun was to be used as a prop in the show, and that it discharged accidentally backstage."

"Do you honestly think that all two hundred girls are going to believe a story like that?"

"Not for long," Constance admitted. "They're going to write to their parents. I can't put a stop to that. Some of those parents will have questions."

"Then you and I have just enough time to skip out of town," Beulah said.

Constance smiled at that offer. "I had Clarence send a wire to Maude Miner this morning asking her to pay us a visit. She'll have to be told the truth. I'll leave it to her to decide what to do."

Beulah sat up in bed. "But you're not going to confess to everything, are you? You'll tell her my name? You'll tell her I tried to shoot Mr. Bernstein?"

"I have to. It's the only way."

Beulah didn't like the sound of that, but thought it best to appeal to Constance's pride. "Doesn't that look bad for you? She'll want to know where I found the gun. What are you going to say about that?"

"The truth," Constance said. "Every word of it. She put her trust in me, and I must do the same."

Beulah couldn't tolerate Constance's noble tone. Police ladies loved to take an honorable stance, and expected warm approval and admiration for it. Beulah wasn't about to give her the satisfaction.

"Go ahead and ruin your own life, if you want to. If I'm found out, I'll go back to New York and pick up where I left off. But if Miss Miner knows that you led a shooting party in the woods, and that you had Beulah Binford living right under your nose—why, it'll be terrible for you, and I suppose it'll close the camp. This is far worse than a few girls sneaking off with their wireless instructor for cocktails and cigarettes."

"Which you did, too, with Hack and Clarence," Constance reminded her.

"Oh, you can't bring them into this!" Beulah had grown fond of those boys. They were so harmless, anyway. Anyone else might've plied them with liquor, but they had nothing but warm beer on offer, which was so bitter and flat that only the boys drank it.

"They brought themselves into this when they went off with you into the woods," Constance said. "They're soldiers, and they know better."

Beulah shrugged. There was nothing she could do for Hack and Clarence. "Am I to leave today, or wait for Miss Miner to come and put me out?"

"I'm not convinced that she will put you out," Constance said. "I think she'll view this the way I do. You shouldn't be punished forever for something that happened when you were not much more than a child."

"Well, you and Miss Miner can believe that, and then I'll only have the rest of the nation to convince." Beulah found it hard to talk with her nose mashed in. She didn't like to accept kindness from the woman who'd done it to her.

"Isn't it better to come clean?" Constance asked. "You can't go on like this forever, can you? Living under an assumed name and making up stories about yourself?"

Beulah bristled at Constance's attempt at fixing her life. "Everyone makes up stories about themselves. Look at you."

Constance managed to look shocked at this, even though Beulah could tell she'd struck close to the truth. "Me? What story have I been telling?"

"It's the story you haven't been telling," Beulah said. "Who are you, anyway? You go around teaching those girls to shoot a gun, and talking about arrests and cases and all the rest of it, and you certainly are good at throwing somebody down on the ground, by

302

the look of my nose. But you want us to think you're just a spin- ster lady from a farm in New Jersey. What are you trying to hide?"

"I don't know why you want to bring me into this," Constance said. "I didn't ask to be camp matron. If Mrs. Nash hadn't taken that fall—"

"Oh, never mind about Mrs. Nash and her fall! You used to be somebody, didn't you? You just don't want anyone to know, same as me."

Constance leaned against the metal rail at the foot of Beulah's bed. "I had a little trouble in my last position," she said. "It was in the papers quite a bit. I've just been hoping that these girls don't follow the crime pages."

"I don't look at a paper much myself," Beulah said, "but why are you trying to hide it?"

"I don't want to have to answer any questions, that's all."

"Why? Are you ashamed? Did you do something terrible?" Beulah felt quite enlivened by the possibilities. "Did you shoot a man? Did you put the wrong girl in jail and leave a criminal out running on the streets?"

"No! It was nothing like that. Only—everything I did was twisted around and misunderstood. Things got blamed on me that shouldn't have been."

Beulah settled back into her pillows with a feeling of satis- faction. "Oh, I know all about that. But what are you going to do about it now?"

Constance quaked a little at that, if a woman of her size could be said to quake. "There isn't a thing I can do. It's over."

"What I mean to say is, what are you going to do next? Are you going to be a police lady again?"

"I don't know why I ought to tell you about it, but no, I couldn't, after what's been said about me in the papers. Every police depart- ment in New Jersey knows my name."

"Then go out West," Beulah offered.

"I couldn't leave my sisters, and we have a farm, besides."

"Then you must have some idea of helping with the war effort, if you're here," Beulah said.

Constance shrugged. "Miss Miner thinks that she might have something for me at the War Department. Or—well, she would have, if I'd managed the camp properly. Now I don't know what she'll say."

"Who cares about Miss Miner? Why are you waiting for her to tell you what you're going to do and who you're going to be? Can't you work that out for yourself?"

"It hardly matters what I decide to do, if no one will hire me to do it."

"But you haven't even tried," Beulah said. "Did you take the wireless class?"

"Of course," Constance said.

"Well, so did I. Did Mr. Turner teach you how to spell that detective's name using different words for every letter?"

"Mr. Bielaski. Yes, he did. I suppose he uses the same name for every class."

"And did he tell you about how Mr. Bielaski marched in and demanded a job going after the Germans, when one didn't even exist?"

"Roxie," Constance said, "pardon me, Beulah—I don't know what Mr. Bielaski has to do with—"

Beulah wouldn't let her finish. "How'd you decide to become a police lady in the first place?"

"I . . . well, I didn't," Constance said. "The sheriff hired me. He saw what I could do when a man was harassing our family, and he asked me to come and work for him."

"And then he asked you not to work for him, is that it?"

"It wasn't his fault," Constance said. "There was an election. Someone else was sheriff."

"All right, so a different sheriff asked you not to work for him," Beulah said. "It's the same thing. And now you're waiting for Miss Miner to ask you to work for her. Why don't you decide what you want, and do the asking yourself? That's what Mr. Bielaski did, and look at him now. That's what I did, too. I couldn't hide from the papers forever. I had to go find myself a job, and make my own life."

"In a strange city, under an assumed name."

"Well, that's because I'm Beulah Binford," she snapped. "The rules are different for me. But what I'm telling you is that I couldn't wait for things to get better on their own. If I'd hung my head in shame every day for the rest of my life, it still wouldn't have been enough, would it?"

"Of course you shouldn't hang your head—"

"Because how much shame is enough? When do you know it's enough? Does somebody write you a letter and tell you? I don't think they do. I never got one."

"Miss Binford, I didn't mean to suggest—"

Beulah was good and wound up now. "What I'm trying to say is, you can't wait for somebody else to decide whether you get another chance. What if nobody ever does?"

⇥ 44 ⇤

"THAT GIRL IS exhausting," Constance said, kicking her feet up on Norma's cot. "They're all exhausting, now that I think of it."

Everyone else was either at sewing or cooking class. Norma had stayed behind to hear what transpired with Beulah. As Norma was the only other soul in camp to know Beulah's identity, Constance hardly had any choice but to talk to her about it. There was no one else to tell.

"If you hadn't broken her nose, we could've put her out first thing this morning," Norma said.

"I'm not going to put her out," Constance said.

"You always go soft for girls with bad reputations," Norma said.

"What is she to do? Her name's been ruined, but she has to make a life for herself."

"She can make a life without stealing a gun and shooting at a man," Norma said. "They put people in jail for that sort of thing, or have you forgotten already?"

"She had a fright," Constance said. "She didn't expect to ever see him again. Apparently he's the one who made sure that she stayed in the papers. She holds him responsible for all her notoriety."

"As I recall, she had a hand in it herself," Norma said.

"She was thirteen when it started. Try to imagine Fleurette when she was thirteen, going with a grown man like Henry Clay Beattie."

"I don't believe I will imagine that. Are we to go on pretending that she's Roxanna Collins from Park Avenue?"

"We are, although she's excused from duties until Nurse Cartwright releases her. I told the nurse to be generous. A few days in the infirmary won't do any harm."

"And you intend to just wait for Maude Miner to show up and sort it out."

"I am not waiting for Maude Miner." Constance couldn't help but sound irked at that. Beulah managed to get under her skin with that talk of always waiting for some other party to decide what her life ought to be. She thought she might put the question of her future to Norma. "This camp of yours hasn't given me any better ideas about what I might do during the war."

"It isn't my camp," Norma said, "and there are a dozen things you could do tomorrow. You're free to choose any of them. Most of us don't have a choice. We're only any good at one thing. Fleurette's going to sew, whether she likes it or not, and I'll be handling the Army's pigeon program."

Constance started to register her doubts about that last bit, but Norma plunged on. "You, on the other hand, could go into police or detective work, or find another jail in need of a matron, or run another camp like this one, or do any sort of work with troubled girls at hospitals and missions and the like. You could take up with a travelers' league like that policewoman in Paterson."

"Belle Headison," Constance groaned. "Don't put me in with her."

"Don't you see?" Norma said. "Belle Headison is probably only capable of doing one thing, which is why she's doing it. You could do a dozen things, but you won't. You'd rather sulk about an election that ended six months ago."

Had it been six months? The wound was still fresh. Perhaps she understood how Beulah, six years after the fact, still wanted to rush at Freeman Bernstein with a gun.

"Your trouble is that nothing else is good enough. You would've worked for Sheriff Heath forever, if they appointed sheriffs for life."

"I might have," Constance admitted.

"If that's the only job that meets your exacting standards, then you're out of work for good. You had the shortest career I've ever heard of, and I only hope the memories are enough to last you a lifetime."

"When do you suppose you'll start running that pigeon division at the Army?" Constance asked, inspired by a sudden eagerness to pack Norma off to another camp.

"Private Hackbush tells me that his commander will be back for graduation, provided this camp isn't shut down in disgrace before that. He's going to hitch my cart to his automobile and drive it around as a demonstration. I'll release what pigeons I have left and show what they can do."

"I wouldn't think Hack would be so eager to help, after the way you treated him in class," Constance said.

"He wasn't particularly inclined at first, but then I reminded him that he'd been sneaking out late at night with one of my sisters, and allowing the other sister to go firing off his guns in the woods, which nearly resulted in a man being killed. He was far more inclined to grant me a favor after that."

THE NEXT FEW days passed quietly enough. Beulah stayed contentedly in the infirmary. She and Nurse Cartwright struck up quite a friendship: one afternoon, Constance had to run over to the infirmary to remind the nurse that she was late to her Thursday afternoon class on bandage-rolling. She and Beulah had been so deep in conversation that she'd entirely forgotten about the class.

Rumors continued to circulate about the mysterious gunshot heard at the end of Mrs. Ward's performance. Those with experience on the stage were more likely to accept the explanation that a gun intended as a prop had misfired: some prop was always misfiring, breaking, or exploding at the theater. Calcium lights were still in use in small towns here and there, and it wasn't uncommon for one of them to burst into flames in the middle of a performance.

Disaster, or the appearance of disaster, went part and parcel with the theater life.

Other girls weren't so sure. Some suspected Mr. Bernstein of firing the gun. He was a German spy, went one rumor, come to extract military secrets from Hack and Clarence. Or perhaps Constance discovered the espionage plot and tried to shoot him, for the good of the country.

Another strain of rumor circulated about Beulah (still known as Roxie to the campers). Perhaps she was Freeman's lover, or maybe he knew of a scandal concerning her. She could've tried and failed to shoot herself over some tragedy, which would explain the lengthy stay in the infirmary. No one had a good look at her that night, when her face was covered in blood, but her confinement lent credence to the idea that she had been on the receiving end of the bullet, perhaps in the ear, or just along the scalp. Enough to wound, but not to kill.

No one knew for sure, and that was fine with Constance. She kept the camp on a tight schedule, invented new chores, and pushed the girls through longer and more difficult calisthenics every morning and afternoon. If she could only exhaust them physically, she reasoned, they might sleep at night rather than stay awake gossiping.

It was three days before Constance had a reply from Maude Miner. Her message came in the form of a telegram, delivered by Clarence, who had by some miracle been able to secure a newspaper as well. The nearest newsstand was ten miles away: as he explained it, the telegram boy carried papers on his country routes to make a little pocket money.

Clarence brought both the telegram and newspaper to Constance in the mess hall one evening, just as supper was being cleared. Norma and Sarah were still lingering at the table. They crowded around eagerly for news.

She opened the telegram first.

ALREADY HEARING FROM PARENTS TOLD THEM NOT TO WORRY GIRLS ARE SAFE WAS ONLY SHOOTING BLANKS AND SO ON CAN'T GET TO CHEVY CHASE YET AS WAR DEPT EXPECTS ME TO PERSUADE MISS RANKIN CARRY ON AS BEFORE YRS MAUDE MINER

"What on earth has Miss Rankin got up to already?" Norma muttered, reaching for the paper.

Sarah, reading over her shoulder, gasped at the headlines. "Is there really to be a war resolution before Congress? I thought it wouldn't happen until this summer."

"The Germans thought otherwise," Norma said. "They've been sinking our ships, while we've been here learning how to march in a straight line and cook dinner for the convalescent. I can't believe we weren't told."

"It's unlike the War Department to keep you in the dark," Constance said. "Only I don't see how Miss Miner and Miss Rankin figure into it."

Norma, still reading, said, "Miss Rankin was just seated yesterday. No one gave any notice to the first woman elected to Congress, because the President marched right in and asked for the authority to go to war. They've been debating it since. Miss Rankin is opposed."

"Did Montana know they'd elected a pacifist?" Constance asked. She'd been so consumed with her own misery since the election that she hadn't paid much attention to the doings in Montana, where women had just recently won the right to vote and the right to run for office.

"They knew they elected a woman, and I suppose it's the same thing as electing a pacifist," Norma said.

"That's not true," Constance put in. "You're not a pacifist. I don't suppose Sarah is, either."

"I don't like to see anyone fighting," Sarah said, "but we can't stand by and let Europe go up in flames."

"Well, it won't do much for the cause of suffrage if she votes against the war," Norma said. "She'll set us back another decade on that front."

"She's not voting on behalf of the suffragists," Constance said, "she's voting on behalf of the people of Montana. Besides, she'll be criticized no matter what she does. If she votes in favor, they'll say that there's no need to put a woman in office if she's only going to vote as the men do. If she votes against war, they'll say that women are too soft to make the difficult decisions."

"I wonder why the War Department is sending in Miss Miner to try to persuade her," Sarah said. "Surely they have enough votes regardless."

"But they'd like a woman's vote. If the only woman in Congress votes for war, every mother in this country will give up her son a little more easily," Norma said.

Constance was sitting right next to Sarah and felt a little shiver go through her at the mention of giving up sons.

"I'll ask Clarence to find some way to arrange for a paper every day this week," Constance said.

⚔ 45 ⚔

THE NEWS ARRIVED a few days later, not in the form of a news-paper, but in the form of a wagon loaded with soldiers, come to dismantle the camp. Although Hack and Clarence had not been expecting the men, they met them at the gate and received the news with whoops and cheers that could be heard all over camp.

"We're going to France, girls!" Hack called, tossing a bundle of daily newspapers at Norma as he went whistling by. "Pack your things."

Not realizing, at first, that soldiers had arrived to close the camp, Constance assumed he meant for her to pack her things for France, which she thought he meant as a joke. She ignored him and sat down next to Norma to read the news.

"The war resolution was adopted by Congress," Norma said. "Miss Rankin voted against it. One account says she cried, one says she trembled, and another says she fainted."

"Then I'll assume she did none of that, and simply cast her vote in a business-like manner," said Constance, who had some experience with reporters claiming that a woman fainted after conducting the ordinary duties of her position.

Norma read on. "Yes, according to the spectators in the gal-lery, she merely stood and said, 'I want to stand by my country, but I cannot vote for war.' There were forty-nine others who voted against, but I don't see any articles about them."

"What happens next?" Constance asked. "Do we have ships sailing for France?"

Norma paged through the other papers, peering at them through the wire-rimmed spectacles that she now required. "What happens next is that we argue over money."

"I'm sure they'll appreciate that in Paris," Constance said. By then she could hear the sound of tent canvas flapping in the wind, and the commotion around camp as the news spread. She stepped outside and saw the newly arrived soldiers pulling down one of the classroom tents, to the loud protests of the campers.

"I'm the matron of this camp," she called, marching over to a man who appeared to be in charge of the others. "We've two more weeks of classes in that tent."

"Sergeant Galt at your service," the man said. "Your classes are over, miss. We'll need this land for an Army camp. Orders are to tear everything down and set it up military style."

"This is the military style! We're a National Service School, training just like the men do."

His expression only hardened at that, as if he were suppressing some remark. "I know you girls like your camp, but the games are over. We have serious work to do here."

Constance bristled at that. "This has not been a game."

"Pardon me, miss, but we're the ones going to war."

Now she was furious. She loomed over him—that always set men back on their heels—and said, practically shouting, "Do you suppose, when you go, that you'd like your wounds bandaged, or shall we leave you to rot in the fields? Do you want a stitch of clothing to wear? How would you like a meal, or do you plan to go to France and starve?"

Sergeant Galt looked ready for a fight. He still didn't realize he was outmatched. "Listen, lady. I'm under orders—"

"Don't think we won't be driving ambulances, too, and running the telephones. You have no idea what we've been doing at this camp."

"In my unit," Sergeant Galt said, "we give a demerit to a man who talks to his commander like you just did."

"You're not my commander. I run this camp. If it's to be torn down, the orders had better come to me directly from Washington. Meanwhile, I certainly hope you're prepared to carry each and every girl back to her home, because if you take down the tents they're living in, they can't exactly walk from here."

Now she had his attention. He looked around at the camp and all the girls running back and forth between the tents, abuzz with talk of the war. "How many of them are there?"

"Two hundred, plus instructors, and they come from as far away as Texas."

"And how were they going to get home?"

"Their families come for them in two weeks' time. Some arrived by taxicab from the train station and will go back the same way."

He spat on the ground and lifted his hat to wipe his forehead. "Somebody bungled these orders," he mumbled.

"I hope this isn't the sort of operation you plan to run in France," Constance said. "Your men are welcome to camp for the night until we sort this out. I can put an extra girl in each tent and that would leave a few empty for you. Pitch them out along the perimeter, away from my girls."

"You don't tell me where to pitch my tents," Sergeant Galt said, but it was only a half-hearted effort. For the rest of the afternoon, the camp was most decidedly back in Constance's hands, and the soldiers went where she ordered them to go.

The arrival of the men and the news of war made for an unsettling evening in the mess hall. It was true that Constance hadn't bothered to keep up much of a semblance of military order during the evening meal—it seemed to serve no real purpose, as the campers were, on the whole, orderly and well-mannered, and tired by nightfall, besides—but with a dozen or so soldiers as an audience, they reverted to the old methods that Mrs. Nash had insisted upon during their first few days at camp. Everyone lined up and filled the tables in succession, starting nearest the door, rather than rushing to the back and saving seats for friends. They stood at their table until ordered to sit, the dishes were brought out swiftly and in the proper sequence, and every girl remained seated until the last table was served and cleared.

"It's just like Plattsburg," Constance heard one of the soldiers say, "except these ladies take it seriously."

The talk during dinner was more solemn, and more subdued. Everyone had a brother, a neighbor, or a betrothed back home who would be readying for war. Most of the campers had, by now, a decided opinion about what they might do next: some intended to volunteer at the Red Cross or for a church's relief project. Many of them lived along the East Coast and thought they might find work at an Army hospital. A few girls of the working class intended to go into factories. "There won't be as many men to build the ships," one of them said. "They'll have to teach us how to do it."

Sarah was notably quiet, and pushed her food around on her plate. That night, back in their tent (with only Constance, Sarah, Norma, and Fleurette present, as Beulah remained with Nurse Cartwright), Sarah said, "I only wish we'd finished our training."

Fleurette groaned. "I finished our training ages ago. If I have to sit through one more class on how to cuff a pair of trousers, I might expire of boredom."

She'd learned that word, *expire,* from Tizzy Spotwood, with whom Fleurette had taken up since Beulah moved into the infirmary. Fleurette still hadn't been told of Beulah's true identity: both Norma and Constance agreed that the risk of an accidental slip was too high.

"I'm talking about the other training," Sarah said. "I'd like to put another round of bullets into those targets, and to show what else we can do."

"You're not going off into the woods now," Norma said. "We have a dozen more men guarding the camp, and I believe Hack sleeps on top of those guns."

"You know enough to be prepared," Constance said. "I hope you'll never need to use it."

Sarah wrapped a shawl around her shoulders. "I only wish those soldiers could see how far we've come. It's awful, what Sergeant Galt said to you. He has no idea what we've been up to at night out there in the woods. Hack and Clarence know, but they'll never tell, and they might not be believed if they did."

It was nine o'clock by then. Taps was played by a more expert bugler than Clarence. It came across the camp in soft and mournful waves, like a blanket coming to rest on top of them. As Constance went out for her nightly patrol of the campground, she thought for the first time that she would miss this camp, and these girls, and what they had tried to do together.

Every one of their lives was about to be forever altered. Constance wished she could keep them all in place, while they were still fine and young and trying to take hold of their dreams. If she could, she'd preserve them forever, right here, in the final moments of their lives before the war.

⪦ 46 ⪧

"I STILL THINK you ought to go see your Meemaw," Nurse Cartwright said from her reclining chair, her feet up on her desk and a cigarette between her fingers. She wouldn't allow Beulah to have one of her own, but she did pass it over so Beulah could take a draw now and then. "Your granny must be—what, eighty-five by now?"

"But what if I go back and she's dead?" Beulah said. "I couldn't bear it. Besides, she might not want to see me."

"You don't know that," the nurse said. "She had no way of getting a letter to you."

"You know who I do wonder about," Beulah said, taking a lazy kind of pleasure in meandering through her own story like this, "is my mother. When I was a little girl, she was the wicked one in the family. But what did she do? She kept a job most of the time, and went with a few men, and got into some liquor. It's nothing I haven't done myself. What's so awful about that?"

Nurse Cartwright said, "Quite a bit, according to a man like your grandfather."

"That's right. He put her out, and that's what drove her to those little brown bottles."

"It might've been more than that," the nurse said.

"Oh, I'm sure it was," Beulah said. "She had her troubles. But what I'm trying to say is that I've been every bit as wicked as she has. The only difference between us is that the whole country knows what I did. Nobody's heard of her."

Nurse Cartwright nodded thoughtfully at that. "I do see what you mean. Maybe you and your mama would understand each other better now."

Beulah considered that. "I wouldn't mind trying. I don't suppose she's still alive."

"I can't imagine how she could be, from what you've told me," the nurse said. Beulah appreciated the frank and straightforward way Nurse Cartwright addressed any subject connected with medicine. "People don't come back from a drug habit like that. It kills them if they try to quit, and it kills them if they don't."

"I just don't know what drove her to it. What was so awful?"

"Must've been something, for her to run out on you and your sister," Nurse Cartwright said.

"I can't judge her for that. I gave my little boy away. Then those people let him die. What I did was worse."

"Don't ever think that way. I've nursed some babies through cholera. At least half of them die no matter what you do."

"I did not know that. I always thought they just didn't send for a doctor in time."

"Not at all. I'm sure the doctor was there every day."

Beulah did feel a half-measure better, having heard that from a trustworthy source. She'd always carried a heavy knot of guilt, down in the pit of her stomach, over little Henry Clay Jr. She couldn't even remember his face anymore, although that could've been from lack of effort. She didn't dare try too hard to summon him up.

It wasn't at all unpleasant, talking like this. Beulah had never had much of a chance to ruminate over her misfortunes in such a leisurely, even friendly, way. Nurse Cartwright exhibited an open-minded curiosity about the events in Beulah's life, going all the way back to that day when she stood on Meemaw's front porch and asked to be let in.

"I'll wager you were starved and small for your age, and eaten up with nits, too," the nurse speculated, sounding as if she regretted not having a chance to get after little Beulah with her nit comb.

"Oh, I was," Beulah said, happy to let her be right. "Claudia and me both could've used some nursing back then."

What a comfort it was, to imagine Nurse Cartwright with her comb, making things right for little Beulah and Claudia. Over those last few weeks in the camp, Beulah's past had leapt out at her like a panther coming at her in a dark jungle. It tore at her and pulled her back down to a place she never wanted to go again. When she went for that gun and pointed it at Freeman, it wasn't really Freeman she wanted to shoot. It was the shadowy, fanged monster of her own ruined past.

But now, after a few peaceful days in the infirmary, with Nurse Cartwright changing her bandages and washing her hair (what a pleasing sensation, to have another person's hands in one's hair), not to mention a smuggled box of chocolate wafers and a shared cigarette now and again as a reward for good behavior, Beulah felt entirely revived. She'd been going through life like a chipped teacup, broken in places and threatening to shatter at any moment if she wasn't handled right, but she felt restored now, or at least glued solidly back together.

It came as some disappointment, then, when Constance arrived to check on her, and Nurse Cartwright announced that she was ready to return to duty.

Beulah's hand flew up to her face. "Oh, but they're all going to ask about my nose."

"You fell down in the commotion the other night," Constance said. "Everyone knows that already. They haven't missed the fact that you're living in the infirmary."

"I saw the soldiers come in yesterday," Beulah said. "Are they really closing the camp down?"

"Not yet," Constance said. "I had a telegram from Maude Miner this morning. She and General Murray will be back in a week's time to give us something like a graduation ceremony and to officially close the camp. The families have all been notified."

"Are the soldiers still here?" Beulah said, rising gingerly from her comfortable hospital bed, as if her injured nose might prevent her from walking upright.

"They've gone back to Washington. They'll return after we leave to put the camp together the way they like it."

"All right, then." Beulah went behind a screen to dress. When she was ready, Nurse Cartwright put her hands on Beulah's forehead as if to take her temperature one last time and declared her well. "Come back once a day and let me look at that nose," she said. "If it starts to bleed again, I'll take care of it."

"It won't," Beulah said. "I've never been much of a bleeder."

"Well, then, you have that in your favor."

Constance looked at Beulah and the nurse, puzzled over the easy manner they had between them. After they left, she whispered, "Did you tell her?"

"Nurse Cartwright? Oh, I told her everything. You have to, if you're staying in her infirmary."

"I can't keep your secret if you go around telling it to other people."

"She's a nurse! She won't tell anyone." Beulah knew perfectly well that Nurse Cartwright would never say a thing. She'd never felt so safe around another person in her life. There was something so staunch and reliable about a gray-haired nurse who had seen everything. She couldn't be surprised or shocked. How she managed to be so kind, and to keep a good humor, after all the malaise she must've witnessed over the years, was something Beulah couldn't fathom, but she did marvel at it.

"I hope you've had some time to think about what you might do next," Constance said, "because we only have a week to go. I don't want to just take you to the train station and drop you off."

"Oh, you won't have to," Beulah said. "I've decided to stay here in Washington for a while."

"But where will you go?"

"I have a friend who wants me to come," Beulah said. She wasn't ready yet to tell Constance who that friend might be. She wanted to keep it to herself, for just a little longer.

Constance studied her for a minute and said, "I have a word of advice for you. I think you ought to change your name."

"I've changed my name a hundred times! I won't be Roxie Collins again. I was thinking—"

"I mean that you ought to change it at the courthouse. Legally. So you don't have to lie anymore."

"You mean like how married ladies change their names?"

"Something like that," Constance said. "You'd have to go before a judge, and they won't all be sympathetic."

Beulah wrung her fingers together as she thought it over. "I wouldn't know how to do a thing like that."

"I can help you with it if you'd like. I know my way around a courthouse. I'm acquainted with a lawyer or two."

"Well, then, I'll think on it. My old name doesn't belong to me anyway. It belongs to a murder trial. I can't ever have it back."

"I'm sorry it has to be that way, but I do believe it's the best thing you could do for yourself," Constance said. "If you don't find a judge here, I might know one in Hackensack."

"Is that where you're going? Back to Hackensack?"

"I'm still thinking about it."

Constance sounded like she knew more than she was willing to say, too. Let her have her secrets, Beulah thought.

"Well, Miss Matron, what are we going to do in our last week of camp?" she asked.

They were on the edge of the training field, looking down at the rows of tents. Constance put her hands on her hips and took a deep breath.

"It's my camp. We're going to train for war."

❧ 47 ❧

CONSTANCE NEVER DID find out how Clarence acquired the extra guns. He must've ridden some distance to collect them, because the trip took the better part of an afternoon. Whether they were requisitioned from a military depot or a farmer up the road was, she decided, not her concern. They were ordinary rifles like any country-dweller might keep on hand.

Neither had she had any trouble convincing Clarence to fetch them. He'd been raised among sisters and was accustomed to women telling him what to do. Besides, he showed a fraternal regard for the women's camp and its inhabitants.

"Decisions are going to be made very quickly in the next few weeks," Constance said when she put the idea before him. "Your own sergeant doesn't think we've done anything here but entertain ourselves. I'd like to show him otherwise."

"My sergeant doesn't think, period," Clarence said, in the tradition of privates everywhere who love to complain about their commanders but would nonetheless follow them straight into the hell of war.

"Then let's finish our training," Constance said, "and hold proper graduation exercises."

"Seems only fair," Clarence said, affably, and went off in search of weaponry.

As soon as she had the guns in hand, so to speak, Constance announced her plans to the campers. She kept them in the mess hall after dinner on a Tuesday evening to explain the last-minute addition of new courses on manual combat and marksmanship, a week before graduation.

The announcement came as a shock to the campers, who thought that the war had granted them a reprieve and their final week would be more like a holiday. Plenty of them raised objections to the militaristic leanings of the new program.

"I was told we weren't to be turned into Amazonians," complained Liddy Powell from a table in the back.

"I hardly imagine we'll be called upon to arm ourselves in Connecticut," said Ginny Field.

"Although I wouldn't mind knowing how to throw a man down on the ground," added Tizzy Spotwood.

"But just who are you to teach us?" shouted Liddy.

Constance thought those were reasonable questions and didn't mind answering them. "A rifle is nothing but wood and metal. It won't turn you into an Amazon. But if you don't want to handle it, you don't have to. You're all welcome to learn how to throw a man down on the ground, or how to break free from a captor. It could be of considerable value to the girls going to France, but you might find a use for it in Connecticut, too. Clarence and Hack have volunteered to play the part of the attackers, as long as you go easy on them. And you're right to ask how I would know."

She didn't even pause before she said it. Beulah was right — she'd been ill-served by the mountain of shame and regret she'd shouldered since the election. What good had it done her? "I was a deputy sheriff in Hackensack. I carried a revolver, and I tackled

criminals and put them into handcuffs, just like any other deputy."

That brought an excited murmur from the crowd. One girl
said, "I heard something about a lady sheriff who got fired last
year."

"That was me," Constance said. "The new sheriff said he
couldn't think of anything for a woman to do at the jail."

There wasn't a camper in the mess hall who agreed with that
sentiment. Every single girl signed on for rifle training, even the
reluctant ones.

The course began promptly at eight o'clock the following
morning: not a minute could be wasted. The grass had grown
long, and the dew was considerable, so that most girls rolled up
their waistbands to raise their hemlines. Constance didn't object,
and in fact imagined that over in France, the women must be
making all manner of impromptu adjustments to their uniforms.

She'd conscripted Sarah Middlebrook as her assistant. The
two of them took the first class and showed them how to stand
with a rifle, how to check it for ammunition, and how to put a target in their sights. There would be no long nights in the woods
rehearsing with wooden substitutes. These girls had to be taught
quickly, out of necessity, which was exactly how Constance herself had learned to shoot, the first time Sheriff Heath put a police
revolver in her hand. She flinched a little at the memory—what
promise that moment had held!—but there was no time for remi-
niscing. Her class was ready to take aim.

"I don't know when I'll ever need to do this," said Liddy Powell, when Constance put the rifle in her hands, "but this might be
the last time anyone offers to teach me."

She hit her target on the first try, gave a little yelp of victory,
and went right back into line to take another turn.

So it transpired that in their last week of camp, in every spare moment, a regiment of young women took part in the training that had previously only been offered to a few of their number, in secret, late at night. Marching practice was cancelled, as were calisthenics. Instead they rehearsed choke-holds and ground tackles. Target practice took place four times a day, with twenty girls at a time aiming at bottles on fence posts near the edge of the woods.

There was simply nothing more glorious than to see what these girls could do, if they were allowed to be a little rough-and-tumble. After a month at camp, their inhibitions and pretenses had fallen away. The uniforms had an effect, of course: everyone was equal in drab khaki, and the differences between them faded away.

As Constance walked among them on the training field, adjusting their stances, and checking that they had the target in their sights, she couldn't help but feel, in some small measure, what it must mean to command a regiment. These girls were hers. They trusted her, and they counted on her to show them what they needed to know.

Constance had the peculiar sensation, during that week, of knowing already that she ought to pack away a memory of those days when they were all together, in the pale lemony sunlight of early April, their feet planted firmly in the earth and their eyes squinted carefully into the rifles' sights, with a round going off and echoing around the camp, to be greeted by cheers and applause from all sides. If there was anything in the world she wanted, it was this. She only wished she knew how to hold on to it.

⊰ 48 ⊱

"'SUNDRY PERSONS HAVE come to the United States during the past year and a half with large foreign credits, by the help of which, it is alleged, fires have been started, factories have been blown up and men and instrumentalities have been subsidized. These credits, when in national banks, can be followed as they are paid out by the accounting and financial detectives in the service of the Government.'"

Norma read the story aloud with great theatricality, then passed it with a flourish to Constance, who was, at that moment, standing on an overturned fruit crate in her petticoats as Fleurette repaired a split seam in her skirt.

"An accounting detective? That's dull work," Fleurette said from behind a mouthful of pins.

"At least the pay's sufficient," Constance said, having turned the newspaper over to finish the story. "It says here that the salaries for investigators begin at three dollars a day, with money for expenses. Experienced men of the highest class receive twelve dollars a day."

"Which means they will offer you a dollar a day, and their thanks," Norma said.

Beulah chortled at that. She was lounging quite comfortably

on Fleurette's cot, enjoying the sensation of a nose liberated from its bandages. It was turning gaudy shades of purple and green and was still quite tender, but the fresh air was doing it wonders.

"I know all about a dollar a day and their thanks," Beulah said. "Don't settle for anything less than five dollars a day, even in service to your country."

Fleurette knotted her thread and ripped it deftly: she never bothered with scissors. "Step into it," she said, holding the skirt up to Constance.

Constance did as she was told. Fleurette buttoned the skirt around her waist and walked around, checking the seams. "Do you have enough room to perform your maneuvers? Let's see you kick something."

Constance kicked her leg out half-heartedly, but she was still engrossed in the newspaper. "Listen to this. 'Mr. Bielaski's business is considerably more difficult than that of the ordinary policeman, inasmuch as the former must ferret out the criminal intentions of would-be violators of law and checkmate them before they can accomplish their purposes. A good example of this sort of work was his exploit in arresting a group of Germans in New York City who planned to blow up the Welland canal. Mr. Bielaski knew all about their plans but he waited until the last possible moment in order to obtain all evidence. Then he made his arrests and the canal today is safe.'"

Fleurette found a loose button and pulled the skirt off. "You've been awfully rough on this uniform. I'm going to do all of these again."

"There's hardly any point. We have only a few days left," Constance said.

"I might as well fix it up. You're going to go right on wearing this uniform when we get home, I know you will."

"I do like a uniform," Constance admitted. It dampened her

spirits to hear mention of returning home. Was she really about to be back on the farm, in her old clothes, sleeping in her old bed again? It seemed impossible, with the war under way. Even congressmen were offering to resign their posts to go into the Army and Navy. It was stifling to think of shuffling back to Wyckoff.

But there was Fleurette, down on the floor, her knees tucked under her, whipping a needle through a wooden button. It occurred to Constance that in every home across the country, siblings were looking at one another and wondering where the war might take them, and when they might again be together.

"Roxanna's made her plans for after camp is over, but she won't tell us about them," Constance said. (Beulah had by then come clean to Fleurette—it was impossible to keep a secret from her—but they'd agreed to stick to the habit of calling her by her assumed name so they wouldn't slip up in front of the others.) "We don't yet know what to do with Fleurette."

Fleurette gave her a sharp glance from her spot on the floor. "Someone has to mind the farm. You'll find some sort of position with Miss Miner, and Norma will be off at an Army pigeon depot," she said as she tied off the last button and shook out the skirt. No one quite trusted the notion that the Army was prepared to welcome Norma into its ranks, but they were all pretending, for the sake of peace within the tent, that she would depart for her military assignment immediately upon graduation.

"Leaving you to mind the farm? You're not going to stay out in the countryside by yourself, are you?" Beulah said. "Aren't there wolves, and snow?"

"There's one but not the other," Norma put in. "Fleurette should go to Francis's."

"Oh, is that it?" Fleurette said. "You and Constance intend to find military posts, and I'll help Bessie on washing day?"

"Who are Francis and Bessie?" asked Beulah, who never did manage to learn much about the Kopp sisters' past.

"Our brother and his wife. They're always trying to take us in," Fleurette said. "He wants the farm sold and the three of us tucked under his roof, or some roof nearby where he has more of a say."

Fleurette wrapped the skirt around Constance's waist again, tested the buttons, and found them satisfactory. "I'll make uniforms, of course. We're so near the woolen mills, I expect they'll set up shops and I'll work in one of them."

There was an odd, uncomfortable silence around the tent. Beulah looked quizzically at Constance, who tried to catch Norma's eye but was unable to do so.

"Well?" asked Fleurette. "Isn't that what you had in mind for me?"

It was—Constance had to admit that it was—but she knew perfectly well that Fleurette had no intention of sitting out the war behind a sewing machine.

⚹ 49 ⚹

WHEN MAUDE MINER and General Murray arrived, a week later, for graduation, they found themselves treated as honorees at a parade. The gate was festooned with bunting, the flags were flying, and the campers lined up in rows three deep to wave them in. A newly expanded viewing platform sat at the edge of the field, where the guests could watch the graduation exercises. Some of the families had arrived as well, and every chair in the camp had been gathered so that they could sit alongside the platform and watch the proceedings.

After lunch the visiting dignitaries climbed the platform and took their seats, along with Constance, the instructors, Nurse Cartwright, and another invited guest: Geneva Nash, still on crutches, but pleased to be asked back to observe the conclusion of the camp she'd opened.

"Why do I have the feeling that I'm about to watch some sort of happening?" Miss Miner asked. "I was imagining that we'd be in the mess hall, handing out badges and patting each girl on the back."

"We prepared something special for you," said Constance. "Has anyone seen Norma? She was supposed to be up here with the instructors."

"She was in the mess hall at lunch," Nurse Cartwright said.

Constance stood and looked around. The girls were all standing at attention, two hundred of them, in rows of twenty. They had wooden rifles at their sides, with the exception of those in the last row, who couldn't be seen clearly by the audience. "I won't keep them waiting," Constance said. She handed her whistle to Mrs. Nash. "Would you do the honors?"

As Constance stepped down to take her place in front of her troops, Mrs. Nash hobbled to her feet and blew the whistle.

"Port, arms," Constance called, and every rifle moved in unison.

"Order, arms." It was a thrilling sight, to see their maneuvers performed with such precision. From behind her, Constance could hear Mrs. Nash applauding each successive move.

"Present, arms."

Now it was time. The girls marched off to the sides, one row after another, and stood at attention once again. Only the last row remained. The girls in that row turned toward the woods, where the targets were arrayed.

When they were in position, Constance gave the order.

"Aim. Fire!"

It happened so fast that Maude Miner nearly fell out of her chair. General Murray was on his feet at once. Mrs. Nash merely stood, leaning on her crutch, watching Constance thoughtfully. Mothers and fathers gasped from the audience.

The first ten girls handed their rifles off to the next. Constance gave the order again.

"Aim. Fire!"

They were hitting their targets as well as any training class might be expected to do, and perhaps a little better. General Murray had forgotten his alarm and was now scrutinizing the women, and the bullet-holes in their targets, with a kind of professional curiosity.

Miss Miner jumped down from the platform and ran for Constance as the next line of women took their place. "Miss Kopp, I must ask that you put a stop to this immediately," she said.

"You said yourself that the generals would need to form a picture in their minds of women at war before they'd consider it," Constance said. "I'm helping General Murray to form a picture."

Miss Miner had to shout over the next round of fire. "He's forming a picture of disobedient women who can't be trusted. Firearms training at these camps was most soundly rejected in Washington."

Constance was only half listening. "Oh, there's Norma. I should've known."

Norma's pigeon cart was rolling out from behind the barn, under the power of Hack's automobile. Norma rode on the coachman's bench atop the cart. They were driving straight toward the training field.

"Parade, rest," Constance called.

The girls put down the butts of their rifles and watched Constance expectantly. When the cart came to a stop in the middle of the field, Norma hopped down and ran over.

"Have them shoot down the pigeons," she said, a little out of breath from her exertions.

"Oh, Norma, I couldn't," Constance said.

"What I meant is for you to have them try. Of course they won't hit one."

"But what if they do?"

Norma looked stoically back at her cart. "It's a war. There will be some losses."

Constance had to fight a smile when she thought of Norma's birds marching bravely off to war. "All right, if it's what you want. Go and release them."

Constance went over to her campers and showed them what

she wanted them to do. "Come around to the side like this, and aim considerably higher," she said. "That's my sister in the cart, and Hack with her. I don't want any chance of them getting hit. The birds are going to fly north, so you can aim your rifles well away from the cart and still put your fire directly in their path."

"Oh, but I don't want to shoot a bird," Fern protested.

"You won't," Constance said. "They fly high and fast. Norma just wants you to make some noise."

Without any more time for discussion—Miss Miner and General Murray were deep into a heated conversation by now—Constance gave the order. Norma released her birds, and the girls fired.

It made a remarkable spectacle, all those pigeons set free at once, climbing frantically higher into a clear blue sky to escape the gunfire. Constance ordered the girls to shoot again, and a third time, until the birds were so high and far away that they could hardly be seen. She felt a little wistful as she watched them settle into formation and set a path for home. They'd be back in Wyckoff tonight, snug in their roost. Having already decided that she couldn't go back herself and sit out the war, Constance felt the first pang of a soldier's longing for home.

There was a mighty round of applause for the pigeons. Norma waved at her admirers, and Hack drove the cart back to the barn. With the field cleared, the rest of the graduates came forward to finish their target exercises.

After everyone had their turn at the targets, five women gave a demonstration of the hand-to-hand moves they'd learned. They'd had far more than five volunteers, but Hack and Clarence protested that they couldn't take much more of a beating. Another twenty paired up and demonstrated with each other, so that the air was full of grunts and thuds and shrieks of victory as each assailant was wrestled to the ground.

At the end—more for comic effect—one group of girls wheeled out the infirmary bed and gave a vigorous demonstration of scientific bed-making, while another group rolled bandages, and a third tapped frantically at a telegraphic machine. Even Miss Miner laughed at the speed and drama with which they performed their more feminine tasks.

Another order to march put the entire camp back into formation. Miss Miner smoothed her skirt and tried to compose herself enough to make a speech. The family members in the audience had settled down, too, after having been on their feet for the duration of the exercises.

It was unusually quiet now, after all the commotion. Even the birds that ordinarily chattered from the treetops had been shocked into silence following the gunfire. Miss Miner stood at the front of the platform and looked down at the rows of women before her.

"I have presided over a number of these graduation ceremonies," she said, "but never one quite like this."

That was greeted by laughter and some concerned rumblings from the parents.

"While you've been at camp, I've been in Washington, trying to make sure that the women of this country have a voice if we're to send our boys overseas. Our only congresswoman voted against the war, but that doesn't mean that we don't see our duty. You girls have taken your obligations more seriously than anyone who has gone before you, and with good reason. I understand from the conversations I had at lunch that some of you intend to go to France yourselves. The rest of you will stay here and help in a hundred different ways. However, it's entirely reasonable for each and every one of you to think that you might have to defend yourself, or to take up arms against an enemy. That's true even if you don't go to France. The Germans have shown us that an ocean is not such an insurmountable obstacle. We already know that we have German spies and saboteurs among us. They've come after our factories and our munition depots. They might yet come after us in our homes.

"There are some who would fault Miss Kopp for encouraging young ladies to behave like soldiers, but I have decided that I won't be among them. I've never been prouder of this country's daughters than I am right now. I wish you all well, and God-speed."

The applause was energetic and heartfelt, although Constance could still see quite a bit of whispering among the parents.

General Murray stood next. "My responsibility at a girls' camp, ordinarily, is to stand here and thank you all for supporting our boys, and to hand you these medals for the completion of your training. This time, it's a little different. First of all, Privates Hackbush and Piper are going to have quite a bit to explain to their commander when this is all over. You couldn't have done any of this without their co-operation."

There came a ripple of protests from the graduates, who were all too eager to defend Hack and Clarence. The general waved them away, suggesting that he meant it only in jest.

"Second, I must have a word with that lady who brought the pigeons onto the field, because I've never seen anything like that in my life. If those birds can do that in France, they can sleep in my bunk on the way over."

Norma very nearly turned purple with delight.

"But to each and every one of you, I say this. You've done something at this camp that you probably thought you never could. Some of you might've been afraid to try. There are men signing up for service all over the country today who don't know if they're equal to the task. Every one of them feels just the way you did when you started. I only wish they could all see you now, because it would give them courage."

He paused for a moment, overcome. "We're all going to need courage."

With that he took his seat. Constance distributed the medals herself.

LATER THAT AFTERNOON, as the tents were coming down and parents were collecting their daughters, Constance walked around the edge of the camp with Miss Miner. They strolled easily, as old friends.

"Your sister put on quite a show today," Miss Miner said. "General Murray has been back there all afternoon going over every inch of that pigeon cart with her."

"She's been working on that cart for more than a year now. We're never going to hear the end of it. She'll be insufferable when she gets home."

"Oh, I don't think she's going home," Maude said. "General Murray wants her to leave directly for Fort Monmouth. The Army Signal Corps has a school there, and pigeons are going to be a part of it."

"Is that right?" Constance glanced back at the barn, where Norma was engaged in an animated conversation with the general. "Then they already have a pigeon program?"

"A half-hearted one, he tells me, put into place mostly because the British have one, and we didn't want to be outdone. I have a feeling it's going to be an entirely different beast once Norma gets hold of it. If she'll agree to go, that is."

Constance was still watching Norma, who was walking around in a circle now, waving her arms, illustrating the birds' flight patterns. "Oh, she'll go," she said.

"And what about your younger sister?" Maude asked.

"I'm not so sure about Fleurette," Constance said. "She's led us to believe that she'll be sewing uniforms, but you know that she loves the stage. I suspect that she has plans to go around entertaining the troops, but she probably thinks she can't tell us about that, especially after what happened with Mr. Bernstein."

"What matters is what didn't happen with Mr. Bernstein," Miss Miner said. "I never did meet the girl involved. Did she apologize, and did the two of them reconcile?"

"A reconciliation was made," Constance said carefully, having found no good reason to trouble Miss Miner about the real identity of the girl in question.

"Then I won't ask anything more," Miss Miner said. "But now we come to you. I promised you a position in Washington if you acquitted yourself well here."

"I'm afraid this wasn't at all what you expected of me," Constance said.

"You did just fine. I'll have a few parents complaining, but with a war on, they ought to be proud of their daughters for showing a little gumption, and I'll put it to them like that. The trouble is, Washington is in worse disarray than I could've imagined. We haven't the time nor the means to raise the Army we need. The Navy doesn't have its ships. We have no aeroplanes to speak of. This is to say nothing of a thousand other problems, from rail lines that don't connect to each other, to commanders who don't speak French, to inadequate supplies and uniforms and everything else an army requires. And don't think the French and British are making it easy for us. This is their war, and they have their own ideas about how it ought to be run."

"Which is to say . . ." Constance put in.

"Which is to say that the idea of finding a few good positions for women is about number eight thousand, nine hundred, and forty-seven on their list of priorities. There will be Army camps all summer. I can put you as a matron in any one of them, but you'd be doing just what I was doing in Plattsburg last year—keeping the town girls away from the soldiers. I know it isn't what you wanted. Take your choice of posts, though, and I'll write as soon as I have more suitable work for you."

They had just reached the stretch of fence that leaned slightly, where Constance had so often slipped between the posts and into the woods. She ran her hand along a gnarled board but didn't say anything about it.

"I will accept your offer," Constance said, "if I need it. But I already have an idea of the kind of work I'd like to do. I believe I'll go along to Washington and put my application in."

"Whatever is it?" Maude asked. "I've been looking everywhere. Don't think I haven't."

"It isn't a position that's been advertised," Constance said. From her pocket she withdrew the latest round of news clippings about Mr. Bielaski. "There's a bureau in Washington out to catch German spies. They could use me. I'm going to go and tell them so."

Maude smiled wearily at that. "It sounds like a life of intrigue, but it's a lot of hanging around factories and listening in on dull conversations. Besides, what they really need are German speakers." She stopped and stared at Constance. "Kopp. You're not a German, are you?"

"Austrian, on my mother's side. New Yorker by birth. All three of us grew up speaking German at home."

"I had no idea! You told me you had some French, but—"

"But we're supposed to pretend we don't speak German. I'm not going to pretend anymore. I can conduct my affairs in three languages, I know my way around the law, I can outrun a man or fight him off, and I know the business end of a gun. I ought to be put to work as a spy."

Maude couldn't have looked more astonished at that. "There

340

isn't exactly an employment bureau for spies in Washington. Didn't I just tell you that we don't even have ships for our Navy?"

"But you have this man," Constance said, pointing to the paper.

"Well, Mr. Bielaski is terribly busy as it is. He's not going around knocking on doors to recruit lady spies."

Constance said, "That's why I intend to knock on his."

Six Months Later

"I DON'T KNOW why you're making such a fuss over a pork chop," Beulah said.

Nurse Cartwright was standing behind her in the kitchen, looking over her shoulder. "I've just never seen you do anything but fry eggs before."

"There's potatoes, too, and green beans. Say, my grandmother used to like to put a little whiskey in the pan when she made chops."

"Well, I don't see the harm in that," Nurse Cartwright said, reaching into the cupboard.

They made a contented pair that night around the kitchen table, with Beulah's nursing school books pushed to one side and Nurse Cartwright's magazines put away. The potatoes were only boiled, but there was plenty of butter and salt for them, and the green beans had baked in the oven with a little cream.

"Are you going to sew up an orange again tonight?" Nurse Cartwright asked as they ate.

"I'll sew a dozen of them, if I have to," Beulah said. "I don't like to stitch a pair of trousers, much less an open wound. I might never graduate from fruit."

"They'll let you practice on pigs pretty soon," the nurse said.

"It's the hardest thing to learn. You have to tell yourself it's a piece of fabric, and go as quickly as you can."

"I just don't want to hurt anybody," Beulah said.

"Oh, they're already hurt by the time you have to stitch them up. Listen to me now. This is where girls always drop out. Don't you be one of them. Once you get past this, the rest won't be so bad."

Beulah remembered the day-old rolls she'd picked up at the bakery and brought them over. "Are you working on Saturday?"

"Only a half-day. I haven't had a Saturday off in a month. Why?"

She felt a little embarrassed to ask after everything Nurse Cartwright had done for her, but she said, "They're giving us units of measurement to study tomorrow. I didn't learn my numbers any better than I learned my letters."

"Oh, it's the same thing," the nurse said placidly. "You just take it slow and do one at a time. You know what happens eventually? You don't even add the sums in your head, or divide them. You just remember them. The doctors ask for the same medicines every time. You'll learn what they're expecting, and it'll all just fall into place. Don't think too hard about it, that's all."

"Is that what you did when you set my nose? Didn't think too hard about it? I can't believe you took a hammer to me."

Nurse Cartwright said, "It was only a little mallet. Believe me, you wanted that nose straightened back out again. Look at you now. You can hardly tell it was ever broken. It has a little bend to it, but it suits you."

Beulah did like her nose the way it was now. It made her look a little different. Her hairstyle had changed again, too, this time into a shorter and more sensible cut that fit easily under a nurse's cap. As time went on, she had less and less fear of ever being recognized.

"It's funny the way they call you Nurse, even when you aren't one and might never become one," she said. They called her Nurse Powers at school now, and she hadn't yet learned to answer to it.

It had taken longer than she'd expected to choose a new name for herself. For a while she held on to Roxie Collins, only because it had grown familiar, but she needed a legal name before she enrolled in nursing school. For a month they sat around the kitchen table and made lists. After tossing around the names of girls she remembered from New York, and names from popular songs of the day, and the names of birds and trees and French perfumes, Nurse Cartwright put the lists away one afternoon and told her that the right name would come to her of its own accord, when she was ready to accept it.

Not long after that, the nurse suggested that they go back to Richmond to check up on Meemaw.

"Oh, I don't dare show my face again," Beulah said. "What would I say to her, after all this time? She might be gone and dead, anyway."

"You don't know that," Nurse Cartwright said. "How about we just stand across the street and look at her front porch?"

"That wouldn't be right either, to go all that way and not pay a visit."

"Well, then, we'll just give it a try and you can decide once you're there."

Beulah agreed, reluctantly, confessing to some longing to see her old home one more time before she stopped being Beulah Binford forever. It was a pleasant ride by train on a Sunday afternoon, and a short walk from the train station to Meemaw's old house. How small Richmond seemed, after New York! It was like a stage set, all the old houses painted to resemble her childhood memories, but none of them looking quite right, some in shambles now, and others polished and shined like they never used to be when she was a child.

Beulah knew the way, nonetheless, and knew how to avoid going past Mayo Street to get there. She recognized her Meemaw's house readily enough, although it had been painted a bright pink, which her grandmother never would've countenanced.

A woman Beulah hadn't seen before was standing on the front porch. Beulah couldn't bring herself to cross the street and make her inquiries, so Nurse Cartwright did it for her. She marched right over, and stood on those old wooden steps, then walked back across the street and gave the news in the stalwart and forthright manner that was her habit.

"Your Meemaw's gone. She's over in the cemetery if you want to see her."

"I don't," Beulah said. They had only been in Richmond for an hour, but it was taking hold of her, with every minute she was back inside of it. She felt herself turning back into that little girl again, the one who stood on that porch and asked to be let inside. "Let's go on back to Washington."

"Not until we see your Meemaw," Nurse Cartwright said firmly. "We have time to walk through the cemetery before our train."

"I don't know why it matters so much to you," Beulah said. "She ain't your family."

Nurse Cartwright stopped in the street and looked Beulah over. It was unusual for Beulah to see the nurse out of uniform. She worked at the Army hospital now, and she was on duty almost every day. On her days off she liked to rest, and stayed in her house dress all day and sent Beulah out to do the shopping. But now she wore an ordinary white shirtwaist and a long broadcloth skirt, not unlike their old camp uniforms.

"You're right, she's not my family," Nurse Cartwright said, "but you're my family, or at least, you're the one I come home to at night for the time being. So let's go see your Meemaw, and tell her how good you're doing, and then we can go on home and have our supper."

It wasn't just Meemaw's grave they found there. Jessie Binford was buried alongside her, in a proper plot, with a good granite headstone. BELOVED MOTHER, it read, under her name.

"Claudia must've paid for it," Beulah whispered.

Carved under a rosette of ivy leaves were the dates: 1869 TO 1912.

"Gone too soon," Nurse Cartwright said, respectfully. "Your Meemaw lived a good long while. 1831 to 1916. That puts her at eighty-five."

Beulah was still thinking about her mother. "She was still alive during my trial. I thought she was dead by then."

"There was no way for you to know," Nurse Cartwright said.

They sat by those graves quietly, taking in the fragrance of crushed grass underneath them. Beulah started to notice the other stones, her grandfather and her uncles, also gone too soon, and even some of the babies who'd been lost. She told the nurse about them, as many of them as she remembered, and then they stood and brushed off their skirts and took the train back to Washington.

It was after that trip to Richmond that Beulah finally chose a name for herself, and went before a judge to have it changed. She took her sister's last name, even though Claudia never did answer her letters. She liked the name Powers, and she liked to imagine that it tethered her, in a fragile, thread-like way, to her only living relation.

For her first name she chose Catherine, her Meemaw's name. Catherine Powers was a name that she would have to grow into. She would have to earn it.

A nursing course took three years. Beulah didn't know if she'd make it all the way through to the end. She'd never done anything for three years. She also didn't know if there'd be any war left to join by the time she finished learning.

"You don't need to be in such a hurry to go off to France," Nurse Cartwright told her, whenever Beulah mentioned the war. "You don't have anything to run from anymore."

Historical Notes

Every book in the Kopp Sisters series (this is the fifth) is based on the real lives of Constance, Norma, and Fleurette Kopp. In each installment, I try to tell their true story as much as I can, and use fiction only to fill in the gaps.

This installment ventures further into fiction than any previous book. In fact, I don't know what the Kopps were doing in the spring of 1917. To satisfy my own love of research and obscure historical stories, I've placed them in a real environment—a National Service School—and I've introduced them to the real-life Beulah Binford.

As far as I know, neither Binford nor the Kopps attended a National Service School, but the idea came from a newspaper clipping about Beulah Binford, written in 1918, about her attempts to join the Red Cross. She was trying to distance herself from her past, and to help in the war effort. I had discovered Beulah Binford already in my research into Freeman Bernstein, who has appeared in previous books owing to a real-life case connecting him and Constance. I found Beulah's story fascinating. By moving Beulah's Red Cross training to 1917, I could place her and the Kopps at a National Service School in the days just before the United States joined the war. I've become fascinated by these early military camps for women and wanted to explore that world.

The National Service Schools were a project of the Women's Section of the Navy League, with a great deal of participation from the Army as well. Many of the organizers were the wives and daughters of prominent politicians and military officers. Their idea was to instill in women a sense of patriotism and national preparedness by teaching skills such as first aid, military kitchen protocols, signaling, and any other tasks that might be considered women's war work.

The first camp was held in Chevy Chase, Maryland, in May 1916. Three others followed around the country. Similar camps were sponsored by other women's preparedness groups. Questions about uniforms arose at every camp: "Women Soldiers Vote for Trousers" was the headline on April 15, 1916, followed, the next day, by "Women Will Not Wear Trousers." The controversy over whether or not women should be given firearms training arose often as well. "Shall Women Shoot?" was quickly followed by the reassurance that they would not.

My version of a National Service School camp ran longer than most did. Many camps were only two weeks long. The camp participants, organizers, and instructors are fiction, but they are very much based on real accounts of the camps as reported in newspapers of the day. The training curriculum, military exercises, and even the mess hall menus are historically accurate. (One camp really did run out of bananas as mine did in chapter 7.) Fortunately, the Library of Congress has preserved wonderful photographs of the training camps. Please visit my website (www.amystewart.com) to see those pictures. For more on the National Service School movement, read Barbara J. Steinson's excellent 1981 book *American Women's Activism in World War I*.

Readers of the third book in the series, *Miss Kopp's Midnight Confessions*, might already be familiar with Freeman Bernstein and May Ward, and I'd encourage you to read the historical notes at the end of that book for more about them. May Ward really was, by 1917, a fading vaudeville actress. Freeman Bernstein was her husband, her manager, and a show promoter. He was, as Constance put it in this novel, "notoriously unreliable, and prone to exaggeration and misdirection." That description might actually be too kind. If you don't believe me, ask his family. His grand-nephew, Walter Shapiro, wrote a fantastic biography of Mr. Bernstein called *Hustling Hitler: The Jewish Vaudevillian Who Fooled the Führer*. Yes, Freeman Bernstein really did try to swindle Hitler. Please do read Walter's book to find out more.

Beulah Binford came to my attention when I was researching Freeman Bernstein. He did attempt to manage and represent her just as the 1911 murder trial was ending. That got me curious about Beulah herself, and pretty soon I'd compiled a complete dossier on her, with hundreds of newspaper clippings spanning several years, a deep and comprehensive family tree compiled from census and other genealogical resources, and even a dive into Richmond's courthouse records with the assistance of Chris Semtner, curator of Richmond's Edgar Allan Poe Museum. I became fascinated with Beulah and her case. Her name was synonymous with sin and scandal—so much so that newspapers didn't bother to explain who she was or what she'd done when they wrote about her in the years following the trial. Everyone already knew.

Although her participation in the National Service School is fiction, her backstory, told in flashbacks in my novel, is almost entirely true, with one glaring exception: I did kill her mother off prematurely. As far as I know, Jessie Binford did not have a drug problem. She died in 1931, not 1912. I also made Freeman Bernstein into more of a guilty party than he might've been in real life

—although it would be entirely in keeping with his character for him to try to turn Beulah into a celebrity, only to make matters worse for her.

If you're wondering what happened next to Beulah Binford, the truth is that I can't be sure—because it appears that she actually did change her name. The record gets murky after that. Perhaps she earned the right to disappear from history.

One historical note about Richmond: Mayo Street no longer exists on any map of the city. The street is gone entirely, replaced by the James Monroe Building. From 1905 to 1915, Mayo Street was a legally sanctioned red-light district. The experiment in legalization was ultimately a failure, but it was extraordinary for its time—and Beulah Binford lived right in the middle of it. For more on this moment in Richmond's history, I recommend Harry M. Ward's book *Children of the Streets of Richmond, 1865–1920.*

Maude Miner is a fascinating woman who deserves her own biography. She was born in 1880, making her just a few years younger than Constance. In 1906 she was working as a probation officer in New York City's night court. Shortly thereafter, she raised the funds to lease an entire building at 165 West Tenth Street in New York, which she called Waverly House. There she housed —and tried to help—some of the women who came through the night court. She then formed the Girls' Service League, which had a mission of helping destitute girls. In 1916 she received a PhD from Columbia, and her dissertation was published under the title *Slavery of Prostitution: A Plea for Emancipation.*

In the run-up to World War I, she visited the training camps and saw trouble brewing between the soldiers and the young women who hung around the camps. She wrote to the War Department and proposed a Committee on Protective Work for Girls, which she ran until 1918. Many of the women involved with that committee grew disenchanted as they saw local authorities use the committee's mandate as an excuse to put "wayward" girls into detention, with no rights or recourse.

Maude continued to run the Girls' Service League until her marriage in 1924, and went on to do service work of one kind or another with her husband. She died in 1967. Her memoir, *Quest for Peace: Personal and Political,* provided many of these details.

Maude's participation in this camp is fictional, as are the specifics of her "business in Washington." However, here's one bizarre coincidence about the intersection between fiction and fact in this novel: The newspaper article that Constance refers to in chapter 39 about Beulah working under an assumed name at the telephone company was, in fact, written by Maude Miner. The real Maude Miner and the real Beulah Binford did actually cross paths.

Two historical figures mentioned in this novel but not actually appearing are Congresswoman Jeannette Rankin and Bureau of Investigation director Bruce Bielaski. Everything I wrote about them is historically accurate.

For readers new to the series who are curious about the Kopp sisters' real lives up to this point, I encourage you to read the historical notes at the end of the previous four books, and to visit my website (www.amystewart.com) for photographs and biographies. The short version, to satisfy your curiosity: Constance really was a deputy sheriff until she was fired after the election of 1916, and Fleurette really was a very talented seamstress, actress, and singer. Norma, in real life, had no interest in pigeons as far as I know. However, her obstinacy, bossiness, and generally disagreeable nature are based on her actual personality, as described to me by members of her own family.

A FEW MORE specifics:

The questions that Geneva Nash asked Constance at the end

of chapter 2 come directly from the National Service Register questions that were used to gauge women's interest in joining a National Service School.

For the speeches given by Geneva Nash and Maude Miner in chapter 5, I quoted heavily from real speeches given at the camps in the spring of 1917, as reported in newspapers of the day. Most quotes come from Elisabeth Elliott Poe, who was instrumental in creating the National Service Schools.

The alphabet code taught by Mr. Turner in chapter 10 comes directly from the 1916 edition of the Army Signal Corps manual.

In chapter 11, Norma gives a version of events concerning the Zimmerman cable that was thought to be true at the time. (The Zimmerman cable was an offer by Germany to Mexico, proposing a partnership if the United States entered the war against Germany. In exchange for being allowed to set up ports and military bases in Mexico, the Germans would allow Mexico to take back Texas, Arizona, and New Mexico after the United States was defeated. News of this telegram was enough to sway American opinion against the Germans and to rally support for joining in the war and defeating Germany.)

Norma's version of events, described in a March 5, 1917, article called "Caught Zimmerman Note at the Border," which ran in the *Evansville (IN) Press* and other papers, suggests that one of Mr. Bielaski's agents intercepted a special messenger at the Mexico border and delivered the secret telegram to Washington. We now know that the British intercepted the telegram and broke the Germans' code, but that information wasn't released at the time because the British didn't want the Germans to know that they could break the code.

The first song sung in chapter 20 is "You're a Dangerous Girl," written by Grant Clarke and sung by Al Jolson in 1916. The second song was written by me (although heavily influenced by murder ballads of the era) and has been sung by no one. "My Little Red Carnation," quoted in chapter 28, was written by Charles Robinson and performed by May Ward.

R. T. Fisher, introduced in chapter 21, really did date Beulah Binford briefly, and she did claim to be married to him. He played for the Brooklyn Dodgers in 1912, just after the Beattie trial, then went on to play for the Chicago Cubs, the Cincinnati Reds, and the St. Louis Cardinals.

In chapter 30, much of what Nurse Cartwright has to say about hygienic bed-making comes from a November 1, 1902, edition of *Collier's Weekly*. The article was "Scientific Bed-Making" by Emma Churchman Hewitt.

In chapter 34, Beulah reads from a newspaper article about herself. That article ran in the *Alexandria Gazette* on August 16, 1911, under the headline "The Question of Affinity."

In chapter 36, I quote from a story called "People Like Anything Salacious" that ran all over the country on September 7, 1911. My copy comes from the *Daily Capital Journal* in Salem, Oregon. I also quoted from "The Barring of Beulah Binford," which appeared in the Louisville, Kentucky, *Courier-Journal* on September 17, 1911. Some of Freeman's dialogue in chapter 38 also comes from his quotes in that same story.

In chapter 45, the discussion about Congresswoman Jeannette Rankin's vote, and how she conducted herself, is drawn from the April 6, 1917, *New York Times* story "Suffrage Leaders Pardon Miss Rankin."

In chapter 48, Norma quotes from an article about Mr. Bielaski that actually ran earlier, on January 2, 1916, in the *St. Louis Post-Dispatch*. The title was "Uncle Sam's $28,000,000 Spy System." In the same chapter, Constance's quotes about Bielaski come from another article, "Minister's Son Hunts Criminals," which ran in the *Lincoln Star* on April 30, 1916.